PRAISE FOR *BENEATH THE RISING*

"A near-flawless debu[...]
and richly rendered, it[...]
romp through unspeaka[...]
also paints a portrait [...]
grappling with their plac[...]
relationship with each other."

Strange Horizons

"Balances horror with humour,
and the banter between the two main characters
alternates between making you chuckle and making
you wince. A thoughtful, well-paced novel with
memorable characters that seamlessly mixes modern
day issues with eldritch horror. "

British Fantasy Society

"A wonderful genre-defying adventure, rife with
strange heart and weird horror. But most notable is its
particular, careful attention to its characters.
Premee Mohamed is a bold new voice."

Chuck Wendig

"A perfect balance of thriller,
horror and humour; reminded me of
The Gone-Away World."

Adrian Tchaikovsky

"This is a great story! I loved the globe trotting,
ancient history and mysteries at every turn."

Stewart Hotston

"*Beneath the Rising* is a fast-paced adventure story. It's also a story of powerful, complex, often difficult emotions, and the tangle of friendship and devotion and other scary things, and honestly I wasn't prepared to have so many feelings."

Karolina Fedyk

"If you haven't read it you should rush, *rush* to read *Beneath The Rising*. Two people who have nothing in the world except one another might be the world's only hope for survival. It's about love, belonging, fear and betrayal. Brilliant."

Leo McBride

"This is not a *Call of Cthulhu* adventure in novel form, or a teenage romance. It is by turns funny, weird, terrifying and full of tension. Above all it is a story built on a dysfunctional relationship, which must be resolved if the world is to be saved. It is very much its own thing. And that, I think, is a very good thing."

Salon Futura

"An enthralling Neo-Lovecraftian read with a strong pair of protagonists, a strong narrative character in Nick, and a detailed world and universe that I was very happy to spend some hours in."

Nerds of a Feather Stick Together

FINALIST IN THE 2021 LOCUS, AURORA, CRAWFORD, AND BRITISH FANTASY AWARDS

First published 2022 by Solaris
an imprint of Rebellion Publishing Ltd,
Riverside House, Osney Mead,
Oxford, OX2 0ES, UK

www.solarisbooks.com

ISBN: 978 1 78618 520 4

10 9 8 7 6 5 4 3 2 1

A CIP catalogue record for this book is available
from the British Library.

Designed & typeset by Rebellion Publishing

Printed in Denmark

THE VOID ASCENDANT

Premee
Mohamed

SOLARIS

Beneath the Rising Trilogy
1. *Beneath the Rising*
2. *A Broken Darkness*
3. *The Void Ascendant*

Solaris Satellites
These Lifeless Things

*For the friends who forgave
and did not forget*

I WILL TELL YOU A STORY

ONCE UPON A time, there was a girl who never forgot, and she killed everybody in the entire world.

Everybody except for me.

Now I am the one who remembers.

Because no one else is left.

CHAPTER ONE

I woke up with my heart already bursting, as if I had been awake and running for hours. Echoes of the dream mingled with the sounds from below as I lay stiff and sweating in the cold bed. And why cold? Soaked in my sweat. The room pitch dark, hearth a banked and lightless heap of ash.

Reality slowly reasserted itself. The sounds remained: but why here, why sounds? Nights were always quiet. The Tower of the Prophet was in an out-of-the-way courtyard for a reason: for silence and sleep, so that the future could speak clearly.

I slithered out of bed, absently wrapping the blanket around my bare shoulders, and crept to the window, peering down through the gap between the shutters. I had dreamt of drums, drumming. A warning of something martial approaching. And so it was: marching footsteps, iron-shod boots badly out of time, likely due to the near-spherical cobblestones that had long lost their mortar. You could break your ankle if you took a bad step in the courtyard. The stones would simply crack the bone like an eggshell.

Marching. Why *marching?* Who would march instead of walk? Soldiers. But our nation had no soldiers. Only the palace guards, who moved like wolves in silent packs on leather soles.

Soldiers marching in the dark. A straggling column, like ants, the shine of their armour dulled in the dust. Hundreds or thousands of helmets, too like ants, like their carapaces, hard and domed.

Make it make sense. We had no soldiers. *No one* had any, not in the whole planet, because they weren't needed, because they weren't *allowed*. Where had they come from? How had they gotten into the compound?

No flag, no insignia, no banners. The palace was being invaded.

I flattened myself against the wall next to the window. The how and why would not matter once the fighting began, would not affect the fires, the screaming, buildings toppling, blood flooding the ground.

Flee, that was it. Wait, no: they'd kill any civilian they saw. Or do worse yet, much worse (don't imagine how much worse!) if they realized they had captured the Royal Prophet.

And supposing they were down there right now, a few peeled away from the column, working silently on the locks of the tower's single door. Supposing they already knew exactly who lived here. They would come up, nothing would stop them, and the door separating my chamber from the stairs had no lock.

I cursed the tower, cursed the ancient architects who had made one way in and one way out. Unless you counted the window, of course... There was a certain temptation to leap to my death, it had to be said. A statement death: *There, I steal myself from you. Do what you wish to my corpse, for you cannot have me.*

But if I jumped and didn't die? No, I wasn't that brave. Not to lie on the ground screaming and shitting myself with broken limbs. Forget it. Have some dignity. For all the times I had wished for death over the last eight years, the wished-for deaths had been quiet, peaceful. Painless. Cowardice and numbness went together like that. I have not had to be brave for a long time.

What else. There were hundreds of guards at the palace. Might I signal for help? But how? No chance anything would be seen from up here anyway.

No, if I stayed here I might be safe for a while, but I would have to come down eventually, and when I did the same fate awaited me as if I had come down fighting. What was owed to the palace was owed; I could at least die in defence of their asset.

Decision made, I shed the blanket (at least let me die in clothes, for God's sake), cleaned my teeth over the basin, threw on robes, finger-combed oil through my hair and beard. Pocketed a handful of protective amulets, which were as far as I could tell bullshit, but might be useful in the event of a half-hearted stab in my chest region.

Even in the darkness I knew where everything was, I had spent so much time in here, there was nothing to do but memorize the place and size and weight of the things around me—not what I would call 'mine,' but at least 'the Prophet's.'

Movement in the cage next to my bed, a soft, worried shuffling, and I hesitated at that; but no. I would go down alone and so die alone.

I silently apologized to the cage's inhabitant, and removed my single weapon from its cabinet, the ceremonial crystal dagger used only for sacrifice. It had a fine edge, which might be good for (who knew?) one stab in the face before the glassy stuff broke on the soldiers' armour. Gingerly, I sheathed it and attached the sheath to my belt.

If invaders were ascending the stairs, they were doing it in miraculous silence. I moved softly down the steps in my own non-iron boots, one hand brushing along the smooth strip on the stone wall where generations of prophets had passed before me, the other methodically fishing amulets from my pocket and passing them over my head, one after another, forming a sort of jingling shield.

The stairs were deserted, just me for three hundred steps in unbroken darkness, and at the base, the barest gleam of a pinkish dawn, lying like a bar of iron on the stone floor, interrupted by the long shadows of those outside. Stamp, stamp, stamp. Armoured ants.

I unsheathed and got a good grip on the dagger, then worked the lock with trembling fingers. It seemed to take far longer than it should, but when the final lever clicked into place, I took a deep breath, flung the door open, and emerged into damp spring air and thousands of marching soldiers.

The soldiers didn't even turn to look.

I stared at them, mouth open. Their armour was black, rusty, raining orange flecks as they walked. Every few steps someone stumbled on a cobblestone, hissed under their breath, kept going. Their spears, swords, and other sundry weaponry were carried at a listless angle. They looked generally as if they had already fought the war and lost.

And a dozen paces away, smack in the middle of the marching column, on the official plaque, sat my Advisor, rising far above the heads of the soldiers flowing around him and mostly obscuring the Mouth of the Prophet huddled behind him. In the dawn light he seemed flat and dark, a low-relief statue of a sphinx on its haunches, his humanish face carved of glitter-flecked black granite, then no light at all along the long, powerful neck, the neatly-folded black wings, the glossy fur of his leonine body. He spotted me cowering in the doorway, and raised one paw.

I waved back instinctively even as my mind kept screaming. What was happening? Did *he* know what was happening? Was the invasion over then, had it happened while I had slept? How had they done it so quietly? And who would have dared to invade *us* of all people, knowing who our protectors were?

He beckoned me, patient and stolid, and the noise in my head died down a little. If they spared him, the soldiers might do the same for me, and it was worth swimming across to him for answers.

The soldiers were spaced widely in their column, so I stepped cautiously into the stream and muttered "Excuse me, sorry, excuse me," in Low Dath as I dodged and skittered between them; the few who looked up enough to see me generally tried to get out of my way, and I crossed with no more than a few bumps and stepped-on toes, both mine and theirs, to the safety of the metal plaque which, not being set above the ground surface in any way, gave only an illusory safety.

"Good morning, Prophet," said the Advisor pleasantly, as if we were not surrounded by inexplicable soldiers. "I hope you slept well. Are you prepared to begin?"

"Am I... What is going on here?" I swung an arm widely, meaning not just the army but the neverendingness of it. "No, I am not prepared to begin! Explain this!"

"Understandable." He had stood to greet me, but now settled back onto his haunches, folding his wings serenely over his back, a gesture he used, more or less, as punctuation. "We will wait."

"Advisor, there cannot be a prophecy this morning. Look at this! What's happening? Who are these people? What nation do they come from? Why are they here, what do they intend with us? Do the King and Queen know they are here? Do the guards? Were they summoned? *What's going on?*"

"Are you prepared to begin?"

"No!" I turned to appeal to the Mouth of the Prophet, as they were, in aggregate, showing a far more reasonable amount of fear and uncertainty. Five of them I knew; the sixth was a trainee, I thought, from her robes. Her antennae trembled constantly as the soldiers continued to pass us, quivering as if in a sharp breeze. I didn't speak Aeliphos pheromones but I recognized in broad strokes the smell of her terror. I was impressed that she didn't bolt. If she did, I would be tempted to follow.

I pictured them clustered behind the Advisor, tiptoeing in his wake as he simply forged his way across the column to this island of metal; I imagined them stumbling to take their accustomed places on the six worn-smooth spots in the carved pattern, trying to find comfort in routine on a morning when the routine had been decidedly disrupted and we were all, as far as I knew, still going to die. "I order one of you to tell me what is happening!"

They stared back at me. The Advisor, pointedly, took out his timepiece, a heavy gold number set into a bisected human skull, tiny as a pocketwatch in his great paw, and flipped it open. "They do not know," he said calmly.

"But *you* know. Is that what you're saying?"

"Are you prepared to begin?"

I put my hands in my pockets and inhaled deeply. Even today they would not break protocol; or, to be exact, they would not break protocol for my sake. Or to be even more exact, there was *nothing* they would break it for, and my mistake was believing that because I was the Prophet, I constituted some kind of reasonable exception to what was not even tradition or custom, but law.

Since I had arrived here I had tried a dozen times to skip the morning's prophecy, but it had been like turning a corner and walking unexpectedly into a wall, something not merely unyielding but absolutely oblivious to so puny an obstacle as the bones of a human face. Even when I had been ill they had simply climbed to my room in the tower and extracted notes from my babbling through fever-split lips or between bouts of vomiting.

I looked beseechingly at the Advisor one last time; he regarded me placidly, his pupils so dilated that they overtook the bluish whites of his eyes. *Stop it*, his gaze seemed to say. *You are balancing on a ledge that is too narrow to hold you, and you do not know which of these loyal servants might report you to the Royal Council for treason. A Prophet is allowed to be eccentric, not blasphemous.*

What *would* happen to me for treason, I wondered? I had never really challenged the Mouth's faith or loyalty. I did sense their everpresent fear of shirking, or being thought to shirk, this duty. Its magnitude worried me, seeming as out of proportion as it did to someone who had quit dozens of jobs in my previous life. They were afraid not for their status or position, I thought, but for their lives. And perhaps mine.

Still the soldiers went on. By this point I reckoned we were past thousands and into the tens of thousands, crossing the courtyard and marching through the arch on its far side, into the main palace compound. Surely towards Backless Hall, the only place large enough to collect them all. And to do what? And why *now*, why today? What did it mean?

"Fine," I said. Maybe if I paid up, the Advisor would give me something in return. "Attend."

"We are prepared to receive your dream, O Prophet," said Phothenth, the second-most senior member of the Mouth after Yalip. I closed my eyes, hearing the familiar rustle as they retrieved notepads and pens from sleeves, bags, and pockets, and turned to a fresh page, followed by the even more familiar reverent hush. Next to me, I felt the air move as the Advisor rose to his feet, his motion wafting the curiously herbal or even resinous smell of his feathers and fur.

Raising my voice over the noise of the boots on the cobbles, I recited the pre-arranged dream I'd prepared last night after supper, as I always did. Lots of colour and texture in it, but totally false. I couldn't remember when I'd decided to stop giving them my real dreams, but it had been a final decision, like a door slamming shut. No more. Never again. What they had of me would be what I chose.

And anyway, it was all bullshit; that the kingdom was still running and hadn't fallen into ruin despite relying on my 'prophecies' for every major decision was proof of that. I suspected that I could say literally anything, true or false, and the books of interpretation would find a way to incorporate it into a reasonable policy decision.

"And that is truly what you recall, Your Holiness?" The Advisor's eyes bored into me; his voice carried an edge like my crystal dagger.

"It is what I recall."

"All of it? That was it, start to finish?"

"Yes, all," I said. Sweat broke out in the small of my back. "You are not accusing me of lying, I hope."

"Never," he said. "I am only making sure. Please repeat it."

I stared at him; he had never asked me to describe a dream more than once. "Very well," I said, and ran through it again, already forgetting small details I'd added a moment ago: something about train tracks, which they didn't have here, and a snowstorm, and a lantern in the distance. Something about birds, which always went over well.

"Thank you, Prophet." I opened my eyes and Phothenth bowed low, blood coming into his beak so that he looked less pale and sickly. He turned and said to the others, his voice trembling, "Let us pray for the wisdom to understand this gift the Prophet has given us. For it is the wisdom of the Masters."

"Let us pray," the others chorused, visibly relieved, and formed a circle around me, joining hand to claw to paw to hand. First Sun crested the rooftops, sliced into bits by the maze of arch and ornament, transforming the pinkish dawn into crimson, then amber, then ordinary gold. Our shadows came into being and grew long and crisp across the pale cobbles and the black-armoured soldiers.

When the Mouth finished its ceremony and recited the Final Gratitudes, they left rapidly and a bit unsteadily, as if (I thought) they wanted to break into a panicked run, hurrying to the Sisur Archive for the books of interpretation, leaving me and the Advisor in the ringing sounds of the army retreating into the distance.

The Advisor gazed down at me, his eyes gradually returning to normal. "Sometimes I worry about you, Prophet."

"*This* you're not worried about?!" I pointed at the last soldiers as if the only thing impeding his explanation was that he for some reason could not see them. "What the hell is going on? Can you tell me now that we're alone?"

"I still cannot."

"I don't like secrets being kept from me, Advisor."

"It seems not," he agreed. "Consider leashing that dislike, Prophet, lest it get loose and attack its betters."

A threat? If it was, it was the first he'd ever expressed to me, and I was as startled as he'd surely meant for me to be. The Advisor was assigned to each incoming Prophet as bodyguard, interpreter, teacher, and mentor, and even though he was, technically, a coworker, he was also the closest thing I had to a friend here. We had never spoken a cross word to each other.

Not a threat, I decided. A warning. To exercise enough self-control in whatever came next, which he clearly knew and I clearly did not, such that I could avoid consequences that even he could not smooth over for me. He had done so in the past, I suspected. Quietly and for my sake alone. An Advisor was a great treasure to the palace—almost more so than a Prophet, for obvious reasons—and he was less replaceable, but not irreplaceable. None of us were.

"Is something terrible happening?" I finally said.

"Yes," he said softly. "Oh, yes."

Somewhere nearby, a joem called tentatively, as if it had just regained both its hearing and its composure after the thousands of ringing boots. Wings fluttered above our heads. An ordinary spring morning.

"But it was not given for me to tell you." He flexed his wings, then tucked them along his back, preparing to walk. "Come."

"Is that an official order, Advisor?"

"It is."

"So I cannot say no; but I'll be told what's happening? By someone who knows?"

"Yes. I promise."

It was a long walk. I called my new home a 'compound,' though the correct name, in High Dath, was an essentially untranslatable term to something as limited as what I had long ago realized English was. What I knew as an immense wall enclosing a few hundred buildings used by the Royal Family, they called the *sithesu-arithsusuir philanu heothesuir*, meaning something like, when you dug into the etymology, 'the fortified place which is not a military fortress which is for good/positive reasons set above the reach of enemies/dangerous things.'

It had taken some getting used to, but I had started out, unlike most Prophets, with the advantage of a certain amount of familiarity. And that was because it looked like several scenes in a movie I had seen about two hundred times back on Earth: like *Mortal Kombat*'s Outworld. When I had been teaching English to the

Advisor, one of the first things I taught him was 'I can't wait to see what the bathrooms look like.' It was the first time I had seen him laugh, really laugh, showing all his sharp and glassy teeth.

"Good morning, Prophet!" someone called; I waved at the little group of guards, unsure who had spoken, as they trooped yawning from a watchtower. Out of sheer boredom one day, as well as hoping to practice my Low Dath, I had asked if I could train with them once or twice a week. Now we were all regular sparring partners, and ate together often after we trained. It was nice to have friends again.

Someone else shouted something I couldn't hear as I passed, and I waved back. Something about a bun? I was hungry, and would have liked one if so, but the Advisor was moving fast and I had to walk at an undignified pace to keep from breaking into a trot.

It was warmer in the sun, cooler in the soaring baroque clutter of arches, skulls, bones, all carved in various colours of stone (or anyway, I hoped all the skeletons were made things; I tried very hard not to think about them *not* being carved and had never been tempted to ask for clarification, unlike the Advisor's watch). In the cold spring morning everything glittered with frost, giving the impression it was moving even in its petrified immobility. Birds flitted back and forth, scuffling over the hundreds of good nesting places in sheltered tangles of ribs and inviting eyesockets.

"Prophet!"

I looked up, and raised a hand to another guard,

leaning over the low parapet of his tower and waving his spear to get my attention. "Good morning!" I called up, pausing.

"Will we see you for cards tonight? Tower Eighteen!"

"Yes, I'll be there! And you know what happens if I catch you cheating this time!"

"No one has forgotten!"

The Advisor turned and came back for me, not impatient, merely inexorable. "Prophet. Come along, please."

"I do apologize."

I began to note landmarks I knew: this garden, that statue, that crumbling arch, a strange cluster of eight joined towers like the columnar pod of a behek plant, topped with the same razor-sharp points. Lichen blinked sleepily at us, not warm enough yet to go crawling across the stones and up the faces and femurs of the walls. Three kalnis looked up at the sound of our footsteps, huge soft fuchsia shrubbery one moment, round-backed animals the next, but seeing that there were only two of us, they shuffled back into the shade and became shrubs again.

In the cobbles I spotted small things the army had dropped: coins, empty pens, other odds and ends wedged between the round stones. I stopped to pick up a piece of paper caught between the leaves of a weed. "I think it's part of a letter," I said when I caught up to the Advisor again. "Someone tore it up. Look, the date is five days ago. They must have changed their mind about sending it."

"Very good, Your Holiness. Please keep up."

"Or someone told them to destroy it. Why would they not want letters to be sent? Why not confiscate it?"

"Your curiosity is a credit to your people, Prophet."

I knew what that kind of bland response was hiding; I couldn't hear the tension in his deep, gritty voice, which simply due to the construction of the vocal apparatus, like a lot of people here (and oh how I had learned to expand what the word *people* meant), often seemed without expression or tone; it had taken me a long time to learn how to interpret what he said.

I kept up.

It occurred to me, not for the first time, that I could spend more time exploring the place that I was all but imprisoned in; but I'd never really wanted to. I spend more time at my window, leaning on the thick sill and staring at the landscape below. The forest beyond the wall, the occasional campfire of some furtive and desperate poacher, the gleam of the sea in the distance. One door, one window, circumscribed my whole life now. Whatever I asked for was brought to me.

And now, I thought with a sudden bolt of fear, someone had asked for the Advisor to bring them something; and I was the thing being brought.

"Where are we going?"

The Advisor glanced back at me as he walked, methodical, not rushing. "Do you not recognize the way, Prophet?"

"No," I said, then corrected myself almost at once. "Yes. Sorry." I had just recognized the long bridge we were crossing, slippery with frost along the curved spines or whatever it was that constituted the handrails, and the platform in the middle planted with golden ornamental grasses. The canal below flowed swiftly beneath a transparent scrim of ice that I suspected would be broken up for good by the afternoon, not to return until late fall.

Yes. To the Auditorium. And I knew what that meant. But it wasn't supposed to happen like this. I was supposed to have been informed a moon in advance: exactly a moon, whichever of the twenty-six tiny glowing pearls had been in the correct spot in the Royal Astronomer's grid on the day it had been decided. There was protocol. There were calculations, even. I thought about pointing this out to the Advisor, then changed my mind.

He was speeding up, lengthening his stride till the feathers along his neck and back streamed in the wind of his moving, and was soon moving fast enough even at a walk that I had to jog to keep up behind him. We were late. My fault. He'd take whatever blame there was for it, but if we could make it a little less noticeable, leniency was likely to be had.

I thought again: We're not irreplaceable.

I thought: Why do I keep thinking that?

The Auditorium, like the other big buildings on this side of the compound, backed onto the cliffs, which I only remembered as we began to clamber rather than walk up the increasingly steep streets towards its windowless white wall of stone. You could only approach it from this one side. Very sensible, really. Didn't want just anybody sauntering in.

The Advisor slowed as we approached, eyeing the huge tapestries dangling from the top of the exterior wall; in a strong breeze, they would occasionally snap out and knock you off your feet. From the open doors emanated the smell of the sea but also of gathered bodies, perfumes and incense, and the murmur of a crowd ordered to be silent but unable to stop itself from shifting. A smell also of burning. Woodsmoke overlying something definitively not wood, touching off a siren inside me that screamed without words. Birds sailed silently overhead, black specks against the green sky.

Don't make me, I thought. Don't make me. I don't want to.

Please.

I said nothing. We emerged from the arched entryway and onto the expected purple carpet, a hundred paces long, its thick nap so far unmarred by any feet, spanning the smooth slate flagstones. At its end hunched the royal pavilion, swagged with thick fabrics shot through with gold thread so that it seemed to capture all the early dawn light, leaving its occupants in luxurious shade. Only an occasional glint of evidence like the eyes of animals in a forest: a crown, a scepter, a ring, a necklace. And below the pavilion, down a handful of shallow steps, waited a wooden platform, and something on top of it, on fire.

To either side of the carpet stood tables covered with trays of food and glass pitchers of wine, and huge bowl-shaped braziers, the flames invisible in the sunlight.

Around us rose step after step after step, pale stone all but covered by the crowd. The walls here were studded with watchtowers, the guards within visible but still: yes, they were for watching within as well as without, the archers were ready to kill—eager for it in fact—and only awaiting their signal: treason, blasphemy, disobedience. Anything the King said. Anything the Queen said.

In the cool air, sweat gathered thickly on the back of my neck, my temples, rolled down into my beard.

As we approached the pavilion and the platform below, the King and Queen emerged and leaned on the edge of the stone box; the crowd fluttered in response, sighed in enforced silence. No cheers, no applause. A thousand soft breaths, stifled coughs. My empty stomach contracted as we passed the food, and again, harder, as we reached the platform.

I noticed the executioner first, but even as my body tensed to run from him, my eyes next fell on the sacrificial victim: Yalip, one of the usual six members of the Mouth. They must have gotten him in the night; they would have waited for him to produce yesterday's prophecy. Squeeze out that final droplet of use.

Yalip was shivering in the light sacrificial robes of white silk; he looked thin, and old, and confused rather than frightened. I had never seen him without his robes and hat of office. And he was bald, or they had shaved him, leaving a dozen small cuts on his scalp. One last cruelty.

He stared at me as the Advisor and I stopped at the prescribed distance, in the prescribed silence. An act of haruspicy had been called for this morning. Now he would be the prophecy.

And they had brought in an outsider to kill him. At a distance I had known this stranger. Recognized him, feared him, so that the blood in my veins seemed to jump back even as I had kept walking. I felt emptied-out by terror, hollow with it. I had last seen him mounted on a dragon, flying after me in an endless darkness. But I had first seen him in a forest, long ago, on fire.

CHAPTER TWO

MY LEGS FELT too stiff to bend. Alone, I climbed the steps to the platform, feeling heat baking off the Burning King as he turned his faceless head to me without any emotion I could discern, including recognition. But of course you could tell nothing without a face. Or I couldn't, anyway.

If he cries out, I thought. If he can speak. If he tells them who I am and where I am from, if he tells them: *It is him! Here is what he has done!*

And what had I done? Even now I felt the weight of years pressing down on the moment: the past, smothered under the layers of stone and mud I poured down on it, till the day came (I desperately hoped) I would not remember it at all, instead of pretending to not remember. Till the day someone would ask and I could say, *I don't remember that. No, that didn't happen to me. It wasn't me. It was someone else.*

Because of all the prophets in all the world in all the...
Because I had showed up here. I, who had schemed and
plotted to betray the rulers of this place, the Ancient
Ones who had conquered it so long ago and now ruled
through Their servants, the King and the Queen. I, who
was alive at Their Majesties' sufferance only because
they did not know my past. My past of treason and
rebellion, of refusing to accede to my proper place in the
universe. If the Burning King revealed me, they would
turn on me like a hunting dog on a rat. That pivot like
lightning: *snap*.

Coward, coward. And is my fear only for me, while
Yalip shivers in his sacrificial silk? My friend? Do I dare
call him that even in my head?

I thought about the crystal dagger, its sheathed weight
banging against my leg. Part of me, cool and clinical,
thought: I could take it out quickly, and kill myself
rather than let this happen. It's brittle but it's sharp.
Meant to take things apart after they're already dead.
And it would be a blasphemy too, wouldn't it? Because
you're only supposed to use it for animals. For sacrificial
animals. Never on a person and certainly never on a
person with some kind of prestige. It's an insult. Makes
the blade unclean. Ha! And if I tried and failed, it would
be like this morning's terrible minutes in the dark of my
tower, wouldn't it. If I had jumped and lived. I thought:
The soldiers would kill me.

Another part of me thought: Now the archers would.
Someone royal would make a small gesture. And that
would be the end.

Yalip's eyes on me like a hand. Clammy against my skin. The eyes baffled, iridescence dulled, as if he were dehydrated.

I cannot say no to this, Yalip, loyal servant of the crown. You know I cannot say no. I know I cannot say no.

The executioner burns, he burns in silence. I too will remain silent. Lest he say anything to expose me.

Not the King and Queen but the executioner chooses the manner of death; that's traditional. I've seen clean ones, beautiful ones. A split second between life and death, the way they measure that here. Once for a festival they brought in a guest executioner from another country, Eulo I think, who carried an axe taller than I was, with a blade about three feet long. Almost as much blade as handle. And as sharp as a piece of broken glass. You see enough messy decapitations, you learn to appreciate a fast, neat one. And it only took one stroke. No messing around with the skin and sinew afterwards. A piece of purple ribbon had been tied around it, I remembered suddenly and for no apparent reason. Purple like the carpet. To show that the honour had been noticed and the executioner appreciated the gesture.

But you. The monster. The king who burns, the thing made of wood and flames, your bloodied no-face, your crown of antlered branches. Why are you here? *How* are you here? When did you arrive? How will you kill the sacrifice? How can I stop you?

What does it mean that you are here?

Like the soldiers, it has meaning, and that has not been shared with me.

My stomach rose, somersaulted, fell. I was forcing everyone to wait: it had been noticed. The King withdrew again into the shade, but the Queen remained leaning on the stone edge of the pavilion, her arms stiff. I was not permitted to meet her gaze but I felt it boring into me as if she had seized my face tightly enough to drive her fingernails into it.

This is how you know you don't want to die. This is the only way you know. You meet the eye of the executioner who has no eyes and you nod. The nod means: *Kill him*. It means: *Don't kill me*.

My only saving grace is telling that voice inside me: Yes, I will kill myself, I will absolutely end my soft and worthless life to make way for something better, but I will do it later. Not now. Later. Don't speak over that voice, don't let the world speak over that voice. It is the only thing that sounds in the emptiness and it is my only companion now, no matter what other voices and bodies surround me with emptinesses of their own.

Is something terrible happening? I had asked the Advisor not half an hour ago, and he had said yes. And this was it.

I still didn't understand how the army came into it; but they had to be connected. Yalip must have been involved with something I didn't understand. Like so much else here. How much did I know about him, really? Not enough. Less than all of us know about each other. Maybe I should take away the word *friend* from him in these moments before his death. He would never know.

I nodded to the Burning King.

Yalip's face went blank with terror and betrayal, but he said nothing; his lips trembled, bluish against the pallor of his face, as he stared at me. I made myself stare back, maintaining eye contact in an effort to tell him I hadn't really left him, that I was still here, that he did understand, didn't he? That there was no choice for either of us but to allow this to happen. The status of the sacrificial victim was directly correlated to the accuracy of the haruspicy. It was a fact; experiments had been done.

It did not correlate, however, to the glee of the executioner, and I hated the way the monster's body moved, gleeful and light, virtually dancing with happiness, as he picked up Yalip and carried the limp form towards the edge of the platform, breaking our locked gaze. And then he leaned down, and the flames roared from his burning crown.

The screams were piercing but, like last time, brief.

When it seemed to be over, I reached for the book and paused, and slowly withdrew my hand, which was shaking so hard I had to grip it with my other hand. My entire body trembled, my teeth clattering together. I should have eaten something. One egg. One fruit. Someone had offered me a bun, hadn't they? I didn't see who. I couldn't think. Proximity to pain is the most terrible thing in the world, because you can do nothing about it. The sickening smell of burnt wood and flesh and bone wafted to me, and I coughed at the smoke, then retched. The only sound in the place. Amplified on purpose. Because we were in an auditorium. *Audit*: so you could hear.

He had killed Yalip; but I had given permission. One nod. No one here was innocent.

I focused on the flagstones as the Burning King returned and laid the headless body on my table, and only looked up again when his wavering, flame-wreathed shadow was gone. Not far enough: he had climbed off the platform to take his place under the Royal Pavilion, in the intersecting shadows of fabric and wall. The flames of his crown and feet illuminated someone—or something, or several things—next to him. I strained to see them, but they were strangely elusive, as if they slipped away once they sensed a gaze upon them.

Then I looked at the Queen: serene, patient, and intent. Because no one ever said no to her; because no one was saying no to her now. She made me think of praying mantises, which they didn't have here. And I was still shaking.

But the incantation had to be read first. I reached for the book again, tugged its ponderous mass from under Yalip's shoulder, the ornate cover now flecked with black ash and curled strands of burnt silk. My hands were slick, moisture darkening the blue velvet bookmark placed at the incantation.

I pried it open, held the cover down with both hands, and read aloud as sweat dripped from my forehead onto the already moisture-rippled pages, soaked and dried a thousand times before today, from other prophets who had wept or perspired as they read. I sensed them behind me in a long unbroken chain of centuries; I sensed them look away from me, and away from each other, murderers, enablers of murderers.

At the end I looked at the King and the Queen in their pavilion, and carefully moved the bookmark, then dried my hands on my robes.

"You may proceed," the Queen said. She removed a small white envelope from her sleeve and handed it to a scribe next to her, who held it out stiffly in both hands in front of him like a shield. "The number of the questions is three."

Three. Last time it had been five. All right. You can do this. You can do this. You have to do this, or they will burn your head off and wait for a new prophet to show up. They don't want that. Do you? (Yes, a bit. But on we go.)

The number of the questions is three. I hefted the sacrificial knife, not my own crystal one; I held up the round whetstone and the vial of oil. For a few minutes there was sound again in the square: the fine high methodical whine of metal across ceramic.

Then I returned to Yalip's body. It too was still shaking—twitching as the last dregs of energy burned in its cells, which didn't know yet that the greater whole was dead. His torso was milk-white, his chest hair long and surprisingly dark, fluttering in the breeze. I had never known the victim before. How could I do this?

Lying, lies. It had worked for years. He's a stranger, I told myself firmly. Don't think of him as a friend. Not even an acquaintance. Without the head he could be anyone, anyway. This isn't someone you knew. It's just a body. In fact, it's a practice body. Made of wax.

Stamp down that part of yourself that is screaming and do what you're fucking told.

I cut, pulled, pinned, reached, sharpened the knife, and cut again. Liver, heart, one kidney: the three. Warm, far warmer than my own hands. As if the fire that had killed him had remained inside him, keeping him at a low simmer after death. His lungs looked terrible— good thing there hadn't been four questions. He must have inhaled the flames, mercifully speeding his death.

I washed my hands in the glass basin of water, dried them on the embroidered towel, laid out the organs, opened the book again. Mechanically, carefully. Blood creeping across the table, dripping over the edge, its sharp metallic animal smell at last covering the stink of burning. Why was there so much blood? Surely the burning had cauterized the big arteries. *Dead stranger, dead stranger. A strange dead man.* Not someone I knew.

I didn't kill him, anyway. Not me. The twitching had stopped. My hands were steady now too. It wears itself out, it burns itself out, whatever is inside us that has a soul and shakes at death. It tires and sleeps.

Gently, I pushed the three organs out of the blood and onto a clean part of the table, and glanced at the book. The diagrams were large and in full colour; anyone could have followed them. It was mere cruelty, I thought clinically, that they forced the Prophet to do it.

It'll be over soon. Come on. You've done this before.

Yes, I have. I have become something that can do this. What I have become is what they have made me. To make me they had to make me do this more than once.

"To the first question, the answer is yes," I said, and nudged the liver aside. "To the second, the answer is no." The kidney. "To the third..."

His heart was so hot. Or was it that my hand was so cold? All the blood in my own body seemed to have drained out and into some cold place, the door left hanging open. The heart was so hot and so small. Yalip had not been a big man, but I had not expected his heart to fit in my palm with room to spare. I could see the lines of my palm past its edges. Heart line, head line. Life line. It was like holding a live coal.

"Prophet." The lightest hint of menace from the Queen.

"To the third..." My throat was closing off, the text doubling, tripling with tears. Yesterday I had almost gotten a smile out of him. Almost. The stain on his robe, I said; was that ink or wine? And he had said, Both, Your Grace, the great poet Lilossa Frich once boasted that he filled his pens with wine and wrote his poems that way, so I thought I might try it out. No smile at all. The Advisor chuckling, though, the wet gleam of his teeth in the dawn light. No soldiers. No flames.

"*Prophet.*"

Not a hint. The table began to sway as if the legs were melting, but I realized what was happening just in time, dropped the heart, and grabbed the edges to stay upright. The book snapped back into focus an inch from my nose. How long had I hesitated? No one spoke.

I picked up the heart again and rotated it delicately in both hands. Last question. Glanced at the diagram; back at the heart. It was all bullshit, all of it. All prophecy.

Dreams, bodies, the flight of birds across the thirty-two segments of the sky, nothing meant anything. Birds flew, they didn't give a shit about us, and they certainly brought no messages from the future, let alone advice.

But Yalip's heart bore something odd: a round, iridescent blue patch, like a coin. Not like a birthmark, more like a tattoo, so clear was the blue against the red. I rubbed it with my thumbs, and it didn't fade. The book was unequivocal. There was *never*; there was *never again*; there was *never for you*. "To the third, the answer is... never."

Now the crowd hissed, a collective intake of breath, as if they knew the question, which was impossible. The Queen nodded.

Is something terrible happening?

Oh, yes.

Breathe, I told myself in a dozen languages. Breathe. Look normal. You don't know that your life doesn't depend on it today. Something is happening. Something was moving and then it moved and now it is here. In front of you. Breathing and alive, as Yalip is not. Whatever it is has come to your door, not by chance but by design. Because it is your door. Because it is the door of this kingdom.

The Queen said, "Everyone must go. Now. Prophet, you and your Advisor are to remain."

I washed my hands again and waited as the Auditorium emptied. This had never happened before; normally, everyone invited to the foretelling went to the tables to feast, and the King and Queen left.

What was happening, what had their questions been? But they would never tell me. To tell was to invalidate the sacrifice.

Were there other clues? I couldn't tell. Both monarchs looked relaxed, even confident, inasmuch as I could tell anything from the King's body language; he was a Lawor, of which Aradec had a vanishingly small indigenous population, and I was sure that the colours on his wings meant something, but audible speech was not something they produced.

Soon it was us and their attendants, and the Advisor, and the opened-out corpse of Yalip, and the smell of the cooling feast mingling with the sea air. We arranged ourselves as if for an ordinary meal, and sat at the very end of one of the long tables. A heavily-perfumed human woman set out four plates, utensils, light silver goblets; another poured out an everyday black wine and placed glass tumblers of water and beakers of honey in their divots on the table. A Turuntu man smelling of woodsmoke began to serve food in order: Queen, King, myself, Advisor. I watched it all without taking it in, my fingers up on the tablecloth where everyone could see them. Etiquette. Manners. Maketh the coward. There was still blood under my fingernails, though I had clipped them as short as I could only yesterday. My friend's blood. No, a stranger's. Perhaps a traitor's. Now they would tell me. They must.

When the Queen finally deigned to sip her wine, we began to eat. I sawed at a translucent red cube of meat that in terms of cost would probably have fed a village for a month, and put a slice into my mouth. It tasted like air and ash. The vegetables dripped a red, oily (*bloody*) juice across the plate. I ripped a piece of bread and dabbed it in the dressing, and chewed, and swallowed.

The Queen said, "I will be brief, Prophet. And I will begin by saying that I was surprised by the answers to my questions."

"Your Majesty," my mouth said, entirely without input from my brain. Surprise was bad. The Queen did not like to be surprised.

"Nevertheless, prophecies show what they show. The answers cannot be changed. Perhaps in due time we will ask something else... Never mind."

I could barely hear her. I was staring at the shadows below the pavilion, the ones that seemed to move and change and shimmer, the ones that seemed to burn. Except for us, everyone had left. Or had they?

The Burning King, when I knew him, had been an errand boy, a bounty hunter. I had not been clear on whose. Only one of the Ancient Ones, as I had called Them on Earth, because what else could you say of Them? The ones who had conquered Earth again and again, frustrated when the dedicated sorcerers of previous ages—and my own age, once—had ejected and thwarted Them.

Here, They were called the Masters. Their conquest of this world, Aradec, had been total and complete; so what else would you call Them? We existed now under Their sufferance, a thrall world subject to Their every whim and demand.

All the same, palace life was good. It always was, I thought, any world you were on: to be near money, even if you had none, and to be near power, even if you had none. But that closeness was both a blessing and a curse; it implied availability, and availability meant requirements, rather than requests. The closer you were to the boss' office, the safer and less safe you were. No in-between.

The Queen said, "For a short time now, we have been receiving the glad news that many Masters are awakening from Their... Their rest. And may all praise Their renewal and return!"

Awakening, I thought, and reached for another piece of bread. Well. True and not true. That made it sound active, as if They were doing it on Their own; when what had really happened was that They had *been* awakened. And I knew who had started it. And I knew you couldn't stop it once it started.

She said, "As is Their way, They have begun once again to bring new worlds under Their benevolent rule..."

Silence. The food sat like lead in my stomach. Across from me, the King unfurled his proboscis and sent it questing into my wine goblet; I did not protest, only watched numbly as the liquid level went down. I was terrified that I might laugh, or scream, or *something*, and I would have no warning of it whatsoever, and that would be the end of me.

"And of course, as loyal subjects of the Masters, we have been waiting eagerly for news that Aradec may join the..." The Queen paused. "The war effort."

This time the laughter actually started, and I held down the rest of it with an effort, covering it with a cough; I knew how it would have sounded, cawing and hysterical, even panicked. The *war effort*. What the hell did she know about this war? I had been there when it started. I had been there at the *moment* it started. Looked at from a certain angle, I had *helped* start it. And now I was sitting here, and she was telling me all about it.

The Masters. Of course you would call Them Masters, I thought again. Of course *we* would. We. I was part of that we now.

Because They ruled. That was what They did. They subjugated planets where They could, destroyed them where They couldn't. And everywhere They went They were ruled by Their hungers and by a mindless, atavistic urge to dig Their claws into order and turn it into disorder, to drag it closer to the state They existed in. To eat, torture, kill, twist, change, ruin. To take anything living and turn it inside out and lick out the living spark of it and laugh. For ages They had slept in scattered places, waiting for an opportunity to wake that would be worth it somehow, a crack into which to insert Their unspeakable tentacles and push till it yawed open.

And about eight years ago, as near as I could reckon, something had cracked. On my homeworld. On Earth. The war that had begun as my old life ended and this one began, a microsecond separating them, or maybe less, separating Earth's death and my birth, or rebirth. One blink and I had come to at the foot of the Tower of the Prophet, where the palace expected a replacement to appear for the old Prophet who had died the day before.

The war had always been moving, creeping towards Aradec, surrounding us as if we were the eye of the storm. But the eye of the storm did not last forever, because the storm was in motion.

I had escaped nothing.

Nothing.

Only for a time. And I had been fooling myself, lying with a force that verged on violence, self-mutilation. It had gone on all along, while I had been safe and pampered here.

The colourful plate of food dimmed in front of me, the shapes beginning to melt and run. The Advisor murmured something under his breath, snapping me back to attention from my daze.

"Prophet," the Queen said, "historically there have been... doubts about our world's loyalty to the Masters. Those doubts have long been laid to rest. We have proven ourselves to be the most dedicated of subjects."

I nodded. Aradec had been conquered about a thousand years ago, as best I could tell from the Archive. The people then had fought back, as everyone fought back against Them; it seemed programmed into the very genes to fight back. But when offered the chance to be a thrall rather than a smudge of dust, all the kingdoms agreed to live as Their subjects, and had spent about two hundred years putting down unsanctioned rebellions against Their presence until finally all resistance crumbled. Periodic flare-ups were put down at once, either by the agents They infrequently stationed here, or by the rulers, whoever discovered it first.

Peace at last. Of course things are very peaceful when you don't fight back.

For years all I had been able to conclude was: *Earth should not have fought back*.

I, we, should not have fought back. I was wrong; I see that now. We made a mistake.

"In accordance with the Book of Syrona," the Queen said, "during a time of war, no actions shall be taken without the approval of the Masters, and all decisions must be in agreement with the augurs, revelations, and portents. Further in accordance with the Book, Prophet, you are now the Head of Royal Military Intelligence. You and the Advisor may act in conjunction with the Guards, if you like. It has been done before."

It was the last thing I had expected; I flinched as if I had been slapped by her smile.

No. No. I don't want to. Please don't make me do this. Please, I have done my duty in every other respect since the moment I came here. I have watched you kill. I have reached inside bodies. I have killed animals. I have condemned men to death. Courteously, relentlessly, patiently, you have threatened me with everything short of death for noncompliance. Have I not done everything you've said? Have you not broken me in ways I did not think someone could be broken?

And I don't *know* anything about military intelligence. And I am no spy. Not any more. I am not a military man. I am soft, and if you see how soft I am, you will declare me incompetent, and then I don't know what will happen to me. You don't know either. Please, ask me to do anything else. Do not involve me in this war.

Quick, say something. Your reputation but also your status, your treatment, your future, your pulse, could end right here. *Quick.* You have already paused too long. Look, she raises her eyebrows at you. You'll need every single word of High Dath you've learned for this.

"Your Majesty," I began, "I... do not think I will be useful to the Masters in this capacity. I know nothing of intelligence or tactics, I know nothing of war. I..."

For the first time the smooth mask of her face cracked, revealing shock so exaggerated and apparently genuine that I was shocked in turn, and the rest of my protest dribbled away and became remorse. Oh God, what was I doing, how had I dared to—?

"Prophet." The threat light, clear. Like a gem. She was not asking for agreement. Agreement was not part of the expected response. Only acknowledgement. Because I couldn't say no. I was no longer in a position where I could say no. The shadows flamed, shimmered. She would forgive this: once. And never again.

I nodded, and blinked sweat out of my eyes. "I am honoured, Your Majesty."

"Yes, I know."

As she spoke to the Advisor, I looked down at the flagstones near the edge of the table, past my trembling hands, the gleaming toes of my own boots, tipped in silver. The thin borders of the stones, fitted as closely as craft could make them, swam in my vision, seeming to form words, like subtitles, as the Queen spoke. Something about the drafted troops that had arrived this morning, where they would be stationed, who to speak to about getting them fed, where they might be stationed (anywhere the Masters needed them, for this war was hungry and both sides consumed soldiers with terrifying rapidity; and the Masters, talented as They were, could not create life, only repurpose it, move it, imitate it, and that was not always useful for war). Magical weapons, artifacts held in museums or universities. The general dearth of magical practitioners who could be trusted. Communications. Ciphers. Payment. Loyalty. Loyalty.

There would not be fighting here, I thought. At least there was that. This planet was already won; They had signed Their name upon it forever, and various of Their minions, agents, and trustees visited from other worlds to collect tribute and magic whenever They wished. We were a company town, existing only to serve Them. They would not let us suffer any harm. The invasion I had imagined this morning would never come to pass.

But everyone else in Their path was fair game. And this was what loyalty meant: to do as They said, or risk our own safety.

I knew that trade. That was a familiar trade. It was one I made every day, and it grew easier all the time.

I inhaled. Exhaled. Looked up to discover that the King's seat was empty; I spotted him fluttering away, already far distant, his spinal spikes catching the early sun and sending rainbows sparking back at us. He would hunt for a few hours and return cleaning fish scales off his fangs, I knew. On the beach below, guards would pace nervously, watching both sea and sky. I often envied his freedom, which should have been less than mine but was more.

"Enemies are already beginning to infiltrate," the Queen murmured, leaning forward. Her heavy gown creaked as she moved, as if to add emphasis. "Are they not, Advisor?"

I twitched, but stopped myself from turning to stare at him. His breath was light and calm at my side. Now we would come to it. What did Yalip…

"We captured six unauthorized trespassers within the royal grounds, Prophet," the Advisor said evenly, not looking at me. The feathers along his neck had risen though, and while this happened in silence, to me it was as loud as a shout. "Five near the gates… whom we suspect to have been trying to deliberately lure us away from the sixth, who was captured inside the Archive of Ashuskroth."

"Wait," I said after a beat, when he seemed to be done. "Inside it? But how? It's…"

"Correct."

"Interrogate them," the Queen said. "Find out what they wished to do here. Why they came into our secret places… whom they serve. They cannot be permitted to interfere with the war. Not even to *attempt* it."

"Yes, Your Majesty," I said. Live through this, I told myself. Live through this and don't look back at it ever again once it's over. Life will be soft and easy again. It'll be all right.

*　　*　　*

I DID NOT dare ask for any kind of delay on my duties, not after my performance earlier. My new status felt like one of our glass tumblers balanced delicately on something, ready at the slightest nudge to fall onto the flagstones and shatter.

The walk to the seldom-used dungeons, even for the Advisor, required stopping twice to get directions, and it took so long that he insisted we also pause at one of the guard stations to get something to eat. I forced down a sweetbun and a riseb, waving away the offer of his penknife and peeling away the indigo skin with my teeth before eating the segments.

"This is good," the Advisor said around his own fruit, neatly flayed with his foreclaws. "You did not eat properly earlier... It is better to have something in your stomach. It settles it."

"For what?"

"You know," he said vaguely, wiping the dark-blue juice on his ceremonial sash. "Interrogation."

"You mean torture," I said, after hunting around for a moment in my head for the word in Low Dath. I didn't even know it in High, and I didn't think I'd taught it to him in English.

"Maybe later," he said. "Now we go this way, and we're to turn right at the three round storehouses. No, you don't start with torture. Initially you simply keep people awake, that's a good start. And it's additive; if you have to do more than that, they break more easily if they have not slept."

"Done a lot of it, have we?"

"There's manuals," he admitted. "In the Guards' Library. What they call the Shed. Handed down, not updated for twenty or thirty years. I don't think the Guards have ever actually had anyone to interrogate beyond a good bout of yelling. Maybe Corporal Polat, she's about seventy and she dealt with that dockyard business."

"But you were here then," I said. His people, the Rhaokor, lived for hundreds of years, and though I knew little about him I did know that he had been Advisor to six prophets before me.

"I was," he said. "I did not participate."

"I don't want to interrogate anyone, Advisor."

"I know," he said. "And I wouldn't ask you to, Prophet. Your heart is a gentle one to be in a war. It was born out of time."

"There's never a good time for a war."

He shook his head. "We're in the best possible place and time for it. You'll see. Now as for the questioning, you can oversee the interrogation while one of the guards takes it on. I'll choose someone reliable. Not one of your friends. Your position is important, yes, and tricky. But no one would judge you for simply managing it instead of getting your hands dirty. Your involvement is necessary, but it can be minimal in that necessity."

Now more than ever before I felt the entire secret of my past hang between us, the truth of this war, the players in it who knew me, whose names I knew in turn, the way the Masters were so far from being a faceless indistinguishable mass of evil. I wished I knew nothing about it, so that I could easily accept the version he knew. But once you know something you cannot unknow it. "I don't even want to oversee it. I don't want to be involved at all."

"I know. Don't let anyone hear you say that. Here we are."

Don't make me betray you, he meant; I knew he would report me if he had to. I pushed it out of my head and looked around. We had arrived at a region of the compound I didn't recognize. The dungeon sat higher than the buildings around it, a stocky circular building of four levels, ringed with a surprisingly deep though empty moat that even now was being filled by a long-suffering-looking junior guard manning a pump that squirted out about a bucketful of water with every heave of the lever. I wondered if he was being punished.

The entire building gave the impression of hasty repair, as if it had just been put back into service last night—which, I thought, it might have been. Valishec, the capital city near which our palace had been built, had its own prisons which we did not use, and we rarely had cause to lock someone up here. I knew a few of the guard towers had a cell for the infrequent capture of drunks or poachers (no lock on the door, only a thumb-latch on the outside, like something you might use on a garden gate). You'd be hard-pressed to find somewhere to put six people at short notice without reopening the dungeon.

The dungeon's interior smelled faintly of old piss, but

not much else; everything was dusty, from the lamps to the registry book in which we signed our titles. Everything was still, silent, except for the small creaturely noise of a guard mopping the floor somewhere. Scrape of wet rags, splash into a bucket. I realized belatedly that I had been expecting screams, prayers, curses, like before an execution or a sacrifice. Sacrificial victims weren't even locked up, merely guarded, and you could hear their pleas from halfway across the compound.

"Where's the spy that was arrested inside the Archive?" I whispered.

The Keeper of Dungeons, a small rattled-looking human dressed in a many-pocketed leather vest, gestured to his right. "Cell Eighteen, your Holiness. You want the keys?"

"No, no," said the Advisor before I could reply. "We're just going to look. And develop a strategy."

"Will you be needing any apparatus?" The Keeper scratched his short, silvery beard. "I think we got them in storage someplace. But I don't know that we can get the furnace going, on account of the chimney not bein' cleaned for, uh. Probably five or six years now. Fill the whole place with smoke. Would a brazier or something do as well? I can borrow one."

"We'll let you know," the Advisor said, and his hackles went up again just as they had been starting to settle flat against his short, gleaming fur.

I whispered, "By apparatus, did he mean—"

"Yes."

"And all that's in the manual."

"Yes, it's under 'Advanced Questioning Techniques.'"
He turned to his left instead of right, and I followed. As
with the outside, the inside was circular, a ring of cells
surrounding a deep central pit, and open to the roof via
another circle that admitted daylight. Each cell was double-
doored, the first set an arm's length from the second,
effectively making a second, tiny cell between them, and,
the Advisor informed me, locked by a separate key. It was
like stacked cartwheels, each spoke leading to a cell.

Both doors had a thickly barred grid set slightly below
my eye level, allowing a view of the cell within: a stone
bunk built into the wall, an exterior window about
the size of a playing card, and a drain in the floor the
same size. Complex, circular wards against the practice
of magic shone from floor to ceiling in the dim light,
glittering like broken glass.

"And it's only the captured spies in here?" I asked the
Advisor in English when we were away from the Keeper
and his desk. "No one else?"

"No, no one else." He looked down at me. "I could do
this alone. With your permission, Prophet."

I shook my head. "I appreciate it. But there's my
position to consider. And yours. During a time of war,"
I added for emphasis. I peeked into the first cell: empty,
as were the next two.

Cell Four held a dark-skinned middle-aged human,
graying hair braided away from his face, who jumped a
little when our faces appeared in the grid, but recovered
to glare at us, and continue to doggedly eat a slice of
thick black bread.

Cell Seven held a Turuntu woman asleep on the stone bunk, her iridescent claws fanned over her face. Cell Nine, a thin young human, head shaved bald, milk-pale, who turned from staring out the window when he became aware of us, but said nothing. Cell Thirteen, a Jokmara man, powerfully built, his face a mass of bruises and a deep, bleeding chip in his beak. He stood briskly when we paused at his door, and took a breath, but did not speak. Waiting to be spoken to, I guessed; he was not from the palace, but the protocols of status and address, while more flexible in the city, were still hard to break.

Cell Fifteen held a small Aeliphos of indeterminate gender wearing blue robes, so resembling, for a moment, the trainee I'd seen this morning under Phothenth that I paused and stared at them in horror. But no, it couldn't be them if they'd been captured last night, and anyway, the robes were different, lacking the palace insignia, and the mandibles orange rather than yellow. It was fine.

Cell Eighteen held the most impossible and the most dangerous of all the spies: whoever had broken into the Archive of Ashuskroth, the vault which only one person in the entire palace compound could enter, locked with both the most intricate locks on the planet and the most unbreakable spells and wards, windowless, possessed of a single door which was watched by a dozen Guards at all times, one to stand in the doorway and eleven to watch that guard, and located at the top of a single staircase, also guarded, nearly two hundred feet above the ground. The architects of the place had said, quite sensibly, centuries ago: If you bury something, someone will burrow in. Put it in the sky, and keep an eye on it. Nothing can burrow through the air.

But someone had.

I peered into the cell, slightly better-lit than the others due to the angle of the reflected daylight. The spy was asleep, or pretending to sleep, clutching a half-eaten piece of bread in one human-looking hand, the left, which was missing three fingers, only index and thumb remaining; the other hand was hidden. They wore ragged black britches that only went to the knee, and a torn shirt that had probably been white once and was now spattered with what resembled black ink. Through the many tears in the cloth their skin was pale, sheened here and there with green and violet iridescence, like bad ham.

"Advisor," I said. "What am I looking at?"

"I don't know, Your Holiness."

The spy stirred at our voice, turned, opening their eyes: mismatched, one green and apparently human, the other a field of blue in which blazed a narrow, red-orange iris. As it turned I saw the intermittent thick, chitinous scales on its back rippling like an unsettled dragon's, as did the spikes along its backbone, a dorsal fin of semi-translucent insect shell. The skin along the shins was blotched with what I first took to be tattoos, but which squirmed as if black and green worms moved below the skin. Bright gray eyes, round and birdlike, peered out of two long scars on the calves, blinking. They had eyelashes.

I took a half-step back, then steeled myself and peered inside again.

"It's not a human," I said, switching to English to make sure it couldn't understand us. "It's… all wrong, it's an abomination. It cannot be natural. Have you ever seen something like this on Aradec?"

"No, Your Holiness," the Advisor said. "In fact, I am not sure I have even *read* about such a species of creature."

"Maybe it isn't a creature," I said slowly. "Maybe it's a… a monster." You did not use the word *monster* lightly here, but there were situations in which it applied.

He shrugged.

My skin was crawling, but I kept my tone light. "And anyway, you're the one who always says not everything is written in books."

The thing's eyes widened, then narrowed, and it crept slowly off the stone bench to approach the inner door. Its matted hair was dark, streaked with what might have been mud, and the face too seemed striped with mud and ink.

"Nick?" it said in English. "Is that you?"

SANITY FLED ME. As if from a distance I watched myself lunge at the grate, try to force my arms through it, hands spasming, ears ringing from my own screams of incoherent rage in languages I could barely recognize, and even after the Advisor dragged me away I did not know what I had been saying, and sat gasping, examining my bleeding hands, for I could not lift my head.

His voice was distant, cottony. "Your Holiness! Prophet! Speak to me. I... What happened?"

My vision returned slowly, ringed with pinkish light. The Keeper of the Dungeon had rushed over, wringing his ink-spotted hands; four guards had followed him, waving their spears as if ready to attack.

Cell Eighteen was silent. I took a deep breath. Another. Another. Spring air flowed through the circular roof. Cold and fresh.

"That one," I said around a mouthful of blood; I had bitten both my tongue and my lips, or ground them against the barred window of the outer door. I spat and tried again. "Here, this creature... "

"Yes, Your Holiness?" the Keeper said, leaning down to listen.

"Wall it in," I said.

"Your Holiness, we are tasked to acquire intelligence from the intruders," the Advisor said, urgency edging his words, though he did not raise his voice. The guards wavered between us. "If you kill—"

"I said wall it in!" I screamed into his face, spraying him with saliva and blood. "Do it! Now!"

He stared at me, then nodded to the Keeper of the Dungeon. "Do as the Prophet wishes."

CHAPTER THREE

THE THING ABOUT being in love is that it's not real until you realize it. The moment you do, that's it: that's where you start the clock. You weren't in love before that.

Hatred is different. Hatred creeps up on you. Winds itself through you, hair-fine, invisible. So that when you realize that you are *in hate,* it's always been there, it's become a part of you, it doesn't belong to you but it is of you.

"Your Holiness."

So let me say that when you come to this place, the Aradeci don't interrogate you or torture you or even question you. They say, *The new Prophet is here.* Then later they teach you the language and you figure out what all those words mean. The 'here' technically exists outside the single door of the tower and its single window. I watch it go and I could shout to it, but I

63

never do. When you come to this place they don't say, *Welcome*. They say, *Thank you*. Because you have come to do a job. The job is to be the one who came to the place.

There have been prophets, they say, who did not dream. A process was developed to deal with that, involving close observation of how they ate, how they walked, what they said when they were feverish or drunk.

There have been prophets, they say, who were animals, or insects, or plants. And a process was developed to deal with them, too.

You had to have a Prophet. The tower itself seemed to control it, and as soon as one died, another appeared to replace them. Though they lacked the vocabulary, it seemed to me they thought of the tower as sort of an antenna, squeezing down the stray wisdom thrown from the Masters like dust and funnelling it into the Prophet, to be interpreted via various codebooks accumulated over the centuries.

We would never presume to know the will of the Masters, oh, no, They would tell us if They wished anything from us; but in terms of general guidance, things we didn't want to bother Them for, the system with Prophets seemed to work well enough. And I had to admit it was uncanny the way the records showed there was never more than a single night between an old Prophet and a new one.

"Your Holiness, can you hear us?"

It still didn't mean I wanted to be one; but I hungered for the protection it gave me. I knew very well I could have ended up anywhere in the universe. (And that I shouldn't have ended up anywhere at all. That I should have been dead.)

So when I came and I seemed a bit more insane than my predecessors, they did not panic. They gave me to the doctors who painstakingly healed my body, they gave me supper and wine, they took me to the bath house, they put me to sleep under warm blankets in the cool of the tower.

No one tried to heal my mind. Too much of it had gone. I keep thinking that what is left is like mould on a wall: after all my efforts, most of it is clean, but a tiny spot of unkillable stuff remained, and from that grew a fresh new coat. But this mould is different from before, coming from something so reduced. It is angry and strong. A survivor.

Interrogate me, I wanted to say sometimes. Ask me questions so I can tell you answers. But they don't want to ask me about what came before. They know what a prophet is; they don't care about anything else except for that.

It's freeing sometimes, but also powerfully lonely and sad. But if you're going to be lonely and sad you might as well be free.

"Perhaps if I try. Prophet? Please, open your eyes."

I watch the people below and I wonder what they worry about, and at night I watch the city lights that make a thing of beauty from what in daytime is little more than a bluegray smudge hazed with woodsmoke, and I wonder what they worry about too. Maybe what

I want is to borrow their worries so that something fills the emptiness inside.

"It's a start… Prophet?"

"Get a water jug."

"What for?"

What did I actually dream of last night? I dreamt I rode on a bus. Something I did thousands of times back home. Around me people wore strange garments: jeans, jackets, runners, sunglasses. One of them played on a Gameboy. I dreamt that I was holding a pole and talking to a demon, smaller than me, a little demon with dark blonde hair. The bus stopped and only the demon and I got off.

And we walked into a field of slaughter, of blood and bones and shells and ichor and broken creatures stretching out for a thousand miles in every direction, because we were in the middle. The bus pulled away.

I dreamt all the dead sank slowly into the ground and I waited for grass to grow from it, but it turned to stone, a dark black-brown stone with a hint of red, churned like a frozen sea below my feet.

And I asked, *Is this healing? Is it healed?* And a voice replied, *No, for the killing will begin again now that you have come.* And it did, and every living creature in every universe arose and killed and died and bled, and any one of them could have refused to fight but no one did, because no one else did, and I thought, *They will all have to say* No, I refuse *together, but they cannot say it together*.

The only thing they can do together is die, and they will die forever and ever and ever and ever.

And the demon said—the demon said something I could not hear, for I woke. And only as I woke did I think, muzzily, climbing up out of sleep like stairs: They fight because someone told them to. Not because they want to. Who told them? Who will tell them to stop?

"Prophet. Prophet? No, stop that. That's not necessary."

Grayness but a dark gray. Slate, not the blackness of sleep. Lazily, fussily, in my head I leafed through a handful of cards placed before me on a table, choosing which language to answer in. What had they spoken to me in? Who spoke? Now supposing they were of lower status than me. Or higher. If I...

"Your Holiness..."

"Of course I can hear you," I said. My eyes were open, I realized, and red and dry; I blinked furiously, waiting for them to focus. I had expected to be in the dungeon, but I was back in my room, in my heavy chair in front of a rekindled fire. The opened shutters printed the window's outline on the wall in crisp golden light. Perhaps an hour or two before second sunset. Some time had been lost, it seemed.

The woman speaking to me was someone I vaguely knew, one of the dozen Royal Surgeons certified to treat the royal family and those of similar rank and association, such as visiting diplomats. She was a short human, broad-shouldered, black hair streaked with silver that glimmered in the half-lit room. She picked up my heavy ceramic wine and water jugs as if they were empty, mixed me a cup of wine, and stirred something into it that sat on the surface like oil, but bereft of any gleam or iridescence.

I sniffed the cup before taking a sip: bitter, salty, more like broth than wine. "What happened?"

She frowned. "We expected *you* to tell us that, Your Holiness."

"Oh?"

"You fell into something of a fit," the Advisor said; I jumped, not having seen him sitting next to the door, framed by the swagged shadows of a tapestry. "In the dungeons, after the spy spoke. We believed that it had ensorcelled you. You were screaming, fighting us."

"Nonsense," I said. "The whole place is full of wards."

"Yes," he said. "It is."

Other shapes moved out from behind the tapestry at his side. Four guards, one of whom offered me a sheepish little wave. And someone else I knew: Brethna, from the Royal Council, whom I technically outranked but who had daily access to the ears of the King and the Queen. And, far more relevantly now, she was a sorceress, one of a very few on Aradec.

Here, as on all the thrall worlds I knew, if They ever found out you could do magic, your choices were to work for Them or die, which generally made for an easy choice.

So she had been brought to see whether the Prophet had been ensorcelled or simply needed to be put down like a mad dog. At her throat and wrists gleamed warded amulets, glittering now as if they were on fire. All of mine, I realized, had been removed.

I felt light, disoriented; I fought panic for several seconds, trying to ensure my voice wouldn't shake when

I spoke again. There was a certain sensation, familiar yet never-before felt, of standing on a beach as a tidal wave rose above me, erasing the daylight, knowing that I couldn't run from it or fight it, that it was millions of tons of power and inevitability and I was a tiny, fragile thing it would crush simply by existing. Water is clear, but the sun could not shine through it. It had that power.

Memory. Everything returning to me that I had kept back. Kept down. "What was I saying? In the dungeon."

The Advisor looked away, giving me the flat, earless side of his huge head. "No one could understand it."

Lying. All right. He was terrible at it.

"Which is why we presumed sorcery," the surgeon said. "But in my examination it appeared to not be the case."

"I'll be the judge of that." Brethna nudged the surgeon aside and approached me. I stood, swaying, and bowed as she did; the motion made me feel seasick. She had me sit again.

I closed my eyes as she pressed her rings to my forehead, my cheeks, my throat. Both the rings and her skin were dry and burning hot. I thought of Yalip's heart, and held down a retch.

"No, a spell was not cast upon him."

"I'll send a message to inform—" the Advisor began, but Brethna cut him off.

"—which means much the worse for you, Prophet," she said.

Giving no indication of my terror, I simply nodded at her, one professional to another. "I was... overcome with anger," I said. "At the very idea of an intruder in the Archive. And, uh, that the creature had penetrated so far into our well-guarded compound. At this crucial time. Of war."

Even to me, my voice sounded brassy and fake, as if I had something to hide, even though it was true. She stared at me for an uncomfortably long time. Like the Advisor, her eyes were black and steady, rich with false depth, like pools rather than surfaces. "Very well," she said. "I will inform the Council, and Their Majesties, that you appear to remain... fit to do your duty. For now."

"Thank you."

"But Prophet," she added in the doorway, "your duties only grow more intense from here. You would do well not to repeat your performance, lest it cost us at a crucial moment."

"Thank you."

The Advisor sent her down with the guards, and waited several minutes before returning to his place next to the door. And that made me uneasy: why did he not cross to join me? It was a statement, of course, there was a multi-layered code of physical and metaphorical position that we all navigated, but I had not been born here, and was still learning it. Was he already avoiding me, since I had been marked with signage saying *Almost but not quite a traitor*? If so I didn't blame him. Loss in status was contagious here, and could be fatal.

My hands hurt. I studied them, bandaged with clean linen from knuckles to mid-forearm, where the iron bars could admit them no further. And still I had thrashed and pushed to reach... to reach...

I shuddered, sipped my wine.

Earth. My family. My home. That was not for Brethna to know. That was a weakness so visible that she and anyone else who knew of it would not be able to resist attacking till it broke. It was a weakness you were supposed to set aside when you came here, as everyone did. No exceptions. None.

There was no more Earth. There were no more people from Earth. Only me.

My stomach rose; I froze, sat very still, until it settled. No vomiting in front of the surgeon.

She said, "While they examined the wards, no one was permitted to enter the dungeon to carry out your order. But they will have begun by now, I am sure. Give me permission to halt them, and treat the prisoner's afflictions. Before the end."

"Permission granted." I glanced at the Advisor. "Temporarily. A pause, not a pardon. But have someone accompany her. No one is to be alone with that prisoner."

"Your Holiness."

He returned alone to stand at a respectful distance from my chair, and we watched the fire. I did not want the wave to crash down on me, but was not sure how much longer I could keep it at bay. Its mere size was terrifying, and fear drank strength. But he did not speak, waiting for me to speak first. Questions hung around his head like a cloud.

Had I called the Advisor, in my head, a friend? Maybe.

Maybe he was a friend of the 'me' I had built here, the person I had constructed so painstakingly from the moment I had regained consciousness at the foot of the tower. Was that friendship, if he had befriended a construct? I might ask the same of him; I did not even know his name, anything about his past. Prestige demanded that we use titles at all times for people above a certain rank, and it had taken me a long time to learn the hierarchy. I did not think he knew my name either, or if I had told him he would have endeavoured to forget. Certainly he never used it if he did know.

"The Council was convened while you lay unconscious, and they were most displeased," the Advisor said.

The phrase was not exactly *most displeased*, once you worked through all the connotations and legacy derivations of High Dath. It meant something like *murderously (wishing to kill or order to be killed) angry*.

I calculated possible answers and tones: conciliatory, defensive, honest. Then I looked at my hands again. A tiny dot of red bloomed over one knuckle. "Mm," I said.

"I was questioned," he said. "About your behaviour, about your time as Prophet. Where you go. What you read. Your training with the guards. All your existing prophecies were ordered to be pulled from the archives and studied. A new Mouth will be convened, starting from tomorrow."

"Will I be replaced as well?"

"They did not say." He sighed. "Brethna is suspicious. Of what, I don't know. Perhaps only that in your sudden illness you overstepped the authority of Their

Majesties. It may be that the Queen will execute the spy after questioning. Not before. But you would not be the one to make that decision, and neither would I. We are military intelligence, Prophet. Not a court."

"As you say," I said carefully, "I was clearly ill."

"I did emphasize that. And I called the Keeper of the Dungeon, too, to say what he saw. But I admit that I cannot understand why you would have commanded such a thing before learning *anything* from the spy. Which is why they all thought..."

We thought you had lost your mind, his silence says. *Or you were under a spell to make us think that. Which was it, Your Holiness?*

"Did you know the spy could speak English when you took it in?" I said.

"No. It did not speak."

"Would you have told me if you did know?"

"I would," he said slowly. "But it is of little import, I thought. There are many lands where English is a tongue, past or future. It is not solely of your homeworld, Prophet."

I got up and went to the window, looking out at the dark forest, a sea of gold in the sunset. No fires tonight. The wine trembled and shimmered in my cup, with its oily surface. That story about pouring oil on the water to calm the waves. That would never work. Maybe just on this scale: a goblet. Not on the wave in my head.

At any rate, he was right about English; humans, as well as myriad other types of people, had been moving between all the known (and probably most of the unknown) worlds for thousands of years, accidentally and on purpose, singly or in trickles or in great hordes. And many languages had accompanied them, and spent generations changing, shifting, evolving, sprouting new branches, just like the people who spoke them. It was a wilder universe than anyone on Earth had known.

He had, however, left something out that needed to be said out loud:

"But not here," I said. "You and I are the only ones who speak it here."

"Yes," he said reluctantly. "I think so."

I studied the forest outside. Had I ever thought about running away, hiding in it? It would be the first place the palace guards would look if I had. I wouldn't be Robin Hood.

"All right," he said. "You no longer trust me. I accept that."

"And you no longer trust me. But hear me out. The thing in that cell," I said, watching the trees move in the wind, "is... looks like... I mean, is wearing the face, has stolen the voice, of someone I... used to know. Someone dead."

"Are you sure this person is dead?" he said at once.

"She died in front of me. I *saw* her die."

"I see."

I gulped my wine and put it down on the table. What had been in it? I didn't feel any calmer or better. Not a sedative.

There was so much more to tell. And I didn't want to tell him. That would make it too real. And anyway how do you say not only *She was dead and now something that looks like her is alive* but *She was the world-destroyer, she destroyed my world, she killed my family and seven billion other people because she was a monster, because she wanted to keep those parts of her that made her monstrous, because she did not want to give them up, not for me, not for them, not for the entire planet. She gambled and she lost and we all lost along with her and only I was spared. Only I survived the cataclysm. Or so I thought. Till today. So you can see, Advisor, why I lost my mind. We are lucky it was only for a few hours.*

I opened my mouth and closed it again. I had to be logical, but how, *how*, Jesus Christ, it was as if my brain itself had been slapped and was still ringing like a church bell. I wanted to scream.

Logic. Stay there. Eliminate all the other possibilities. If you can. If. I said, "Have you ever seen that?"

"Seen what?"

"Someone dead returned to life, but... but changed."

"Yes, but I don't think we're talking about the same thing, Prophet." He poured himself a water, no wine, and came to stand next to me at the window. "I've seen y'tans, but I've never heard them speak. I was under the impression that they could not."

"They *can't.*"

"Well, our knowledge must be incomplete. We cannot be so certain of the powers of the Masters. Can we?"

"No," I said. "I suppose not. I..."

"Then maybe it is as simple as that," he said soothingly. "We do not know how the Masters work, we never have.

75

They have more power than we can conceive of, more than our little minds can understand. We, being mortals, think y'tans are not truly alive, they do not possess the true spark of life, and so they can be distinguished at once from the living; but in truth, that is just what we have seen. Clearly we have not seen everything."

I gnawed on my lip. Ow. "All right," I said, and dredged up one memory from the past, dim but clear, like a miniature painting. Too small to hurt, I hoped. "And... I once saw someone that was dead... moving around. And speaking. Even answering questions."

"And they were certainly dead?"

"Dead," I said. And what had his name been? I couldn't remember. French. Bernier? Maybe Bernier. A scientist. And he had come at us and...

"There," said the Advisor. "See?"

It's not her. It can't be her. It doesn't even look like her. It's an imitation made by somebody and sent here to drive me out of my mind. That's all. They did it. Why?

No. It doesn't matter. They want me to ask why. For whatever reason. They want me to dig into this. And I won't. I won't. I will do as much as I am asked as Prophet, and nothing more.

"Where this creature went," I said, "death followed. Always, no exceptions. This thing, the copy... should be killed, not interrogated. And how did it get into the Archive?"

"That's one of the questions we need to answer. So it needs to live."

"Yes, but..."

"You would disobey the Queen?"

I hesitated. The wine shifted and burned in my empty stomach. While you could not use the word *loyalty*, exactly, for how They treated each other, you could certainly say that They did not like people crossing Them. Especially not people like us: the subjugated, those brought low. Told we were brought high, because now we were allied with the most powerful beings in the universe. No, I didn't want to cross the Queen. But I didn't want to interrogate the thing in Cell Eighteen, either.

The Advisor would do it for me, I knew. Without question and without judgement. But the right questions would never be asked.

"It's a trap," I said. "I know it is. Because otherwise there's no way to explain why that thing and I were ever in the same place at the same time ever again. Someone is using its imprisonment as bait. Perhaps it's me they intend to catch. Perhaps it allowed itself to be captured in the Archive to get into the compound. We should kill it quickly, before it can carry out any other parts of its plan, so we can circumvent the trap. You understand? The Queen will respect that. It is for all of our safety. In this time of war. We must be swift. The longer it sits there, the better it is for our enemies."

The advisor shook his head dubiously.

"We can refuse to be trapped," I insisted, aware that my voice had gone up an octave. I tried to shove it down. "You see? It's counting on us holding it prisoner. That's part of its plan. So it doesn't matter how it got into the Archive."

"Prophet," the Advisor said. "It still does matter. You know that."

I could not reply and our silence lay heavy on the room, building as if it were slowly filling with water. The light on the far wall changed from gold to crimson to pale blue. I wanted to say: *Kill the thing anyway. Kill it because it trespassed. Let its knowledge die with it. The others will know things too. And you can torture them to death if you like.*

"I have never seen you like that," the Advisor said. "Never once since the day we met. You seemed like a stranger to me."

"Well," I said heavily, "perhaps you don't know me as well as you think you do."

"Well enough, I think, to know that you have a good and kind heart. And that you would never react like that unless there was a good reason." He paused significantly. "Nor that you would order a death, let alone such a cruel death."

"Unless there was a good reason."

"No, not even then."

"As I say. You do not know me. I'm not the man you think I am. I'm... It doesn't matter. It won't be a cruel death. There's a window there for air. The spy will die of thirst in a couple of days. No more. It won't be a long, monstrous process."

"No. It will be short and monstrous. That's something *we* do, Prophet. Not you."

"Till now."

He raised his voice at last. "Why are you so resistant

to letting it live even one more day? It cannot be that dangerous. It's imprisoned. You saw the shine of the wards; no magic can be performed in there, none."

"It deserves to die," I said. "It deserved to die the first time. It deserves to die now."

"For what reason? For trespass alone? For spying during a time of war?"

"Not just that."

"Then what?"

I paced the length of the room, came back. What I wanted to do was go downstairs, find the dungeon again, and throw a grenade into the cell. But bombs hadn't been invented here. I'd have to do that first. The Advisor flinched a little at my pained smile, but said nothing.

Had I blacked out from rage earlier? I had been screaming, he said. But he understood English, so he knew very well what I had said, whatever it was, and had lied in front of the Surgeon. If you have a secret, he seemed to say now, I will help you keep it. And yet he *wasn't* a friend; merely an acquaintance I saw frequently. I knew nothing of his life or mind or heart. Or vice versa. Not that there was much to know, I thought now. I was empty inside. I had been emptied out. The void was filled with other things: fine robes, good food, prestige, ceremony, ritual, respect. The tone people used when they spoke my title.

This thing in the cell, this copy. And the Burning King, who had been so near when I had last seen the spell done to double a person, who perhaps had done it himself.

Here together, all of us. Why? And if he was responsible for the abomination, why not make a perfect copy, as he had done last time?

What *was* that thing, that half-alive creature with the face so close and the voice so close but neither of them remotely right?

"She died," I said again. "The thing in the cell is something else. Whatever it's here for, though, you can be sure it is meant to harm or destroy us. That's why it let us catch it. It had to look convincing. It had to fool the guards. I'm the only person who would see a greater connection. Only me."

"Prophet, you are very tired," the Advisor said quietly. "You have had a long day."

"I'm going back down," I said. "I have to know."

"Whatever you need to know, the Interrogator will find out."

"She will not. *I'm* the only one who will know." I crossed to the heavy, open cabinet next to my bed and rapped my knuckles on the roof of the intricate brass cage occupying its largest compartment. Its inhabitant scrabbled out of the thick pile of woodchips and peered up at me in a posture that I would have said was expectant in a cat or a dog.

"Ah!" the Advisor cried. This creature was a favourite of his, I knew. He dug in the pockets of his sash and extracted a paper bag, spotted with grease. "Who's a good boy? Have you been a good boy?"

"I think so," I said cautiously.

"Not you."

The Advisor extended one claw through the brass wires, balancing a salted nut. Inside, the large beetle, pink and violet as a flower, stared as if triangulating, then lunged up and snagged the nut, shuffling back down under the woodchips. For a moment we listened to the crunching. The Advisor had never asked me about 1779, whom I had been carrying when I appeared at the foot of the tower. I gathered that other prophets had arrived with stranger cargo. And since he had never asked, I had never explained to him the beetle's more peculiar properties, those that made it more than simply a pet and a souvenir from a dead world.

I opened the cage door and scooped the beetle from the wood chips, putting him in the topmost pocket of my robe. "Let's go," I said.

"Now?"

"It cannot wait," I said. "I told you. The longer you leave that thing alive, the longer it has to plot against us."

I WAVED AWAY the guards who called out that I had missed both my sparring sessions and my card games, and ignored their playful laughter and taunts. Was that how they saw me? The Advisor, the rest of them? A soft man, a soft big man with my big soft beard (yes, this is what she does to you, she poisons you against yourself: she makes you step out of your head, look at yourself and see someone lesser than, someone inadequate, someone laughable, compared to her). A man with a soft heart. And that was all right; a Prophet did not have to be a hard man. He only had to be in the tower, an antenna pointed at the skies, cycling through the stations as he slept, when whispers of futures might seep through.

Even in times of war, a Prophet did not have to be a hard man. Did not have to fight. Did not have to kill. And here, unlike down in the city, you could still survive. Stay on the right side of the wall and you could be as soft as a poached egg.

The dungeon already smelled more of use: of piss, armpits, cooked food. Not much; the great central well still brought air and moonlight into the place. A ring of rings within another ring, like a trick.

This time I went to Cell Eighteen first, where under the eye of the Keeper a mason and his scrawny assistant were mixing a wheelbarrow full of black mortar. The mason followed my gaze down, then sketched out a perfunctory bow, seeing the insignia on my robes and the marks of my station. It only lasted a moment before he fell back into the rhythms of a tradesman.

"That's clay from the Furtunus Mountains what gives it that colour," he said proudly. "Finest mortar in the land. I keep a few sacks of it special in the workshop. Them bricks'll stay up till the last moon falls out of the sky."

"Very impressive." My voice seemed to come from somewhere else. Stomach rather than mouth. "Open the doors."

"Both of them?" The Keeper blinked; the clutch of heavy keys clanked against one another on a fresh chain hung around his neck.

"Both."

"Want us to go?" said the mason, squatting next to the wheelbarrow.

"Stay," I said.

The Advisor took the ring of keys, worked the locks and stepped inside before I could stop him. With one brisk movement he smoothly shackled the sleeping spy's wrists to each other, and then to the iron ring set into the wall. It came awake with a startled snort, too late to do anything but hiss at him as he returned to the corridor to allow me to enter the cell.

It. She. Pick something, I scolded myself. Gender is for people, and 'it' is for objects and monsters; and they don't often say monster here.

Fine. Perhaps it's not a monster. But is it a person? It could still be an object. A made thing.

I felt cold, as if my robes were soaked and clinging to me. An illusion of the skin, I realized. The air wasn't eating my warmth; it was just that my blood was retreating to its warm core, as if I were in shock, as if it wanted to hide. Maybe not from the spy, eighty pounds of bone and scale, spike and spine, various things sticking out through its clothing. From something else. From the meaning it carried.

The Surgeon had shaved its head, the skin underneath maggot-pale and gleaming, crisscrossed with old scars; blue ointment gleamed on fresher cuts. Whatever had happened to its fingers had happened to both hands and not recently, for the stumps looked healed over. Still angry and reddish though, even in the weak light of the lantern hanging outside the open cell. Three fingers gone from the left, two from the right. The edges of its mouth were smeared with fluid of a couple of colours, like paint. Was what I had thought of as ink on its clothes actually its blood?

It wasn't important. I would know soon enough whether I had to ever spare one more minute's thought on the thing.

I took out 1779 and held it flat on my palm so the spy could see it. We both watched as its antennae quivered, as it sprang into the air with a roar, launching itself straight up like a songbird.

It circled the cell once, twice. Searching, sensing, its antennae vibrating so fast the thin strands resembled feathers. A third time, a fourth. It shot out the tiny window into the open air and then back inside, whirring past my face so that my hair blew in its wake. Out the two open doors, around several people's startled yelps, back inside. One last orbit around my head, and then it crashed into my shoulder and ran around agitatedly, the tiny claws on its feet pinching so hard I could feel it through the layers of fabric. It had not once gone near the spy.

Something washed over me, thin, lightly luxuriant, as if I had stepped into a warm shower: relief. So it really was an impostor. But how? And (this was the part I didn't want to think about) what had gone wrong?

Wait. If there were... I stepped fully into the cell from the space between the two doors. Holding down my revulsion, I reached down and flipped the spy over despite its screech of protest, then pulled back the filthy shirt.

No scar. No coin, where mine was a crescent. Nothing. I flipped it around again and examined the skin just under its collarbone, avoiding the snapping teeth. Nothing.

"What are you?" I said quietly.

THE SPY SNORTED. "Doesn't mean anything," it croaked in English. The voice wrong, too. I had heard that voice more, growing up, than my own. More than any other voice of family, friends, teachers, television, radio. I would have known the real one from hearing it speak a single syllable.

"Answer the question, spy," I said. And it was wrong: it meant *everything*. The lack of the scar was one thing. The beetle that Johnny Chambers had engineered so long ago to carry messages between us, the only survivor of the pair, that would have known her instantly and instead had treated this person like a stranger: *that* meant something too. Stranger. False.

"You *know* who I am." It struggled to sit, pulling itself weakly up the stone shelf till its head came level with the iron ring. Now I could see two fresh, still-bloody sockets gaping in its mouth—upper right, lower left—where the Surgeon must have pulled rotten teeth. The blood was dark blue, opaque as paint.

A fresh wave of nausea at the words, the stolen voice. I held it down. "Then say it. Tell me who you are."

"You were dead," it said. "I saw you die. Torn into a million pieces. I thought..." The croaky little voice trailed off.

They had trained the thing well, I thought dazedly, whoever had done it. They had told it just what to say. How to say it. Perhaps assuming that I had forgotten, in my shock, more than I truly had. That was their downfall.

The beetle didn't know it. And I too, who had once killed the thing's doppelgänger, a supposedly exact copy down to her cells and her memories, knew it wasn't her. So neither of us could deny that it was a monster after all: both a monster and a made thing, and I was right to say *it*. The tables turned so neatly on the original monster-maker that the original, if she weren't dead, might even have appreciated the slickness of the trick.

"Tell me your name and what you were doing here," I said as gently as possible, "or I will ask the Advisor to come in here and knock out one more tooth."

The spy narrowed its eyes. The teeth thing: that'd do it. A punch in the face was one thing, but teeth didn't grow back. I supposed I could have said *finger*. It was running pretty low on those and it might be a point of sensitivity.

We stared at each other in the reflected half-light of the hallway, searching for familiarity. There was a time when I would have seen no more than an elbow or the fringe of a scarf in a crowd and I would have known it was the real her. No more than her silhouette from a mile off. On a rainy night. On TV with bad reception. I would have thought: You, you, the other half of me.

But I reached for that surety now and found nothing. A void of uncertainty. The thing looked less like her than a sister or a cousin: the bones all different, the skull different, let alone the scales and the eyes and the missing scar and the dorsal fin.

"You're going to have me bricked in anyway," it said. "I thought it was a bluff. But I can smell the mortar. So why should I tell you anything?"

"Because I could have them stop," I said. "And we could have a conversation like reasonable people. Or I could have them stop and I could have you tortured. And now I see you cannot say your own name. Why? Did you forget it? Did you forget your line? Didn't practice enough?"

It turned away to cough up a black blob of blood, streaked with other colours like a glass marble. The clot wriggled disconcertingly before sliding down the floor drain.

I stepped backwards. I wanted to scream at the spy, attack it, bound as it was, and close my hands around its throat. I could already imagine how the scales there would feel as they cut into my palms. The thing would fight back, but I was bigger than it was, far bigger, and it would be so easy to not even feel it as it kicked and thrashed. *You dare! You thief! Impostor!*

No. What was important was the war. Not that this thing could interfere with the war, but that it had even *tried*: that was what was important. I would just have to set aside the human in me and focus on being the Head of Royal Military Intelligence. Be like the Advisor: a job, not a name. Just get the information and everything would go back to normal. Remember, there wouldn't even be any fighting here. It would be a war far away. And I would be safe and warm in my tower.

Behind me I sensed the presence and weight of the two masons, the little man and his assistant, waiting. The best mortar, I thought. The finest materials. Kept aside specially in case of a request by someone illustrious: like a Prophet.

I stepped back outside, shut and locked the first door, shut and locked the second, handed the keys to the Advisor.

"What were you looking for in the Archive?" I said through the grate. "Tell me, and maybe there will be mercy."

"Are you... Why do you keep talking like that?" the spy said.

I gestured to the mason. He and his assistant meticulously began to lay the first layer of stones across the doorway. I paused long enough to hear the scrape and clink of their trowels, so that the thing in the cell could hear it too.

"The war, creature," I said. "You expect me to think it's a coincidence that six spies were captured in the Royal Compound the day it was announced? Just tell me. How did you get into the Archive? Who sent you? What were you trying to steal?"

"I wasn't trying to steal anything!" it finally burst out, twisting on the short chains of the shackles. "They didn't find anything on me. They can tell you that!"

"Then what were you doing in there?"

"None of your goddamn business!"

"It is," I said. "It's war. That's all my business now."

The thing writhed, seeming to waver between genuine laughter and tears of rage. "*You!* What a fucking joke. You coward, you hypocrite. What did they do to you?"

"The stones are up to my waist now, spy. Maybe if you prove that you know something, I'll ask them to stop. And we can have a conversation as if you were a person, and not a monster."

"Fuck you. Torture me then."

"Why do you think I won't? Is that what they told you to think? That I would be fooled by you, that I had no power here?"

It turned again on its next rotation of the chains and stared at me, the mismatched eyes widening. "Wait a minute. Are you doing spells here? Do they know you can do magic?"

The Advisor stiffened next to me, then went still, the kind of stillness that only his people could hold, pupils fixed, feathers unmoving. My heart gonged in my chest like a bell. "An interesting lie," I said, but my voice sounded weak even to me. I threw my shoulders back and attempted a sneer. "Of course you know I meant the power of my position. Not magical powers. I cannot do magic. Only the Royal Sorcerers can, with the express permission of the Masters."

It wasn't even listening. "Did you tell them? Or did they test you? They didn't, did they? Oh my God. Look at your face. They really don't know. You've really kept it hidden all this time. Incredible."

The masons could go no higher while I stood there. The thing's face was inhumanly smug. Even then I thought it was not too late to change my mind and take it out and have it tortured. It's what the Queen would want, part of me said calmly. It's what's good for the kingdom. The thing's pain traded for safety and peace. For lives. Yes.

And then kill it at the end. A mercy. If I had a soul, my soul would be washed clean in its blood. For being so merciful. For doing the right thing.

Yes. Information first. Then death. The stones were unreasonable. But I was a reasonable man. And the thing had forced my hand; really, it was making its own decision on what happened next, not me. It was the one who had slammed shut every door leading to its salvation.

"Very well," I said, "you leave me no choice but to..." Outside, faint shouts rose up from ground level, cries of alarm rather than fear. A moment later a strange bell began to ring, not one I recognized. The Advisor cocked his head.

"Fire," he said. "Someone—" He stopped short, glancing at the hallway that led to the stairs. The bell had fallen silent, its last clang still reverberating, but the shouting had become screaming, and the air was filling with smoke.

"Well," I said to the spy, "you may have a quicker death than thirst, it seems."

"Your Holiness," said the Advisor. "We should go *now*."

"Just a mom—what was that?"

A shadow flitted overhead, too large for a bird, just

a dark shape interrupting the moonlight, barely visible behind the clouds of choking smoke rising up the stairs and, impossibly, the central well of the dungeon, which led only to bedrock. I instinctively covered my face with the sleeve of my robe. The Advisor was already at the top of the stairs, beckoning frantically as he flapped his wings to dispel the smoke around his face. "Prophet!"

"Keeper!" I coughed, ducked low to get out of the smoke layer. "Get the prisoners out! The spies! They cannot die until we have questioned them!"

"Forget them, Your Holiness!" The Advisor galloped back and took my arm, entirely against protocol; I hadn't actually been touched by someone for so long that I jumped and yanked my arm back, coughing loudly.

"Shackle them together!" I shouted. "Christ! Where did he go?"

"The lower level is on fire," the Advisor said, his wings buffeting my shoulders. "He must have gone to get his men out. Please, Prophet! Forget the prisoners. Your life is more important."

"The war is more important than any of us, for fuck sake!"

"What?"

The mason and his assistant had fled too; I snarled as I ran back to Cell Eighteen, where the spy was looking around interestedly, coughing as the smoke began to filter in. Its exterior window darkened for a moment and I leapt backwards, finally putting it together.

"It's an escape attempt!" I shouted. "From the outside! Find the Keeper, or at least the keys!"

The Advisor's reply vanished in the noise as the building shook, and a low rumble began from below us. Was something bombarding the masonry? Well, good fucking luck, I thought wildly, looking around at the unmoved walls.

Footsteps sounded from the stairs, people running up rather than down, and for a second all I could do was watch in horror as a dozen guards emerged, pursued by a handful of strangers clad in loose brown and gray clothing with masks tied firmly around their faces. The Advisor spotted them at once and swept me behind him with his wings, a sudden slap of feathers as hard as stone, so that I fell onto the floor. "Protect the Prophet!" he cried.

"Protect the Prophet!" one of the guards repeated thoughtlessly, and only then realized his mistake, as the strangers looked up, almost as one, and spotted me still scrambling to rise. I could see the wheels turning in their head: *The Prophet? What is he doing here?*

Kill the Prophet!

"Oh, forget me," I began angrily, staggering to my feet and seizing the Advisor's wing to stay upright; he began to speak before the building rocked again, more drastically this time, like an earthquake, and our voices were drowned out by the crunch and thud of falling stone meeting cobbles and walls. Something landed on the roof and scrabbled there, sweeping smoke down the light well and darkening the entire dungeon. The guards shouted in anger and pain as they grappled with the strangers, metal clanging.

The building took one more enormous hit and tipped for good as one side collapsed, sending me and the Advisor sliding around the circle towards the melee. I screamed in nothing more than sheer rage as moonlight and wind broke in from the wall next to Cell Eighteen, where something had smashed a hole from the outside in.

"Him!" someone shouted in Low Dath, a new speaker. "In the red robes! Kill him!"

The Advisor leapt up, snarling; I got out my crystal dagger. My eyes burned, my throat burned, I had coughed so hard that my stomach was starting to hitch, but I'd be fucked if I went down without a fight.

Wait, I could do one better than the flimsy crystal blade: on the floor gleamed a handful of weapons dropped either by the guards or the intruders, including a double-handed sword like the one I'd been training on, though longer and heavier. I pocketed the dagger and held the sword in both hands: Position Five, Stance of the Leaf.

The strangers rushed us, splitting up to break down the iron-hard wooden doors of the other cells with some kind of small explosive, or spell, I couldn't tell which, exponentially multiplying the noise levels alongside the rising screams of the prisoners and the guards.

Bombs? Wait, were those—

Something flew at my head and absolutely by reflex, not thinking at all, I swung my sword and batted it back the way it had come; shrieks rose in a chorus before I even registered the sound of the explosion. As if in answer, someone ran at me—a cloud, muffled in his baggy brown disguise. In a split second the fight became a mere matter of physics. My arms were longer than his and so was my sword and I swept it down and bludgeoned him across both forearms, spraying bright blood into the air and sending him screaming to the floor.

I fought back towards the torn-open Cell Eighteen, slipping on the tilted floor and the fresh pools of blood. The intruders had expected resistance but I still took down five or six of them, dimly registering, from the corner of my eye, at least one of them pursuing me not to attack but to drive his dagger into the throats of the fallen. Like me, I thought, in the microseconds of coherence between thrusts and sweeps, just like me, saying No, *they will not have you, they cannot have you alive.*

The air pressure changed abruptly, sending my hair and beard streaming past my face. Something had finally torn away the rest of the wall, ripping open the spy's cell and those next to it like a shoebox diorama. The spy dangled from its shackles in grim silence, moonlight glaring off its pallid skin, as a set of gleaming claws longer than it was tall closed on either edge of the broken stone. A creature that had climbed up the tower, I thought dazedly, or flown there, or... As I snapped back to reality, I realized it didn't matter. Whatever it was, it had come specifically to rescue the spies.

Or not all of them.

Not all.

"No!" I screamed. "Not that one! Advisor! Don't let them get it! Kill it!" I raced towards the hole, the claws, the dangling spy, the man climbing awkwardly down the creature's sloped neck towards it.

The creature swung one clawed paw with ponderous grace and smashed out the thick iron bar that the spy's shackles were attached to, like someone scooping a seed out of a ripe tulmar. No time, no time, I was running out of time, but I scrambled up the broken stone, stepped on a limp body, raced through the two doors and into the gaping cell.

My entrance startled the stranger for a second, just long enough for me to begin to reach back with my sword, but my swing was stopped short with a teeth-rattling *clang* that at first I could not even understand. Only when someone seized me by the throat did I realize that the spy had thrust its shackles in the path of a blow meant to kill me. Dagger or short sword, I thought clinically, still too shocked to think for a second; they had both moved very fast. The building sagged again, as if in warning.

"Take him too!" the spy shouted in Low Dath to the man who held me, grasping his free arm, which still held the dagger, with its shackled hands. "Take him with us!"

"What?" the man screamed back as I thrashed. "Have you lost your *mind?*"

The spy yanked hard at his arm, startling him enough that he slackened his grip; the bar and chains crashed to the floor of her cell, now disintegrating stone by stone like the wall behind us, as the flapping monster thrashed for its own grip on the edges of the hole. The spy was free, though still chained at the wrists. It shouted, "I'll explain after! Take him or we all die here!"

The Advisor shouldered his way in front of me, putting his body between me and the creature, and for a split second I felt torn between gratitude and fury. That the creature should fucking *dare* to try to kidnap *me* in this disaster, that—

The clawed flying thing outside tensed, and I only had a second to think *Oh I was so wrong, I assumed too much, of course I did*, before the limb—not a bird's limb at all but a long, boneless, writhing thing—whipped out and slapped the Advisor aside with a sickening crack of bone and flesh, and then clenched, fist-tight, around my midsection and snaked me through the hole.

I flailed at it uselessly with my sword, vision already graying from the crushing grip, the blade rebounding without any visible effect from the thin glistening layer of scales, and then we were outside, a clear night sky, white clouds, moons, and everything went dark.

CHAPTER FOUR

LIGHT RETURNED MOMENTS later, along with several other things: noise, stench, pain, the ability to draw in a full breath, and the strange sensation of being lightly slapped all over my face. I snarled, shook my head sharply, and waited for my senses to give me something to work with.

"Stay still, motherfucker," someone said conversationally in Low Dath, so near my ear that I recoiled from it. "Ropes can go around necks too, you know."

"Itzlek," said someone else, "don't kill him. We need him."

"So *she* says," the voice said. The pain continued along several axes, but my eyes were adjusting and I stared around the confusing, pattering darkness. Hands tied, feet tied, and hands tied to feet where I knelt. What was hitting me in the face, aside from Itzlek's threats, whoever he was, was clots of dirt and small stones. The air was cold and close and smelled of soil, and all around was a continuous loud rumbling, regular as machinery. Nothing made sense. I waited, and kept my lips and eyes shut against the onslaught of dirt.

"It's pure madness," someone said distantly, "taking him. They'll…"

"I know what I'm doing." The voice of the spy. So it was here. Had survived. I snarled with rage, all unheard.

Someone said, "You said you'd explain."

"When we're safe. Not before."

Typical, I thought. Cagey as fuck. They trained the thing well, whoever trained it. That sneer in the voice: I knew that sneer.

The rain of dirt and stones on my face slowed, then stopped, as did the sound of crunching and crashing. A lantern bobbed towards me seemingly on its own in the darkness: no, just held by someone tall, whose long insectile arm carried the light far before his masked face could be seen. Behind him were two others, also in masks, stinking of blood; without comment, they dragged me out of whatever we had been in. I glanced back once, seeing what looked inexplicably like a mud-covered wicker basket.

It dawned on me that we had indeed burrowed out of the compound, and had been travelling in something towed behind the burrowing animal. If guards had been searching for us, they would be looking at the sky, not the ground. Like swapping cars during a heist, I thought, and almost laughed out loud. All right. No chance to escape down here, who knew how deep we were, and

I couldn't go anywhere except straight back into the tunnel where we'd come from. But we couldn't stay down here forever. I closed my eyes again as they hauled me away. Okay, outnumbered, disarmed, tied up, and surrounded by enemies. Stay calm. Regroup.

When the chance comes: run. Get back home. And then hunt these bastards down and make them talk.

WE SWAPPED 'TRAILERS' three more times, and finally they cut the bonds on my feet so we could walk up a stone ramp, splashing through shallow stagnant water. Someone unceremoniously threw a piece of cloth over my head and secured it with rope just as we entered the complex-looking metal door at the end of the ramp. Hooded now, I was manhandled for a long time with muttered swearing, occasionally thrown into walls or doors, usually accompanied by dark chuckles and sarcastic apologies. The spy never interceded.

Stay calm, I repeated to myself, clenching my teeth so hard they squeaked. Stay calm. Rummage through the memory for something useful from the old days. Only chance now. You know something that will help. You know a *little*, down there under all that denial.

When we finally stopped, the makeshift hood was untied and I blinked dirt and sweat out of my eyes, feeling tears stream down my cheeks in an effort to wash out the filth; I half-instinctively tried to wipe my face, forgetting that my hands were still bound.

The place was dimly lit, and stank of smoke and

unwashed bodies, like animal musk. It made me think of the cats scent-marking things in the palace, arrogantly lifting their chins and staring at you as if daring you to protest that this was your palace, not theirs. A small fire burned at the far end, an obvious concession to the need to boil bandages for the wounded spies and rescuers now being hauled in behind me.

Shadowy forms were silhouetted by the low, reddish light of a dozen tiny lanterns and the fire. Sparks spat onto the dirt floor, sending insects scurrying. Like a broken necklace of pearls: moonbugs. No wonder our surgeons had shaved the spy's head. Very contagious, moonbugs.

Heads turned as we moved, but it was too dark for me to see faces; only the posture of wings, shoulders, backs, tails, hackles, stiffening with distaste at the stranger in their midst. I don't want to be here either, I wanted to shout. Don't look at me like that. You don't want to see me and I don't want to be seen!

They pushed me to an empty corner, far from the fire's meagre warmth. The man who had climbed down the flying creature, who I hated already for he had come personally to free the spy, ripped off his mask and tossed it aside. The spy ducked absentmindedly.

I retreated without looking as he came at me, and hit the wall with my back hard enough to rattle my teeth. He seized my throat, pressing me hard to the wall. His fingers dug not quite deeply enough to cut off my air but with enough pressure to suggest both that he wanted to and that it would be easy, so easy. I knew that already.

I'd been at a sacrifice once where the chosen method of execution had been strangling and it had only taken a moment. The inside of the trachea is sticky, you see; it adheres when it's crushed, and that's that. What a thing to remember now.

With his free hand he snatched a knife from inside his clothing, the blade short but sharp, chipped edge glinting. The spy glanced at it, then back at me, not moving.

"This is Ksajakra," the spy said in English. "Leader of the resistance for the city of Valishec. He is not your enemy."

"Speak properly, Yenu," the man growled in Low Dath, not looking away from me. He looked like he might be human. The parts I could see of him, anyway. I had been here long enough to know that there was no certainty just by looking at someone; there were simply too many kinds of people out there. His skin was an ordinary dark brown, and his teeth and eyes seemed human. He was tall for Aradec, the top of his head nearly at my collarbones. Thin but big-boned. A fighter. I became very aware of my pulse hammering against his thumb.

The spy switched to Low Dath. "I'm trying to introduce you. This is—"

"I don't need to know him," Ksajakra said. "And *you*, what's wrong with you? Why did you insist we take this... this turd from the palace? We could have died! Explain yourself. Now."

"What's wrong with her is that she's working with them," someone said quietly in the darkness, a stocky

Turuntu with pale lilac scales. "As we've said from the start, Ksajakra. To lead them back here. Him. Specifically. Don't you know what those robes are? That's the Royal Prophet she brought here. Brought upon us."

So. They doubt her too. And now this. What if I can use that somehow, what if...?

Yenu looked unperturbed. And where had I heard that name before? In the silence, the crackling of the fire seemed very loud. Footsteps and cartwheels rumbled above us, briefly darkening what I hadn't noticed before: a single grimy window, set at what would have been street level, letting in almost no light at all. Glass. A weak point. How...?

Ksajakra released me. "Him, I would kill in an instant," he said grimly, turning to her with the knife still held high. "You, though... you are my second, you were the beating heart of this cell. You, I would take a minute before I killed. But you insisted on going to the palace."

"Yes," she said, "*and* I insisted that you not come to get me if I was arrested."

"Your arrest put us all in danger," he snarled. "They would have tortured you. Found us. Killed us all. And now this, him, the Prophet. You had us take their *Prophet*. Talk!"

"Not here," she said. "Too many people are listening."

"They have the right to listen. They are with us." His eyes narrowed, and he glanced up at the Turuntu standing by the wall, arms crossed, leaning back casually on her tail. Ksajakra's face had the look of a man suddenly putting several unrelated things together. I suspected that mine did too. And Yenu's expression of serenity was crossing over into arrogance; it was bothering him, and me, that she did not seem more fearful, or at least conciliatory.

"Not here," she said again.

"Fine. Then I will kill him."

She shrugged. "Then the resistance stops here. We can no longer resist."

She had said, it seemed, the magic words: he hesitated, then stowed the knife. I straightened up to my full height, putting my shoulders to the wall. My shoulders hurt from having my hands bound behind me, and I hated being unable to stretch. In the dim light all I could see of either of them were their eyes, the movement of their teeth.

That was some threat, I thought. It was almost funny. Resistance to what? To the war? There were no more than twenty or thirty people in the room. It was like someone trying to put out a forest fire with a paper fan.

Just like that, actually, and my stomach revolved queasily at the image. Precisely like that. Not just because it would do nothing, but because it might even bring the fire closer. It might burn them up before they realized that they had gone from hero to victim. Because this was it, this was 'the resistance.' And what they were resisting was not the crown or the guards or anything like that. It was not a revolution to overthrow the King and the Queen. What they were resisting was the war.

How they had learned of it didn't matter; I had only learned of it this morning, but the war had been going on for years. Just because the palace did not speak of it did not mean that the rest of the planet did not. Long enough, at any rate, to decide to resist it...

Yenu wandered off a ways and murmured to someone who worked on the locks of her shackles for a moment till they fell away. I could not see who she had spoken to, only their hands, small and dexterous, like the hands of a raccoon, and then the jingle and scrape as they dragged the fallen shackles towards themselves. Probably sell them for scrap metal; iron was valuable here.

Freed now, unselfconsciously, hidden by the shadows, Yenu began to undress. She was so pale that her skin still gave away every movement, the lanternlight glittering off the scales, the sharp dorsal fin, the blinking eyes on her legs. "This is it," she said unhelpfully, pulling on a dark pair of full-length britches, then stepping into a proper pair of boots. "This is what makes the rest of the plan possible."

"This? What this? Speak straight," Ksajakra snapped.

She threw on a shirt and over that a knee-length black coat of some stiff stuff, like what the guards wore at the castle, though with brass toggles instead of buttons. "Him."

"The Prophet? We do not need prophecies."

"Not his prophecies." A creak in the darkness: a trunk, a drawer? Metal gleamed as she began to slot daggers, knives, and other small items into the coat's pockets, ending with an intricately-carved rectangular case that she slung across her body like a messenger bag

yes the brown canvas messenger bag remember that yes she used to have it always on her

it's not her!

on its long chain. She rubbed a hand across her shaven head, then began to head for the fire where the wounded lay. "Come on," she said. "Let's clean up first, and then we can talk."

Ksajakra moved in front of her. "You think I am so easily distracted? I am the leader here," he said. His voice was soft, but everyone turned to look at him once more. "And at my word, no matter what you can do or you say you can do, Yenu, they will remove you from this resistance and from this life. Lives hang in the balance here. Our lives."

"She doesn't care about your lives," I said. Both Ksajakra and Yenu glanced at me and I felt, with delirious, smug glee, something shift between our gaze. The creature's eyes were different, but I had seen that look a thousand times before in the eyes of the original. It said: *I've got this. Don't say anything.*

"Do you know what she is?" I said rapidly, pointing my chin at the spy. "Her. Notice I say *what*, I don't say *who*. Her name doesn't matter."

She began to speak; Ksajakra cut her off with a brief motion of his long hand. Empty of weapons, it still resembled a weapon. "You think you know something about her we don't?"

"I think I know something about her that *nobody* else does. So maybe for your sake it is for the best that you took me, out of anyone at the palace, hostage. What a coincidence! Or maybe not. Maybe it's not a coincidence that she demanded I come. Maybe she *is* working with me. How would you know?" I was babbling now, and his gaze suggested that I should come to a point, before he demonstrated exactly how I could be induced to confess. It would be a familiar speech, I thought. One I had very recently delivered myself. "That thing was made by the... by the Masters. The very ones I suspect you plot against."

Several people couldn't help but gasp. Yenu's face went still, only the barest flicker of hatred behind her expressionless mask.

So I was right. I had been right from the first moment I saw it.

I plunged ahead. "Never mind what it looks like. I'm not saying that's proof of anything. I'm saying that They patterned it after an original. A girl I knew, a human girl from my homeworld. Named Johnny Chambers. Who was also Theirs, who belonged to Them. They offered her a covenant, They made her what she was. Just like this thing."

More gasps and whispers. People were shuffling closer. Not a few, I noticed with pleasure, were holding weapons. It might be over soon, all over, if I could just get this right. Eyes glittered in the darkness. Yenu did not move.

"Johnny never would have told you this," I said. "Because she had to control the narrative. What did this one tell you? What did she show you? Let me guess. Secret powers. Intelligence beyond belief. Magic and wonders. A genius, a hero. You said: Look at this. We cannot do any of this.

"And let me guess further. She always said: You can lead; I'll support you. But listen. It's an act. She does this not only because she wants underlings to rule, but also because she knows she will need many, many people to sacrifice on the way. Could she do this alone? Probably. Would she *rather* grease the cartwheels with your blood? Certainly. So she has gathered you as protection to throw you away later.

"And what is her purpose? She is a trap. She was made to infiltrate you, betray you, and draw the Masters to you. I know. Johnny did the same to me. To all of Earth. And in so doing she destroyed our planet. Seven and a half billion people. This thing isn't here to fight the Masters. She's here to give Aradec to Them."

"If that's so," Yenu said, "then why would I take *you*? The one person who supposedly knows about this... this trap? With me as the bait?"

"Because Johnny would have trusted me not to say anything," I said. "Because she would have expected me to keep my mouth shut and protect her. Even now. You're just doing what you're programmed to do."

"This Johnny," Ksajakra said quietly. "What happened to her?"

"She died," I said. "In front of me. Almost close enough for me to reach out a hand and touch. I saw everything. Everything. I saw her blood. I saw her bones. Everything flew apart into pieces. And then my world..."

The silence was thick, solid; for a moment I lost all bearings, felt the dim room spin around me, remembering the thing, the void, hungry for matter and light, crowded with jostling eyes, tentacles, tearing fangs, screaming mouths. Ready for Their prize. The prize she had given Them: a whole planet. My parents, my brothers, my sister. All dead. Everyone else dead. Because of her. Because of her. And me only miraculously spared by being thrown through the void into somewhere else.

I sagged to the floor; Ksajakra hauled me back up by the front of my robe, teeth bared.

"She'll betray you," I said wearily, not caring who I referred to. "It's all she knows how to do. She brought me here to bring the palace down upon you. You know they won't rest while their Prophet is gone. Not during a time of war. And to bring the palace means bringing the Masters. They're here, you know. On Aradec. Now. Because of the war. I saw one just this morning, at a sacrifice. He played executioner. They're here."

His breath was fast, harsh. But he still did not reply.

"Let me go," I said softly, addressing only him. "Look at you. You never trusted her, did you? She can talk the ear off a statue. Believe me, I know. But this is it. Where you get to decide whether you want to let me go, so I can bolt back to the palace. *You* know I don't know where this place is and could never lead them here. Or whether you want to do as she says, which will mean the guards do come here and arrest, question, torture, mutilate, and kill every one of you. Except her. You'll see."

He said nothing.

"What was she there for?" I said. "What was she there to steal? She didn't tell you, did you? Then something 'went wrong.' How could someone with her abilities get arrested by ordinary palace guards? Hm? Think about it. Take as long as you like."

A cart rolled past the window, shaking loose dust and cobwebs from the low ceiling. The other people weren't quite crowding us, but were obviously listening, and looked weary, hurt already, as if this had happened before, as if they had been betrayed before, as if each of them had an image in their head of someone who had let them down, or been let down, and come to a sad end. So did I. The semicircle of listeners stopped crisply about three yards from Yenu. As if a force field protected her, an invisible dome. Many of them were armed.

Good, I thought. Good. This is what you do when you have been betrayed. This is how you operate. Or should operate. Your first priority should be ensuring it doesn't happen again. By whatever means necessary. And they wanted to, I could sense it. Or perhaps I just hoped I could.

For a moment I wondered whether Ksajakra was the one holding them in abeyance, then noticed, with a twist of displeasure and even confusion, that they weren't looking at him; they were looking at her.

"I'm not a made thing," Yenu said mildly. "His whole argument hinges on it. You know They can't create life."

"They are the only things that could make something like you. An abomination," I retorted. "Look at you. What's your middle name, hm? What was Johnny Chambers' middle name?"

She looked away, her face twisting, the mask gone. It returned when she looked back at us, and stroked a hand again over her shaved head.

Knew it. "You don't know," I said. "You're a thing. They made a copy and they didn't even make a *good* copy. The original had a perfect memory. More than perfect."

"You, shut up. Now the palace's dog has said his piece," said Ksajakra. "Maybe we let him bark too long. But what he has said makes sense in my bones. You may say your piece. And we will see if it is any better."

"Leaving aside whether you'd believe him over me," she said, "after everything I've done for you, you really want to know why we need him? Why I insisted we take him? It's because he can do magic."

The crowd murmured; the weapons stayed raised. "He killed ten of our people," someone said: a half-familiar face over a powerful square body. No I didn't, I almost said. *You* killed at least three of them, I saw you. I only wounded them.

"She lies," said someone else. "Then she tells us it is for our own good. She doesn't trust us."

"If Ksajakra trusts her, that's good enough for me, and it should be good enough for the rest of you," a woman's voice said stoutly.

"Ksajakra, kill the royal dog," someone else said, pushing forward: a human, slender and dark-haired with a scruff of beard. "Let me do it. I will, if you only say."

"Get back!" the woman snapped. In a moment they were all talking at cross-purposes, though taking care, I noticed, to keep their voices down.

"She lies," I agreed. "Everyone knows the Prophet is a conduit only. A pathway."

Yenu ignored me. "You remember what happened at

Sharatar. It could be worse next time. Now we have a backup. He is maybe the *one* person who can do magic in all the city, perhaps all the kingdom, that They haven't found out."

I stared at her, stunned. Ksajakra glanced briefly at me, then back at her. "Prove it," he said to her. "He says you lie."

"He would say that," she said, then looked at me, shaking her head in false regret. "I saved your life, you know, Nick. They would have killed you."

"Stop pretending you're her!" I shouted, unable to stop myself; several people flinched, and everyone fell silent. I saw the glint of blades in the dim firelight. "You don't know me, monster!"

"She lies, you lie," Ksajakra said again, his voice grim. "I suspect. Yenu, make him do something we can see."

She shook her head. "You know what happens."

I didn't know, but I could guess. In a system reliant on the monopolization of magic by the ruling bodies—the Masters, Their minions and thralls, and Their conquered worlds—any unsanctioned use of magic would be like a wildfire on the landscape: visible for hundreds of miles, even if the spark where it had started was not immediately evident. Do it enough times, though, and They would know exactly who to watch for when the fire raged up again.

I thought again, a dog worrying at a bone: *But the Archive. How, if not magic?*

Wanted me as a backup. To do what? What were they planning?

I said, "Don't listen to her. Ksajakra. What has she been telling you? About this 'resistance'? She doesn't save lives. She takes them. And if you people fight the Masters, you'll all be killed yourselves, *and* you'll provoke Them into killing innocent people. She wants that. Listen, cooperation is the only way to save lives. You want to end the war? Then help the Masters win, quickly and bloodlessly. Don't fight Them. The war ends when They win. Not before."

His face wavered for a moment, as if seen through water. Yenu shot me a look of pure hatred.

"No," she said. "We fight Them. Somebody has to. They can't keep doing what They're doing."

"You *can't* stop Them," I said. "Hear me. All of you. Billions of ghosts haunt me. They always will, they'll never stop. Imagine all that death for a second. Memory is not resurrection. I couldn't stop her. But you can. The war will end the sooner for it."

"We are going to end it our way, not Theirs," she said. "Now that we have you."

"You don't have me," I said, and the room filled with light.

THE CITY ROARED and broke upon me like an anthill, all stench and gleaming motes of light, dust and filth, mud, darkened chambers filled with wriggling life, the thick and sluggish canals burping their gases into the air, and people, more people in one place than I had seen in years, and I was running while trying to look as if I was not running, and my heart was going so hard that I thought it was going to stop any second now, hard and irregular, all out of rhythm.

But it was still beating. That was the important thing. And me, I could barely breathe, I coughed and gagged, but I could still walk. Fast, uphill, towards where the tiny carved bones and skulls of the palace gleamed in the early sunlight, white-hot against the green sky, too far away, too far, my gods, how far had they taken me underground, how long had we travelled? The whole night had burned away.

The spell I had cast was mostly show, normally producing something like a brief set of fireworks; but it had had two things going for it. One, that it was the only one I had been able to remember and therefore mark its relatively simple sigil on the wall behind me, unseen, using the piece of charcoal I'd spotted earlier and picked up when I slid to the floor; and two, that it produced a shockwave, and that had bowled everybody over as well as knocking out the window and part of the wall. I'd eeled up and out in a split second, sheer adrenaline propelling me through the hole, and gone sprinting out into the street like a spooked cockroach.

There had been pursuit; I had heard it. But that had ceased an hour ago, after the sun had come up and I had ditched my red robes into a canal, leaving me in loose gray underclothes, linen shirt and britches that protected my skin from the scratchy brocade. I hadn't had much in my pockets, but I had kept the bit of charcoal, the crystal knife, and 1779 before bundling up the robes and flinging them into the thick water. Red was too noticeable in a chase, it was as bright as a shout, and anyway, the weight had been slowing me down.

Were they still after me? I turned a dozen times, seeing nothing. But part of me hoped they were, because I had set my wildfire: in a world where magical practitioners had been winnowed down to a leashed, muzzled handful, one of that handful, a Royal Sorcerer, would certainly be able to pinpoint where that spell was cast. The palace guards would find me before the so-called resistance did. And even though I knew the 'rebels' would have fled to another bolthole before the guards found that one, it pleased me to think that some of them at least would be captured.

A fucking *resistance*. Unbelievable. And because of that here I was, the Royal Prophet, rattled, starving, emptied-out from magic, scratched-clean within by it, gasping for air, power-walking through the crowds before I was recaptured and tortured. Yesterday morning at this time I had held in my hand the heart of a friend. But you could get used to anything. Anything, really, if you just had the time to process it. Keep walking. Get home. Process it there.

People stared as I went past, but maybe I didn't look worth robbing, in my plain underclothes that resembled everyone else's outer clothes, and anyway I'm a big fat motherfucker now, yes I am, I'm taller and heavier than everyone here and I don't walk up and down thousands of steps every day for nothing or train for twenty hours a week at lance and mace and sword for nothing, and I knew I looked like I would put up enough of a fight to make robbing me not worth it.

A resistance. Think it again, the word not even making sense. There hadn't been a resistance for hundreds of years here, not to the Masters, not to anything. Perhaps at one point there had been a kind of slow seeping flood scenario, but then after centuries of locating the leaks and plugging them, of cementing over spots that didn't leak but looked weak, I would not have even believed the people had it in them.

Christ: they probably hadn't. Not until Yenu showed up. And where did I know that name from? It was bothering me.

I bumped and dodged through the streets, seeking somewhere busier, trying to keep my bearings towards the palace on its hill. Little blocked my view; the city of Valishec was mostly wood and brick, single levels, a few buildings of three or four storeys, plus a few higher, wretched-looking towers poking out of the morass like sticks in a swamp.

Workshops were mixed in with apartments, everything higgledy-piggledy, here an abattoir washing blood out of its doorway into the canal, here a shop selling hats and gloves, here a glassworks set above what looked like an alehouse, everywhere crisscrossed with catwalks, ropes, pulleys, clotheslines, arches, and scaffolding. The air smelled of a hundred types of shit and stagnant canal water, overlaid by woodsmoke and charcoal smoke that eddied over the street in the cold breeze. And it was loud, louder than I'd ever heard anything at the palace, though nothing unusual seemed to be happening: just people talking in a dozen languages, shouting to each other across streets, yelling at the harel and chamos pulling carts, offering things or themselves for sale, begging for alms, ordering food, getting children out of the way, complaining and gossiping and celebrating.

It was a beautiful riot of colour and light and though I was overwhelmed, I dimly realized that this was only because I had so infrequently left the compound, which for all its baroque imagery, I now thought, was as gray and sterile as an empty book, and had reduced all my senses to perceiving only its gray sterility as normal. Whatever parts of the compound might look like this had always been hidden from me, so that my life, the lives of the nobles and the royals, could rise above it all like clouds looking down on no more than a colourful smudge on the landscape.

But even as I thought that, I also thought, with a kind of grim certainty, that now there was nothing I wouldn't do to get back to it. Nothing. Back up to where this was all a smudge, and I was safe and protected and respected and valuable. Where I had friends. Food. Wine. The security of the tower I only now realized I loved, with its single door.

That our ethereal existence in the place of carved bones was made possible only by the work of the people down here was something I knew academically, but had not really experienced, the same way that back on Earth I had only rejoiced over being able to buy back-to-school hoodies for the kids for ten dollars, without ever thinking of the suffering of the people in Cambodia or Uganda who worked in their sweatshops to produce them for so cheap.

That's the way it goes though, and it has to, if you want to stay above instead of below. That's the way it goes: you think of the benefit to yourself as being greater than the cost to someone else; you always do the analysis in your head and come up with a positive number that justifies it, because it's easy to discount the cost when you've never had to pay it.

But I was paying them back somehow, wasn't I? My role in the system was to take and take, but now I was giving back, and none of these people would ever know. I lived the soft life and would return to it, and they would continue to live the hard life, but that was the key: *they would continue to live.* Because the Masters were like an avalanche, a lava flow, a lahar. To stand in front of Them meant death. You could not protect yourself, you could not protect anyone standing behind you. The best you could do was to step aside and let it flow, and clearly pass on the knowledge that it could not be resisted, lest some poor ignoramus step in front of it expecting to stop it.

No one had the power to stop it. No matter how many. A revolution of any kind, a resistance to anything, was predicated on the unspoken idea that *You can't kill all of us!* But They could. And They would. The number of *all* wasn't important. Against the Masters, one nation, a dozen nations, a world full of people, entire galaxies full of people, mortals had no more weight than a breath.

If They were provoked, if you fought Them, if They simply felt like it, They *would* kill all of you. There were always more of you to go around.

Appeasement had saved many lives. It was just a fact.

The Masters were disorganized and capricious, as a rule. They answered to no central spirit; you simply could not tell what They would do next, even to a world as loyal as Aradec, and that was where the danger lay. It was better to avoid all attention. *That* was heroism. The true, quiet steel at the centre of the softness that was the palace. The steel core that I contributed to.

They had wiped out entire worlds for nothing. For speaking disrespectfully to a representative of Their rule, for graffiti, for thrown stones. They had made sacrificial demands sometimes of entire demographics—all the women in a certain city, for instance, or all the children under five. And the things I had read in the Archive... oceans boiled dry, terrifying floods, the instantaneous removal of the atmosphere. Some worlds destroyed by a hurled moon. Some imploding into nothingness. Some that seemed as if they were all right, but everything living on them *changed*.

The Masters had had more power at times, less at others; They went quiet, then rose in fury; They were defeated by sorcerers and spirits and gods, who might be defeated in their turn; They fought amongst themselves, killed Their own, leapt through gates and doorways and rode rivers and seas of time and space to steal and possess what others had or might have in the future or had once held briefly in the past.

In the face of such power and unpredictability, all I could do was save a handful of lives in the only way I knew how. And that meant getting back to the palace. The Masters shut doors on you, They closed off options. I would walk through whatever They had left us instead of trying to smash through a wall. I had learned my lesson long ago.

The 'resistance' hadn't seen what I had seen. That was their great mistake, and why they would never succeed.

At last there was a crowd ahead, and I plunged into it with relief, then hesitated, realizing I was stuck fast. At least the resistance couldn't ambush me here in secret, but I couldn't keep going either. People weren't moving, as they had been for the market stalls and around the canals; it wasn't a crowd that flowed. Everyone was standing still, craning their necks to see something. I tracked their gazes and saw nothing, although I was taller than the people I stood near.

No one paid the slightest attention to me. I tried to move again, stopped short when I realized I would have to shove, and then crept awkwardly around the edges. The snatches of conversation I caught along the way painted a picture, slowly at first, making more sense as I reached the first corner of the square I hadn't realized I had entered.

All the spectators faced the centre, where a clot of soldiers in black helmets, like the ones I'd awoken to yesterday morning, had formed a kind of cordon, though I couldn't see what they were guarding.

For no reason at all, my stomach dropped. It should

have meant safety, seeing those soldiers; I should have run to them, explained my situation, begged them to escort me back. But something inside me screamed to just keep walking. *Get to the far side. Get out. Don't look.*

Why? It hit me in a moment: a smell from deepest memory, the sour, rotten smell of magic, something you only smelled when an enormous spell had been performed and enough of it had built up in one area. The wind would blow it away in a moment, but for now it stank of disaster.

Calm down. Not disaster: far from it. It means safety. If anyone is doing magic it must be sanctioned magic. No one else but a Royal Sorcerer is allowed to do it here.

I had to be sure. I looked for something to climb onto, seeing that kids of various species had taken all the easily accessible vantage spots, on rooftops or clinging to window ledges or arches. I spotted a wooden crate with a couple of kids standing on it and edged over, nudging them aside to reach up and grab the decorative stone lintel of the door next to it, then hauling myself up, boots scrabbling at the brick, till I could sit carefully on its wide top.

"No fair," muttered one of the kids below my feet.

"Nothing's fair about being tall," I pointed out. "You just get what you get. What's happening here?"

"Dunno," said the other kid. "We just saw everybody looking, so we came to look."

"Me too," I said. But it hadn't helped; it was still just a tiny singularity in the middle of the square, a black hole of black helmets and armour, tightly guarding something too small for me to see. Their spears bristled unmoving, the ends jammed between the square cobbles.

They were waiting for something. But what?

No. There. No. Not smell alone or sight or hearing told me the thing was coming, but something else, some deeper sense I had not always had, a cold pull on my viscera, a terrible stinging crackle. Dread came before it, and the common people in the square, who did not know how to interpret what their bodies were telling them, screamed and wailed, collapsed, tried to flee, failed to penetrate the crowd, fell where they stood. I waited for a stampede to begin, but no one else ran now; they froze in fear.

I white-knuckled the stone lintel so hard I half-expected it to turn to sand in my grip. It. Something.

Them.

CHAPTER FIVE

At first I thought wildly, *It is only fog, it is only a dark fog blown in from the sea, that's all right,* but too soon it became visible: hunched between the buildings and straightening as it reached the packed square, something I could not look at directly, a moving strip of darkness, a shimmer around it as if it were gas rather than solid, darting spurts of plasma and light, violet and red and amber.

A groaning hum came off it like heat, a vibration that shook the air and the stones and the flesh and bones of the crowd, and all the brick and wood and glass around it, generating a terrible chorus that hit the backbrain rather than the ear, a resonance that made my teeth ache. People covered their ears, and so did I, although it didn't help.

Remember, I thought grimly, almost laughing, these are your employers. Show a little respect.

But I had never seen anything like this before. They did not come here in person; They let us rule, and simply swooped in now and then far from the palace to take what They liked. Yet here was something—some *thing*—in the middle of the capital city. Like the Burning King. From outside our world.

"Let it be known—" someone shouted, then lapsed into a coughing fit. The crowd quieted except for an undercurrent of sobbing, poorly stifled in sleeves and shawls. "That the Royal Draft is underway; that representatives of Their Majesties' Army are now in every city and every town; that any who oppose the draft and will not fight for the Masters will be punished. Let it all be known. There are no secrets in Aradec. We are open to you all."

Who was talking? One of the soldiers? Reading off something by the sound of it. As they moved aside I saw more clearly the dark object that they had been guarding: a dog? No. Someone curled up on the cobbles, someone who had perhaps openly opposed the draft, or tried to dodge it, or just some poor fool who had been in the wrong place at the wrong time when They decided to send a message.

It didn't matter. His fate had been sealed the moment he had been captured, not when he had done (or not done) his crime.

The shimmering being, apparently aware that the speech was over, lunged down and seized the man, lifting him screaming and kicking into the air. He had not been bound or shackled.

Part of me thought, clinically: Look away. Do not let this into your mind.

Part of me thought, more distantly: There must be ten thousand people here. And there are fifteen or sixteen soldiers. And no one is thinking: We could rush forward, smother and overwhelm them, rescue this man, by sheer force of numbers. Because numbers meant nothing. They know that. Why does the 'resistance' not know?

Then again, maybe everyone thought, as we were supposed to think, that the draft dodger did not deserve rescuing. Many people looked away, covered their eyes or ears, closed a flap of skin across their sensory organs, shutting their wings, as the monster tore the man apart. The weeping and whispering continued.

This time the screaming went on and on, long after I expected his death. For minute after minute I thought wildly, *But he* must *be dead. He has to be. No one can be like that and live. His intestines are hanging in loops. Maybe all I am hearing is the echo of his screams. Maybe he did stop.*

He will *stop.*

Stop.

Please stop.

Please die.

The crowd fell silent only when he did. The dead man still floated a moment in mid-air, held up by a kind of glassy glow, which disappeared abruptly, sending the body to the stones with a wet and final thud. Was the creature gone? I could not tell. The mark of the Masters, generally, was a certain lack of definition when it came to things like physical laws, the visible spectrum, things like that.

"It is done," one of the soldiers shouted unnecessarily. "Tell all you see. We *will* take whoever is needed to fight. It is your duty to fight."

Idly I wondered if the so-called resistance was still in pursuit, and if so, whether they had seen this. What lessons would they draw from it? I hoped the same as the rest of us: that life was sacred and should be preserved; that the Masters did not care, particularly, about ours; and it was up to us, not Them, to keep people alive.

And that the resistance had therefore positioned itself against all that. Not merely on the wrong side of history, but the wrong side of life itself.

The crowd was dispersing, silent, shocked, too slowly for me to catch up with the soldiers, who vanished down a side-street. Still, I could move again, and the palace on its hill still winked in the light. All those polished bones. Home.

I tried to take the straightest path, but just as on the way to the square, the streets zigged and zagged around natural features, boulders, hills, where cobbles or flagstones could not be laid. The right direction was always possible, but only by taking three times as long in streets and alleys that went the wrong way. The dead man's screams seemed to echo in my ears. Something the Advisor had told me once: *What you see can never be unseen. There is no way to uproot it from your mind.* Good or bad, I knew he had left unsaid. If only he had known the things I'd seen before I came here.

At least I was getting closer to the palace; I could smell the sea, and the palace sat on the cliffs of the shore. If I could get closer to the shoreline, I could turn and walk until I hit the road that led to the supply-way, and...

Three men blocked the path ahead of me, laughing and chatting; one held something on his shoulder that looked for all the world like the head of an ant, but an ant the size of a pig. The hard, red surface gleamed in the half-light of the alley. "Yes, so then I thought I'd get it bronzed," he was saying, "but it turns out there's only one place that can do that."

"Where's that?" said the other man.

I barely heard them. I was watching the third, who was smiling and nodding, and looking at me. I didn't recognize him, only the look in his eyes.

The whole interaction was the work of a moment. I turned abruptly and moved down the alleyway to my left, heart hammering. No, I hadn't seen his face in that dim, smoky room, had I? I hadn't. But he looked at me with such knowing.

A few streets later I was back on track, and close enough to the docks to feel genuine relief. If I had not in fact evaded the so-called resistance, at least I would be in the open soon, away from this tangle of streets and stairs. They could chase me then if they wanted. I didn't think they would; what they wanted was secrecy, not to be known.

The end of this alley was blocked with pallets stacked high with bulging canvas bags of salt; I sighed, and went to climb over them, then paused. I could see not only daylight but sea to my right, down an open alleyway that led straight down to the docks. I could even see a little gleam of red: the signage pointing traders to the hard-paved track leading to the supply-way.

Later, I could not believe how oblivious I'd been; in the moment though, my eagerness felt entirely forgivable. A clear way! An open path! Nothing easier! And in a couple of hours, I'll be drinking wine with the Advisor and telling him in serious tones about what had happened to the draft dodger over a meal of...

They didn't run towards me, only walked, smiling as if they had just spotted an old friend. Ksajakra carried my sword, the heavy one I had taken in the fight at the dungeon. It was too long for him and he held it awkwardly at his chest. The others, too, made sure to show their weapons. Even little Yenu, the only one not smiling.

"All right," she said in Low Dath. "While no one's looking. Come on. Quietly."

"You wouldn't kill me," I said. They were still coming; I turned and glanced at the alleyway behind me. No, too easy. They'd have stationed somebody at the far end. I backed away and turned, back down the alley still blocked with the salt bags. She was right that no one was looking. No witnesses. They must have warned people a while ago to clear out rather than get involved. How long had they been tracking me?

"Kill you? No. Some folks want to, mind you. You killed our people."

"You killed more of mine."

"It doesn't matter. We might hurt you though," she said tonelessly. "You don't need all your body parts to do magic. Basic fact."

Notice how they don't say *Join us*, I thought as I kept backing up. It was all I could think of. *The villain is supposed to say 'Join us.' I saw it a million times. But all they're saying is 'Let us use you, or else.'*

Something landed with a thud just behind me, and I whirled, hands already up, useless against the blow I expected, but it was a palace guard, his bright uniform the gladdest sight I'd seen for hours, a big Chithuz man holding a pikestaff. "Halt!" he bellowed, aiming it over my shoulder. "Arrest the traitors!"

A dozen other guards climbed down from the rooftops, many dropping on the pile of salt on their way, a few bags breaking open and spilling into the alley. They were followed by an even gladder sight: the Advisor himself, leaping straight down and landing at my side. "Prophet! Are you harmed?"

"No, thank fuck. Why did *you* come to get me?"

"It is my duty to—Watch out!" He pushed me low and something whirred over my head, embedding itself into an unbroken bag. Without even looking at it, I shouted for everyone to run, though that meant running into the resistance fighters arranged across the end of the alleyway. No time to explain what a bomb was, or how gunpowder worked, or how Yenu, the wily fucker, had invented them in secret, or—

It went off with more force than I had expected, sending everybody sprawling and showering half the block with salt. Something, bomb shrapnel or stone, had hit me, though I hadn't felt it; blood trickled down my cheek. My ears rang.

Still, the resistance was outnumbered, and was rapidly being outfought. Their only advantage was that the guards had clearly been instructed to capture them alive, and so they were retreating as they fought, down alleys and over canals, and at last were beginning to draw a crowd.

I began to follow them, wiping at my cheek, and the Advisor tugged cautiously at my sleeve. "Your Holiness, stop! The guards will have them. We cannot risk you being harmed again."

"I'm not going to fight them all," I said, breaking into a run; he padded behind me, his anxiety so thick it almost came off him in waves. "I just want to kill one of them. Just one."

"Prophet, *please*."

Despite the guards' orders, one of the rebels had been killed and lay in the gutter in a thick puddle of green ichor; I stooped as I ran, and snatched the sword he still clutched in death. Good thing too, the stickiness of the blood on the grip. Thanks, pal. Doing me a favour and you didn't even know it.

I joined the guards, slashing and swinging, only vaguely aware of the stalls through which we fought, the people screaming as they fled, knocking over tables of shellfish that clattered to the ground like gunshot, spilling bags of vegetables and fruit, abandoning the day's fish. My sword went through a heap of spices that exploded into the air and burned everyone's eyes, but the stinging didn't last long, and my target was small, and moving, and easy to find.

This time. This time. I've had so many chances, but this time I know...

Someone slashed at me from one side; I feinted away, then simply lowered my shoulder and slammed into him, knocking him flat. From behind I still heard the Advisor calling for me in despair, telling me to stop. He knew me as a soft man, a good man, and I would have to shatter his illusions in a moment, and—and—why were we on the actual docks now, why had they led us so close to the ships?

Too late I realized the trap. The first snares I had spotted; this one I had not guessed in time. Even though the guards were still fighting, several of the rebels had somehow managed to snatch the Advisor and drag him up the gangplank to a small three-master made of dark wood, flying no flag. He wasn't struggling, I realized in horror: drugged, or dead.

Drugged. Stolen. If I thought my rage had been murderous before—

"To me!" I shouted. "Everyone to me! Forget the others! They have the Advisor! The Advisor to the Prophet!"

We charged up the gangplank and even before the first blow I staggered at the choking stench of magic. The real hit came a moment later, a pulled punch, I could almost feel the exact level and angle of its pull, from someone I didn't see, across my cheekbone. I fell, rose again, caught a boot to the ribs—*They don't want to kill me, they won't kill me, fight, fight*—another, and then one square on the side of my head, sending everything into a bright, ringing place.

Through the new light I saw them simply hurl the remaining guards over the railing, knock down the gangplank, unwisely, how will you climb down again, didn't think of *that* did you, ha ha, and with a shocking jolt, we snapped loose from the mooring and were out to sea.

CHAPTER SIX

I GOT UP again despite the thudding pain in my head, hearing a strange noise: a kind of grinding snarl. Startled to realize it was coming from me. The Advisor was guarded by a half-dozen people and I still struggled to reach him, and was restrained suddenly by something looped around my throat. My world went from white to darkness again.

Clawing behind me did nothing, nor did trying to pry the thing off my throat; it was a rope, or something worse than a rope, something sinuous and steely that I only shattered my fingernails on. Yenu pushed through the others towards me, reeling, bloodied blue from a dozen small cuts, her teeth bared and the wet gaps making their arrangement strangely disquieting, like the mouth of a dangerous fish.

"The guards will not stop," I croaked. "They will take

boats. Commandeer. Sail out after us. We are still within sight of the shore."

"I'm well aware of that," she said. "Jak, tie him to a mast. We're getting out of here."

As Ksajakra and others slapped and kicked me into position, Yenu snatched a piece of chalk out of a box bolted to the deck and began to draw. Everyone scattered away from it as if she had started a fire, but I knew it was only to avoid stepping on the chalk-marks. Any change you made to a sigil changed the spell, and nearly always for the worse. If they did not know that by experience, she must have put the fear into them some other way.

These people. How had she gathered them around her? Did they follow her out of love or fear?

"Where are we going?" Ksajakra stood behind her, to my eyes angry and bewildered, but not so much that he could ignore whatever warnings she'd fed them about magic. "Our plan was to—"

"We are adjusting the plan," she said. Sweat dripped from her forehead as she drew, and she corrected several curlicues with alarming speed, barely looking at them.

"We—"

"*I* am, fine," she said, raising her voice over the slap of waves against the wooden hull. I thought fleetingly about the fishing ships the guards would have to commandeer. Even if they had sent a runner back to the palace the moment the Advisor had been abducted, the handful of armed ships of the Royal Navy would take hours to mobilize. Even their weapons were few and mostly for show. We were not a warlike people, I thought, and repeated it to myself with fresh anger: *We do not go to war! We do not fight! And now she is forcing a fight!*

But the little ship we were on didn't appear to be armed either; there were no weapons on deck, anyway. Perhaps belowdecks they had some, those big crossbows like we—no, worse, because she had figured out bombs, and the ship might hold dangers that the guards would never foresee. Was it rigged for a long journey? I couldn't tell from where I had been bound. You could tell, though, at least approximatwly, by looking; I knew that from the few trips I'd taken with the King and the Queen. Now I had Ksajakra's question too: Where *were* we going?

My most immediate worry was for the Advisor, but calling to him produced no response except someone kicking me hard in the thigh, then vanishing with a laugh when I turned my head, the only part of me I could move, to see who had done it. "Fucker!" I shouted in English, which made me feel slightly better.

Yenu's sigil was huge, and hideously complex; I'd never seen anything like it. Even Ksajakra fell silent, staring at it. Sometimes they had that effect on people even before they were activated, I knew. A spell that complex...

Of course. Wherever we were going, we could not sail there. And she could never do this alone.

When she finally finished and approached me, I was ready for her demands, and even before she had begun to speak, I said, "No. I won't do it."

Ksajakra stepped between us, swinging a sword. "You are a tool," he snapped. "Tools don't talk."

"Bullshit," I said in English, then switched back to Low Dath. "Tools can't refuse work either, can they? And I refuse. Whatever it is you're doing at her say-so, it's a suicide mission as well as a homicide mission. You will die and you will cost many more worthwhile lives than yours. I refuse to participate. And you all should do the same."

Again that look of terrible doubt and clarity in his eyes. He had a button, I thought, and I had pushed it several times already: he didn't trust Yenu. And he didn't like it. *Stop it*, his face said; *go on*, his face said.

Don't push your luck, something inside me advised.

I glared at them both, though the angle hurt my neck. "The guards are already coming, aren't they? I can hear oars. So no."

He glanced over the railing and tightened his lips. "And if we convince you? Using your friend here?"

"Convince me to do what?" I snapped. "Listen to yourself. You sound like a child reciting a nursery rhyme because you heard your grandmother say it once. Just words, no meaning. Do you know what one of the first words I learned in your languages was? *Sacrifice*. I told you, she'll sacrifice me; she'll sacrifice any one of you. And for what? Her plan? You don't even know where she wants to take us, do you? Where she wants to take your people? The ones who trusted you to lead them?"

"I still lead them!" he shouted.

Yenu said, "Yes. The guards are coming. And yes, I don't intend to let them take us. Interpret that however you like. But I'm the only one who can get us out of here. You'll have to transfer magic to me to make this work. The others can't do it."

The guards are coming: so I was right. I allowed myself a single moment of hope, like the golden flare of a lit match. "And if I say no?" I said.

"Dead weight will be tossed overboard."

"Then good luck getting your spell to run."

"I wasn't talking about you."

Behind the ring of weapons, the Advisor lifted his chin groggily, but otherwise gave no indication that his life had just been threatened.

"Do it, then," I said, steadying my voice. "What is he to me, except the minder assigned to me by the King and Queen? He and I are merely fellow bureaucrats, not soulmates. All of you are excellent at empty threats, I notice."

"Good effort," she said. "Points for trying. You only came aboard because we had him."

"Stalemate, then, if that's what you think." I cocked my head theatrically. "I can't see, are they here yet? Are they close? Are they in fishing boats? Or did they commandeer the troop ships?"

Ksajakra looked again, unable to stop himself; so did several of the others. Yenu didn't. Instead she got a dagger out of her coat, a small one, and replaced the piece of chalk into the same pocket, making sure I was watching.

I glanced at the Advisor, entirely against my will. My head seemed to weigh a thousand pounds. "The rest of you cannot possibly be considering going along with this," I said. No one replied.

"What are you doing? Are you so devoted to her cause? Look, take the ship back to the docks. The Advisor and I are of high status at the palace, we will argue for clemency: we'll tell them that you should be spared because you chose to defy this creature and spare our lives. You could live out your lives in the dungeon. The dungeon isn't that bad. You *don't have to die*." I raised my voice over the thrillingly near sound of someone hailing us. "They're almost here anyway. Arrest is inevitable. But you don't have to *die* because she tells you to die. We could be on your side. She's not."

A few people exchanged glances. Could I buy a few more minutes if I changed tack? Some I had with promises, I knew, but the others might listen to logic. "It's a trap," I said. "All of this, all of it is a trap. Did you not hear all the other doors closing behind you? No, because Yenu told you the open door was the best one, and she could get you safely through it. She can't. Us being on this ship, here and now, is part of it. Can you all not see it? Why would you see the trap and let yourself be caught in it?"

"What They would want us to do is surrender, to be still," Yenu said, her voice level and deadly. "Because we are the resistance. Do you see us doing that?"

"Yes. We haven't moved, have we?" I looked around angrily, writhing in the thick ropes. The shouts were getting nearer. "What are you doing, letting her think for you? Is that how a sane person speaks? Or is that how the Masters speak?"

"They won't listen to you. Now stop talking to them," she said. "Pick a side."

"Why wouldn't they listen to me?" I said. "Have you done something to them?"

She narrowed her eyes. This is what Johnny did to me, I said with my gaze, meeting hers. Do you understand that? She taught me to find the weak spot and go in with my sharpest blade. Never show weakness. Only find it and use it. It's so useful. She taught me so well. If only you could have met her.

No, maybe for the best that you didn't. What universe could handle two of you?

"Not picking a side picks Their side," she said so that only I could hear, in English. "You know that."

Look away, I thought furiously.

She didn't.

"All right," she said in Low Dath, turning away and pointing at the Advisor. "Bind him properly. We'll start with fingers. That's traditional, after all. And he won't need to walk."

I stared, heart hammering. They wouldn't, I thought. After the speech I gave. They're not really considering obeying her. They're not—

They made sure I could see. The Advisor didn't cry out or struggle, but the blade had reached bone when I shouted, "All right! All right, you motherfucker! I'll do it!"

The Advisor's blood trickled across the deck towards the sigil; Yenu put her boot in front of it, smearing it to one side to give it a fresh path.

The voices hailing us were so close they sounded as if they were on the deck now. I swore and nearly wept: we had been so close, so *fucking close*, I shouldn't have said anything, it's only one finger, it...

She held out her hands and spoke in a language I didn't know, something heavy and old, instantly recognizable as words of power to activate the spell coded into the sigil. The air bent and shimmered around it in a dome, then a cone, narrowing to an impossibly dark dot above it, like a fleck of dust that sucked all the warmth from the air; frost sprouted abruptly in the centre of the chalk circle, radiating outwards from it.

"Now," she said.

"Untie me," I said, moving my shoulders.

"You don't need to touch someone to transfer. Do it!"

I closed my eyes. Someone screamed behind me and I heard the familiar sound of the Advisor's heavy wings, and something clinking or jingling. More screams rose, and a few heavy thuds.

Just wait. Just wait a minute longer and the ship would be swarmed with rescuers. Just wait.

"It's not working!" Yenu shouted over the increasing noise. I opened my eyes again to see the dark dot bobbing ominously in mid-air, dimming everything around it, but the sigil had not begun to glow.

"For fuck sake, *you* do whatever it is!" I yelled back. "Just take what you need!"

"That's what I'm saying! I can't take anything! You won't let me!"

"I am letting you!"

"Well then *it* won't let me!"

"I fail to see how that's *my* pr—"

A sound like a bell drowned out my next words; her face went blank with surprise and panic as the tiny void at the top of the chalk circle billowed out like the silk of a hot-air balloon, enveloping the ship in glistening pink light.

When I dared open my eyes again we were motionless in an unending plain of gray stones and thick white grass.

THE STENCH OF magic filled the air, chokingly thick, like smoke. I coughed and spat, indistinct forms reeling around me on the ship's perfectly-still deck. My legs against the dark wood were scraped, bloodied, glowing faintly violet. Each hair of my beard was limned with blue lightning.

The chalk circle was still visible, though the design was blurred with blood. Fresh gouges marked the ship like hieroglyphics, as if hundreds of tiny impacts had torn away the black-stained surface wood to reveal the lighter brown below. In the distance, huge shapeless forms strode slowly across the pale grass, some on four legs, some on six, some on none, so far away that all that could be discerned of pattern or colour was that they were darker than the gray sky, and their heads vanished into the crawling clouds. The air was thin and cold—so thin, in fact, that I began to feel dizzy.

Behind me, something sawed patiently at the ropes, not bothering to untie the knots. When they fell away, I turned painfully to see the Advisor, who simply lay down next to me and put his head on his forepaws, breathing hard. For the moment, it seemed, we were alone. And we were no longer at sea. And I did not know where we were. I held down a wave of terror, and flexed my hands slowly both for something to do and to bring the blood back into them. My shoulders ached worse than anything.

"Is she dead?" I croaked.

"Who?"

"You know who."

He craned his long neck and the face returned. "I am not sure, Prophet."

"I'm sorry," I added, looking at his cut paw, in which whitish-blue bone visibly gleamed like a droplet of mercury. It had stopped bleeding, at least; but it would be an ugly, permanent scar, and now he would not be able to walk without pain.

"I'm sorry about that," I said again when he did not reply. "I shouldn't have even let them touch you. I should have agreed before they touched the knife to your skin."

Both feathers and fur rose vertically in shock, a full-body twitch that even I recoiled from. "Should? You *should* have let them take me apart, Your Holiness," he said, sounding only mildly offended. "The drug they used to capture me dulled my pain as well as my mind, and the guards were nearly at the ship. In a few minutes we would have been safe, and these people arrested or killed. You know that, you heard them. You did not have to acquiesce to the threat!"

"They might have killed you!"

"Perhaps."

"You really think I would have bought my rescue with your life?"

"You believe it is an unreasonable thing to do?" he asked, baffled. "I would have done it, Your Holiness. Only a little more time was needed to avert this disaster." *And you were too weak and soft to hold out even that time*, was the subtext there. I appreciated his decency in not saying it.

"This is all my fault," I murmured. "I'm still sorry, though, and I want you to accept it."

"Do not apologize." He lowered his head and licked at the cut with his long, pointed tongue. "You did not wield the knife yourself."

"A technicality." I looked around. "You know, they're not watching us. I am still armed, I have the sacrificial dagger. You and I could…"

"I advise against it," he said. "We are greatly outnumbered. There are more below… at least a dozen."

"Flee, then. If not fight. Do you advise against that too?"

"I do." He wiped his mouth reluctantly against his shoulder, the blood invisible against the iridescent black fur just where it became feather. "We will watch. And wait."

I touched a scrape in the wood next to me, a full inch deep. What had made it? I felt as if half my brain had been left behind at the docks. I rose awkwardly, keeping one hand on the mast to steady myself. Panting helped more than long, deep breaths, but I still felt lightheaded.

Yenu wasn't dead, but a glance told me that was a technicality; she appeared to be dying. I kept my distance as the others wearily took turns pounding on her skinny back to make her cough up what seemed like gallons of thin, particle-flecked golden fluid. From their muttering I concluded she would probably live. Pity.

Ksajakra went belowdecks and returned with wrapped packets of food and two canteens, silently giving one to the Advisor and one to me while we watched them strive to keep Yenu alive. Nobody's faces suggested that they wanted to.

Just smother her, I wanted to say. It'll be a nice, quick death. Then we'll all figure out how to get home. We'll pretend this didn't happen, and the war can continue to sail over our heads like a kite, until it's gone, till even its tail is gone, its string is gone, and everything will go back to normal. You don't have to fight against a war happening, you know. You could just let it happen and look away. The soldiers in the draft might even come home. After all, do *you* know what they'll be fighting? Or who they'll be fighting alongside? I don't, but I've seen what the Masters can do, and believe me, They can fight when They want to. Okay? Be reasonable. Just kill her. She's so close, it would *barely* be a murder.

I said nothing, and ate what I had been given: a spongy bun with a thin layer of ithel leaves inside it, and a wedge of preserved kolros, full of salt and sugar. The canteen water tasted like copper; I allowed myself a few mouthfuls despite my thirst, then poured a little into my

palm and let 1779 out of my pocket to drink. I stowed
him away again quickly when Ksajakra returned.

"What did you do to her, Prophet?"

"What did *I* do?" I repeated, unable to come up with
anything better; that was the last thing I'd expected him
to say. "Whatever was done, she did it to herself." I
paused, thinking. "She did say she couldn't do the spell
herself, didn't she? I wonder why it still ran. It should
have fizzled out, not killed her."

"She is not dead."

"She ought to be."

I waited for him to say *I wonder why she isn't*, but
we both knew there was only one answer: the Masters
had bestowed powers we hadn't seen yet upon Their
creation. She would have surprised the resistance before,
I was sure. For maximum impact and theatre, revealing
some new and amazing ability whenever she sensed
doubt creeping into her followers. The Ancient Ones
knew how mortals worked; we were simple beings, and
that would be our downfall.

"Throw her over the side, Ksajakra." I folded up
the waxed paper wrapper and put it in my pocket; he
watched my hands the whole time. "Don't think of it as
killing your second-in-command. Think of it as getting
a mad dog out of the village. She's bitten enough people
already."

His face wavered between uncertainty and anger. Did
they have rabies on Aradec? Still, something had sunk
in; I had again managed to reach past his logic and touch
some part of his gut instinct that told him, had told him

from the beginning, that she wasn't to be trusted.

"Not yet," he finally said. "We still need her."

That at least was true. I couldn't get us home, and I suspected he hadn't asked me to because he already knew that. And frustrated rage boiled up in me again, hot and inexorable, and all the worse for not being able to do anything about it. "So. From now on we'll all have to go wherever she tells us to go, and we'll never go anywhere else. Because she's the only one who can move this thing between worlds."

I glared at the horizon rather than her inert body on the deck, trying to calm myself before I rushed over and did something unreasonable. They'd dogpile me without question, not so much to protect her as to repel an outsider; it was a human instinct. "What *is* this thing? This ship. How did you build it without getting caught for doing magic?"

"Yenu had the components assembled elsewhere," he said vaguely, also looking at the horizon, where the huge dark shapes moved with apparent leisure, uninterested in us. "I don't know how they came together. It took four years. She was often away, seeing how the war proceeded in other places. Then she would come back and work on it."

"You didn't see it being built?"

"No. We only saw it intermittently. She kept it in a secret place so that you people would not find it."

You people being the palace, presumably, and from there, the Masters. Made sense to me; but further confirmation that we were as firmly under her thumb as she could wish. "Her people," I said. "Not yours. Her spell, her boat. Her plan. While she told you that you were the leader."

He said nothing.

"It's like a…" I began, and trailed off. I didn't know the word *cult* in Low Dath or High, which he wouldn't speak anyway, or in any other language except English. Religion had died out on Aradec when the Masters showed up, and not even as part of Their conquest; it simply became impossible for people to believe in unseen gods when real ones were present, visible, and destroying your village. But I wanted to explain to Ksajakra that Yenu was a cult leader, not a resistance leader; she wanted followers, not comrades, not peers. If she had gathered all these people around her with a combination of magic, charisma, and whatever else They had stuffed her with, it was not going to be to overthrow her benefactors.

"What did she tell you the plan was, anyway?" I added.

"I am tired of you talking," he announced, and walked back across the deck to the knot of people gathered around Yenu's sprawled body.

As the Advisor and I, though orders of magnitude bigger than everyone else, were apparently unarmed as well as unwilling to start a two-man mutiny, we were left alone to wander the deck. Despite my frequent stops to gasp for breath, I had to admit we had been lucky to arrive at a place with breathable air at all. When you thought about all the worlds in all the known universe and how many of them were hospitable to lungs like ours... or maybe we hadn't?

I thought back to a long time ago, a nightmarish flight through the darkness of space in nothing more than a sphere of soil and air. Maybe the ship too carried a sphere of air with it and if we left we'd suffocate at once. I felt pretty sure that Yenu would have planned ahead for that though. Just as she must have planned for us to land here.

The ship was about thirty paces long, with a square stern and a blunt, fat prow; where I would have expected a proper ship's wheel was a saucer-sized one, so small it seemed ornamental, blooming from a narrow brass column bolted to the deck. Surely not wide enough to contain the necessary lines or chains. The wood was stained black, except where our passage here had chipped and scratched it, and I couldn't see any wards or sigils. Which wasn't to say that Yenu hadn't crammed the place with them; maybe they were in the hold, or on the underside of the boards, or something.

There was something odd about the ship's proportions, but I was not enough of a nautical man to figure out exactly what. It was too short, or too high, or too wide or something; it felt like it should have been unseaworthy, though it had floated all right in the harbour. It definitely felt too short for the three masts, and they also felt too close together for my liking. The sails were tightly furled as if they'd never been used, as solid as tree trunks, and also black, like the shrouds and rigging. The railing was close with balustrades, its top rounded rather than square, like the few ships I had been in. There was no capstan on the deck, only a dozen boxes of the same dark wood nailed and bolted into place here and there, and a trap door that would lead to the hold.

It was *basically* ordinary. And somehow also *extremely* wrong. Yenu had designed it to seem unremarkable when surrounded by similar ships, I surmised, because you would never see it on dry land... sitting perfectly level instead of toppling over.

When I circled back around, Yenu was groggily sitting up and feeling her face with bleeding fingertips, the ink-dark blood mixing with the transparent, straw-coloured fluid that flowed from her eyes, nose, and mouth. Was that... what did you call it... the stuff that cushioned your spine? I hoped not, as it would mean that her current consciousness was only forestalling her death for a couple of minutes. I was sure you couldn't lose that much of the stuff and live. Maybe it was something else. Maybe her physiology was more inhuman even than it looked on the outside. The fluid glittered slightly as it flowed, as if it contained gold dust.

"Respectfully, Ksajakra, brother," wheezed one of the rebels, "where are we?" He clearly wasn't getting much air—medium-height, narrow-chested, thin. His lips were turning lilac and his voice was faint. I felt bad for him. Surely whatever he had signed up for had not included this, or else he wouldn't have asked.

"I am finding that out now, Liandan," said Ksajakra, looking meaningfully at Yenu. She looked up at him clear-eyed and unafraid, and held out a hand; someone put a cloth into it, and she pressed it to her face and stood as he addressed her. "Yenu! You said the plan was changing. And now you have brought us to this place. What are we doing?"

"It's not changing *much*. And we wouldn't be here at all if I had managed to get what I needed from the Archive." She glared at me as if I was the one who had arrested her. I glared back.

But there was a kind of change in the air, a quickening amongst the rebels. I tried not to gloat too visibly. She really hadn't told them, I realized. They had been operating on faith, and the last of their faith was about to run dry; so she was either about to tell the truth, or lie for her life. What had she told the other five spies to get them to act as decoys while she broke into our Archive? Knowing that they might be discovered and tortured as a result? They must have been absolute whoppers. Lies as big as a planet. She was more like her prototype than her makers could have hoped.

"I am not interested in why we are *here* rather than somewhere else," Ksajakra said. There was an edge in his voice. "I asked you what we are expected to do in this place."

"It sounds to me like I'll have to do it myself," Yenu said coolly. She moved a dry part of the cloth to one ear. "Since the rest of you sound like you might be having doubts about our goals."

"What does that mean?" Ksajakra snapped. "And what is happening to you?"

"It's nothing. Side effect of having to move the ship

alone. Saving all of our lives from the palace guards. That's all." She switched the cloth to the other ear. "Anyone here is welcome to go home on their own if they wish. Any takers?"

The temperature on the deck seemed to drop a dozen degrees. Wrong answer, I thought with something like glee. On Aradec, they had been metaphorical hostages to her whims. Here, it was literal. And no one wanted to be a hostage. They had thought of themselves as more or less equals. Contributing as much as anyone to her plan. I could have told them this would happen sooner or later.

"All right," she said, checking the cloth, then stowing it in a coat pocket. "Let us all remind ourselves why we assembled in the first place, hm? To end the war. To topple the Masters. To make sure They never, ever harm anyone ever again. Didn't we?"

Murmurs of assent, but not with, I thought, a rekindling of an original faith. Not with the same holy fire as when they had been safe on their home planet, scheming and conspiring in a smoky cellar.

Most just watched her with an expression somewhere between hatred and awe. I knew how they felt. *We* could do that, their faces said; she said we could. Just us. We're the only people who could do such a thing, and she's trusting us with the mission.

It always starts like that, I wanted to say. But wait till she tells you the cost. She hasn't yet, I don't think.

"Yenu isn't my real name," she said. "Most of you know that. Most of you don't know why I chose it, though." She glanced at the Advisor. "He might."

The Advisor shook his head, refusing to be pulled into her play.

"No? It's in *your* palace Archive, after all. That's why I came to your planet. To Aradec. Thought I'd be more famous." She laughed bitterly, and then in apparent pain sat back down on the deck. "Instead I find I've picked a name nobody knows... Get back. Move your boot. While we get used to the air, let me tell you a little story.

"Dobeltai Yiemki lived in Aradec when the so-called Masters arrived there. She led the initial resistance against Them with the kingdom of Beycrod and its allies. Six kingdoms. The general, you understand, of an army of millions. The Masters didn't like that. Killed her. Easily. Killed her armies. The flames of resistance against Them appeared to be snuffed out. *You* know they weren't; *I* know they weren't. They smouldered underground for two centuries. Organized initially, and in the wake of Yiemki's death, by her daughter. Yenu. Who had a plan."

Her breath came hard; sweat ran down her forehead. It was a nice story, I thought tiredly. The resistance probably hadn't known it. They thought they were starting something all new because the war was new, having started less than a decade ago. History lost all its definition and delineation and became a muddy smear past a certain point. There was no way to learn about something that happened a thousand years ago.

"And her plan—?" said Ksajakra.

"Failed. Obviously. But I thought you'd get the

reference." She got out the cloth again, wiped at her still-streaming face. "She was missing too many pieces. But it was a good starting point. Mine is better." She studied the cloth, then briskly wrung it out. "We're going to free the Quevereld."

Silence fell. Yenu looked up at me and only me. "The Elder Gods," she said in English. "Now do you understand?"

I had to sit down. For a long time I waited for someone to say, *You're joking*, or *You've lost your mind*.

The Elder Gods. Defeated and imprisoned who knew how long ago, or in which *where* or *when* the Masters had intersected with (for there were many) after the last war in which They had fought, the decisive one that took the Elders out of the equation in all the possible futures. Once, a long time ago on Earth, Johnny Chambers and I had begged the Elder Gods for help and received only a last gasp, the best something's spirit could offer, in an underground tomb. Hardly the cavalry coming over the hills.

Or so she'd told me. And I had believed her. About that, and about everything else...

Yenu said, "What's happening right now isn't rightly called a war. You'd call it something else. The Masters were... Well, let's say something happened quite recently, on the immortal timescale, to get Their dander up."

I opened my mouth and closed it again; the Advisor glanced curiously at me.

"The earliest stages of this current conflict began when They awoke, woke others, massed for an easy invasion

at an opportune alignment when all the doors opened to
Them, and were, um... thwarted. When They regrouped
and invaded again, the planet They wanted most was...
taken from Them."

Very diplomatic, I almost said. Weaselly, passive
language. Notice how she doesn't say who else played a
role in that.

"That was when They decided to take up expansion.
But not like the old days: chaos and factions. It's very
different now. This is not a war," she repeated. "It's
a process, and it's being carried out by a *machine*. An
inanimate device composed of animate components. It
is fuelled by, fed by, greased by, the people on the worlds
They have not yet conquered. Civilians. Noncombatants.
Not as collateral damage, but as part of the machine.
Because mortals can't fight Them, ordinary people
become nothing more than collections of chemicals and
energy to power the destruction of more worlds, so the
more They conquer, the more They can conquer. Do you
understand?

"But the Quevereld *will* fight Them. That creates two
sides to the war. And if the Ancient Ones are fighting
the Quevereld, They will not be conquering worlds. And
then They will be defeated."

I put my head between my knees. All around me, as if
transmitted through the mast at my back, I could hear
the breaths of the others, the distant whoosh and hum
of the walking creatures. "You're not stopping a war," I
said. "You're starting a war."

She shrugged.

154

"A jailbreak to free the gods," I said. "This really is a suicide mission."

"No it isn't."

Ksajakra, who had been looking between us with growing concern, frowned. "Where are we? Are we in the place where the Quevereld were held?"

"Oh that," Yenu said carelessly. "No, of course not." Her entire posture changed: weary but arrogant, chin up. The familiarity was like looking into a cracked mirror, and I felt sick for a moment. "As I said, I wasn't able to get what I needed from the Archive. And may our brothers, sisters, and others who assisted me and did not return, sleep in peace," she added, somewhat perfunctorily, though it seemed to satisfy at least a few of the rebels, who nodded at her. "But there is one other place to find it, and it's here. Near here," she amended. "A copy not of the entire book, but of part of the book. This world is called St. Chirkenai, not that it really matters."

"So we are not fighting? No more lives will be lost here?" said Ksajakra.

"Is that what you're worried about?" she said disdainfully. "I thought we all agreed that we would give our lives for the cause."

His face seemed to slam shut like a door. *Wrong answer*. "What is in the book?"

"What the original Yenu didn't know she needed. The shape of something missing."

"We're... looking for something that's *not* there?"

"Glad you get it," she said, and stood unsteadily. "Come on. It's a long walk, and we need supplies."

"Have fun," I said. "Bring me back a souvenir shot glass."

"Oh, you're coming."

CHAPTER SEVEN

KSAJAKRA CARRIED YENU strapped to his back with a spare piece of sailcloth as we climbed down from the ship; she murmured directions into his ear. I could see she was pissed off at the indignity, but there was no avoiding it: as soon as we had reached the flat, stony ground, everyone had cried out in surprise, and with the exception of the Advisor, had been flattened to hands and knees. Walking was a struggle for all of us, and too much for the magic-weakened Yenu.

To explain to them that the gravity here was perceptibly and annoyingly higher than on Aradec would have meant nothing to anyone but Yenu; nor was there much point to explaining that we were all light-headed and semi-deranged because there was too little oxygen. At any rate the combination rendered me both high and leaden, and I clumped along behind Ksajakra as if I were drunk. At least, I consoled myself, I could blame future bad decisions on the lack of oxygen; I'd feel better about it later. Less guilty.

They had found a sturdier pair of britches for me in the hold, as well as a proper leather belt and a long coat, dark red, almost maroon, like dried blood. I had also found a piece of twine to tie back my hair; the breeze was constant and I hated having it brush across my face. It made me think too much of the sky, filled with squirming tendrils occasionally visible through the thick clouds.

The Advisor padded silently next to me, limping a little. I hadn't wanted him to come, but he didn't want to stay on the ship with the others, reasonably enough; and moreover, he had worried for my safety with these people in turn. We were safer together.

In wonderment we watched the forms on the horizon, ponderous shapes of creatures we did not know. Monsters in silhouette, taller than mountains, faces vanished in the clouds. Better for us, I hoped. I pictured them sniffing us out, rearing in anger or hunger, turning, galloping towards us, now that we had left the protective bubble of the ship. How long would one of their paces be? How long till they reached us, nine tiny specks like ants in their sight? No, better not to think about it.

I glanced back at the ship, impossibly upright on the stony plain, its curved keel appearing to bear the whole weight of the thing on a beam of wood no thicker than my thigh. The distant creatures could crush it like an egg with a single step.

No one had bothered introducing me to the rebels who had come with us, though I had heard a few names I remembered. They still called me 'Prophet' when they deigned to speak to me at all. Saloc, Itzlek, and Liandan were humans, though I couldn't remember which of the three men was which. Liandan, I thought, was the skinny one who was having the most trouble breathing after Yenu. Ceth and Rhakun were a Turuntu woman and So'it man respectively, which was a bit easier.

Ceth, too, was the closest so far I had come to thinking of as an actual person rather than a faceless kidnapper, by asking me if she could please hold 1779 on her palm for a minute back aboard ship. *We have these back home*, she explained as he trundled around between her claws, *but we didn't always have them; they showed up one day when I was about ten. Much smaller than this. And less colourful, mostly black and green. Isn't it strange?*

I had wanted to tell her about Earth and all the different kinds of insects there and their various colours, but Yenu was yelling at us to go, and Ceth regretfully gave the beetle back. He rode now in my coat pocket, the antennae just visible when I looked down.

Except for the reverberating calls of the distant beasts, which I could 'hear' more in the soles of my feet than my ears, it was almost silent. Just the never-ending wind, which should have been refreshing but was so thin as to be unhelpful, and our gasping breaths.

"What is our destination?" I asked Ksajakra under my breath. "Did she tell you?"

"No," he grunted.

"There isn't even a city around here."

"Prophet," he said, "I understand that you are not accustomed to being spoken to with disrespect. But shut up, or I will shut you up."

"So you do trust her," I said, ignoring the threat; they had overpowered me once, but there frankly weren't enough people in this party to try it now. There is a certain privilege in size that I had not needed to take advantage of at the castle, but fully intended to lord over all of them now. Except for the Advisor, who weighed around a ton and was thirteen feet tall from toe-tip to feathered scalp, I was far bigger than any of them. And he and I would both resist if they laid a hand on me again.

"She has never given me reason not to," said Ksajakra, keeping his voice low. Yenu seemed semi-conscious, but I knew she was listening. I didn't care.

"I keep telling you," I whispered, "she is Their creature. She'll do what benefits Them. Now ask yourself how taking the so-called resistance to this place helps you resist? You don't know. Maybe all she wanted was to get you all here, and strand you."

"You think she would come so close to death simply to eliminate a handful of people?" Ksajakra's voice was even. "Working for the Masters has rotted your brain."

"Maybe," I said. "Maybe not. Maybe those were her orders. And at least I'm questioning her. I notice none of you are. Is that a sign of a whole, sound brain?"

"You're Their puppet," he said quietly. "So you think everybody is the same as you. And you cannot understand why we are doing what we are doing."

"I know what the term *arrow-fodder* means. And that is your purpose to her. It always has been. No matter what she tells you."

"And you, were you her arrow-fodder once? This girl you say looked like her."

"No, I..."

I concentrated on the ground beneath my boots, the heaviness of my body: my shoulders like stone, my head like stone. The straining of my neck. There was that tide again over me, blocking out the sun of Earth, clear water of memory turned dark with churned silt, rising, rising, like everything I had tried to push down and hide instead of gather it into my hands and feel the shape of it. Don't. *Don't don't don't not here not now—*

my father my mother my sister my brothers everyone i knew everyone i ever loved all the strangers in the world every single person every single animal every single heart that beat and mind that dreamed smashed under Their boot enslaved murdered mutilated sacrificed eaten torn bloody on the ground if not transformed twisted into image of conqueror image of monster dropping down onto our clear green blue world rippling across it like poison like death itself like death itself like mother father brothers sister

They did this
she did this
They
she's not different from Them she proved she wasn't she's the same it's her it's Them what the fuck does it matter any more all that matters is this is a trap they

made this thing as bait and we all fell for it and nothing, nothing will bring back the ones i love and nothing will bring back my love

The wave crested and crashed down; voices filled my head, laughing, shouting, talking, conversations I remembered in warm bedrooms, in cars late at night, under trees, looking up at the star-filled sky, small voices, older voices, calling my name, drowning out everything around me.

I put one boot in front of the other. Heavy. Walk.

I thought coldly: There's nothing you can do. Just walk into Their trap along with the rest of them. Pick a side, the impostor had said. Then I will pick the side that dies. Funny thing. It's both of them. It's both. Your deal with the devil will not keep you safe if the demons don't know you made it.

You are no one here, you are nothing. Just a tool in a toolbox to be used as needed. And you don't know what you are building. And neither do these people.

Walk. Through what remains of the wave. Walk. Force it back down again. You cannot let this overwhelm you again, perhaps in a crucial moment. Be grateful that it happened now, when you are doing nothing but walking.

"I just wanted to have the things she took from me," I said quietly. "A home. A safe place. You don't know how much of my old life I spent wondering if I would have a home or not. How many times we moved desperately from place to place, pretending things were getting better. How much I wanted a home for myself and my family, a place to stay still, be together. And those were all taken from me. Then I had them again in Aradec, when I never expected to. The palace, the tower."

"Even as you speak, you know you only got anything from the Masters by taking it away from others," Ksajakra said flatly, unaffected. "You wanted Them to want you. You were seduced by usefulness. And if you have dealt with Them before, as you say, you do not have innocence as an excuse."

"Whatever I was doing, whatever I am doing now, I just want to save lives."

"Appeasing Them will not save lives. They must be eliminated." He glanced at me over Yenu's shoulder. "And you have not seen what she can do. Why we follow her. What she knows."

"I've seen enough. And I know that she's a copy of a very dangerous person," I said. "For the hundredth time, I don't trust her for *that reason*. That she's a copy, that someone made the copy. Ask yourself why They would do that. Why They would try so hard to fool you."

"Several possibilities come to mind," he said. "But would They expend even the smallest amount of effort trying to eliminate a resistance that had no chance of succeeding? I do not think so."

"I do," I said. "I've read the history books. They would expend effort on literally anything. They killed *children* who threw stones at Them from windows. It's not the size of the offense. It's the magnitude of the offended. Trust me. I thought I would have to spend the rest of my life escaping Their retaliation and revenge. But They let me live. They showed me mercy. They *do* know mercy."

"Then either They did not know who you were when you came here, or They knew precisely who you were and have spent years arranging the trap you say we are walking into," he said. "Both cannot be true. Pick one."

"This isn't about me. It's about her. And what she is. And what she hasn't told you."

"If it were anyone but her," he said, lowering his voice again, as if it would make a difference with her head a few inches from his mouth. "Anyone. Let's say. Would you help us then?"

"I... I don't know."

"Fine," he said. "Now I know everything about you I need to know. And as for what we do not know about *her*: it's a risk we'll have to take. And I will not take any further insolence from you. I repeat: shut up, or I will shut you up. I do not fear the truth you are telling me, because it is a supposed truth. This conversation is over. We will not have it again."

The Advisor took two lazy paces and caught up to Ksajakra, his great obsidian face expressionless, the only movement the iridescent flecks that caught the light. He gave the impression of stepping into the argument and therefore directly upon it with all his weight, pressing the life out of it. "Let me carry her," he said.

"...Why would you offer such a thing?"

"Because you are having trouble breathing."

Ksajakra stopped; behind us, everyone backed up into a clump, wheezing and steaming and reeking of blood and sweat so that I was sure anything for miles around could smell us. At last, he unbound the scrap of sailcloth and transferred Yenu's limp form to the Advisor's back, where he enfolded her smoothly with his wings so that she would not slide off. Her eyes opened for a moment, focused on me, one pupil dilated and round in the bile-green iris, the other a thin slit in a small fiery-red jewel, then closed.

"She still may die," the Advisor murmured as we began to walk again. "I can feel her heart beat and it is not normal."

Ksajakra nodded, and looked at me. *This is your fault*, his eyes said. *You should have helped.*

"Let her die," I said again. "If Their tool is broken, Their notice will no longer fall on us."

"And then what of the war?"

"We take our chances," I said. "Same as everyone else."

"Not good enough," Ksajakra said, folding the sailcloth and tucking it into a coat pocket. "Not an answer I will accept."

YENU HAD NOT died by the time we reached the cliffs that she claimed were our destination; but her directions had become fewer and fainter, so that sometimes Ksajakra had to lean down and press his ear nearly to her mouth.

Deep inside I felt for even the slightest hint of worry that she might die, and didn't find one. True, we'd be stranded here; but there were worse places. You could make a life here. There was air, anyway, and what else did you need? We had brought supplies. *Robinson Crusoe* or whatever. Shipwrecked with an intact ship. As long as we steered clear of the things in the distance, probably...

The cliffs towered above us skyscraper-high, a creamy white stone face tinted pale blue in the eternal twilight. They were beautiful in a strange way, the craggy formations studded with huge fossils of half-recognizable things—curled shells, twisted spines, neatly triangular teeth, all slightly darker than the white stone around them. Above them, the things dangling and twisting in the sky seemed close enough to brush against their bare tops. I looked down again as quickly as I had looked up.

"This is no city," said Rhakun, worry flaring all over his sensitive, bluegray skin in dots of white and pink. "Where are we supposed to—?"

The Advisor listened for a moment, then shifted his weight carefully and lifted a paw, extending his index claw. "She says it is inside the stone."

I stared along the line of his forelimb, spotting it at last: a small, rectangular doorway at the very base of the cliff, a fleck of blackness that from where we stood looked no bigger than a postcard, with two carved statues faintly visible next to it. If you took your eyes off it for a moment it blended back into the shadows and angles of the vertical surface.

"Inside?" said the skinny man, wheezing.

The stocky one, whose name I was fairly sure was Itzlek, shrugged uneasily. "Makes sense," he said. "Supposing you lived out here. Always worrying about those... things."

"We go on," Ksajakra said. "Everyone, weapons at hand."

*　　*　　*

INSIDE, THE AIR changed at once—strange to the nose, even to the tongue, the skin. It clung to my face like cobwebs. In the misty light of the entrance I saw the others swiping at their faces and hair as well, then looking at their hands as if they expected to see something there. The floor was flat, carved into the stone of the cliffs itself, not paved or flagged. The walls, too, were smooth, forming a narrow corridor; the Advisor had to squeeze himself in last, and even with his wings tucked tightly around Yenu and shoulders bowed, he was both almost too wide and too tall for the corridor. But the atmosphere was rich, damp stuff compared to outside, and the tightness in my chest eased.

"You know," I said to no one in general, "in a horror movie, this would usually mean that we were walking into a mouth."

"Shut up," said someone.

"Saloc," said Ksajakra.

Saloc rummaged in the pockets of his baggy purple robes and emerged with a flat metal device, which he squeezed with both hands until it unfolded into a small box, something inside it clicking into place. He pressed a lever on the side, scraping something along it into a spark, and handed the glowing lantern to Ksajakra. It was a clever device I thought I hadn't seen at the castle, and I wondered if Yenu had invented it. One of the amazing signs and wonders she'd used to recruit them, probably.

The corridor led gradually downwards with sharp right-angle or even more acute turns to the left or the right. Every time I turned along one of these I thought: A good way to escape something big, isn't it? To make the way in small. And to make it so that it cannot reach straight in.

What are those things outside, anyway? No, best not to think about it.

The city, when we finally reached it, had been built inside a dome-shaped hollow in the cliff, its apex hundreds of paces above our heads; colourfully painted and tiled buildings threw back the light of small, jellyfishlike illuminations floating around like dandelion seeds. The place looked like a Christmas tree display, I thought, and almost laughed. But then if you did live inside of a cliff, I supposed you had two choices: get used to the darkness, or light it up as much as you could. The effect was breathtaking, and made me think of old textbooks I'd seen on Earth: circular space stations with rotating gravity, and fields and houses and factories and trees on every interior surface.

The reason the air was better down here became apparent as we walked: plants grew everywhere, mostly hanging vines but also pillows of lichens and mosses, many attended apparently by their very own jellyfish, illuminating the delicate crenellations. Our footsteps on the stone were moss-muffled as we crossed a stone bridge over a dark, still body of water.

Not many people were out; I wondered if we had come in the middle of their night. Glancing at the Advisor, I saw that Yenu had recovered enough in the thick air to kneel on his back, clutching the scruff of feathers along his neck to stay upright. A painfully familiar golden haze surrounded her head, as bright as candlelight near the shorn scalp.

Green posters had been slapped up on the walls around us, some so new that glue still drooled from their bottom edges. I couldn't read the language, but Yenu whispered, "Draft offices."

"The war is here, too?" Ksajakra said.

"The war is everywhere and has been for years," she said firmly. "Did you think I would take us to a place that was free from it? Well, I don't know where those are; it changes by the minute. The moment They find a place with bodies They can throw at Their foes, that's the moment They take it over."

"Then we are not safe here," Itzlek said, pausing to study a poster. "We should—"

"We are not safe anywhere," Ksajakra cut him off. "And safety was never the goal. Do you wish to return to the ship?"

"No! I want to do whatever is needed. As best as I can." Itzlek glanced at the others, uneasily but with a certain hope. His eyes were large and a curious shade of blue in the lanternlight, almost slate-gray. "As we all do." *Don't we?* was the unspoken question.

Liandan, Saloc, and Rhakun nodded. Ceth swallowed, the scales on her throat whitening for a moment, then returning to their ordinary colour. But fear came off us in waves. The quiet meant nothing to me; the draft posters were like someone yelling into a megaphone. We were in a place that the enemy had left only minutes ago; and we were likely being watched now. This was a city, I reasoned, that did not get many visitors.

And why would they, I wondered as we walked, keeping as best we could to the unlighted ways. There was nothing here, was there? Only this place that Yenu said contained the book she needed. A copy, I thought bitterly, like her.

Ahead of us, something vaguely humanoid crossed between two houses, pausing to glance at us then moving on; a couple of Jokmara girls came our way, forelimbs linked, giggling. They veered away from the Advisor with a little cry of surprise. From the gold-lit stone doorway of what I could only assume was a bar, judging from the smell, an apparently human woman called to us, then helpfully hiked up the hem of her robe to reinforce the message.

She vanished in silence with a whisk of fabric as three burly forms lumbered down the alleyway toward us, indistinct in the low light but immediately identifiable to the back-brain as *Cop, Unspecified*.

"Split up," whispered Yenu. "Quick. You two to me. The rest of you, draw them away if you can. Quietly."

I ended up with Yenu, and tried to watch unobtrusively as the others confidently approached the three whatever-they-weres, then darted into another alleyway so fast that the floating lights whirled in their wake. Footsteps echoed around us, the sound of boots on hundreds of stairs. The few people out paused to stare.

We went on, though my heart was pounding. Were we really going to *sneak* our way through this? Well, maybe you could, if it was a library she planned to rob. One of the jellyfish lights drifted down to hang over the Advisor's head, orbiting him in small circles like a moon.

"All right," Yenu finally said. "Over there. The fountain. I read about that. Landmark. Good place to hide."

It was a big round multi-tiered thing, too high to be useful as a water source unless you were ten feet tall, in the middle of an empty stone square bordered with vine-hung buildings; water splashed ceaselessly down the tiers, making my throat contract to watch it. I sipped from my canteen while Yenu slid down from the Advisor's back and grabbed Ksajakra's arm to stay upright. We gathered in the shadow of the bottommost bowl, where the warm air was even more humid.

Yenu turned to me. "We have to break into a museum."

"Why am I not surprised."

That actually made her smile, revealing the still-bloodied gaps. "This one won't be guarded."

"And why not?"

"It's a book that does *not* contain the information you need," Ksajakra said again, as if he still could not believe his ears. Shouts rang around us, and we drew further into the shadow of the fountain.

"We'll have to be as quick as we can," she said, ignoring us both. "If there's spells needed, or wards to break, you'll have to do it."

"Me?" I said.

"Why do you think we brought you? I'll have to draw the sigil and give you the words of power. I don't trust trying to transfer again. And if I try something significant, this time I could die."

"I don't understand it," Ksajakra said doggedly, shooting me a glance as rife with envy as confusion, though I had no idea why he'd envy me of all people. "He can do magic, but you never explained what happened back there..."

Ah.

She waved her hand, irritated. Unfair of her, I thought. People didn't know how magic worked, even people who could do it. The history of magic was no more than millennia of more or less disastrous guesswork. And particularly on Aradec, how could anyone learn about it? People who could practice magic were limited to twenty or so, and they all lived in the palace compound.

"Spells run on magic," she said, "obviously. But aside from all the other parameters magic might have, which I'm not sure about—speed, direction, mass, force, I don't know—it definitely has quantity. If a spell calls for more magic than exists within some radius, I'm not sure what, then it... makes up for it with the next closest source of, I suppose you'd call it, inexplicable energy. Which is something inside the practitioner. Magic-*adjacent*. So that's why for very large spells it's best if you can share the load with a few people. Shutting a great gate, for instance, and putting a lock on it, you might need twelve or thirteen people for that."

He stared at her, putting things together; the Advisor blinked slowly. Footsteps were scraping the flagstones of the square, fast, purposeful. Random passers-by? People looking for us? I couldn't see anyone, only hear them.

"We should go," I whispered.

"Just a moment," Ksajakra said, leaning down to hiss incredulously at Yenu. "You, you designed and built that ship. But you cannot move it by yourself?"

"Not the way I did back at the harbour. It's meant to sail somewhere else, if my calculations are correct. We just didn't get there."

"I..." He shook his head. "Sail?"

"Not on water."

"This is *insane*."

"Mm," she said, on firmer ground now. "Yeah. I'll explain later, maybe. Now come on."

"Just one more thing," I said. "Supposing *I* can't do magic here?"

She glanced at me opaquely, and I felt a brief jolt of fear. "You can," she said.

How do you know? I almost said, then shook my head. "Very well. But after this, I want you to send me back to Aradec."

"No deal," she said, moving cautiously out from under the bowl of the fountain, not looking back at me. The footsteps had faded into the distance, but not far.

"Just a fucking minute," I said, reaching for her and missing. Ksajakra smacked my forearm back down with the edge of his hand; I barely noticed. "That spell nearly killed you. You're hardly in a position to be negotiating."

"Neither are you," she said. "You'd never get home alone. So stalemate, okay? Now move."

* * *

YENU INSISTED ON leaving the Advisor at the fountain. I argued; he did not, only sat placidly as I pointed out that we would be leaving him to the mercy of strangers, and entirely alone. Robbing the museum, she insisted, would not benefit from the services of my bodyguard; if anything, he was a liability. Theft was apparently something she did semi-routinely now, and she knew to a nicety what was needed and what was not.

I wished he had argued to stay with me. I looked back uneasily until he vanished into the darkness, still with the little white light bobbing loyally above his great, impassive face. He lifted a paw briefly in farewell, then dropped to all fours and padded to the far side of the fountain's bowl.

"All this," I said quietly in English as we walked, her clinging again to Ksajakra's coat sleeve. "How do you know what we're doing? Have you been here before?"

"No. I read about it. Took some doing. The book is about the last moments of the last war. A rarity in and of itself: almost *everything* about that final battle is gone. Lost, censored, burnt. What remains is the barest shreds of Their propaganda, on worlds where They gave a shit about it. And even fewer shreds of real information. Some by people who didn't even know what they were writing down. Took me a little while to find it all, puzzle it out. Build it into a plan."

"A little while."

"Years, I guess. I don't know. When you move around places that experience time differently it's hard to tell how long it's passing... about two years in Aradec." She looked ahead steadily, her face glistening in the lamplight. Tears? Sweat? "This, you know," she added, waving her free hand before putting it back into her coat pocket, "doesn't all happen at once."

"This what?"

"Well, generally for a first offense, getting caught in one of Their information repositories, the guards break a finger," she said conversationally. "As a deterrent. And you get put on a special shit list if they ever see you again. Just gotta get sneakier. But there was so much I needed and there was so little time... anyway, I picked up some first offenses. I forget how many. And then for repeat offenses, They cut off a finger."

I stared down at her, feeling sick. Five fingers. "You... Just to get into Their libraries?"

"It's the only way the dead have to speak to us," she said. "And in some cases it's the only way the truth survives, among the lies. You know that saying about how a lie gets around the world twice before the truth puts its shoes on? Lies aren't just fast; they're heavy, too. They're big, beautiful buildings and they weigh a lot and they have a lot of room inside them and they're very pleasing to the eye. You build one over the truth, you'll never see the truth again. It'll be dead, buried under there, a little insignificant thing.

"But what I needed was the truth. They know someone would, that's why They tried to hide or destroy it. The thing is, it still speaks in the things They think *didn't* have it; you just have to read enough of it to put together the clues. A hundred lies, each with one percent of truth, if you want to think of it that way. Or like putting together a picture based on a thousand other pictures that were each missing something small. Like the dark spaces lining up just so, to form a shape if arranged a certain way."

"So you did that. You found your picture."

"No," she said patiently. She teetered, then let go of Ksajakra's arm and cautiously caught herself on the wall next to us, her hand sinking deep into a tuft of lichen. "Gah! I found the *missing* spaces. And back-calculated to certain coordinates and times. Look, the things They censor the most diligently? Those are the things that They least want people to know. On their own, they seem to not mean anything, they're not useful. But absent information has meaning. The Ancient Ones, They're not diligent about *anything*, I mean, not really. They're lightly-organized chaos at best. So the more effort They make to erase something, the more I want it."

"So they were censoring... " I prompted when she did not go on, clearly assuming we had finished the train of thought.

"Any hint of where the prisons might be in which They placed the Quevereld," she said, pausing us at an intersection. I peeked over her head at the empty four-square, lit with only a few dangling lights. "It didn't matter to Them that no one could break the prisoners out. Or that the prisoners themselves could not get out. None of that mattered. They just wanted to be absolutely sure that *no one knew where they were*."

I shook my head. You had to admire her cunning; and

in this respect only, I gave her the barest hint of awe. It did look like a miracle, it would have looked like a miracle to the members of the resistance, and what made it miraculous was that even after she had explained it, all you could conclude was that there was no way you could have done it yourself.

"Anyway," she went on, as we scuttled across the intersection and into another darkened alleyway, splashing through what I hoped was water, "I didn't have enough time in the Archive. And the books wouldn't answer any of my questions."

"Pardon me?" said Ksajakra.

I felt an abrupt but definite chill, memory clawing up again through the dirt in which I had buried it, not deep enough: The books don't want to talk to you, someone's voice said. *Not her. Never her.* They had told me that themselves. Why not? *No, not her. We want to talk to you. Not her.* Why, why? She was the genius.

No. Another life. Different books, different time, different dimension, different girl.

The museum had been built high in the dome, probably a coveted spot, far above the drainage and slop of the lower levels. It was a small two-storey building faced in yellow ceramic, with just one of the jellyfish lights floating outside of it. Broken glass glittered in the modest sign above the door, a language I couldn't read. I thought about the regional museums we had back home, and waited out the familiar and inevitable pang of pain at letting myself do so. It had a similar feel. Run by volunteers, a handful of exhibits, curiosities found in farmers' fields, postcards in a spinner rack by the door, a sweet smell of dust, hay, and wood. Cloudy glass, smeared by children's fingers. Two-dollar admission fee. Free for under-twelves...

I shook my head, and looked down at Yenu where she was crouched next to Ksajakra behind a thick bulge of lichen clinging to the edge of the wall.

Not on Earth. Gone forever. Focus. Maybe there will be no home left on Aradec either, but best not to think about it. Just do the next thing. Do what you do best, not what's best to do.

1779 distracted me, thankfully, by crawling out of my pocket and fluttering to the lichen bulge, landing with a thump and sending up a little cloud of who knew what, dust or spores. "Hey!" I whispered. "Don't eat that stuff, you don't know what it is."

"I'll get him," Yenu whispered back, and reached for the beetle; it avoided her hand easily and flew back to me as if she had frightened it. She blinked, murmured something I couldn't hear, and ran her hand over her head, where stubble had not quite started to grow back yet. It glistened as if oiled.

"Keep that thing under control," Ksajakra said.

"There's no one here," I pointed out.

It was easy. Too easy. But then if it was like she said: like a war museum. Everything made free from danger by either the war itself or by some misadventure afterwards or by the curator's art, taken from a veteran or scavenged from some ditch or trench, and put behind glass. A broken cannon, say. A shattered rifle. You wouldn't steal it because it wasn't valuable to resell, and you wouldn't steal it with the intent of doing harm because it was incapable of harm. If I went along with this, it was her logic I trusted, not her.

"Come on," said Ksajakra, and we slid out of the alleyway, hands trailing along the stone wall, soft hiss of lichen, touch of moss. The museum had no windows to break and, it seemed, only one door, facing onto the narrow street that formed the collective roof of the tier of buildings below it. The door was solid stone behind its coat of bright blue paint.

"Huh," she whispered.

"What?"

She shrugged minutely, and pressed down the latch; with a creak and a clonk the door opened, and we moved quickly inside, latching it behind us. Less nerve-wracking than being out on the 'street,' but not by much. The lantern illuminated exactly the kind of place I had imagined: a small desk and chair near the door, exhibits of strange things under a low ceiling on either side of a central aisle, each exhibit not under glass but enclosed in a little stone corral, knee-high to me. It looked very human. Very Earth.

"Everywhere you go, you see that people have created a cabinet of curiosities," Yenu said as we walked down the aisle over a colourful, geometric-patterned rug. "On Niornal-27, they have a museum that's just three million individual crystal bubbles, each containing a smell, and the fungus-people of Torulia have a gallery in their capital just for... It's not here. Let's go upstairs."

"What if there's a guard?" Ksajakra fumbled for his sword with his non-lantern hand.

"In here? They didn't even lock the door."

"Or a guard d... animal," I said.

"We'll deal with it."

There was a small staircase at the back of the room, twenty cramped steps up to the second level with my shoulders touching the walls on both sides, folded nearly in half to avoid cracking my head on the ceiling. If the Advisor had come, I reflected, he would have barely been able to fit his face in here. I wondered if he was still at the fountain, if he had climbed or flown to a higher level to watch.

Even after such a short climb, Yenu was panting for breath at the top; we waited for her to recover, and Ksajakra lifted the lantern high to illuminate the small room. It glittered glassily off something large at the back of the room, not an enclosure of glass or crystal but a sheet of it, mounted on the stone wall above a small display.

"There we go," Yenu said breathlessly. "See? No problem."

Ksajakra grimaced. I wonder how many times she'd said that in front of him a moment before disaster. All the same, he led the way with the lantern as we found the display and peered over the low stone lip.

The book was not at all as I had expected—I had been picturing something like what the real Johnny usually trafficked in (and therefore stole). Battered, ancient, curled from age and damp and too much handling, undoubtedly full of woodcut illustrations ready to steal your memories, sanity, or free will.

Instead this looked like... well, frankly, a popular science fiction book from around the time Earth had last existed. The title, in large silvery font, wasn't in English, and was blazoned diagonally across a black and navy cover with a few silver stars on it, above a couple of red and pink blobs that were probably supposed to be planets. It might have been a book penned by a popular astronaut about one of the Mars missions.

"Don't like *that* much," I said before I could stop myself.

Ksajakra gazed at it leerily, holding the lantern steady while the rest of his body seemed to edge away from the display. "Are you... sure?"

"Pretty sure," Yenu said. He and I both winced. "Jak, give me that cloth you had earlier," she added. She laid it flat on the floor and drew on it as best she could with the remaining stub of chalk from her pocket, then beckoned me over. "We have to ward something to carry them, they can't be handled otherwise. And by 'we' I mean 'you.' The words of power are in Krorunkarr. Do you know that one?"

I studied the sigil, which had taken no more than a minute to draw. "This is a small spell. Do it yourself."

"It's more costly than it looks."

"I said I would help *if necessary*. You're just sandbagging."

"Oh, okay then," she said airily, "I guess we'll just hang out here until I feel better, how's that? It might be a couple of weeks."

Ksajakra started to say something, but I didn't think he had gotten the full impact of Yenu's passive-aggression and I talked over him: "This is your resistance, and your spell, and your crime. At some point I'm going to be held accountable for helping you, and I want to be able to say *Only when I was forced to.*"

"You fucking coward," she said, getting up; Ksajakra backed away, as one would flinch away from a spider on the wall. But she was a spider without venom now, essentially a clot of black lint, and I looked down at her impassively.

"I've heard worse," I said. "Go on, yell louder. See what happens."

"That wasn't an insult," she said. "Just a statement of fact. I mean to say, you fucking coward. You're a coward who's so afraid that even your own *fear* isn't letting you pick a side. You're just... you're just washed to and fro in the currents, you won't help your 'Masters' by sabotaging our plan, you won't help *us* because you still think They'll throw you a bone someday, you're letting the entire world push you around and use you and that's the funniest part of all. It's that you're *useless*, you *have* no use. You can't prophesy and you won't do magic and you're just a fucking *lump*. You really think you can go on with life just leading you by the hand until something happens that resolves all your problems for you one way or another, don't you? You really do!"

"Yes," I said. "Because you know what? That's how *life is.* Only somebody as terminally fucking narcissistic as you thinks that everybody's lives revolves around yours. Only somebody who runs on arrogance instead of actual *oxygen* thinks it's as easy as *Pick a side*. Look at you, rushing around without looking, dragging all these people into it behind you! You're going to get them all killed, you've already gotten dozens killed, you don't care, and for all I know, the *reason* you're crashing around the universe like a fucking drunk driver is that you *want* Them to find the resistance and end this, and give you your payoff. So yes! I am waiting to pick a side! I'm waiting for a side that doesn't have you on it!"

"The longer you wait to pick a side, the more time you give Them to destroy all the other ones," she snapped. "You *know* that, Nick! You've seen what They do whenever anyone else hesitates!"

"Don't call me that," I said. "Don't use my name. Get my name out of your mouth. And I don't want to hear you say it ever again."

In the pause as she wound up for another volley, a sound filtered down from above us, where I had not thought there was another floor: a soft, surreptitious scraping, followed by silence. Someone moving, I figured, then freezing when they realized they could be heard.

"Do this," Yenu whispered quickly, "and I'll send you back to Aradec. You and your bodyguard. All right?"

"He's my advisor, but deal. And thank you for being fucking civilized for once."

She grumbled under her breath, glanced up at the ceiling, from which no more noises had come, then dug in her pockets again, coming out with a slender black cylinder. "Does anyone have any paper? No, thought not. Black sails, what were we thinking. No, this won't work on stone."

I sighed and rolled up my coatsleeve, turning over my forearm. She grasped my wrist and wrote out the words of power phonetically in English with what looked like a grease pencil extruded from the black cylinder, careful black letters against the paler brown of my skin avoiding the fresh scars under the bandages I had gotten fed up with and peeled off when I had changed clothes.

It ended up taking both arms; she circled a '1' on my left, a '2' on my right. Ksajakra gave me the lantern, looking pained. I looped its small wooden handle around my thumb and began to read, thinking nothing more than *Home. Home. She promised.*

The spell built gradually, the tug and shuffle of energies crossing from inside to outside of my body, pressures shaping themselves around the words and the sigil, creating the invisible scaffolding that would channel the magic into a shape that did work, *oh she was right, this is bigger than I thought*, the sickening pull of something deep inside, deeper than organs or bone, grasping and clawing for whatever was needed, drawing it out in skeins, the pain building as I read, building, a dizzying heaviness, the light of the lantern dimming, a faint roar from somewhere—and then it was done.

I looked dazedly at the sailcloth, where the sigil had vanished, replaced by the faintest shine of light across its weave, as if it had been sprayed with water. I felt hungry, empty, even more sleep-deprived than I knew I was. The air stank of magic for a moment, and then it faded as if a breeze had come through the warm, still air.

Yenu was watching me closely, her face unreadable. Behind the bright-red pupil of the blue eye, something flared hotly, then vanished as if a door had slammed shut. She picked up the shimmering cloth, knotted its ends to form a pouch, and handed it to me. "Hold this open. We still can't touch it, I don't think; but this should let us carry it."

She got a dagger from her coat and leaned over the stone lip of the shelf; I held out the sailcloth bag as she gingerly reached for the book.

And light filled the room, erasing the walls, blazing through us so sharply that I threw up my arms to protect my face, eyes burning like staring into the sun. Next to me Yenu cried out, and there was a single high, distant chime. As the light faded the walls closed around us and twisted, changing, leaving us teetering at the top of a flight of glistening white stairs of wet marble, and at the bottom a deep green ocean in which terrible things glared up at us and snapped their jaws, the steps disappearing under their silky bodies.

"It's an illusion," Yenu gasped. "We didn't move. It must be a... It's something it's doing as a defence. The book."

I touched the cold marble wall, drew my hand away glistening with moisture. The waves licking at the steps splashed our faces with water, tasting not of salt but something else, acid, electric. A thing like a shark with a half-peeled away face, translucent cartilage under the gray-pink flesh, stared up with dead sockets and settled itself calmly on the steps, half-in and half-out of the water, its gaze fixed upon us as if a string connected our faces.

Yenu backed away and grabbed the sleeve of my coat. "It's not real," she said.

"It looks pretty real." I shook her off and looked down. "And the water is rising."

"We could... step back a little bit. In the illusion."

"Let's do that." I moved backwards, still staring at the peeled shark thing, its rotted tongue hanging over the lower teeth, at all angles but sharp enough. Our boots crunched into dead leaves, twigs, and I turned before I could stop myself, finding myself alone and empty-handed in a dark forest of impossibly tall trees. Ahead of me, thirty paces up, shone a gigantic pair of golden eyes.

It's you, it said, not entirely reassuringly.

"I'm an illusion," I said at once.

The eyes wavered, retreated, returned. The trees rustled softly at first, then all at once, branches rattling and clacking till I was surrounded by their towering noise. Distantly someone called my name: my full, real name, not 'the Prophet' or 'Your Holiness.' I turned uneasily, knowing the voice. Not Yenu's. Whose?

Something was coming through the trees, something big. At first branches cracked and snapped, then whole trunks, clouds of birds and leaves exploding into the dim orange sky. The eyes vanished: fled, it seemed, in fear. And I too turned and ran into the dark, *it's not real, it's not real,* my boots loud on the dead leaves, tripping over rock-hard roots, till the light faded entirely and I stopped.

Pitch dark, heart pounding. Smell of rot, fungus, but also growing things, broken wood, sap. *Not real.*

A gray light grew ahead of me, firefly-small, and I ran for that, watching as it became closer to amber, the colour of Ksajakra's lantern. Instead I flew straight over a cliff, icy air smelling of fresh snow, and landed on my back in a drift. I scrambled up, panting the clean air, apparently unhurt, though of course I had fallen only eight or ten feet and... and it was an illusion and I... Mountains. Mountains.

And something else. Watching me. Unseen, hidden in the pale gray stone. Silence, the sound of wind hissing across stone and snow. No eyes this time but you did not need eyes to watch.

No. He does not. His face is covered.

Where did that come from?

And then a voice much closer, rough, audible over the sound of the wind. "Yenu! Yenu! What is happening? Speak! Tell me what I can do!"

Ksajakra. Close. Because we hadn't moved, we had gone nowhere, the book was protecting itself, but illusions were both more and less real than anything else we called real, I knew that, *shoes full of black sand so long ago*, and they could trap, kill, rob you of reason and sense and memory, they could—

Something scrabbled against my face, and I instinctively batted at it... and came to, lying on the floor of the museum, 1779's mandibles sunk deep into my upper lip. I pried him off, wiped away the blood, and stood to see Yenu still rigidly tranced by the book, her hands inches from it, not even touching it, eyes wide and staring, a small, eerie buzz emitting from her throat as if an insect had gotten lodged there, not as if she were making the noise at all.

Ksajakra lunged for me, seizing the lapels of my coat. "You, Prophet! What is happening?"

"I don't know," I said mushily, and pushed him away without effort. "The book doesn't need guards because it protects itself. It pulled my mind into... never mind, I don't know. It's doing the same to her now. I think she must have fallen further than I did." I dabbed at my lip with the back of my hand again. "Wow, hope this doesn't get infected."

"Do something!"

I put 1779 back into my pocket, then got the sailcloth sack. "Give me your sword."

"Absolutely not."

"All right," I said. "I can't reach it then. Perhaps you'd like to try?"

He unsheathed his sword—formerly mine, I noticed, and before that some palace guard's—and glanced at the book, then back at me. Then, with a snarl, he handed it over. "If you—"

"Shut up. I'm trying to concentrate." I held the enchanted pouch at one corner, then reached gingerly around Yenu and prodded the book with the tip of the sword.

Pain. Lightning. Images flashed and screamed past my head too fast to see, the sword twisting in my hand, my wrist screaming, tendons and bones creaking, *hear it hear it* over the sound of the moving colours, *stop it, fucking stop it I said!* and I instinctively formed something inside myself into a battering ram and gave it a tremendous shove, recoiling as it slammed into something invisible and so solid that the impact threw me to the floor, Yenu atop me, the cloth-trapped book thumping very satisfyingly into her face.

We got up, dazed. Before I could say anything, Ksajakra held his hand out. "Give me back the sword."

"You're welcome to try to take it back," I said, and put it through a metal bracket on the side of my belt; it bobbed ridiculously along my leg as I walked towards the staircase, but felt secure enough. "I'll have to sleep eventually. Oh, and you're both welcome."

Yenu said something garbled, perhaps unable to work her mouth properly after the ordeal, but it did not quite cover the noise of footsteps on the stairs. Of course. Someone coming, after all the ruckus. Blocking our only way out of a windowless room.

"Motherfucker," I whispered.

Ksajakra said, "Will you give me the sword now?"

"Still no." I drew it instead and dropped to a crouch, everything aching. Beaten up by a book: what a day. Ksajakra pushed Yenu behind him and stood next to me, drawing a dagger from his belt.

A voice drifted up, presumably saying something menacing; I didn't know the language. It sounded like a woman, which wasn't any help—I'd been in fights with a wide variety of genders by this point and it made no difference in the amount of damage either dealt or received. I sighed, and got a better grip on my sword. Just get through this, and go home.

The voice continued to rise, along with a small circle of pinkish light, so that we saw the hovering jellyfish first, and only then the head. Too stunned by the latter to move, I didn't see what she was holding at all until it had almost hit me, and only by instinct brought my sword up in time. The impact reverberated all the way up my shoulder, but as the light joined the light of our lantern, she finally got as good a look at us as we had at her.

She lowered the cricket bat. "There is just," said Dr. Huxley, "*no* fucking escaping some people, is there?"

OUR NOISE HAD attracted more than just the curator, as it turned out; a couple of city guards showed up as well, and as Huxley spoke to them downstairs, we huddled in the back of the room, weapons at the ready, waiting for them to come charging up the stairs anyway. But she eventually returned alone, shaking her head, and beckoned us to a doorway hidden behind a hideously gaudy set of enamelled armour, which did indeed lead up to a third floor not visible from the street.

From a door at the back of this room we entered a series of small tunnels carved through the rock, dripping with water but carefully sloped so it ran off into drainage gutters on either side. It must have taken a long time—but then again, I thought deliriously, what did you have in here except time? Anything beat going outside and taking your chances with the tentacled sky and the distant monsters. At any moment they could become less distant. Better to stay hidden. Always better to stay hidden. Chisel your city into being one chip of cliff-stone at a time, pausing always to listen for danger.

And Huxley. Of all people. Of all *possible* people. She was being so militant about our silence that I hadn't questioned her, but I was nothing but questions now. And yet, no matter what she might say, I could not think of any answer that would not point to this being a setup. Another one. Or part of the same trap. Or a trap *within* a trap, meant for us to see and evade the first one only to step straight into another, as we were meant to... Yenu had a pretty good patter about us finding our own way, doing our own thing, but we were being moved, all of us. Either she was in on it or she wasn't; and the same was true of Huxley.

There was simply no way to explain why we had again been brought together. It was far too much for coincidence. I would not accept it. Could not.

Something powerful moved us all, and this was proof.

Eventually we reached the end of a tunnel and found ourselves back in the open at an immense height, looking down over the entire city. Next to me, Yenu and Ksajakra gasped softly. It was impossibly beautiful from up here, I had to admit: the shapes of the buildings, the lit windows, the coloured flecks of the drifting lights across vines and leaves and moss, the graceful curves of street and stair, the glitter of the canals. You'd wait your whole life for a view like this. And it was just as dangerous as it was lovely. We had to go.

My head ached and my lip hurt, and it was strange that the jelly lights seemed to be ignoring us now. Actively avoiding us, possibly. Yenu refused to let Ksajakra carry the bag with the book, and I didn't offer. I had the unnerving sense that we had been seen not solely by the residents of the city, and not by the book itself, but something else, at a great distance and a great remove—certainly not in our space, perhaps not even in our time—and that the thing that had seen us had not in fact been looking for us.

I hoped it was too confused to know what it had seen, as I had been. But you never knew what people knew.

The Advisor leapt down from the top tier of the fountain, landing front paws then back paws, so that for a moment, with his wings folded, he looked like a human-faced black panther, a heavy and threatening predator. "Prophet, what happened? Who is this?"

"Bit my lip. Are the others back?"

He shook his head.

"I told them it might take a while," Yenu said, though she sounded uncertain now. I wondered what she had seen when the book had fought back, and couldn't help but look at the bulky black sack she carried. I wondered if the book was screaming for help in there, as I knew from bitter experience some books could do. Or just telling war stories, embellishing them maybe. Discussing this great indignity. Retirees rehashing great battles, old injuries.

It's you, something had said to me in the great trees.

The Advisor looked up, the feathers on the back of his head springing upright and curving into two dished cups. "Someone is coming."

"The others?" said Ksajakra, squinting into the darkness and holding up his lantern.

"No." The transparent eyelids flicked across his eyes. "Armed people. Many of them. Moving quietly."

"Ah, a mob," Yenu said, in much the same tone as she might have said *Oh, it's raining*. "Back to the ship. Go."

"But—" Ksajakra looked around, horrified and angry. Voices could be heard now, and the flavour if not the words of their dark intent. I'd dealt with mobs before, and Yenu was right; we had to run. Mobs had projectiles. You could count on it. And any little change in direction was like a flock of birds: they would all follow a leader even if there was no clear leader, and that led to overreactions in the great, unpredictable mind of the group.

"The others will catch up," Yenu said.

"I will not leave them! I will stay and fight! And you—"

"All right. Then *we're* leaving."

He stared at her, genuinely shocked. The soft glow of the floating lights was closing around us; in a moment we would be visible, even here under the shadow of the fountain. Yenu could navigate us back out; I probably wouldn't be able to, and neither would he. *You would leave me to the mob?* his face said, and hers, neutral, cool, familiar and unfamiliar in its utter hardness and lack of charm said, *I got what I wanted.*

He swore harshly, and Yenu led us back to the street at not quite a run, the bag tied across her chest like a child, then glanced back at Huxley. "Doctor—"

"Not that way," Huxley said. "They'll know you're runnin' back out the way you came in. I've lived here for twenty years. Follow me."

"What's she saying? Can we trust her?" Ksajakra whispered incredulously.

Huxley ignored him and pointed at Yenu and me. "Move it, all of you, and your pet lamassu or whatever the hell that is, too. *Now.*"

CHAPTER EIGHT

"Now do you believe it's a trap?" I demanded.

Yenu sighed. "I need a drink."

"*I* need a drink."

"I need a drink more than either of you need a drink," Huxley snapped. "One minute I'm about to deal with some asshole breaking into my museum, and the next minute it's *you* two—is anyone going to offer me a chair?"

"It's not exactly a cruise ship," I said. "It's a little hard to keep chairs on the deck, Dr. Huxley."

"Knock it off," she said briskly. "There's no living any more unless it's with a fake name. I'm going by Sudworth now."

"Does that mean something in some language I'm not aware of?" I said suspiciously.

"It means my maiden name, so mind your business." She sat down on a box, ignoring Saloc's feeble protests about the need to access its contents. "Now do you mind explaining why the hell you robbed my museum of the single genuine artifact in it?"

"Doesn't the question suggest the answer?" said Yenu.

Sudworth glared at her.

I sat down too, on a coil of rope, and held my head in my hands. Sudworth-once-Huxley had helped Johnny and me a long time ago when we had accidentally fallen into the pocket universe containing the archive she had been sentenced to steward. (And come to think of it: had we ever established just how accidental that had been? God, how long had They been running this con, anyway?)

Sudworth had been picked up by the Society, technically not for helping us (which was also against their rules) but for contravening the terms of her sentence. What her crime had been I was not sure; and the full extent of her sentence had also been a mystery, though we knew guarding the Archive was part of it. And her husband being taken hostage by the Society to ensure her compliance I had guessed, though never confirmed. Worse yet, we had been unknowingly followed to her Archive, and it had been destroyed in our escape from our pursuers.

The last time I had seen Sudworth she had lost everything, and it had been our fault: her books, her home, her work, everything she owned. All she had had left was her irascible dignity, and her anger at the Society of Watchers.

Sudworth refused to speak again until Itzlek went

belowdecks and returned with a small thick-walled bottle of clear spirits, tinged faintly pink, like the fluid that seeped from a burn. She drank first, three large swallows, said, "Nice beard, by the way. Almost didn't recognize you at first," and passed it to me, then tipped her chin at Yenu. "And what the *hell* happened to you?"

"It's not really her," I said, when Yenu looked away instead of answering. "I thought the same thing. But..."

"She tell you that?"

I shook my head.

"She tell you she's her?"

"She won't say either way."

"Spill," Sudworth said, snapping her fingers. "You owe me more answers than I owe you, Chambers, if that's really you."

"It's not," I said again.

"You, shut it. Let her talk."

The others were watching us and—thanks to our rapid-fire English—looking bewildered; even the Advisor was visibly having trouble keeping up. And whether they could understand us or not, Yenu was reacting the way her prototype would have: embarrassment cloaked under what she probably thought was either a mysterious or stoic silence. Sudworth wouldn't stand for that.

"Talk," she said. "If you're running a con, everybody has to be on the same page. Or people die." She glanced around shrewdly. "People have died already, haven't they? You wouldn't take a ship this size with a crew this small, magic or no; it must take thirty or forty people to run this thing, eh?"

Yenu lifted her chin. "Thirty-five."

"And now this. You didn't come here like this; you were *chased* out of somewhere. Weren't you."

I sipped from the flask, which felt like putting out a burning twig with my mouth, and swallowed with some difficulty, then passed it to Yenu.

Yenu held it in both hands, rubbing the glass with her thumbs, and looked at Sudworth. "I don't know," she said at last. "I think I'm me. I wish I could say something more certain than that, believe me. I *wish*. The last thing I remember from Earth was... the control room. At the reactor. From far above. I was in the air, I knew my spell had run, I knew I had miscalculated..."

"Hold it," I said, more loudly than I had intended, my voice already trembling with anger. "*Miscalculated?* Christ! Tell the fucking truth. She—*you* told us you were going to do one thing. And then you did something else. Just *say it*."

She cleared her throat and looked down at the flask in her lap. "Fair. I... I knew my spell had run. It wasn't the spell that I told you all about. Instead, the spell was meant to draw Them into a microsupermassive black hole that They'd never escape. It should have worked, just like the original spell. But something went wrong."

"What?" I said.

"That I still don't know for sure. I know I did create the black hole, and when gravity started having problems, I did see the gate They were coming through. Maybe there's simply a mechanism by which those two magical things couldn't exist in the same place at the same time.

And I didn't know it. So I didn't compensate for it." She looked up, not quite at Sudworth but over the ship's railing behind her shoulder. "A second later I saw Nick disappear... There was so much blood..."

"That was yours," I cut in.

"But I... But you were..."

I shook my head. "I was covered in blood when I landed at the tower, but I wasn't hurt. It was all your blood. He can tell you, he found me."

The Advisor sat back on his haunches and stared at the three of us, unmoving.

"Okay, maybe he won't," I amended. "Anyway. Obviously I didn't die." A playing piece, I thought again, on a board. And where were you? Playing? Being played? "But you... *you* definitely died."

She winced. "Maybe I did," she said. "When I woke up I was... like this."

In the two words I heard untold vastnesses of shock and despair; but I still could not bring myself to feel sorry for her. After all, it could still be part of an act. Neither Johnny nor Yenu struck me as someone who would shy away from a con for being too complicated or requiring too much acting.

"I was on an island, a little one," she went on. "A few months later when I was really starting to freak out about living there forever, a ship spotted my signal fire. When they took me back to their home city, I found I could do magic there, so I learned the language and picked up some, uh, odd magical jobs for a little while. Moved around. Had an idea. Tried to pick up a team to help me with it. Didn't work. Tried again. And about five years ago, Aradec time, I came to the capital, because I finally figured out it's only on the planets where the Ancient Ones hold sway that you can find anything still written down. It was hard. I don't know." She drank lingeringly from the flask and made a face, the scales along her arms standing straight up for a moment to display their chromed undersides. "I still think we can do it. Because..."

She handed the bottle to Sudworth, and in that moment I felt again that tsunami of memory, the weight of it more like concrete than water, or like molten lead, crashing down, burning me from my skin through to the marrow of my bones.

If it was really her, she had destroyed our home; and only we three here on this ship had survived. We three, out of seven and a half billion people. We had no home. We had tried to make homes in other places. Find jobs, find new people. But all our people were gone. Everyone we had loved. Her too. If she had loved anyone but herself. Distantly I wondered why I didn't simply get up and throttle her to death; the crew might stop me this time, or they might not, but it would be worth it simply to try. She did not deserve to live after taking so many lives.

Then again, who was I to take hers? Grief empties you out, and I had grieved for a long time; but anger, of course, fills you up. And now I felt dense and heavy with it, like a city-destroying monster with uranium bones. Full, filled up. Alive again.

"How did *you* get away, Sudworth?" I said quietly when I felt I could speak without screaming.

"Never you mind," she said. "I left before your little party trick and that's all. Heard about what happened later. I was looking for... it's not important. But you two, you're saying, you weren't just *there* at the end of the world. You ended it."

"She did," I said.

"Figures." But her voice was trembling at last, and I knew the same thing I had just felt had happened to her. For years, like me, she had thought she alone had escaped the destruction of Earth. And I knew. I knew. At a certain point you found yourself thinking about it not every waking hour but maybe every waking hour plus five minutes. Then ten. Then six months later you'd find that you'd gone two hours without thinking about it. About how alone you were, how all those millions of lives had been erased for a single person's hunger for power. Then two years later maybe you could go a couple of days. And finally, now, I barely thought about it at all. What I had loved. What I had had taken from me. But it was back.

"So it is you," I finally said to Yenu. I wasn't sure I believed it but I didn't know what else to say.

"I don't know," Yenu said, which didn't help. "Maybe. I have holes in my memory... places where I look for things and they're not there. I know my name was Johnny Chambers. I don't remember my middle name. You were right."

"Meredith," I said, and looked away, feeling sick.

"Here is what may have happened," the Advisor said slowly, choosing his words with care; Sudworth jumped, splashing liquor onto the deck. "It sounds as if... you were separated into your individual, smallest components, which is the normal way of travelling through a gate of any size. But at that same moment, so were many other individuals coming through the gate—simultaneously, not sequentially. It is possible that the thing you created, which I admit I do not fully understand, stopped all the movement in the gate. The suspended components became... combined. And so what eventually did cross through the gate when it operated again was you, and less than you, and more than you."

"Oh my God," I said, "it's like *The Fly*," at the same moment that Yenu croaked, "Just like *The Fly*! I'm Jeff Goldblum!"

"You're not Jeff Goldblum," I said. "You're the fly and Jeff Goldblum."

"Awwwk! I'm Brundlefly!"

"You're Brundlefly."

She made a noise in her throat.

"All right, calm down," I said. "Maybe that explains why 1779 couldn't recognize you." I paused, unable to help myself. "You know, that might mean there's a monster out there that's all monster except it's got your other eye."

"Shut up. That's horrible."

I turned back to the Advisor. "Have you ever heard of this happening before?"

"Truly, I have not. So this is why I say *may* have

happened. And you yourself," he added, gesturing at Yenu, "admit that you cannot remember. I think you were not alive for a time. Maybe a surprisingly long time. But your spark of life remained intact enough to reanimate the body that was assembled on the far side of the gate. Your body."

"But what if it's not hers?" I insisted. "What if it's someone else's? What if it's just using her voice and stealing her mind?"

"I don't know. It could be."

I stared at her again, and tried to make myself say *Johnny, Johnny* in my head. It was terrible: painful, rusty, like trying to unstick something corroded beyond recognition. I heard instead, very clearly, the voices inside me saying: *Johnny's dead. You saw her die. This is a stranger. You know this isn't her. As much as you know yourself, you know this isn't her.*

Maybe They trained her to say this. Maybe she had handlers, maybe They said: Pretend you've got memory loss.

Yenu accepted my stare, unmoving. *I don't know. I don't know.* Even the green of the one eye different. Literally even the green. More yellowy and with that unpleasant gleam like bad meat. How had that happened? Even the hair different before it had been shaved: black instead of blonde. And no scar. No scar. I used to know every square inch of her from any distance, from across oceans. *This isn't her.*

She said, "You killed a czeroth once that had been made of me. Because you knew the real me. And that's supposed to be impossible... Do you feel like that now? Like you're looking at the real me?"

"No."

Sudworth passed me the flask again.

I took a long swig and tried another tack, speaking past the molten-metal burn of the drink going down. "There are other universes, right? Not just other worlds. Universes full of worlds of their own."

Sudworth nodded. "Conventional thinking is that every time there's a spell cast, it divides into pre-spell and post-spell universes."

"Okay, so the old one. The pre-spell universe. Couldn't this one... Yenu... be the Johnny from one of those? A lot of spells were performed on our Earth. There must be hundreds, maybe thousands of alternates..."

"Nope," Sudworth said, not even pausing to think. My stomach sank. "Each time it happens, the old one is shoved into its own universe. *Certain* things can go between universes if they've got enough energy. Light, for instance. Magic. Some lengths of radio waves. Not matter, never matter. They're all locked off from one another in that respect. The act of division, of creating that new universe, leaves most of the energy and the magic on the side where the spell was carried out. A universe has to be a certain shape to work a certain way; and after the division, it messes up the shape just where the spell is. So that one goes on. And the other one has to go into a place where it's the right shape, or it destroys itself."

I opened my mouth and closed it again, then gave her

the flask before I simply drank the entire thing. I had had a couple of theories about what the Yenu/Johnny person could have been, and they had been, in order, a new type of czeroth, a y'tan (gruesome but possible), and an alternate-universe Johnny. They all still seemed possible to me and no one could definitively shut the door on any of them and I wished everyone would stop using words like *probably* and *most likely* and *in general*.

And I didn't *want* it to be the real her, to get right down to it. The real mass murderer. The real destroyer of the world. Who had killed my family and sent me spinning into exile, doomed to live in Their cage. Even if Their cage was exactly where I still wanted to return. Even if that.

I didn't want to spend the rest of my life like this: hunted, a war criminal on the run on a bizarre magical ship with the person I hated most, several people who hated *me*, and only one person I trusted.

"Me, I've spent years studying the bastards," Sudworth said. "Years, I mean, on St. Cherkenai. And real quiet, too. Don't want to attract any unwanted attention."

I nodded; one of the first things I had done when I had come to my senses in Aradec was scour my chamber for anything interesting, clues about past prophets. I had found a hidden drawer next to the fireplace holding hundreds of years' worth of journals, most of which I couldn't read, with accounts from at least three prophets who had arrived from Earth. The most recent one, from 1826 (according to her) was written in French, but I picked up enough. By counting as best she could and making a crude water clock, she had estimated that an Aradec day was about twenty-six Earth hours, and their year around both suns about three hundred Earth days; she had even drawn a devilishly complicated double-sundial in the journal. I hadn't bothered checking it. It wasn't quite one to one, but when I said eight years I meant 'eight-ish' and that was always good enough for me. I assumed Sudworth meant the same and had done the same for her years.

She went on, "I'm just known as a researcher now, you know. A 'scholar.' Nameless, no planet of provenance. And *that's* exactly why you ended up below my goddamn bedroom again."

"Pardon?" I said. "That was some tangent."

"Look, the way They pick the places They want to colonize and the order They do it in—you know what, I'm going to call that the Chambers Equation."

"Oh come on, I published that when I was six," protested Yenu, who I still couldn't quite bring myself to call Johnny. "The caloric consumption of any bacterial colony less than—"

"No. And don't interrupt. This is *my* Chambers Equation."

"You can't just name an equation the same as an already existing equation!"

"Watch me." She stuffed the cork back into the bottle and concealed it somewhere in her voluminous robes, all dusty-gray and pink, like the plumage of an Earth pigeon. We were all panting from the effort of the conversation. I didn't like the great striding things at the horizon, but I found myself missing the city, its breathable air, the softness of every corner with all that moss and lichen. And it was safer out here from the mobs inside; I didn't think the ship could be easily seen from the door in the fossiliferous cliffs.

It occurred to me, weirdly, that this was the most I had travelled since I had come to the Tower of the Prophet. True, I had been on a handful of trips with the King and the Queen to the capitals of our neighbouring countries to perform haruspicy for them, but had seen very little outside the windows of our slow, luxurious ship or our slightly faster carriage; and we had returned home after just a few days of sacrifices and speeches, ceremonies and celebrations. Now I was awed and disoriented at the size of everything, at the openness of it, the lack of walls. I had been too long inside, cooped up.

The others looked impatient as well as nervous; Yenu had already told them that we'd gotten what we needed, so it made no sense for us to sit on the deck and talk to the old woman who had apparently followed us here. I knew how they felt, but there was no rushing her. Sudworth moved at her own speed, and as tempting as it was to kick her off and send her back, Yenu clearly wanted to know what she knew.

I got up and wandered around anyway, stretching my legs while I listened.

Sudworth said, "Now this theory. All I know about is this universe, all right? All the books say the same. Billions or trillions of stars or whatever, millions of worlds around those stars, some with life that evolved there, endemic-like, and some that got colonized by other worlds." She paused, sucked her lips. "You know, like mould. Wherever it spreads, the next thing it wants to do is spread some more. It's why you keep finding the same dozen or so species on most worlds except Earth. Now there's worlds that They want and worlds that They want less, okay? They can live in the void between worlds, but They don't like it any more than we do. It's a place to inhabit, not to live.

"Now from looking at the worlds They want, the ones They used to make a special effort to conquer, my theory is, They want any planet that can be exploited for more and more gain for Them... *up to a point* at which the populace figures out how to destroy either itself or Them.

"If They can figure out when this is about to happen—which They can't always do, 'cos as discussed, there's a wide range of what I guess you'd call critical thinking skills among these things—They'll try to stop it. However that looks depends on what the threat is. Maybe that means ending scientific research. Or ending a civilization. Or physically destroying part of the planet. Or just depopulating it, something like that. Now in Earth's case, that's exactly what happened, and very suddenly too; but the problem, or what They'd call Their problem, wasn't really solved. Normally it would be! But in this case the single thing that could, maybe for the first time in the history of sentient life, destroy both the civilization that produced it, and Them, escaped." She turned to Yenu. "You."

Yenu pressed her lips together but said nothing.

"On any other world, if there were folks still alive they'd be knocked back to a state out of which that ability or technology could never develop again. And you know, if They weren't living there, if They were doing the absentee landlord thing and just stopping by occasionally to terrorize a few towns, snatch up a few sacrifices, siphon off some magic... maybe They wouldn't know if it ever did. You know the monitoring They do was always kind of erratic, sporadic, done by a wide variety of bored or nosy individuals, it wasn't coordinated or anything like that, looking to entertain themselves. Like people were video games or books or movies or whatever. A very few were more like talent scouts. All assholes, of course, you know, no matter what they were doing..."

I waited for Sudworth to catch her breath again, then circled back around and said carefully, "So do you think They know, or don't know, that Yenu is still alive?"

By which I meant to say: *Do you think that what we're looking at here is a trap or not?*

"Well, hard to say," she said, giving me a frosty look. "But you got it in one, kid. Myself, I'd say They don't. Or else we wouldn't be sitting here havin' this conversation. On the other hand, if Little Miss Genocide here has swapped sides and is trotting about the universe free as a bird with her special Eldritch Horror Passport and hasn't told anyone..."

"Which was my theory," I said, "and I'm not sure I don't still subscribe to it."

"Call that the Prasad Equation then."

"You can't just keep calling things 'the whatever equation'!" Yenu protested.

Sudworth ignored her, uncorked the bottle again, and took a swig. Her lips were turning blue.

"Look," Yenu said, sighing heavily. "I know how this looks. I know how this all *looks*. So with that said, I'm very sorry that we stole your book, I'm not giving it back, and you're free to go back to the city and back to your museum. He's a prisoner here. You're not."

Sudworth narrowed her eyes. "That book doesn't even have all its pages," she said. "What are you plannin' to do with it?"

"End the war."

The ship trembled slightly, as if to emphasize what she had said, but sheer instinct as well as experience made me survey around us anyway. Was one of the things in the distance, higher than a mountain, coming closer to us? It seemed that way. Slowly, stride by stride on four exaggeratedly stiltlike, skyscraper legs. Still hazy and soft with distance. "Hey," I said.

"Beg your fucking pardon?" said Sudworth to Yenu.

"Find one of the prisons of the Elder Gods. Start setting them free to fight against the Ancient Ones. I've almost worked out where the most powerful one is imprisoned, and that should start a chain reaction that will allow them to free the others."

"You think you found one of Their *prisons?*" Sudworth said.

"It's a long story, okay?" Yenu wheezed as she moved her hands in the air, burnt and pink from whatever the book had done to her while she was frozen, holding it. I winced to look. "And this ship, yeah, it's a part of it. I can see you looking at it. We'll be on our way in a minute," she added in Low Dath, as Ksajakra came up respectfully behind Sudworth. The things in the distance were getting closer; it wasn't just my imagination.

Yenu said rapidly, "Look, the thing about space, right, is we were just figuring it out when... we were just figuring it out, physicists back home, I mean. It was a theory, how could you confirm it? But the shape of space itself, the idea that it's just empty, a void, a vacuum, not really, it isn't really. I don't think.

"*I* think it has a structure, it has shapes in it, channels, rivers, roads, of varying... you could say solidity. Not a very useful term. But phases, types. Flavours. Maybe how you think of water being able to be liquid and solid and gas, but not *water* phases, *space* phases. I haven't worked them all out yet but anyway, it's not just empty, it has a shape, and shapes within shapes, shapes that can only fit within particular shapes. And things can flow around them and through them and in some cases they're restricted, channelled, squeezed, slowed, sped up, I think, some shapes have limits and impose limits, some don't. So things go through."

"Things."

"Light. Heat. Dark matter. Ordinary matter. Time. Magic. Gods. Monsters. Minds. Information. Other shapes of space. I don't know. Things. I set up the ship to be able to sail along certain of those structures. Fast. Nearly the speed of light. Not *through* but *on*."

The ship trembled again. The thing in the distance, vaguely pyramidal, was still approaching. Ksajakra stared at it, his eyes fixed with something beyond horror, more as if he feared something would happen if he broke his gaze. The others were nervously playing with their weapons, and eyeing the gouged ship, its tightly bound sails, as if we could sail away on dry land. Hell, maybe we could; who knew what kind of thing Yenu had designed. Dark spots danced in front of my eyes: no oxygen. They looked like elongated blobs, like dark, sleekly furred rats running freely up and down the rope-cluttered deck.

"Now I know I've heard you say it before," Sudworth said, putting her palms flat on the boards below us as if gauging how close the walking thing was. "But you wrote a spell to do all that. Didn't you."

"Yeah?"

"Not discover. Not adjust. Make up. You *made up* a spell."

"She's done it a lot," I said.

Sudworth didn't look at me. The ship shook so hard this time that a few people fell over, and a coil of rope next to the centre mast simply uncoiled itself like a snake, sending people scattering. "Neohexonomics," she said, making it sound like a curse.

"I had to," Yenu said. "I could tell right away I'd never find one to do what I needed. And I had your book of conversion factors to clean up the transition calculations between matter and magic."

"You still got that?"

"Oh sure." She burrowed in the pockets of her coat and came up with the little book, blackened with filth and the edges crumbled away on each corner, so that it was nearly oval-shaped and barely two-thirds of its former size. "I memorized it before it looked like this, of course. I guess I keep it for sentimental reasons."

"What have you been *doing* to it?"

"Well, I couldn't always keep it on me. Especially if I was about to be arrested. I buried it a few times. In a bag to try to keep the water out of it. Then went back for it later."

"How much later?"

"Two years, at one point. Anyway, it doesn't matter. The numbers are important, not the book. Which reminds me. Are you going to tell me where you got it?"

"Maybe later." Sudworth looked longingly at the book, then slowly stood up and dusted herself down, beating fluff and lint from her robes and glaring at us as if we were the ones who had covered her with it. The ship was trembling steadily now, quivering hard enough for our teeth to knock together, and the thing was still coming towards us.

I felt no fear, only a faint, strange sense of resignation. What could we do against it anyway except leave? We couldn't fight it. We couldn't play dead, pretend to be not here, pretend to be something we weren't. Story of my life. Should be used to this by now.

"Yenu," Ksajakra said, raising his voice slightly.

"We're going," Yenu said. "Dr. Sudworth, I'll have them put down a ladder for you and—"

But I knew the look in the old woman's eyes: calculating, sly. "Where are you headed next?"

"Well," Yenu said cautiously, eyeing the horizon, "if we survive this, the prison."

"Tell you what," Sudworth said, ignoring my groan. "I'll help you get the ship going again. Onto the Violet River. That's what you're talking about, those currents in space, those shapes. Even if you didn't know the term."

Yenu stared at her, for once lost for words.

"Yes, it's real. I'll put us on the River," Sudworth repeated, "and show you where you can get something you'll want before you go for that prison. And then I'll take myself home. You'll need all the help you can get if you want to end this war."

"Get... what?"

"Weapons."

Yenu stared at her for a long time, now hanging onto the ship's railing to keep her balance. I spread my legs wide, taking deep breaths and keeping my eye on the thing. Was it speeding up? I very much feared it was.

"Come on," Sudworth said again; it should have sounded coaxing, coming from her grandmotherly face, but I heard it as faintly sinister. "You'll need me to take some of the weight of the spell. One look at you and I can see how getting here wrung you out like a dry rag. And you didn't use this 'un, or else you would have by now."

"Wait a minute, wait a minute," I said. "Why would you help her?"

"Because you're against Them. Aren't you?"

"Of course we are," said Yenu.

"That's not the real reason," I snapped. "It can't be as simple as that. Nothing ever is. No. I don't know what it is, but until she tells the truth—"

"You're not in charge here, Prophet," Yenu said. "Ksajakra, tell everyone to go below and we'll—"

The creature in the distance stopped, and I realized dimly that it was not really in the distance any more. Or it was and it wasn't... It was probably still a few hundred miles away, but it was so big now that we could see virtually nothing else. It filled the horizon from ground nearly as high as I could see by tilting my head all the way back. Tiny white flecks, maybe birds, flew past its lower limbs like snowflakes.

And far up, in the clouds, even further, nearly at the writhing tentacles above the clouds, it lifted its head back and began to bay. Not merely loud, but felt physically in every cell of our bodies, in the boat—in every molecule of air, I was sure, on the whole planet.

The other creatures, still far distant, began to join in. It didn't seem to get any louder, at least through the hands clapped over my ears, but I felt it more and more deeply, as if that were possible: in my bones, in their marrow. In the pulp of my teeth. My eyes trembled, but it didn't matter that they weren't focusing. The things simply stood and howled and I didn't know what they were doing or what they were

(calling)

trying to do, or whether they would come after us, or whether they had even noticed us, but none of the answers were meant for us, I was sure.

I staggered across the deck with the others, following them through the trap in the hold. The ship shook, rocked, began to list. The last thing I saw before the door shut overhead was Yenu and Sudworth tearing a piece of paper from a notebook in Sudworth's robes, and the strange, every-colour-no-colour glow of the opened bag of cloth that contained the stolen book.

The ship's hold held a faint, high scent of magic, like spoiled fruit on its way to becoming amateur schnapps; it was bigger than it looked, and emptier, almost worryingly empty, instead of the packed rooms of supplies I had been expecting. Wards covered most of the wooden surfaces of wall, support beams, and ceiling.

The Advisor came last, squeezing down the stairwell and blocking out the last of the gray-blue light; Ceth and Liandan moved around lighting lanterns until we stood in a little circle of wan light, the ship jumping now. We wouldn't know if they were successful up top; we'd only know they had failed if the thing stepped on us. Might be a nice way to go. A split second and then death, not some long drawn-out process of pain and terror. In the uncertain light no one looked committed to the resistance any more; everyone's faces gleamed with sweat and the effort of breathing the air. *We don't want to end the war*, their faces said. *War has just been declared on us specifically. Our little ship on this endless plain...*

Ksajakra watched me closely, the light swinging back and forth across his tense face. "The old woman knows you," he said flatly.

"Yes."

"And Yenu."

"Yes."

"And how does she know you both?"

I studied him. What had Yenu told him? I had no doubt she had created an image for the resistance. Not even necessarily mysterious, opaque. Just very carefully crafted. Once, I would have simply told him everything; but now there was no simple narrative, nothing that unbraided the twisted strands of her life, my life, the decisions we had made, the ways we kept getting thrown together, what had turned out to be a trap, what had turned out to be a setup, what had seemed like free will, what hadn't. The game we were in wasn't over, and there was no way to explain the size of the board, the identities of the players. "Ask her," I finally said. "Sudworth. She will tell you the truth."

"And you would not?"

"No. I would not. I don't know it."

He took a lantern down from the wall and held it near my face, steadying himself with the other hand as the ship jumped and groaned. For only a moment I thought: He has left his own people in the dark so he can see the slightest trace of a lie on my face. Who is this man?

"I did not trust you, Prophet," he said quietly, so that the others could not hear, even though a few people leaned closer to listen; the Advisor's brow furrowed in concern. "I trusted Yenu. But now I listen to you doing what she never does, which is admit that you don't know the truth. *She* is the one we cannot trust, isn't she?"

"Correct. In my experience. Sometimes she used to pretend she was trustworthy." I met his eyes, the pupils pinpricks in the lanternlight, beads of sweat glittering under them. "Maybe she's changed."

"But you don't think she has."

"No. I don't think so. Look at this: she said she'd send me and the Advisor home, and here we are."

"But you did not ask her to when we returned to the ship."

"I don't think she can," I said. "I think she lied to me in the museum to get me to do the spell. She had no intention of keeping her promise, not only because she does not wish to, but because she *can't*. That's why I didn't ask. If you must know."

His lip lifted, but he said nothing.

"Why do *you* follow her?" I whispered. "Where did you come from, Ksajakra, that you have dedicated your life to her cause?"

"It was my cause," he said. "She stole it."

I waited for him to go on, but he turned away and hung the lantern up again, vanishing into a dim corner. The ship juddered, scraped along the ground, jumped again. It seemed to be fighting against two opposing directions of *up* and *forwards*, and with every jolt tossed us around the floor of the hold until we found something to hang onto.

And then with a stomach-flipping lurch we did rise into the air, and the howling outside ceased, and the thumping and scraping and scratching too, and there was only silence. I wished I could shake the idea that the things outside had been calling to each other or something more distant (in particular I did not want to think of what that far-flung recipient could be). A wolf's howl was a message, a bird's song was a message. Information was being transmitted. But what, and to who?

"Is it over?" someone said.

"I'm not going back up there," someone else replied.

"Me neither."

CHAPTER NINE

Wherever they had taken us, we were high up, but not as high as the strange structures surrounding us: tall, wobbly-looking towers of some slate-gray stuff—not stone—supporting thousands of buildings crowded onto their tops and dribbling down their sides. Golden lights glowed in tiny round windows. From roofs, walls, and the tower stuff itself sprouted wires, spires, spheres, strange things on stalks tipped with what resembled feathers or wings, long arrangements of shapes that gleamed in the strange, dull blue light. It looked like those slime moulds you saw growing in forests, a webby thing on its own and further decorated by whatever odds and ends had stuck onto it from the litter. The air was thin and cold.

As I watched, a wire snapped up from a narrow, pointed roof and snagged a bird out of the sky, dragging it back inside. A window opened and closed again and the wire coiled itself back up.

"Uh," I said to no one, and stepped away from the railing, bumping into somebody, I wasn't sure who, and apologizing under my breath.

I huffed on my hands to warm them, then stuffed them into my pockets. The ship drifted slowly through the middle air; all around us was a kind of heat shimmer, the air bending around something I couldn't see, as if we were travelling in a soap bubble. Other vehicles glided above the towers as well—nothing like ours, sensibly enough; everyone had avoided things with our open deck and exposure to the elements. Most looked like zeppelins and blimps, even a few bulbous hot-air balloons with enclosed cabins slung beneath them, everything in dark blues, purples, and grays. Not a place you wanted to call attention to yourself, it seemed, and for a moment I was glad of our ship's dark hull and black sails, if nothing else about it.

It was eerily silent, not even wind. "What is this place?" I asked Sudworth, who had come up from the hold and was scanning the towers with a clumsy spyglass that someone had dug out of storage for her. It was longer than her arms and looked like it weighed as much as a cannon.

"Here? Bejurru. Weird place. Full of, what d'you call 'em. Like thin spots. They've got a real name though." She lowered the spyglass to the deck and rubbed her wrists, wincing. "Not gates, but with a hard enough push you can get through all the same. Without *too* much loss of life, usually. Anyway, that's not how we got in. But you can see how this place picks up"—she waved vaguely at the other aerial vehicles humming past us—"well, the kind of folks that go through the window instead of the door, if you catch my drift."

I nodded. Thieves, pirates, fugitives, refugees, assorted people on the run or merely striving to go unnoticed for a little while. On the one hand, I could understand why these weapons she spoke of had ended up here; on the other hand, I couldn't understand why they hadn't already been stolen and sold. "Where are we going?"

"An armoury. If what we're lookin' for is still here, I mean," she added, practically. "Kind of in a historical exhibit... like my museum."

"I can't believe you ended up running a *museum* after you left Earth. Why would—?"

"Stay on task, kid," she said briskly. "That's your problem, always has been. Too distractible. Not to mention I heard you switched sides and I shouldn't trust you further'n I can throw you. Here. You got young eyes." She hefted the spyglass and gave it to me. "Bloody thing feels like it's made of lead. We're looking for one of them towers with a big building right at the very tip-top of it. That's the most prestigious spot in this place, up at the top. Way of the world. And it'll have something on it that looks like a church. Ten or twelve big pointy towers and a central steeple. It ain't, though."

I sighed and lifted the spyglass, focusing it with the stiff ring around the second lens. "I didn't *switch sides*, I just... Anyway, so these will be pretty heavily guarded, do you think?"

"The rest of the place should be. These, well, we'll see. To most they'd be considered worthless."

"Worthless? The weapons of the *gods*?"

"Worthless to everybody but them," she said. "'Cos mortals can't use them. A bit like handing a spider a grenade and saying *Here, use this to catch a fly...* Well, and maybe they'll be worthless to the gods too. These are..."

She fell silent for so long that I eventually lowered the spyglass, which was making my shoulders ache anyway, and looked down at her. "What?" I said cautiously. "Dangerous? Being watched?"

"Old," she said. "Broken. Depleted. Almost... mementos. From that final war. They would have been trophies if they hadn't been so ill-treated when they were recovered, the way the Adversaries don't show respect to anything They loot, you know how it is. Now they're curiosities. Like finding a piece of a rusty cannonball on a beach."

"All right," I said, picking up the spyglass again and bracing my elbows on the railing, although that meant I had to hunch down awkwardly to put my eye in the right place. "So they're considered worthless because they're considered useless. But if we knew a god, we could say..."

"We might say 'Wotcher, here's your stuff.'" She paused. "Maybe, you know, with more fancy words."

I panned the spyglass slowly to avoid vertigo, pivoting it around my elbow. The towers had an oddly spongy appearance, like the pumice stone you got from air bubbles in lava, but I still didn't think they were stone. What it looked like, actually, was the texture you saw when you cut into a mushroom. Were they stalks of some huge fungus? No weirder, I supposed, than that fungus concrete Johnny had been working on when we were kids. Mycrete or whatever she had called it. Hycrete? I couldn't remember. She had brought me a sample cube once: light but indestructible, the weave densely satisfying to the touch. Maybe this was the same stuff.

"Who're *these* assholes, anyway?" Sudworth added, sotto voce.

"You don't need to whisper," I said, adjusting the focus ring again with a loud squeak. "Nobody speaks English except me and Yenu. And the Advisor."

"He got a real name?"

"It's 'the Advisor.' Anyway, as far as I can tell, Yenu there... sorry, Ksajakra, the tall brown one with the braids... started pulling people together a few years back to, you know. 'Rise up' against Them. The Adversaries. On Aradec, where I'm from. But the resistance was going nowhere until Yenu showed up and convinced them it was really possible. As opposed to, you know, hundreds of years of history saying it was suicide... I guess she was supposed to tip the scales. So they followed her. They had this plan, see, and then I got into the middle of it, and they kidnapped me and threatened to hurt the Advisor if I didn't help them."

"Like one of them doomsday cults," Sudworth said disapprovingly. "Well, I suppose I'm not surprised at either of you. See anything yet?"

"Nothing like what you said. Why aren't you surprised?"

"Well, she needs the attention, you know that. Likes having people fawning around her if she can boss 'em around, likes going it alone if she can't. Plus," she added with brutal honesty, "it's hard to climb to the top unless you got a solid foundation of backs to step on. That applies wherever you are. All the worlds're the same."

I looked down at Sudworth, swathed serenely in her gray and rose robes, the face I remembered: hard because it had to be hard, tired of the rawness and newness of everyone around her who disregarded her wisdom because it so often came with the sting of insult or disdain.

"If you think all of that's true, then why are *you* helping them?" I said. "You didn't have to leave your home."

"Lots of reasons," she said. "Keep looking. I'm going to go get a drink."

THE ARMOURY WAS absolutely guarded; even from our height you could see people moving about both outside and in, and since it was an armoury, I couldn't imagine they wouldn't be armed to the teeth.

"I'll stay here and watch the ship," I said helpfully.

Yenu glared at me. "You're coming. I might need you to run interference while Dr. Sudworth and I look for stuff." *Besides*, her face said, *you may think I don't like you, but* these *people* really *don't care whether you live or die.* I felt their eyes on me now, hard, cold, impatient.

All I could think was that she'd managed to convince them that despite also having Sudworth, my ability to do magic was still needed.

Ability, I wanted to inform them, that was directly caused by proximity to her. Like getting a tumour from living near low-grade radiation. I didn't *ask* for it.

In the end she left Ksajakra in charge, and took a few of the others who had come to get the book—the stocky Itzlek, who I was still a little uneasy about, even though in his position during the dungeon rescue attempt I'd have been silencing the wounded too; and Rhakun, the young So'it who she said was good with non-magical locks and barriers. Everybody remaining aboard had been tasked with causing a noticeable, though non-destructive distraction at the other end of the armoury from where Sudworth believed ('hoped,' I thought, was the more accurate word) the weapons were stored.

Yenu and Ksajakra had argued for hours about the nature of the diversion she wanted. It would have been more effective, he said, to make it as destructive as possible, to draw the maximum number of occupants to both watch the spectacle and try to help. Something more subtle risked people deciding it wasn't worth getting up to watch, or that their presence wasn't needed. Yenu, meanwhile, wanted to trade effectiveness for subterfuge. Blowing up half the building (say) would mean the theft would be discovered at once; disasters had a way of drastically increasing the scrutiny of the whole building, not just the affected portion. But if everyone was on one side of the place saying 'What's that?' we might be able to sneak in and sneak out. I had fallen asleep and woken up and they had been fighting on both ends of my nap.

"Well, what do we care if the Masters find out?" Ksajakra said, annoyed. "They're the enemy. We should *want* Them to know that we are in possession of things that could hurt Them. So They will fear us, maybe even avoid us. I would."

"No we don't," she said patiently. "Because it betrays our intentions. If They discover we've got weapons only the Quevereld can use, what do you think They'll assume we're doing next?"

"Oh."

"Paranoia," she said, getting up from the firepit, "is your friend."

"Excuse me," I said, "I am a civil servant. I am not qualified to do what you are asking me to do."

"Do it anyway."

I sighed and took the rope Yenu was holding out. We hadn't been able to position the ship to get a ladder down to the awkwardly-shaped armoury, which covered practically the entire top of its fungal tower (and how was that good design, I ask you?); but several of her people working together had managed to anchor ropes to the outer wall below where the guards would spot them, and as they walked back and forth we did have, I admitted, a fairly long window of time to slip down unnoticed.

It's just that it was a long slide, and it was dark, and I weighed twice as much as our next heaviest person, and I didn't want to.

"This is bullshit," I said, wrapping my sweaty hands around the doubled-up rope knotted around the main line. In theory, this would let me slide instead of just fall. In practice, I was pretty sure I'd panic, let go, and drop off like a rock. Maybe if I thought of it as a piece of playground equipment. They had something like this at the park near our old house, I thought distantly, balancing on the edge of the gangplank. Like a zipline. Yeah.

I took a deep breath and stepped off, clutching the handles, the wall approaching at terrifying speed even before my stomach had quite figured out that we were falling, the cold air rushing past me and freezing the sweat on my face. Five seconds later I banged into the weirdly soft wall, pulled myself up the last few feet of parapet, and dropped down on the other side, feeling like a raccoon caught in a motion-activated light while raiding trashcans. The thud as I hit hadn't been terribly loud, but to me it had sounded like a car crash. Surely the guards would come to investigate.

The others slid down one after another, and like me, grunted and flailed as they hauled themselves over the edge of the wall. The metal hook at the end of the main line, triple-barbed—a lot like an actual fishhook when you looked at it, in fact—seemed to be holding steady enough.

We didn't have long; in minutes the ship would sail to the far side of the place and start lowering Yenu's weird homebrew grenades on strings, detonating them harmlessly in mid-air. In the dark and the quiet and the gloom, I suspected the combined noise and flame would draw rubberneckers from all the surrounding towers, not just the armoury. As the ship drifted off, I saw one of the black cables snap out from an adjacent tower, but it wasn't long enough and reeled itself back in, as if sulking. They'd have to watch for those too. Imagine if one of them grabbed a grenade before it detonated... and how the hell had Yenu made grenades in the first place? Aradec hadn't discovered gunpowder, it was practically a violation of the Prime Directive, not that she cared, or that the Prime Directive was real...

The guards had marched to the end of the parapet and were turning back; I could just see bits of metal gleaming on their outfits in the blue light, as if at the bottom of a pool. Rent-a-cops really, and I felt bad for them as Itzlek and Yenu pounced, going for the heads and faces, then quickly tied them up and gagged them.

Inside, we trotted down a short flight of spongy steps and into a corridor with lanterns set into the gray walls at long intervals, leaving deep pools of darkness between them.

Historical artifacts, I thought again, trying to distract myself from the adrenaline that made my lips and fingertips buzz and made it hard to think. What if they were damaged beyond repair, even if we did manage to get them? And supposing somehow we managed to find the gods (a very weird thought, almost too large to angle in a way that fit in my head so I could think about it), would we hand them these broken things? What an insult. Better to say we had not even tried.

"This way," Sudworth hissed, pointing us down another hallway.

"How do you know where these things are?" I whispered. "You've never been here, have you?"

"Read a book sometime."

"Do you and her just coordinate on these things?" I demanded. A moment later I heard the first distant explosions, and braced myself for people to appear in our hallway, but nothing happened. Through the small square windows I could see people rushing back and forth in other wings of the building.

"Okay," Yenu said, peering out a window herself, then beckoning us to follow her. "Go, go, go, go."

"Hey, how are we getting out of here?" I said.

"The room should be marked," Sudworth said, not speaking to me but Yenu, who was looking up at the small, dusty signs on the wall. "Yes, that one."

"I was just wondering if you've noticed that we can't climb back *up* to the ship?"

"No, not that door. This one. "

The door—quite ordinary, made of the same dense, spongy stuff of the towers—was locked, but Rhakun got it open with a few minutes' work of his boneless, nimble fingers. I was still nervous; a few minutes might be all we had. How long could anyone stand outside looking at fireworks before they got bored and went back to their station?

There were four items, presented not exactly with

reverence, in an open-topped square platform, but at least not stuffed into a drawer somewhere. None of them, to my eyes, remotely resembled a weapon: three solid columns of green metal, attached along their vertical edges like pan pipes; a faceted piece of something that looked like bone; a clay dish containing, admittedly, what appeared to be a very small thunderstorm at sunset, all golden and red clouds and tiny flashes of lightning; and what looked for all the world like a wristwatch, with a blank white face inside a steel rim, on a plain black leather strap. I didn't like the featureless face, the lack of numbers. Something about it made hair prickle on the back of my neck.

Itzlek tucked his arms to his stocky chest, so tight his leather coat creaked, and said, "I will carry whatever you ask, Yenu, but I am *not* touching them first."

"Sensible," I said.

Yenu reached out tentatively, perhaps waiting for something to attack, as the book had defended itself, but nothing happened. Or at least nothing we could see. Outside, the muffled bangs continued; here all I could hear was our panting breath.

"At least they're small," Yenu said, drawing her hand back, then shrugging and reaching out again. Dust rose in clouds as she stuffed them into her satchel: the columns first, then the watch, then the bone, and finally, gingerly, as if it were an open dish filled with liquid, the bowl with the storm. Inside, the miniature flashes of the lightning could just be seen through the fabric.

"I know they don't look like much," Sudworth said as

we left, "but that's definitely them. Now, can they still be used? If a god got their hands on 'em? I couldn't tell you. There's no way to tell, as far as I know, because that's how they were designed: not for the, you know. Unworthy."

"They're better than nothing," Yenu said. "And I'm glad we did get them. We need any advantage we can get, and there aren't many."

We left out the door from which we had entered, stepping out into the cold eternal twilight that dimly lit the parapet. It had all been so easy. Too easy? Well, who cared. "How *are* we getting back?" I repeated, looking around.

"Opposite way," Yenu said, holding her hand horizontally above her head, then dropping it to the middle of her chest. "Like that. The others cut the rope loose from the railing, but it's still anchored at this end, so all we have to do is get back to the rope and Jak will fly the ship to below the top of the tower. We climb down to the deck." She paused. "Uh, ideally."

"Where did the guards go?" Itzlek whispered.

"What?"

They came at us from both sides, not many, but you didn't need many to outnumber us—and as we closed up automatically around Sudworth, who hadn't even brought her cricket bat, the Equalizer, all I could think was how *obvious* it was, how we should have planned for it from the beginning, how strange it was (or suspicious it was) that we hadn't. And by *we* I meant...

I drew my sword and squinted into the darkness. I didn't want to kill anybody for the things we had stolen, but I was far more interested in not being killed myself; and would they *actually* kill us to get back a couple of stolen historical artifacts? I doubted it.

They answered that with perfect clarity, coming at us with screams far more aggrieved than I had expected from rent-a-cops—and none of them wore the uniforms we had seen on our way in. "Wait a minute, these aren't—" Rhakun began, and then they were on us.

The fight would have been nightmarish in broad daylight. Worse, maybe. But it still felt surreally terrifying in the deep-blue light, unable to see what we were fighting, only able to smell the rotten odour of magic emanating from them, feel the slap and sting of their tentacles, see the feral glitter of eyes and fangs. They had not brought weapons; they *were* the weapons. They were, in fact, as far as I could tell, *Them*.

Something clawed my leg, deep and sudden, and as I growled and struck out for it, vanished into a cloud of sulphurous mist. I swung my sword through it anyway, staggered, slipped in my blood, and just managed to fend off something tall and gaunt that loomed over me. It swayed away, recovered, and fingers like exposed bone sliced across my face and neck, luckily stopped from a worse wound by my beard.

Next to me, Itzlek cried out in pain, and something cold splattered across me, quickly becoming hot. Acid, or some venomous chemical, and I wiped as much as I could from my bare hand and ear, listening to its sizzle fade on my coat. There was no time to do anything more, and it continued to burn my skin as I fought off something like a dog (and also very much not), oddly familiar, where had I seen it before? Wolflike, but with a hot throatful of bluegreen fire like a dragon, the claws and teeth like glass.

"We can't leave witnesses!" Yenu said through gritted teeth; her small body bounced off my side as she swung at something, and then she was off again, daggers flashing. We were gradually being pushed back towards the doorway and I did *not* want to get trapped in the narrow hallway inside. "Not one! If They report that we were here, if They identify us—"

"How did They know we were here in the first place?" I hissed back.

"Who cares? There's a war on. Oh, fuck this. Cover your eyes, folks, I didn't want to do this, but—"

I extricated my sword from a bubbling carcass, retched at the smell, and just managed to get my arm over my face as the world filled with light. A moment later the concussive crack of the explosion hit, throwing us all to the ground in tangled confusion—had she thrown a grenade or a spell? It didn't matter, she'd gotten all of Them, or almost all, but there were more where those came from, that was the big thing about Them, They were *legion*.

Sudworth shouted, "You just better hope they're down there, because we're goin'!"

"Hey!" Yenu croaked; was that smoke coming from her actual mouth? "No! Wait, there's a signal—"

"Help me over this," Sudworth gasped, snapping her fingers at Itzlek, who couldn't understand her but luckily got the gist. Yenu rushed over to stop them, fumbling in her coat for something; the signal, I hoped. More things were coming and I so desperately wanted to say *people* but They were not, and we had to go. I ignored Yenu too and followed the others over the edge of the wall, hanging onto the thick rope and bracing my legs on the tower.

The signal was something that was and wasn't a flare, almost like a bird, but glowing, or even aflame, and it fluttered around frantically as if its wings were broken. It fell from Yenu's fingertips like a burning sheet of magnesium and illuminated the blunt crags of the fungus tower, the tar-sticky rope we clung to, and various items of blood, gore, and anatomy stuck to our clothes and weapons.

And not the ship. Strain as I might, from my position nearest the top of the wall, I couldn't see anything resembling it. My arms were beginning to shake as voices gathered above us. Would the hook hold? And where was Yenu, with the bag of stolen weapons? I had seen her a second ago; now she was gone. And in a minute they'd do the obvious and look over the side of the wall, and then it was only a matter of a single creature swinging a blade at the rope and—

—there, thank fuck. It was a long drop from the end of the rope, and as the others leapt down into the nest of sailcloth that someone had thought to put onto the deck, it seemed an impossibly small target. But it wasn't getting any closer, and the signal was starting to fade, and I needed that to see, and for some reason I looked up suddenly, as if someone had just cleared their throat.

No one had, but just a few feet above my head, a head was watching me, in silence, unmoving, unlike the others rushing around behind it. The head was silhouetted, but something in the eyes held a deep green glow that froze me in place. Not the sensation of being seen, but being *seen*, no matter the physical darkness. We stared at each other as the shaking in my arms and legs grew worse, till my teeth began to clatter against each other. Seen. Known.

"Prophet!" someone screamed below in Low Dath. "Jump, fool!"

The head withdrew, still in silence. I gasped for air— one, two, three, four breaths—and then jumped.

WE WERE ALL wounded, some worse than others, Sudworth the least; but the chemical burns Itzlek, Yenu, and I had sustained were by the far the most concerning. As we sailed through the cool darkness, rushing to put distance between ourselves and the armoury, all our deck lanterns unlit, we patched ourselves up as best we could in the hold.

The burns weren't deep, but they were painful, and they were weeping blood, lymph, and a bluish-green fluid that I didn't much like. Yenu went back and forth soaking bandages in some thin, solvent-smelling fluid from a keg (was it actually alcohol, I wondered, or something she'd cooked up as part of a first aid kit?).

As the others muttered and ate and passed around a big ceramic bottle of wine, Yenu jerked her head at me and we headed up to the deck, shivering without our coats. Dozens of the crew were moving in silence around us, trying to let down the sails as quietly as possible for our jump onto the Violet River that Sudworth had talked about. I wanted to point out that you didn't need sails in space, because there was no wind, but decided it meant there was something both physical and magical about them. What a strange thought, though: being *pushed* along the River, the shapes and current propelling us along.

"I think we're being tracked," Yenu said. Her teeth were chattering and I could barely understand her.

"Tracked?"

"Maybe. I don't know." She winced as she put one burned forearm along the railing; several of the metallic, chitinous-looking scales had snapped off in the fight, and the edges were like razors. "Something in the ship. I should search it for anything I didn't put in here myself. Or it's... well, the obvious."

"A spy?" I said. That was pretty good coming from her, if she was working for Them; I'd almost stopped suspecting her for a minute there. "How would spying work here? Could a spy even communicate with the Masters?" I said, playing along.

She shook her head, seemingly too distracted to notice my bad acting. "The ship is *particularly* warded against anything like that. It's not hard; They do the same thing. Or used to, anyway, when They still had enemies. But They've got them again and I can't help but wonder..."

"You think They showed up back there because They were tipped off?" I glanced at the others, who seemed to be too far away to hear us, but you never knew. Well, there was no helping it. "I guess it's possible. But don't you think it's more likely that, well...?"

"What?"

"That you're just..." I sighed. "That it's just *obvious*, what you're doing? I really don't think They would need to track us or follow us or spy on us if they could just *guess*. Even coming to this place... how many of these weapons are still out there in the universe? How easy are they to get to? Maybe They just, I don't know. Eliminated the possibilities and made an educated guess as to where you'd be and when."

"Could be," she said reluctantly. "I mean, when you put it like that."

"You said as much to Ksajakra," I said. "You said if anyone knew we were here, they'd know exactly why. Not figure we were... doing a fungus sightseeing cruise or were zeppelin enthusiasts or whatever. And suppose someone saw us back at St. Cherkenai and knew we had stolen that book. The Masters aren't mindless beasts, you know. They can be intelligent."

"Maybe. Maybe it's as simple as that."

"Why are you telling me either way? What if I'm, you know, the spy?"

She snorted, which wasn't an answer, but declined to go into detail.

"It's a single incident," I said, after a minute. "Maybe it doesn't mean anything. Maybe all it means is that They're everywhere."

I couldn't quite see her face in the blue darkness, only

the glare of her mismatched eyes, and the fresh ointment where it had been dabbed onto her face, sitting up in little hills of grease. "Come on," she said. "We'd better help get those sails down. After we get onto the River, I'm changing the plan."

"How?"

"Zig instead of zag." She looked up at the sails, at the near-invisible birds and zeppelins that shared the air with us, everything moving in silence. The cool darkness seemed to be holding its breath. "To go for the prison would make sense now that we have weaponry the god could use. But supposing we did something else."

"Something else?"

"I'll need to redirect the ship." She chewed on her lip. "Where's Sudworth?"

"She was below last I saw." *Why?* I almost said, then frowned. Would Sudworth, of all people, be passing information to Them? It had been her idea to come here to Bejurru, true, but that didn't mean anything. Yenu had eagerly agreed. And Sudworth's claim of studying Them didn't mean she was allied with Them; she hated Them too much for that. I couldn't imagine anything They could offer that would be enough to convert someone as ascetic as Sudworth was. Or had been.

Or had been. When I knew her.

But we had all changed, hadn't we?

"Look, can we get any light up here?" I finally said. "I'm losing my mind in this darkness, I feel like I'm underwater."

"Soon. We just need to get out of range of the—"

But whatever she was going to say was cut off as a black wire, glistening with thick blue spikes, shot out of nowhere and entwined itself around the third mast. The man below it yelped and ducked, saving his life but not his back; wounds opened like mouths through clothing and skin. Someone next to him fell in silence, and someone else, thinking much faster than me, brought the blade of their heavy pike down on the cable, severing it so that it snapped back like an elastic band.

The air hissed; I spun from the railing, seeing first two, then three, then a dozen of the cables springing at us from rooftops and towers. "Get us out of here!"

"Then get over here!" Yenu shouted; everyone leapt into action at once, and everyone tangled and stalled at the same time. Cables webbed the entire ship, snagging the railing, masts, figurehead, everyone running back and forth chopping at them. The ship lurched, tilted, sent people spilling towards the railings and back. Had that been a faint, despairing scream off the edge? Jesus, what if we—

"We're not close enough to a river mouth," she said rapidly in English. "I need you to take some of the load for this spell—watch it!"

I ducked automatically, something scraping across the top of my head. I fumbled for my sword; Yenu snatched a dagger and hacked as it went past, sending something like a football-sized spiked seedcase tumbling to the deck, where it stuck in the wood. A runnel of blood wormed towards the steering column; she blocked it with her boot before it could seep into the mechanism.

Maybe it would work this time; I held out a hand, and Yenu pincered her fingers onto my wrist, cold and bloody. There was a heavy, thunderstorm sense of potential, and I held my breath, yelling at something inside me that I could not even identify, *Come on, come on, move over, let her use you, it's not like last time, we're all going to die, we*—

"It's not working!" she cried. "Go get Sud—"

And the ship simply flipped like a carnival ride and hurled us all into emptiness. My scream was cut off along with all the breath in my body as I thudded into a rolled lump of sails, and without even thinking I cinched my arms and legs tightly around the cloth and ropes, looking up at the deck above me rather than down at the bluish darkness, its muffled, unearthly silence into which the screams of the fallen now vanished. The cables enclosed the ship entirely now, worming across the bloodied wood, pulling us inexorably towards the towers.

I gasped for air, burying my face into the rough weave of the sail, the burned patch on my cheek screaming with pain as if it was being burned all over again, my heart pounding. The bare deck. I couldn't see anyone. To be fair, my vision had narrowed to a tiny hole, but still. What the fuck. Everyone had been lost when we had flipped, everyone but me. How would... if I...

The ship jolted away, nearly breaking my grip, and flipped again so that my ribs rang with the impact like a drum. The entire structure shuddered as if we had crashed into something solid, then strained, creaking, against the cables; distantly I could hear some break, with high single notes, as if they were piano wires. And at last, in a wash of white light, we were free, and all around us was darkness and stars, and below us, the half-visible silky current of the Violet River. So it was real.

It seemed to take forever to unlock my arms and legs from the spar, and even longer to climb the snarled man-lines down to the deck. My limbs refused to obey me, and when I finally dropped to the boards I simply collapsed onto my ass, shaking from the adrenaline, the effort, and whatever had just happened. I hadn't seen that, right? All those bodies, remote and anonymous, not real people with faces, homes, no, don't think about it, all those people, I didn't even know them, after all, *all those people falling into the darkness, the things sniping at them from the towers, feeding...*

Eight forms still stood or lay on the deck. Far more than I had expected, which had been none. Maybe they had spotted the cable that had ultimately flipped us over, and had managed to grab something just in time, or maybe they had been belowdecks and had gotten away with just being smashed against the ceiling.

The Advisor had made it, though he was holding one wing half-extended, as if it hurt to fold it normally. I went to him first and we simply sat on the deck together, wordless. I was still shaking. Thought we had gotten away. Not clean, okay, sure. Not a *clean* getaway. But gotten away from the worst thing. And now this. In the star-bright void around us I still could not see who was sobbing, softly, on and on and on somewhere.

As before, Yenu was barely clinging to life; Sudworth—

who had indeed been in the hold—and I took her down into one of the bunks and propped her head up so the thin glittering stuff could drain out between each shallow, bubbling breath.

"That's what happens," Sudworth muttered. "Supposed to find a river mouth. Can't just hop in anywhere, or you'll drown." She looked at me sharply, the back of her hand on Yenu's bluish-white forehead. "Why didn't you help her? Do you hate these people so much, hm?"

"I tried. I couldn't share the load."

"But you *can* use magic."

"I don't know what happened."

"Well, you better get over that performance anxiety," she snapped. "I can't take the same hits as I used to myself, so if we only have one working sorcerer on this tub, it's as good as having none. A spell's going to kill her one of these days and we'll be right fucked no matter where we are if we can't move this boat."

I nodded wearily and went back up. Ksajakra was the only one in motion; the others seemed half-catatonic with shock, and were clinging to ropes and the bolted boxes on the deck as if they were afraid we'd flip again. The River was stable, Yenu had told us; it acted more or less like a real river, simply carrying you along without intent or malice, a shape made out of all the spaces around it just as the spaces around them were, and in motion because of those shapes. We took our orientation with us, just as we had taken our gravity and our air. We wouldn't capsize here. But I could understand if her reassurances seemed very far away now.

"Help me," Ksajakra said harshly, and I turned, startled. I hadn't heard him come up behind me. He was limping, his face a scratched and bleeding mask. "There are... remains. We must give them proper rites."

I was exhausted and felt as if I couldn't even carry my own weight, but I didn't see how I could refuse him; he hated and mistrusted me, he would flinch to see me touching his dead friends, he still saw me as one of Them, uncertain of my loyalties, but... there was no one else up and moving. It had cost him more than I could guess to get those three sentences out. "Fine."

All in an instant. And the ones who had fallen were lost forever. Terrible to think of them being eaten by the towers and their feeding cables, if that's what they were. We weren't even *in* the war, there shouldn't have been casualties yet.

Yes, said something inside me, but you've already killed several of his friends, so stop fretting about these ones.

"Shut," I whispered, lifting a broken body and pulling it across the stained wood, "the fuck up."

Ksajakra glanced at me. "Is Yenu alive?"

"Last I saw." I hoped we would not have to place her with the dead, and I also didn't want to think about what would happen to us if we did. "I... we *were* friends once," I said, before I could stop myself. "You wouldn't know it now. I mean, she did actually *kidnap* me and torture the Advisor and threaten us both with death. But once, a long time ago."

He nodded.

"It doesn't mean anything any more," I said. "She

was someone else, I was someone else. I still don't even think it's really her, if you want to know the truth. She doesn't have the scar that... Look, I just... I don't know. Let's just do whatever we have to do next. The war will happen anyway. And I just want to go home."

"I want to go home," he said, "if I can go to a home that is not contaminated with those creatures."

Well, you won't, I almost said, then nodded. "So we can agree at least on one thing."

"Yes. And we agree on doing the next thing."

We wrapped the pitifully few bodies in extra sailcloth, and got needles and a huge spool of black thread from a box on the deck to sew the shrouds shut, making sure there were no gaps. Ksajakra and I needed two lanterns each for the work, and it still wasn't enough light. All around us was something like starlight—beautiful, silvery, but faint. My burned fingers ached as we worked.

"You said she stole the resistance from you," I said quietly, not looking at him; it took most of my concentration to knot the thick thread.

"She agreed that I was our leader," he said, also not looking at me. Every now and then a droplet of blood fell from his face, glittered an instant in the lanternlight, and fell with a *pap* onto the sailcloth. "She said, *I will be your second*. My most loyal lieutenant, my shadow. *Together, there's nothing we can't do*. The others didn't trust her; she wasn't an Aradeci, how could she know what the Masters were like. How bad it was. We knew nothing of her past. She came out of nowhere."

"She didn't tell you about herself?"

"No. The rest of us knew a bit about one another; she was a zero, a blank page in a book. She knew..." He looked up at last, wearily, his hands going still. "The Masters destroyed my city when I was very young. Half of us died. My parents died. They were the lucky ones. The creatures, They came, They filled up the whole sky. We asked Them what They wanted as tribute, worship. You know They want things sometimes. They did not reply. They put up a wall around what remained of the city and cut off the river. Then They hunted us. For sport, I think. Like noblemen trying to kill a ciargar, you get the prestige as well as the horn for the trophy."

I nodded. Nothing he could tell me about the Ancient Ones would have surprised me any more. They were so much worse, and so very different, from what I had thought They were when I first learned about them back on Earth, all those years ago.

He put his hand flat on the shroud before him. "People came to me first," he said. "Secretly, quietly. They wanted to fight back. We had plans. Then she came along and she had new plans. And soon it was her they were following. I told myself it didn't matter; we were all fighting for the same thing, no matter whose plans they were. This," he said, spreading his long fingers on the cloth, "is Zhybur Nuing. My friend for the last two years. A good fighter. Until you, the biggest man I'd ever seen. He broke his neck in the hold."

In my head I heard the Advisor's voice: *Your heart is a gentle one to be in war.* But I was a killer.

"I don't want anyone else to die, Ksajakra," I said.

"I do," he said softly, beginning to sew again. "If it means we can defeat the Masters. They will be worthwhile deaths. You, you still think 'life' is all, and so you want the war over quickly and the Masters to win. I am telling you, your logic is broken. You must think of life in the future. Not merely now."

"Those lives don't exist yet. We should safeguard the ones that exist now. As many as we can. Or there won't *be* any future lives."

"Then we still disagree," he said. "And you are still a tool that will turn in our hands."

I could not reply. His face was so still in the wavering light, though his voice was full of anguish. Another drop of blood fell, soaked into the black cloth, vanished.

I said, "Pass me the spool, please."

He did.

CHAPTER TEN

I COVERED MY eyes, which didn't help. In the damp darkness I heard a gratifying thud, which I hoped was Yenu falling senseless to the ground. I ground the heels of my hands into my eyesockets to make sparks and said, "You know what the problem is with all these places."

"Yes," said a voice near my ankles.

"The problem is. Their problem is. That they are all the wrong scale. They're the wrong scale for us, obviously. Humans. But they're also the wrong scale for whatever built them. They always are. I mean what the *hell* would you need a wall that high for. What would *anything* need a wall that high for?"

I uncovered my eyes, but reluctantly. This world gave me vertigo in my soul, it ruinously affected my inner ear. At least there was both gravity and air; I did not take those for granted now. We stood, or I stood and Yenu lay, in the middle of a small, green-turfed courtyard, seemingly the only flat place for miles around. I pictured her spell hovering like a helicopter circling a metropolitan downtown, looking for somewhere to land that wasn't the pointy top of a skyscraper. The three of us—her, me, and the Advisor—barely fit in it.

The walls of the courtyard rose above our heads, but a round window pierced each one, showing us how high off the ground we were. All the same, there was something out there higher still: sickeningly, impossibly high, *miles* high, disappearing into the atmosphere, too high to have been built by human hands unless it had taken ten thousand years, zigzagging over mountains and valleys, black stone of unsettling smoothness like a trickle of ink across a watercolour painting of a landscape.

Far below us and all around us were towers, sharp and dark and narrow, like upturned knives. But these at least seemed comprehensible. You could see windows, doorways. And at their bases, if that was ground level, the slow and unalarming movements of a population mostly on foot. From here they did not even look like ants. They looked far, far smaller. Like a spill of black pepper.

On the far side of the wall, nearly at the limit of my fairly good distance vision, were what I initially thought were white stones protruding from the ground. But the longer I looked at them, the less I could convince myself that they were so smoothly shaped by weathering... Bone, that was what they really looked like. Strangely clean though. No bird had nested on it, and nothing else—lichen, moss, plants—seemed able to gain a foothold.

I remembered Johnny once saying that bones, being a sort of stone, would be likely to survive many human cataclysms; and so would teeth, even likelier. Glass. Fired ceramics. "Toilets," I had said, and she had nodded. Stands to reason. The mountain-sized ones I didn't much like though. Too big for bones.

Supposing that wasn't a big load-bearing bone there, sticking through the far-off greenish dirt. Supposing its full length was twice what we could see, or ten times, but nearly buried, and we saw only the very tip of it; and suppose it was just a fingerbone. Or an earbone. Or something that something much bigger had picked out of its dinner, the way we would pick out the fine pinbones of a fish.

But even something that big would not be able to get over the wall. Would it? The wall was so high it seemed to distort the land itself, and time and space around it.

Yenu, up again and clutching the edge of the window, said, "Those things..."

"What?"

"Nothing." She shivered, and slowly did up the toggles of her coat, then patted herself down back and front, gently, as if making sure all her weapons were in place. "Uh, let's go. It's just..."

"Spit it out," I said.

"It's nothing... Just, you know the story about Omunia?"

"I do," said the Advisor.

"Yeah, well," she said. "Then you know how it ends. Or doesn't end."

"Someone could tell *me* the story," I said.

She cocked her head as if listening to either a shoulder angel or devil, then crossed the courtyard and stood in a tall, narrow arch, through which a flight of stone steps led down, hemmed in on both sides to hip height with more cut and fitted stone.

"This way, I think. We'll have to get down to ground level. Anyway," she said, putting her hand on the wall as she descended, "there was this world, Omunia. Don't ask me how long ago, the books are a little vague. Range of thousands of years. People living there in relative harmony, or at least not actively trying to murder each other all the time. And something showed up. Something big."

"An Ancient One?"

The Advisor, walking next to me, winced. "In the stories *I* know, it was never said explicitly that it was a Master," he said.

"But it might have been," I said.

"I suppose."

Yenu said, "It might have been, yeah. There's things out there that aren't, you know. They always said it was the thing exactly halfway between a god and a beast. Do I have any idea what that means? I do not. Anyway, the story goes that it was just a... a very, very big... thing. Some kind of animal. No one knew where it came from, no one saw it coming. There was no comet lighting up the sky, no earthquakes from below. It didn't seem to burrow there, it didn't seem to fly there. It just appeared. And it was so big that it affected the planet's orbit—"

"Jesus!"

"Yeah. Horrible. Threw it off by so much that it moved towards their sun and destabilized everything. A lot of people died, they say. Earthquakes, volcanoes, giant storms, the atmosphere got stripped away, magnetic fields got fucked up, the weather systems shut down, it affected gravity, heat, light, everything. And then it—"

"Did it say it had come there to take over? Did it want them to worship it? Give it tribute? Something like that?"

"No," the Advisor said. "It did not speak. Then it vanished."

"It did? What the hell. How do we know all this really happened, anyway? Is it a made-up story?"

"There were survivors," Yenu said vaguely. "A few got off-planet right after the thing came. Not sure how, because they didn't have interstellar flight. The accounts leave that part out. Not your standard refugee story. But anyway, the thing..."

"Let me guess," I said. "No one ever found out where it came from. And after, no one knew where it went." I paused at a landing, and looked out through the thin blades of the towers to the plains where the white bones gleamed against the darkness of the wall. "Can we talk about something else?"

"Oh sure."

We walked and walked; Yenu stopped often to rub her thighs, and the Advisor and I waited for her. The Tower of the Prophet, if it did not actually do anything useful for the palace, did at least train you for climbing a truly unbelievable amount of stairs every day. The air was cool, and up here smelled wet and fresh, like the breeze off a rain-damp mountain. It was enough to tempt you to linger, but we had to get to ground level, if Yenu's reading could be believed.

They will not be up in the towers, she had said, and we said *What towers?*

She said, *They will be down on the ground, where they can run. That is all I know for sure.*

So of the envoys, the things we had come here to get, all I had was a mental image of something that could run, and nothing else. Would they have legs? Terribly inefficient. Even something that looked like a cheetah, a greyhound... but in fact we didn't know how they looked. None of Yenu's research had turned that up, and Sudworth, despite her years of eldritch research, said she didn't know either.

No wayfinding spell had worked, though she and Sudworth had banged their heads against it for days as we sailed. The best we had been able to do (and they had seemed tremendously proud of it) was this pleasant green world, and this walled city.

Needle in a haystack time though, I thought when we had been dropped off the River; there were thousands of these towers, and envoys were deliberately difficult to find. Notorious for it, and necessarily notorious: to scout, to spy, to courier messages and weapons, flit back and forth over enemy lines, warn and rally opposition on the planets next in Their sights. Envoys, Yenu said, could find each other, usually, and so could the gods they served; but for their own protection, as well as that of their allies, they made themselves difficult to pin down either by magical means or otherwise.

But she had assured us that there were some here, and that she could find them for us. All the same, no one had volunteered to come, not after what had just happened. People were wounded, grieving, almost no one was left anyway, and the *look* in their eyes, even Ksajakra's...

It was strange that we had seen no one on the steps—not ours, not on the thousands or millions visible around us, winding around and through the dark, knifelike towers. I had not even seen a glimpse of movement in the windows or doors, and we had again passed more than I could count. I wondered if the others were thinking it too.

I shook my head, and paused to re-orient myself. I was used to stairs, but something between my eyes and my inner ears was calling out for a break. Enough stairs and you just stop being able to judge angles and heights; your body gives up on panicking that you're going to fall, and that's when you fall. And if we fell, we'd be falling for a long, long time. We had been up so high I had been able to see the curvature of this place, far in the distance where the land met the sky, still with its black swooping brushstroke of wall.

As we descended, the noise level rose and broke into individual sounds: footsteps, shouting voices, the occasional scream of commerce or danger, hoofbeats, the creak of wheels, the whine and thud of pipe and drum busking somewhere. Well, if I lived here, I wouldn't want to hang out inside these creepy, silent towers either; I'd live down here, on the ground.

I looked up at ours when we hit the street, Yenu and the Advisor hanging back under the arch of the stairway. Yes, very like skyscrapers, with their small regular windows, the fine-grained stone, but impossibly high, and tapering to a point I found unpleasant. Again I thought of knives, blades. They thrust through the paler dirt of the street with no demarcation of foundation, as if they had grown there. Sprouted overnight like mushrooms. Still there was no hint of movement up there. All the stairs and all the doorways and all the windows and all the courtyards, and not one single occupant.

At street level, it reminded me of Valishec, though I had experienced the city for barely an afternoon what felt like a thousand years ago. Humans and humanoids and a hundred other types of person carrying out their daily business, mopping their front stoops, hawking cooked food, waving away flies, sharpening knives, shining boots, pissing against walls, guiding wagons both open and covered down the relatively clear centre of the street, which was unpaved but reasonably dry. Cats darted in and out of the shadows between the towers. I hoped the Advisor's appearance would not cause a riot.

I beckoned to Yenu and the Advisor, and we began to follow a wagon loaded with bolts of black cloth.

"How will we find the envoys?" I murmured. "Will they find us, maybe?"

"No," Yenu said, not turning to look at me. "How

would they know we were looking for them? We'll have to find them."

"Stop scratching at your head. People are staring, they think you have fleas."

"I've never had a shaved head before. The stubble feels *weird*."

"Has the war reached this world?" whispered the Advisor as best he could; his vocal cords, unlike human ones, were not set up for whispering. I had no idea. I couldn't see any obvious soldiers, posters, stalls reading *REGISTER FOR THE DRAFT HERE*.

Yenu came to an answer at the same moment I did, as we moved into a small square with carved stone statues at the four corners and a larger one in the middle, everything crisscrossed with the shadows of the towers, blue and black and gold. It was not so much the square itself but the statues, and not even them alone (the Advisor and I were used to strange statues) but their plinths, each inset with a plaque of white marble, bright and clean against the black, and carved with a dozen lines of a language I recognized at once.

The old tongue, the tongue They used for Their own spells and communication, Their oldest speech.

"Of course," I said. "It's a thrall world, like ours. If you've traced the envoys here, then you've traced them to their prison. The whole place might be packed with the... Masters. Got Their own restaurants. Sports bars, probably."

"Not necessarily," the Advisor said; we moved behind one of the statues to get out of the crowd, putting our backs to a tower. My mouth felt both dry and sticky. I felt a bit as if I had sneaked out of work one afternoon, gone to the arcade, and spotted my boss. The instinct to hide was nearly overwhelming.

The Advisor said, "On Aradec, the Masters rarely appeared Themselves, you know that. There's no need if the rulers are loyal."

"*Loyal* is some way of putting it," Yenu said. "And you already know it's not like that on every world They invade. That's exactly the way They keep everybody in a permanent state of exhausted terror: because you just *don't know*. Are They going to show up today and disembowel everybody for the sheer joy of it? Change us all into monsters and make us fight for their entertainment? Or will it just be another day? I don't know how you can live like that. Yes, Aradec was lucky. Luckier than most. It was a good place to start a resistance."

"Hold that thought," I whispered. "You can keep arguing later, it's fine. Yenu, what do these plaques say? You know They usually don't make images of Themselves."

She nodded; They had a certain disdain of the physical form. That was something mortals suffered because we could not change it, and Their status increased in some ineffable way the further They were from the limitations that a sculptor might capture in stone. The laws of physics were for lesser beings; if you had to obey them, you were a joke. Mortals were a joke. Inherently close enough to non-entities for Them to simply regard us as raw material, the way we'd look at coal or livestock.

Yenu crept to the better-lit side of the plaque, and

read in silence with her lips moving, running her fingers along the carved letters, deep in the hard white stone. I wondered what the literacy level was around here.

"It's not words of power or anything," she said softly. "Not a warning, not wayfinding, not names or commemoration or a curse. It's just a list of... things. I don't understand."

"Things?"

"It's different on each side. This one says *the door the knife the eye the heart the hand the river the stone the—*"

"Yes, all right. Nothing useful." I looked up at the statues, pitted and blurred but still hideous in the half-light, and shivered.

What if they're on some uninhabited world? That's where I would go if I had just lost a war.

No, they'll be in disguise. And to keep up a disguise you have to have things around you that resemble you. You can't be anything but what you are in an emptiness.

We shuffled out of the square, trying to keep up with the crowd. Were people staring? I would have to stare back to know, and I kept my eyes down. The market stalls, I noticed, were not built against the backs of the towers, but a few paces away from them, and some even further, crowding into the road. It would have been easier to build a three-sided stall and use the stone as the fourth side, but no one had, and that made me uneasy in a way I could not even put my finger on. Maybe it was just a local tradition, but even as I thought that, I knew it wasn't.

No one had even moved into the lower levels of the buildings, with all their invitingly open doors and arches, promising sturdy, waterproof shelter with lots of room inside. Everything was in the open.

How would we know the envoys? Something in the eyes, maybe? A gleam, a spark. Or something secret. If you were hiding out on a planet ruled by Them, and you were Their greatest enemy, you wouldn't want to draw attention to it. Living in enemy territory. The audacity! Or the courage, if I was being generous.

Or hell, maybe they didn't worry about it, the envoys; maybe they had all switched sides. Maybe they were safe here. Treasured defectors. Maybe they would turn *us* in.

I absently dodged a fancy gilt carriage drawn by a pair of six-legged chamos, like the kind we had on Aradec. "You'd think more places would have cars by now," I said under my breath. "Haven't some of these places had people in them for hundreds of thousands of years?"

"I think that's part of Sudworth's theory," Yenu said.

"The Chambers Equation."

"It's *not* the... anyway. I know on a population level They're not the brightest, in the way we'd think of as intelligence—the ability to comprehend existing information, extrapolate or generate new information, and use it to correctly solve novel problems. But on an *individual* basis, the ones who pushed for invasion and expansion were cunning. Cagey, I think you'd say. There's a great word for it in Low Dath: *bybazuz*. Not driven by fear, but pragmatism. Like Sudworth said: They prefer to keep worlds at a point of development where the population *cannot* threaten Their rule. Magic included; in fact, magic first, because everywhere discovers that before they discover, say, gunpowder.

"So if They show up and magic is already being practiced, They stamp it down—you saw that in Aradec. They monopolize magic by killing or controlling whoever can practice it. If there's a rogue practitioner, everybody nearby is incentivized to turn them in *immediately*. It's a good system." She spotted the look on my face, and amended herself. "I mean it's an effective system. If that's your goal."

But that's like you, I almost said as I followed her through a narrow alleyway and into another packed street, the Advisor padding behind me so close I could feel the fire of his breath on the backs of my ears. That's what you wanted on Earth. You gave speeches about it: prettied up a little. You wanted to be the *only one* who could do what you did, by virtue of what you did being impossible. And then you bought up everyone even remotely at your level and stamped your name on them. So that whatever they did, you would still have control.

That was why she had broken her promise, and refused to send me and the Advisor back to Aradec when I had asked, back on the ship a few days ago. She hadn't said that was the reason; I just knew it. She just wanted to control us *in case* we could be useful later, and she could be a hero later.

Was she Theirs? I wished I could stop thinking it. I wished I just had a simple yes or no from someone that wasn't her.

We turned again and again, moving like slow, random pinballs; the streets were emptying out by degrees, and we walked through what looked like camps or field hospitals but were, I was pretty sure, permanent habitations.

And again I looked at the solid, weather proof towers behind them, knifing into the pale gray sky, and again down at everyone determinedly crawling into their tents for the night, cupping their hands around lanterns and tying canvas flaps shut, and I shook my head and we kept going.

"We're..." Yenu whispered, and I nodded. *Being followed:* I knew. Something had shifted a little in the air, something that had intent, not just people travelling in the same direction as us. And the suns we had seen from the top of our tower (twin, small, close together on the horizon, like back home) were setting, flooding the streets with thick blue light like deep water, studded with the twinkling fish of lanterns and candles. One by one these disappeared into the tents, winking out behind the thick fabric. Soon it was so quiet that all I could hear were Yenu's and my bootsoles on the road, the Advisor silent on his velvet paws.

I glanced behind us, then automatically up at the towers for any hint of movement, the shine of a light. Nothing. But something was after us despite the silence. I could feel it. I put my palm on the hilt of my sword, casually, as if protecting the coat pocket next to it.

Pickpockets, ordinary cutpurses? Possible. Following us because they knew precisely who we were and why we were here? Equally possible.

I thought again of Yenu's rapid, hissed speech. Again there was no easy answer. A spy could have figured out where we were going, or simply asked Sudworth (if she herself was not the spy). Alternatively, Yenu's plan of zigging rather than zagging had been more obvious than she thought, distracted and deranged as she was with urgency.

Or *feigned* urgency. She was doing a very good job of pretending that we needed to raise the Quevereld army before the general of the Masters figured out she was alive and came after her again, *or* she was in genuine terror and that was why she drove us without rest. And I didn't know and no one would tell me the truth and I was losing my *mind*.

It was all academic now; we had more pressing issues. Something was after us, and we could only go forward, not back.

"I see them," the Advisor said softly. "Behind us on the street. And above to the right."

"Above? You mean in... the buildings?"

"Yes."

I glanced back at him in the deepening blue light, seeing the wet glitter of his eyes, the dark irises completely displacing the sky-blue whites, the way they did when his adrenaline ran high. Yes: a flicker of movement on a staircase above us, and a hushed scrape, a tiny hint of metal against the fine stone. They were trying to be quiet. An ambush. Behind us, only a dark shape flitted between the tents, gone again even as I watched, no more threatening than a cloud of smoke.

"Sonofabitch," Yenu whispered. "I definitely saw something." She reached into her pocket; in the lowering darkness, as if we were sinking through deep water, I could only hear. First the slick rustle of her deck of spells, then the squeak of her short sword being pulled from its sheath inside her coat.

"How many weapons do you *have* in there?" I said.

"Look, you know how it is, sometimes you stab somebody and you can't get your knife back. It's important to have backups." She took a deep breath. "Stay behind me. You'll rip open all your burns."

"I'm sorry, can you repeat the part about *whom* I'm supposed to stay behind?"

"I too will fight," the Advisor said. There was what I would have called a surprised silence from Yenu, but she just nodded instead, nothing visible now except the faintest glisten of the last of the light on her scalp.

Another scrape, and then the ground trembled, slight but perceptible. I looked around wildly again, still seeing nothing: towers, walls, stairs, arches, doors, circles and squares of darkness with nothing behind them, but something heavy had just taken a step near us, and I could not see it. Light, we needed light. I thought about Rhakun moving around in the hold, climbing effortlessly into the bunk next to mine, one of the few resistance members who spoke directly to me rather than through Yenu: *Humans like light, don't they, Prophet? Darkness is the real gift. It gives you everything.*

It didn't feel like a gift.

Whatever hit us got the Advisor first, in silence and

evidently with incredible force, sending him to the ground in a confused tangle of limbs and wings. Yenu cursed in a language I didn't know, then shouted something. A grape-sized sphere of pink light burst into life, illuminating, for a moment, no more than a morass of incoming forms at ground level, all legs and snouts and fangs, before she tossed it upwards, suspending it above us like a flare.

Statues. They were *statues*, carved of the same dark stone as the towers, some even familiar: we had passed them on the way here, we had read their plinths.

Yenu's sword rang against the first one that loped slowly but inexorably towards us, the blade kicking up white sparks; the sound pained my ears and teeth. I dove away from another that leapt for me, a heavy-set thing like a scaled sphinx with three heads, and the Advisor's paw met it with a deceptive, almost leisurely slowness, sending it into the wall with a crack that shattered its back legs.

Spell! Spell! Do something! Fire! The one you did back at their fucking stupid headquarters!

But there was no time to draw the sigil, simple as it was, and another statue was already galloping towards me, like a long-legged alligator with a tangle of roughly-carved tentacles for a face. I kicked out at it, turning to avoid the worst of the tentacles. The kick did no damage, only knocked it sideways, tripping another thing. Yenu spun and sent a stream of lilac fire out of her free hand, bursting a crater into it but not bringing it down.

And they were coming faster now, scuttling down the walls, clattering from side streets and the stairs, and we did not have the high ground. If just one of them figured out it could climb and leap down, bringing the full weight of stone onto our pitiful bodies—

Just as I thought it, Yenu's little pink light was blotted out by something huge and flat, careening towards us from several storeys up. In a split second, I dove flat and rolled, Yenu raised her hand—so small, so wounded already—and something *else* shot towards it, connecting in mid-air and shattering it against another tower.

Broken stone pattered against my face as I scrambled to my feet, stunned from the impact and the noise.

A dozen statues fought now, perhaps more, but they were fighting *each other*, and three had taken up stations around Yenu, the Advisor, and me, so large that the three alone almost formed a circle. They were strange, asymmetrical things that should never have been able to stand as a statue and seemed even less stable in motion, masses of carven claws and exposed muscle and bone like the statues of flayed saints you sometimes saw in museums.

The envoys!

Their battle was silent now, only the sound of stone colliding against the walls and one another, and in the fading pink light it was impossible to tell who was winning, if anyone was. So that was how they had lived here! In plain sight, blending in with all the other agents and cops of the Masters.

But now that they had exposed themselves, they were like us: having chosen a side not so much out of desire to join it as by the sheer audacity of having defied the other side.

"There's an opening!" Yenu gasped, dodging a flying stone tail that missed her head by two inches. "Run, go!"

We went for it, thankfully not alone but flanked by the three great guardians, two behind and one in front, squeezing in single file down the narrow alleyway, Yenu's light following us like a firefly, visibly dimming. She began gasping for breath despite the relatively short distance, and we stopped perhaps two blocks later. In the new, uneven darkness, footsteps clattered on all sides—maybe the envoys, maybe the enemy—a constant restless rattle, like the first moments of a landslide.

"We can't stop here!" I stared wildly around us, again seeing nothing; her mote of light had vanished, and far above, the distant stars gave no light between the closely-packed blades of towers. "Come on, one of us will carry you."

"Something else," she panted, clutching my sleeve. "Happening."

"What?"

"Can't you feel it?"

I lifted a boot, felt it slammed back to the ground with teeth-rattling force, like powerful magnets reuniting. And then I saw it: ahead of us, just beyond the two giant guardians, two more small statues had leapt down and pressed their flanks together, uniting the carved halves of a magical sigil into the necessary circle. It burst into an intricate tracery of light even as we watched.

I only managed to get out, "There—" before the ground dissolved beneath us.

* * *

A DARKNESS BUT not a perfect darkness, which would have been the true gift. As it was I could see just enough to make my blood turn to lead: the flicker of an eye here, the glow of a throat there. Yenu shakily dug out the lantern from her pack, and I almost stopped her: *We don't need to see to know where we are.*

But I said nothing, and the clear amber light revealed all. The place between, the place that was neither here nor there, dragonspace composed of rooms and corridors, cathedrals and theatres, built out of tessellated patterns of flesh. The floor upon which we huddled, the walls at our back, all was dragon, or what the mind generally processed as *dragon*.

The air stank of musk and acid, and a low undercurrent of something burning; it was like sitting in front of a smoky trash fire. Yenu's lantern bobbed as if we were at sea, rocking and tipping as the scales under it shifted. Not restless or agitated, but continuous, a perpetual motion machine. I couldn't distinguish heads in the minimal light, but every now and then I'd spot a nostril, a half-open mouth, a startling eye that seemed to carry its own light.

Think about that. Without us here and our pathetic box of fire, they would be in the dark here all the time, in silence. Slithering around in the dark.

I shuddered, and looked down at the apparent miniature thunderstorm between the Advisor's paws. Unable to keep up their disguise, the envoys had reverted to their original forms: very useful for long-range travel, I was sure, and for moving without being detected. But the half-cohered bubbles of cloud seemed terribly vulnerable here. And there was nowhere for them to go.

But I knew this place. I had been in this place before. I knew whose place this was. It was comprised of magical beings, but no spells could be performed here, nothing. It was a trap, and we had fallen into it with perfect ease.

"What really annoys me," Yenu muttered, "is that I can't *see* any anti-magic wards. That's how they work, you know. Design's so powerful they draw all the available magic to themselves and there's none left for other spells. Like parking an ice-cream van next to a playground... Maybe they're just tiny, I don't know. Maybe they're *on* the dragons."

"Figures," I said. "He must've learned from last time."

"Last time?" the Advisor said politely.

When neither of us answered him, he tried again: "Have you... been here before? How did you get out?"

I didn't want to tell the story of this place, the Burning King's kingdom; Yenu seemed not to either, or had forgotten, and began muttering to herself and shuffling through her useless deck of spells. The Advisor curled up and put his chin on his forepaws, folding his wings tightly and tucking his tail in. The envoys panicked and fluttered away, then returned and settled at his flanks, so that he seemed to be lying half-submerged in a cloud bank.

It's all right, I wanted to say to him. Now that we're here, we can finally say what we were thinking, and no one can gainsay us. We can say: Everyone *knew* this wasn't going to work. You knew it, I knew it. The Masters will therefore understand that we were only complying to preserve our own lives, and because we knew all Yenu's crackpot schemes were useless, no threat to the Masters Themselves. The time she could have been dangerous to Them was long, long ago; she does not have what she needs any more. She is a wild boar that destroyed one too many plantings and has now had her tusks drawn. Last time, yes, I fought on the wrong side. *This* time, you and I have credentials to present. We are known to the one in charge here. We saw him only a short time ago presiding over Yalip's sacrifice. He will recognize us as one of his own. Only the 'resistance' will be imprisoned. Her, and these.

No point in restating the obvious. Yenu would be scheming to escape. Let her. I would stay.

It felt like a strangely shaped but heavy weight had been taken off my shoulders, and below my instinctive fear of the dragons (you couldn't predict dragons, and I didn't like that) was something cool, slow-flowing as a stream: relief. At last.

Called into the boss' office? Sure. But I had done nothing wrong; and I could point to the 'coworker' sabotaging the company. The Advisor and I might be back home today, both of us, back at the tower. The Burning King could take us back. He moved, it was said, in mysterious ways, which never failed to make me laugh.

I said nothing, and stared into the flame of the lantern, which cast square-framed, dancing shadows of our bodies onto the rippling walls behind us. The place glittered extravagantly but somehow did not communicate beauty or grandeur or even mystery, the way it would have (I felt certain) if it had been made of something else. Anything else. Birds. Snakes. Aradec had beautiful snakes; if you watched the walls long enough you often saw them climbing on the carvings, like coloured inks dripping upwards. They were good climbers, the palace snakes. Strange to think of them now.

"All right," Yenu muttered, and put away the card deck. "Think, think. That son of a bitch. Should have known he'd come for us. How did he know? How?"

One of the envoys, a grayish cloud shot through with strange triangular shards like broken glass, drifted over and touched my eyebrow with a dangling tendril; it smelled of smoke, overpowering the musky stink of the dragons. "Hello," I said cautiously. "I—"

The impact of its message rocked my head back like a slap, and I flopped onto my back. Yenu and the Advisor stared as I hauled myself upright again, rubbing my forehead. Of all the ways to communicate that I'd experienced, that was a new one, and took top prize for being the most unpleasant.

"The envoys think that not all of them were caught in the trap," I said. My mouth felt strange and numb.

"Oh?" said Yenu, not paying attention. She was going through her pack again, as if she had brought something else and simply forgotten about it. ACME Corporation, I thought, almost laughing. Can of tunnel paint. Portable hole.

"So they may have been captured back in the city; or it may be that they escaped. This one does not know for sure."

"Mm." She scratched at her head again, absently. "Not useful information, then. What we should do now," she said, "is wait."

"For what?" said the Advisor.

"For him to show up."

"Him who?"

She hesitated for a long time, then said, with genuine curiosity, "Don't you know where we are?"

"Should I?"

"Hm." Incredibly, she tugged off her coat and her pack, folded them up, and lay down, hands under her cheek. The scales of her forearms clattered against the scales below her like castanets. "Well, I'm going to close my eyes for a minute. Suggest you do the same."

"What are you up to?" I said suspiciously.

"It's fine," she said, not opening her eyes. "We move when he moves."

WHEN I WOKE, it was definitely lighter, the dragons more agitated; it was their movements, I thought, that had woken me. The 'ceiling' had expanded upwards while I slept, which was to say that the intertwined dragons had rearranged themselves and locked claws, tails, teeth, and limbs together to form a different structure, like ants.

A dragon much larger than the others, its orange-and-red head the size of a house, had emerged from the morass and lay on its belly no more than fifty paces from us, staring fixedly with about sixteen large, pale-amber eyes, each with a crisp black slit of pupil. I stared back at it, stomach somersaulting with shock and fear, but the dragon didn't move.

"How long has *that* been there?"

"Uh, not sure," Yenu said. "At least half an hour, because that was when I woke up."

"Does it ever blink?"

"It does not."

"What were you dreaming?" the Advisor said to me. "You shouted out... you tried to keep something away."

"And that was when this thing showed up," Yenu added, jerking a thumb behind herself.

"What did I say?" I said cautiously.

She shrugged, and the Advisor shook his head. "We did not understand it."

"Well, maybe it didn't mean anything. Maybe it was just gibberish. I'm only the Prophet when the Mouth of the Prophet is there, you know. And knows what books to look in."

The Advisor fell silent, glanced at the dragon, back at me. "Some do say dreams are meaningless," he said. "Maybe some are. But dreams can also be gates. At any rate, they can be openings that things may pass through. When they do, where do they go? Sometimes nowhere. Sometimes only into another place that the dream connects. But who can say? The Tower of the Prophet is designed to focus and amplify all those things that come to us when we do not know we are gates. Maybe you saw something that was real, Prophet. What did you see?"

"It was only for a second." I shook my head, trying to recapture it. A photo glimpsed once in a flickering book. "He was surrounded by words, somehow. I thought they were birds or insects or... sand. White sand. There was a mountain. Swirled like marble, and the markings in motion. I thought something was crawling on the surface. Or the clouds were moving and allowing sun to fall on it only sometimes... and near the summit, the opening of a cave. And at the mouth of the cave, someone sitting, not clear behind the words, wearing a gray robe and a golden crown. And attached to the crown, something terrible."

I hesitated. "I don't know why I thought that then. It's not really terrible. A piece of yellow cloth, like a veil. Fine, very light. Moving in the wind but not so as to reveal his face. Maybe silk. I don't know." I did not add that I had felt *known* by the small unmoving figure, even though I was sure he could not see me through the cloth. It had had the same sense, cold and final, as the hallucinations from the book we had stolen from the museum. *It's you.*

The Advisor went still, and somehow I could sense it even in the constant subtle movement of the things under us, the pitch and yaw of the lantern. His face froze, his wings locked into place. Like shutters doing down.

"Do you know who that is?" I said. "Who I dreamt?" But even as I asked, I knew he did. If he didn't tell me, that told me something too; and we both knew it. His entire body radiated it. A smooth, numb fear, instead of his hackles going up. Yenu edged away from him.

"Yes," he said. "He has no name. He is not mentioned in the texts. If ever he is, the book is burned and the author is killed and pulverized so no part of them may return in any form. Most people, really, have the good sense not to write about him at all. Not even hint."

"Then how do *you* know about him?"

"From speaking only," he said. "Mine is a long-lived people. And we pass on what we fear most, so that the children may fear it too. And when I tell you that we have feared him for fifty thousand years, as far back as we can recall, maybe you will not believe me. But he is the only thing that everyone fears. Some worlds know of him, some don't. But even the ones that don't are afraid of him."

"Why?"

"No one knows."

"...Is there any water?"

We ate and drank as best we could and I, with a certain vengeful glee, went into a corner to piss against the head of a dragon, which blinked in annoyance and submerged itself in the coils and scales. I felt light, emptied of guilt, but also of other things. That dream. So real. The cold and the wind and the soft dim light, and the little pat-pat of words hitting my cheeks like sand, getting caught in my beard. I felt as if, while sleeping, I had had a shock so tremendous that it had driven everything else out of me for a little while.

The war would simply go on as planned. Yenu's

resistance had been no more than a speed bump, easily surmounted with not even a single army division diverted to it.

But even as I thought it, I thought also: Not *all* of me believes that. I wish I could with my whole heart, but I don't. I still feel sick, because the Burning King doesn't know her. His master doesn't know her either. They think They do, but They don't, They can't. What They fear is that she is a being of chaos, even more than They are. And on top of that, she is a weapon They do not understand how to use. They wanted it once because They believed They did understand; now I think They are too afraid to see if it can even *be* used in war. They wish it destroyed.

Was I so truly on Their side after all I had seen? Even now, I didn't know. But for *once* in my goddamn life, I did want to be on the side that survived.

"Prophet?" Yenu knelt next to me; her human eye blazed as if a bonfire had been built behind it. "Can I borrow your sword?"

"What for?" I said, immediately distrustful of her formal, sweetly courteous tone.

"I need something with more surface area than anything I've got."

"...Okay, while you *technically* answered the question, you *non*-technically—"

"You'll get it back."

"Are you going to stab the big one?" I said, pointing at the orange dragon that still stared at us.

"Maybe later."

I pulled it from the scabbard. "Don't make me regret this."

She returned to the far side of the lantern, got something out of her pack, and frowned: a black ink stick, like the kind Sudworth used. "Mm. Too wide. Advisor? A word."

They conferred for a moment, then he nodded and suffered her to pluck a feather, small and leaf-shaped, from the ridge running from his head down the back of his neck between his wings. She knelt again next to the lantern, sharpened the end of the feather with one of her knives, glanced around, then dipped the newly-made quill pen into the half-coagulated blood that pooled in the cupped scale next to the lantern. We were all bleeding a little from glancing wounds sustained in the fight with the envoys, but I had not even noticed her losing so much blood.

"That is disgusting," I said interestedly.

"Needs must," she said without looking up. The design expanded, though not much, across the metal, slightly wider than her palm. A sigil, and a complicated one.

"But you can't do magic here. You said so."

"Me? No. Definitely not."

Aren't you going to stop her? I demanded of myself, then followed that immediately with, Why bother trying? This won't work; she just said it won't. Followed in its turn by: You should try, at least. But you're still trying to not pick a side, aren't you? You still want to be placed onto a side by one or another player. The

Masters put you on one square of the chessboard and then she showed up and put you on another, on the far side of the board.

Yes. That's what game pieces are for. I'm not a player. I'm a piece. I always have been. Who in the hell would *want* to be the one moving the pieces around on the board? Egomaniacs and psychopaths. Like her. Like the Manifestation. Their general, the one who's always wanted her.

You could change that.

What, and become one of them? No thank you.

Not like them. It is not inevitable that you would become like them.

"Everybody shut the fuck up," I said out loud. The Advisor looked up, as did Yenu, then she continued to draw. The envoys hovered around her shoulder, wafting their strange scents as they moved: smoke, ozone, fruit, rot. Zig instead of zag, she'd said; instead of going for the god, go for the envoys; send them out to find the others, fly through them like flak, use them as distraction and disguise. It had seemed sensible enough. I should have remembered the word *flak*: which was not alive, and which should have told me not only how she thought of the envoys, but the rest of us around her.

"How come you can still use your covenant if you can't do spells?" I said, studying the haze around her head; the envoys surrounded it as if they were butterflies drinking from a salt pool.

"Oh, that's not a spell," she said, continuing to draw. "Never has been. We're in a universe and a dimension where it works, that's all. I pay up, I get what I'm owed. And if I don't use it here, we're doomed."

"*We're* not," I said, meaning myself and the Advisor.

She looked up and smiled, a bleak thing like a fresh scar across her face. "You? You're transparent, Prophet. You think His Royal GhostRiderheadedness will just show up and welcome you back? You've been helping the resistance. They'll *never* take you back into the fold. And your loyalty was questionable anyway, given your history; if anyone's been waiting for you to slip up, renounce it, switch sides, it's him, 'cos he was there last time. And you know how They feel about second chances." She chuckled coldly. "We're all doomed together. Stop trying to deny it."

She stood, and held the sword close to the warmth of the lantern to dry her design, the blood sticking alarmingly well to the pitted metal. "Plus," she added, "you think I've spent all this time getting my fingers chopped off to read books about manners and meadmaking? I know things nobody else knows. Including things about this place."

I stood too, more slowly. The weight resettled itself on my shoulders, ten times heavier, clawing at me. My stomach filled with ice. Knew it knew it knew it, *knew* it, she *always* finds a way to do this... "You knew we were going to get trapped down here," I said, no question mark at the end of the statement.

She nodded.

"No. It gets better. Doesn't it? You... you *wanted* us to be trapped here."

This time her smile was a definite sneer. "Didn't you? Different reasons, of course."

"No! I mean..."

The air changed abruptly, a pressure-laden *thud* that hit in the lungs and the membranes of the ear, and I wavered but did not fall. Behind the great flame-coloured dragon that still stared unblinkingly at us, an aperture opened, hair-thin, and for a second the air sprouted mirrors all reflecting the wrong thing from impossible angles.

And through the opening strode the Burning King, a darkness, a flame, the twisted branches of his crown throwing great flickering shadows that writhed like living things, and his feet too afire, smouldering columns that seemed too burnt to hold him up but did all the same, and between them breathed the mass of wood and fire and hunt and abyss that seemed not at all out of place here the way it had in the great Auditorium where he had killed my friend and I had looked away.

He balanced atop the head of the great dragon and grasped one of its long, twisted horns, and angled his crown down at us.

The dragons came to a halt, hissing, and it was as if sand had been falling quietly and constantly somewhere and had finally run out. His flames burned in silence. He had brought something with him, a pleasurable burden: the dragon shifted its head, sending something spilling down it like a trickle of mercury. Chains and shackles, bathed in a greasy-looking green light. Trap. Easy. Succeeded so well. *Easy*.

Lacking a face, he could not smile, but I sensed him

smiling as he came towards us, marching proudly down the dragon's stone-still head, the chains pattering after him like so many tame snakes. Johnny's voice in my head from long ago: *Something evil, somewhere, is laughing at us; our pain is amusement to the things that know.*

We stared up at him. Would he speak? I had only met him three times in my life and each time he had been silent. For a moment, the entire cathedral of dragons seemed to hold its breath.

Then, with a perfectly natural movement, Yenu hefted my sword, spun on her bootheel, and hurled it at the Burning King.

CHAPTER ELEVEN

LIGHT FLOODED THE space, light and chaos and noise and shrapnel, as if she had set off a bomb. The dragons writhed, screamed, roared; limbs sprouted out of gaps and unravelled from the floor, revealing only more dragons below in a confused tangle.

But I could still see Yenu through the confusion, and charged after her as she ran towards the Burning King. Whether she had killed him or not, she knew *something* about how he had gotten in, and therefore how we might get out. As we scrambled up the sudden hills and valleys of the writhing worms, dropping to our hands and knees and cutting our palms on the edges of scales like broken tiles, as we neared the ball of heat he had become, it seemed he had been pierced clean through. The sword was glowing white, and he had collapsed onto the heap of chains, the thick branches of his limbs clawing weakly at the handle, recoiling as if the white was heat rather than magic.

The big orange dragon slowly raised its head, as if under some massive weight it was unused to carrying, and even more slowly began to open its mouth, the fat, pointed tongue lolling, covered in its iridescent and flammable venom. Yenu was slowing down though; at last I could see where she was going, and she wasn't going to make it.

I tried to speed up, but couldn't get enough air; every breath was shallow, constricted, like a hand were around my ribs, squeezing. She turned back desperately, seemingly about to say something, then yelped in genuine alarm, the noise carrying with supernatural clarity over the noise of the worms.

I began to turn, was stopped dead by something slamming into me from behind; I felt talons clutch and flailed backwards trying to break its grip, waiting at any moment for the noise of the dragon's claws punching through my coat and then my shoulder, but heard instead a sound I had only heard a few times before: the ponderous, muffled flap of the Advisor's wings.

In a few wingbeats we had caught up to the Burning King, and Yenu snatched at my sword as we passed, yanking her feet up to avoid a swiping claw, and then the Advisor banked hard through an invisible membrane, sending us in a trumpet-blare of heat and light onto solid ground, real ground, not a dragon.

I hit and skidded, crashed into Yenu and over her, then leapt to my feet and ran for the Advisor, slumped in a heap of feathers with his wings over his face. The pale brown earth, already dry and cracked, audibly rumbled and began to collapse a mere handful of paces away.

But he was my first concern. I thrust away his wings, slapped his cheeks, which were dry and hot, the skin minutely abrasive, like the skin of a shark. He was panting, eyes open but unseeing, breathing harder than I'd ever seen him. Yenu followed me, something vague around her shoulders, as if she were trailing a cape of mist—the envoys, it seemed, had had the good sense to follow our lead, and I felt a moment's relief, increased when the Advisor managed to focus his eyes on our faces.

"What's wrong with him?" Yenu knelt next to me, then glanced ahead of us. The shaking was getting worse, bits of white rock spraying out from the widening crack and pattering to the ground like rain.

"Nothing, not really, except that Rhaokor can't fly, I mean, the wings aren't *technically* vestigial, but he told me that with each generation fewer of them are actually *able* to get off the ground, let alone carrying two people, and with the diaspora they're moving to planets where the gravity is too high anyway, they live mostly in—"

"All right, all right, shut up, you need to breathe too, can you get him up?"

I held a hand out for my sword, but she drew away from me, shaking her head. The blood sigil was gone now and the length of the blade was smeared with what looked like ordinary ash. The ground rocked so hard that she immediately fell over, then scrambled up again, wincing at her bloodied palms. "There, towards those rocks. We have to—"

We dove behind the outcrop of pale bluish stones, and barely in time, as the ground erupted all the way to where we had been standing, waterfalling into the fresh crevasse. The great orange dragon struggled to climb free of the gap, swivelling its great head back and forth and scenting at the air with quivering, almost prehensile nostrils. The air grew perceptibly warmer as the dirt sloughed away around its back, revealing smaller faces, dozens of them, snapping and wricking their jaws and scrabbling at each other's bodies in their efforts to get up the writhing back.

"Hey, what the fuck do we—?" I whispered, and turned to Yenu, who was scribbling something right on the rockface with one of her wax pencils.

"Blue," she said breathlessly, and pointed, as if it made sense. "Get down and don't make any noise!"

I dropped flat, poking one eye out at the orange dragon, which had risen to its full height, blocking out the depthless, pearl-gray sky as it visibly scanned the field of stones in which we had hidden. It would see us in seconds. Yenu whispered something, her lips pressed to the stone.

And our rock trembled on its own, shivered like a cup of water, and seemed to collapse or liquefy all at once. I scuttled away from it, dragging Yenu by her coat, as something began to pour out of its throat: sluggish at first, then a fast roaring stream like a breached dam. Flying stones? Each individual mote was dark blue, gleaming inside as if it had swallowed a star, glassy and sapphire-thick. No, insects... *bees*. Blue bees with large, clear wings, their blue bodies striped neatly with black, pouring for no damn good reason I could think of out of the solid rock.

They paid us no regard, but flew and flew and kept flying, a swarm without end, straight upwards in a ragged cloud, and then down towards the struggling mass of dragons still extricating themselves from the earth that crumbled around them and slowed their climb.

For a terrifying minute the air filled with a jet-engine sound, then began to grow hot, even the air behind our rock heating up, somewhere nearby a dragon was getting to flame and gods help us if we were in its path... and then it stuttered to a stop, and there was only the sound of the bees, faint and persistent.

I pushed Yenu flat with my elbow so she wouldn't follow me, and peeked around what remained of the stone. The bees had found their target now and paid me no mind. The orange dragon writhed in silence, flecks and spots of light appearing on the stones as if projected from far away, or like the sun breaking through clouds, so that we could see at irregular intervals the dragon's shadow. Like a play, like a toy was being destroyed instead of a real thing.

But it was real, and the humming bees began to buzz, then roar, an angry snarl moving up and down the scales until it became a scream of rage.

The dragon began to scream too, thumping its body frantically on the ground, crushing them in their thousands, to no avail. The bees were systematically taking it apart—and there was something hideous about the word that had come to mind, *systematic*, yes, because bees were like that, methodical, each a little flying factory with one set of inputs and outputs, and they were tearing into the dragon's oozing wounds and flying away dripping and triumphant with gobbets of flesh the same curious dark blue as Yenu's blood. I glanced back at her briefly; she was staring, transfixed, at the shadows on the stones around us, golden and red, not dark like a real shadow.

"Where is that light coming from?" she whispered.

"Uh," I said, unhelpfully, and turned back. The answer was 'inside the dragon,' the glow bursting through like a different kind of blood and raying out of it, searchlights piercing the sky for nothing, growing brighter by the moment. "I think we'd better get out of here."

"In a second," Yenu whispered.

"Why, exactly?"

"What, you don't think it'll still attack us if it spots us?"

"Yes," I said. "I also think it's about to explode, and we're very much inside the blast radius."

"Just one more second," she repeated, pushing me aside and peeping past the edge of our rock. "Oh. I see. I mean, on the plus side, I can use magic up here, so—"

Later, trying to reconstruct the minute or so that followed that sentence, I could only conclude that the dragon had indeed exploded, and Yenu had managed to put something around us that had deflected the blast; when I could think clearly again as well as see, the horizon was half-filled with a mushroom cloud of dust and bees as high as a skyscraper, and more dragons successfully fleeing the opening in the earth, its edges glittering dangerously, like obsidian.

"They have made a way," the Advisor gasped, rearing back. "Run!"

"No!" Yenu got up and shook her head once, hard, as if to clear it; her nose was bleeding and her coat was visibly smoking. The envoys clustered behind her as if another blast were coming. "We're getting a ride out of here. Prophet, you've *got* to help me share the load on this one, or we're not going to make it."

"What, so you can... fly us into another trap?"

"Can we fucking discuss this later?"

"Just tell me what to do this time."

BUT AS BEFORE, no matter what, the spell did not function between us; it was like a door not just shut but locked, and I felt as if a spark inside me had been snuffed out permanently from trying. The air boiled with shadows and scales and we collapsed at the same moment, gasping at the hot, sulphurous air. The dust below our feet smelled and tasted of salt, coating our dry lips, as if this had once been an ocean, now long dry. A nice thought. Seaside vacation.

"Okay," Yenu croaked, waving the blood-sodden spell card. "One more try. No, you stay down. It's not working." The envoys crowded her, obscuring her face. She waved them away, but gently, with her other hand. "It's okay. It's okay. Plan B. I might not have full control, but *you* guys know where we need to go, right? Right. Back to the ship. Back to the River. So I'll put my foot on the gas, and you steer. Maybe if we split it up, we'll survive this."

"What in the hell are you talking about?" I gasped, staggering up again and looking around at the approaching dragons. "Give me back my sword!"

Instead of replying, she put the card in her pocket and murmured a word of power, a long uninterrupted string of syllables that tumbled out like water.

The closest dragon jerked, twisted as if it had been tased, and then to its obvious confusion found itself being dragged towards us as if on an invisible rope, its horns digging into the ground and kicking up clouds of glassy crystals. It was green-black like a magpie feather, and its huge jaws snapped futilely at us.

The Advisor and I backed up, but Yenu thrust her hand palm-down at the ground and the dragon flopped down as well, visibly straining to open its mouth. Its eyes, bigger than my first car, rolled furiously.

"Get on," Yenu gasped. "Quick."

"Are you *sure* you can control this thing?"

"Dragons can go between places," she wheezed.

"That wasn't an answer!"

I hurried to catch up with her, as the other dragons were clawing and snapping their way towards us, more by the moment. Where had the bees gone? Ah: still picking apart the first dragon. Disgusting.

She said, "That's why they're his kingdom and *in* his kingdom: a liminal space, neither here nor there. Not anywhere. He controls those things that go between."

"So you're just hijacking his ride?"

"I'll give it *back*." She struggled to crawl onto the dragon's immobile but trembling foreleg, and I pushed past her, climbed up onto its shoulder, then hauled her up and pushed her ahead of me between the two rows of ridged, back-swept horns. The scales were hot, several inches thick, and ridged on each sharp edge; I opted to grab a horn instead. The Advisor scrambled up and lifted one wing to allow the envoys to huddle underneath. As we lifted off, for a moment I caught the scent of spring flowers.

"Find them," Yenu whispered over her shoulder to the envoys, wrapping one arm around the dragon's thrumming horn; the animal seemed to vibrate with pent-up rage at our presence, the insult of we three tiny motes of mortal tissue on top of its head. "Find the others. Find the way back to the Violet River."

And then we were rising, beat by beat, above the squirming mass of multicoloured scales and snapping teeth; higher, to see the whole rock-flecked white plain, tiny mountains in the distance lavender and glittering faintly with snow; higher, the air growing thin, and then darkness and warmth under the stained-glass membranes of the thing's wings.

"JESUS CHRIST! YOU almost got us all killed!"

"Can you please stop exaggerating?"

"What part of that was exaggeration?"

The others were staring at us, particularly Sudworth and the Advisor, as we were arguing in English, and my skin crawled at that: I hated being stared at. On the other hand, what *was* I doing? Yenu wouldn't admit she was wrong, and since we had survived, I had no proof as to the exact level of danger our lives had been in.

Still though: I switched to Low Dath, which I felt bad about as it would shut Sudworth out, but the others deserved to hear. "When you split us up to look for the envoys, you already knew we were walking into a trap. Didn't you? You knew the Burning King was there, waiting, ready. Just say yes or no, traitor! You *wanted* us to get caught. You could have stopped us any time, and you didn't."

"Do you think I would let us be trapped down there without a good reason?"

"Yes! And do you know why? Because what you consider a good reason is that you're a fucking—" I hesitated. There was no straight translation for 'control freak' in Dath. "Is never what *anyone else* would consider a good reason."

"I needed information," she said. "No part of a resistance works without information. Otherwise we're just... wandering through the darkness, swinging our fists at nothingness. How can we stay one step ahead of the enemy? *They're* staying several steps ahead of us, and the trap was proof. So is that what you were looking for? Yes. I knew there would be a trap. Yes, I knew where we'd end up. Yes, I knew it was him. *And* I got this on our way out."

She unbuttoned her coat with a flourish, revealing the incredibly dirty brown lining. Everyone stared at it.

"You got... what?" I said.

"For fuck sake," she said, and gestured impatiently at one mark that looked darker than the rest. "This."

We continued to wait.

"When the blade hit the Burning King, it got his blood on it," she said slowly, as if speaking to a child. "That was the purpose of the sigil I drew: I can get information from that. I won't get much detail. It would have been better to capture and interrogate him. But dangerous, too, for us, and the danger would be from both him and from the higher-ups the moment they realized he didn't check in. I think he's one they keep very close tabs on. I'll get a snapshot. But a clear one. And recent."

"And *that* was worth almost killing us?"

She shrugged, her face hard, disdainful. "Everybody here is ready to die to prevent this war."

"And I would too. But that's not what you're trying to do. You're trying to build an army that will cause *far* more damage than just letting the Masters have Their way. An unfathomable amount of damage. But what do you care?"

"What do I care? I care about the people that I'm giving a *chance*. You'd take even that away." She lowered her voice; no one moved closer to listen. They seemed transfixed, each placed in their spot of sun or shadow on the deck. "And you. You *still* haven't picked a side. Instead you're sitting there like you're staging some kind of nonviolent protest, as if doing nothing was the decision you meant to make all along. People are already dying and all you're doing is lying there on the ground, greasing the wheels as They roll over you to get to Their victims. You're *helping* them by doing nothing. You're being dragged along and you think there's something *noble* about it. Fucking get up. Pick a side."

"You're making a hell of a case for it to be yours."

"Am I? Take it out of the equation, then." She fumbled furiously in her coat, came out with a dagger, tossed it at my feet, drew another from somewhere, pointed the blade at me, unsmiling. Ksajakra's jaw dropped.

I almost laughed. Johnny fought dirty, Yenu would fight even dirtier, but even if I had been unarmed, I would still win. The Advisor thought I was so *soft*, so *gentle*; but he had never seen me in my natural element, bathed in the thin, spitting rain of her anger.

I kicked the blade back to her and switched to English. "Fuck you. You're still a spoiled little shit who always wants the camera to be on you so you can look like the hero. I'm not going to be in your show. Your plan is shit. You're going to get all of us killed. *That's* why I'm not helping. It's stopped being ideological now."

"Fine." She picked it up, put it away, then slowly buttoned her coat back up. "Then you're never going home."

"According to you, they'll lock me up the minute I set foot back on Aradec anyway," I said. "So you can't even use that on me now, and it's your fucking fault. Congratulations: perfectly engineered. You finally got what you asked for all those years ago. A pet that can't run away from you."

She erased me with a gesture, and began to head back towards the hold; and I should have let her go, it would have been so easy to let her go, but I reached for her coat. "Give me my sword back," I said quietly. "You've taken enough from me."

"It's not even yours. You stole it. Back at your dungeon." Our faces were inches apart, and something startling, unexpected, swept across hers the way cloud shadows sometimes cross a field. "Whatever he knew, I don't want the spy to know," she said softly and very rapidly in English. "Pick a fight, say we'll settle it below."

I took a deep breath, blew it out hard over her head. God, *why* would I play along? It was that flicker, I knew, even as I asked myself. That brightness that had truly never left her, whatever she was now: that brief flash of my home, souvenir of something I had loved, and the promise of a secret. For me and for no one else. And I had to admit the curiosity was killing me. "I asked you *civilly* to give it back," I said loudly in Low Dath. "Should I ask you again?"

"Did you talk like this at the palace?" she retorted, rising onto the toes of her boots, which brought her head not quite to the bottom of my breastbone. "I won't have you disrespecting me again in front of my people."

"And it won't happen again if we settle this below." I folded my arms. Was that a real hint of fear in her face? "Keep the sword. It can be daggers if you wish."

"Daggers, then."

The trap door leading to the hold had no lock; still, there was a strangely final feeling about the way Yenu thumped the door into place, despite our flimsy acting, and it came with the certainty that no one would follow us down to witness the 'fight.'

There was a sense in the air of a thunderstorm that would be heavy with lightning. *She will kill him*, I think some of them were saying. *He will kill her*, said the others. They looked at both of us—me, six foot five and three hundred and fifty pounds, and her, about the size of a ferret—and said, *We don't know who will kill who*. A sense of urgently looking away from the resolution of the question.

Yenu uncovered something in the ceiling I hadn't seen before, a chunk of crystal or glass faceted like a gem that gave a surprising amount of light. "Can't use those on the River," she said, seeing my face. "It works best with a point source of light. Sun or moon. Part of the reason I parked us here and sent the dragon back onto the River. Blurs our tracks back."

She took off her coat and we sat across from each other; from a cabinet, she removed a thin piece of what looked like slate. I dimly remembered something from my training with the Ssarati: as far as we knew, magic moved better in some interstices than others, and magic had to move to work. Glass, clay, stone were all good. Not metal, but otherwise always better inorganic than organic, except for certain types of shell and horn. And there were other rules, exceptions, but I couldn't remember them now. I watched her resentfully, hating her memory.

"It's no good sending the envoys ahead now," she said.

"All they'll find are locked doors. We need to go for that god, and I need to know what... what the Burning King's master is doing. Wherever he faces, we need to face the other way."

"The Manifestation," I said. "That's who he's working for, isn't it? What's the thing's real name?"

"I don't know. Probably nothing we can say. He called himself Nyarlathotep on Earth once. A joke name, almost an insult. Doesn't mean anything in the language he stole it from and doesn't mean anything anywhere else."

"Names don't have to mean anything," I protested.

"They do if you give them to yourself," she said. Moving quickly, she sliced out the lining of her coat, laid it on the sigil-marked slate tile, and held her hands over it. "Watch out," she said. "Could be proximity effects."

"Watch out for wh—?"

My vision filled with sparkles from corner to corner, bordered with black, so that Yenu's scarred, serious face swam behind it like a TV show seen through static. She kept talking, though I could only hear an occasional word; my ears had filled with static too, buzzing so hard they itched. I imagined magic crashing around the enclosed space, manipulating things it found like an unfamiliar dashboard, pressing accidentally on the little bones of the ear while it was trying to turn on the wipers or cruise control.

The smudged cloth writhed and pulsated on the slate as if it were trying to escape her, spitting sparks that smouldered out on the wood around it. Occasionally my hands moved on their own. I let them; if she didn't like it, she'd say something. I felt oddly off-balance, and that was her doing too. We had started off with a real fight, and then it had turned fake, and now I was the only keeper, aside from her, of whatever the Burning King knew. She clearly didn't think I was the spy. Was it just a test, then? The way they did it in movies, I thought suddenly. They give fake information about serial killers to the newspapers, and then all the weirdos out there who call in to confess say they did what was in the news, not what was really done.

"Do you *really* think we can break a god out of prison?" I said. "And that he'll just... end the war? Just like that?"

"No, of course not. He's the start, not the end, of the army of the Quevereld. We just need to kick-start it, because we're the only ones who can."

"We can't at this rate," I said. "They're onto us. Whether thanks to a spy or just guessing... They'll *know* exactly where you're going. They'll get there first, and that'll be a trap you can't just fly out of. We can't make this army of yours. We just can't. This isn't going to be like..." I shut my eyes, trying to remember. A cartoon? Something. "...Like lighting the beacons and waiting for help. No one's there to see the beacons any more except the enemy. The last big war took care of that."

"There are survivors," she said. "Veterans. More than you think. And prisons scattered all over the universe. The envoys can find them when the time comes."

"I know. I do know that. I'm saying there aren't *enough*."

"The Ancient Ones can't be everywhere at once," she said doggedly. "And They're not." The cloth twitched, twisted into the air, a snake for a moment, startlingly real, then slumped down again. Static fuzzed in my eyes and I blinked it furiously away.

"Everything you're saying applies to us too," I said. "We can't be everywhere at once either. The envoys are better, but there aren't an infinite number of them. Whatever you're doing is starting to look less desperate and more totally fucking insane. Okay? Can we agree on that?"

"Nope."

"You're like a drunk driver at this point," I hissed. "They're going to take away your keys. You cannot keep this up. You've killed so many people. Just stop, okay?"

"Stop and what?" She looked up, her face very still, cold; only her eyes burned with hatred and disgust, as if I were some piece of filth she had found in her food. "And what? Give up? Give up on all Their future victims? The ones They're killing right now? Wait to be captured, tortured, and killed?"

"They..." No. *They would do the first two things to you*, I had nearly said; *They won't do the last. Because they want you, and they want you alive.* We keep saying you're 'like' a weapon, but you *are* one. It is *what you are*: the weapon that ends the world.

What wouldn't They do to get one of those weapons once it had been discovered? Especially if it had come about by fluke, and was the only one that had ever existed? What if that weapon had no plans and no blueprints, and would only ever exist once?

"No," she said when it was clear I would say nothing more. "No. Fuck surrender, and fuck you. I'm going down fighting. I'll fight with whatever I have. I was hoping that would be an army. Maybe it will just be words, in the end. I don't care. And you don't have to come."

"We have no way of going home unless you take us home."

"I don't have a home. Yours is overrun by monsters. Aradec is part of the war effort, remember? Is that where you want to go back to?"

"Where I *want* to go back to was destroyed by a fucking maniac with a black hole."

"Better than having it conquered by Them," she said implacably. "Is that what you wanted? For Them to come into the world They had resurfaced to look like one of Theirs, and enslave your parents, and rape your sister and your bro—"

For once she had not been expecting the punch, so it hit fair and true; the back of her head bounced off the wood behind her and she slumped sideways. I rubbed my fist, panting, half-daring her to get up; my vision was back, and it was red around the edges with rage. I settled back onto my knees and folded my hands in my lap.

But she did sit up, nose and mouth bleeding, and spat into the corner, and without looking at me held her hands over the slate again. The cloth rose, fell, sank into the chalked sigil as if it were a carving, each curlicue and line and triangle visible below the dirtied weave. At last, it simply fell apart, into a little heap of dust.

Footsteps sounded on the ladder. "Are you getting what you need?" Sudworth said, peering through the trap into the little octagon of light from the deck crystal. "I can try a transfer, if you..."

Yenu waved her away. "It's fine."

"Are you sure? Maybe I'll just—"

"Go back above. Now."

Sudworth paused, holding the door handle; her gaze went from Yenu's face to mine, back. There was no blood on my hand, the just-healed scars had not even split open, but Yenu's blood-smeared face looked as if she had dipped it in ink. Sudworth backed away.

Yenu waited till the door was shut and looked impassively at me.

I said quietly, "I thought you were dead. I was *glad* you were dead, if I thought about it at all. Was that repayment—I mean redemption—for you having destroyed Earth? Far from it. You killed everyone I loved. That you killed everyone you loved too didn't make up for it at all. If you died now, if I *killed* you now, you would still not be redeemed. Or forgiven. Not by me. But because you can't unhappen it, there's nothing we can do. So I am going to wait until the hatred fades again. But you should know it's there. Always. There's nothing else inside me now but that."

She watched me for a long time, then finally nodded. "Like you say," she said muzzily. "What happened can't unhappen. And for me... what's made cannot be un-made. They'll spend forever trying to recreate it... me. The weapon. Unless we stop Them. We can't bring the Earth back, but we can *try* to prevent a thousand other Earths from happening. Help me," she said, meeting my gaze steadily. "Help me *try*."

I rubbed my knuckles again. Shame was catching up to me, the sensation like a slow rising tide of cold water soaking into my clothes. I had never hit her before in my life. I had wanted to a thousand times and still hadn't. And now I had, and it hadn't solved anything. I couldn't even answer her plea with a yes or a no.

I sighed. My head ached. "Do you think Sudworth is the spy?"

"I still think it could be anybody."

"Anybody but me."

"Yes."

"And why not me?"

"I don't know," she said. "I hope it doesn't get us killed." She wadded up the cloth and used it to scrub away the sigil on the slate, then replaced the tile in its storage slot and put the cloth in her pocket, slow and methodical. "Okay," she said, holding her shirtsleeve to her still-bleeding nose. "We're going to have to rehearse this."

"Rehearse what?"

"What we tell the others. Versus what's real."

CHAPTER TWELVE

WE HAD ZIGGED to test our pursuit; now we were zagging again, and the anxiety was palpable. Or mine was, anyway. First off, I couldn't think of why the Ancient Ones would not have simply built the prison in the middle of space, with nothing that involved mass or gravity or water or (you had to say it) any of that mortal stuff.

Instead, according to Yenu, They had chosen this world: admittedly without air we could breathe, though she'd packed something like spacesuits in the hold for just such an eventuality. We had all declined the suits, though, keeping only the light, strange helmets. "This *is* glass, isn't it?" Itzlek murmured doubtfully, scratching it with a fingernail. "Just glass?"

"Why would I trust my brain to ordinary glass?" Yenu had replied reasonably, although as often happened, that wasn't really the answer to the question she'd been asked.

The light here made my exposed skin prickle. It wasn't painful exactly, but certainly perceptible enough to make me wonder whether I had just increased my risk of skin cancer some huge amount by not covering my hands and the modest triangle of exposed skin at the top of my shirt. But if no one else was wearing Yenu's spacesuits, I wouldn't either.

Still, as we climbed down from the ship, I felt a moment of optimism: the ship was hidden in the thick jungle around us, and nothing seemed to be attacking. We were safe.

The landscape corrected me a second later, sending a small rock hurtling up with my first step onto the ground that, despite my best dodge, clipped me on the underside of my helmet so hard it left a quarter-sized spiderweb of cracks. I touched the spot cautiously, trying to see if I was leaking the good air generated inside it by Yenu's highly suspicious magical technology; if it exited faster than it could be replenished, I'd suffocate. But it didn't seem to have gone all the way through the not-glass. And what the hell, I thought belatedly as the others came down, had *caused* that?

Two steps away from the ship, Itzlek was caught in what appeared to be a high-gravity spot and screamed as he was flattened to the ground; Ksajakra and I dragged him out of it and gave it a wide berth as we went on, Itzlek nursing his bruised ribs and gasping for breath.

It became slow and cautious going. The land was tortured, a crowded tangle of pale stone spires mobbed by shrubs, vines, and trees of various sizes, coloured in a range of blues and purples. The dull orange sky was crowded with thousands of stars in paler yellow, blocked here and there by hovering stones that might have weighed a couple of tons each. There was no trail; we squeezed between the stones where we could, climbed them where we could not, following Yenu's shouted directions.

"Why didn't you invent radios for these things?" I complained.

"You, shut up. You're already wearing a technomagical impossibility over your head."

As we climbed and swore and slid and flailed, I recognized nothing, but couldn't stop thinking about what Sudworth had said about colonization. Had humans, or other races, founded a colony on purpose here, or accidentally slipped through and found themselves part of a colony? Had anyone planned it like real colonizers did—taking animals and plants with them? Or if you did a spell that went wrong and woke up, shocked, in a world where you could live, did you just work with whatever had evolved there in the first place? Some of the fruits and vegetables on Aradec had looked temptingly close to recognizable.

"This way!"

"We can't *fit* that way, Yenu," Ksajakra shouted back.

"Are you going to argue with the map?"

"...No."

As we had sailed here, Yenu had, to everyone's fascination except mine, cooked up what looked for all the world like a stone-age GPS unit; Rhakun had been tasked with hammering a spare canteen into a sheet of copper which she framed in pieces of spare wood and enclosed in a small metal cage. It had taken days, none of her helpers knew what their individual tasks would involve, and I had enjoyed watching them trying to puzzle it out.

The wayfinding device produced small dark patterns on the copper that flickered in and out of visibility and gave me a headache to look at; Yenu wore it on a leather neckstrap, like a tourist with a heavy camera, and refused to let anyone touch it.

There weren't many people to spare now, and the ship needed guarding. After Ksajakra and Yenu had asked for volunteers and come up empty, Ksajakra had simply told Itzlek, Saloc, and Rhakun to come along; and Sudworth had insisted on coming—to make up for, as she said, my uselessness. "You can be the muscle," she'd said airily.

I felt more like a pack mule. We carried packs with food, water, and weapons; wisely, Ksajakra had insisted we split everything as evenly as possible, so we wouldn't be too screwed if one person lost their pack or... well, best not to think about it.

Scrambling through the stone was exhausting work, and our labours attracted swarms of pea-sized, bright-red bugs that sipped the sweat off our skin and crawled up our sleeves and down the tops of our boots, where they pressed their revoltingly soft bodies against us. They particularly plagued the Advisor, whose fur and feathers shuddered constantly as he walked, his body shaking them off automatically.

"Rest break," Ksajakra gasped after what felt like two or three interminable hours. "Everyone stop. Stop, or our bodies will stop themselves."

"But we're close," Yenu wheezed, somewhat hilariously, as she looked closest to the verge of collapse. "The map says—"

"You are responsible for the stupid parts of this plan, and I am responsible for the parts of this plan that will keep us alive. This falls under my jurisdiction. Rest or I'll tie you to one of these rocks," he snapped.

We crowded into a relatively flat spot beneath one of the huge trees, where the roots had broken up the stone enough that we could at least sit in a group and in stable gravity, albeit uncomfortably. The constant shifts in gravity were far more exhausting than I would have guessed from how relatively subtle they were; things were constantly flying up at our helmets, or flattening us into the shrubbery or stones; we had even encountered a few areas of zero gravity, and hung mid-air in a panic, flailing our arms and getting little movement, until the Advisor, flapping nearly to the point of exhaustion, had been able to tow us out. My imagination kept throwing up terrible visions of taking a wrong step into one of the high-gravity spots and just having both my legs break, shoved up into my pelvis somehow, though even before we sensed them with our conscious minds, everyone's bodies seemed to automatically throw us down to take the impact horizontally instead of vertically, even Rhakun, who technically had cartilage that would bend rather than bones that would break.

While we juggled our helmets, drank water, and dried our faces and necks, the biting bugs backed away. For a moment there was only the sound of distant birdcalls (I hoped they were birds) and our panting breath, and I sincerely envied those guarding and repairing the ship, even if it was hard and boring work and some of it would have to wait for Yenu's return. I still didn't understand how precisely it was and wasn't a real boat, how it was and wasn't held together by Yenu's magic, and how the ways in which it was currently damaged or weakened would not be apparent right away, which made them all the more dangerous. Unless every fault could be searched out and repaired, something might fail catastrophically later on, at the slightest stress. And it was all we had; every step of the plan hinged on us having a getaway ride.

"This isn't much of a jail." Sudworth gulped from her canteen and quickly replaced her helmet, streaked and spattered with the blue sap of the trees. "People can just walk right in."

"You call this walking right in?" I protested.

"I'm seventy-one and this place hasn't managed to kill me yet." She sniffed. "Not even trying, if you ask me."

"Look, don't tempt it." I glanced at the branches closest to our heads, smooth-barked, the grayed blue of the bark scored with thousands of tiny scratches. Even as I watched, what resembled a long, hairy centipede, as thick as my forearm, shuffled rapidly along the branch, spotted us, and contorted itself trying to double back and head towards the trunk. "Why's it always gotta be centipedes?"

"What?"

"Nothing." I scratched the back of my neck; my coat was smotheringly hot, but it protected me enough from the bugs that I didn't want to take it off.

"The elder is right, though," said the Advisor in Low Dath, inclining his head fractionally towards her. "I find it hard to believe that any prisoner, either of the Masters or the Quevereld, might be imprisoned *here*."

"It might be a better prison than it looks," Yenu said. "This side of the universe isn't even populated. By mortal things, I mean. And it's under a cloaking ward. It must be a big one. Miles wide. No one else could have found this but me."

"But why would anyone bother to find it?" he persisted. "Supposing a being of such power were in a prison. Even one designed by the other side to secure such a prisoner. After so long, surely they would have determined a way to escape? They were considered gods, after all."

"Could be," she conceded, then tapped her wayfinding device. "But this spell's showing that there's something still here. Something powerful. Like you say. A being of power."

"Why do you keep saying 'either side'?" I said, turning to the Advisor. "I've never heard that before. Why would one of the *Masters* be in prison after the war? They won."

"That's what They want people to think," Itzlek blurted fervently. "Because They lie, and the Quevereld cannot lie."

The Advisor looked at him without expression. "The war was like any war. A succession of many battles. It may be that there were individual battles where the Quevereld won, and put away their prisoners of war in fortified places."

"That's not what happened," Ksajakra said. The others nodded, light glancing in sheets off their helmets. "Yenu researched it. The truth."

Yenu shrugged. "What I read was that the Ancient Ones and the Elder Gods had had several skirmishes, with no decisive winner. Then, when They embarked on Their last period of conquest and invasion, the Elder Gods gathered a real army, and organized it, with battalions and generals and weapons and forts, and went to put an end to Them for the last time. It had to be the last, because they realized They wouldn't stop. But the two greatest Elder Gods were sent false messages each purporting to be from the other, saying they had gone to the other side, and because it was war, and because neither of them believed each other, they fought one another. While they were fighting, the rest of the war fell to chaos; and the Ancient Ones swept in, ensorcelled and imprisoned the generals and the gods, and killed the rest."

"Killed them?" Itzlek tapped his wrists together reflexively, a childhood sign of protection I had seen in Aradec.

"I don't know." Yenu closed her eyes and leaned back against the tree. "It's hard to kill a Quevereld. Maybe impossible. Even for Them. To kill them in the sense that *we* would say kill. And vice versa. Beings of lesser power could be destroyed in a way that they could not regenerate, but for the two greatest participants, maybe not. So they were put away. Asleep. Restrained. Maybe dreaming. Maybe going mad. Who knows? It was a long time ago. Maybe they won't even be useful now if we find them. But it's still our best bet. Trust me."

Itzlek and Ksajakra exchanged a look of terror— as much at her as at what she'd said, I thought—and Ksajakra met my eyes.

It is all as you said, his gaze said.

I know, I tried to say back.

Things rustled and slithered in the undergrowth; as night fell, I imagined, we would see the glint of eyes in the vegetation, reflecting the strangeness of our lanterns and torches. My limbs were leaden with exhaustion and hunger already, even though we had eaten before we set out. We were armed with weapons and magic, but anything here would only look at us and see easy calories on the march. Hardly a formidable rescue party.

"Let's go," Yenu said impatiently, struggling to her feet and brushing leaves from her clothes. "Do you want to be out here when it's dark?"

"Will we reach the prison before dark?" I said bluntly.

"...Let's just go."

NIGHT DID FALL as we walked, the orange sky darkening until it was a red so pure it looked like dried blood, the stars standing out in pinpricks around the pink disc of the sun till it slid below the horizon. A light rain began to fall, and Ksajakra lifted his helmet to taste it from his hand, then insisted we try to refill our canteens. We pressed them to the stones and stood in the silence and the darkness, and the patter of the rain. The Advisor pressed close to me, absently wiping his helmet with the velvety backs of his forepaws.

"The story *I* was told was not one of treachery and trickery," he said quietly, gesturing for me to give him another canteen. I handed him mine, half-full, and got an empty one out of my pack to fill. "The Masters wished to keep peace in the universes in which the war was being waged. Because the Quevereld were about to embark on their own campaign of empire. And so to avoid wars in the future, which would take many lives, the Masters decided to put an end to the Quevereld's ambitions in the only way possible: by imprisoning them."

"Advisor," I said, "at this point in time, knowing what you know of the Masters, does this act of apparent altruism make sense to you as something They would do?"

"Yes... I... Maybe the... the lesser beings of the Masters, Their thralls and servants, Their minions have been... more or less considerate of the lives in their care," he said diplomatically. "But the Great Old Ones, the Masters Themselves, the all-powerful, the immortal, the incomprehensible... They treasure life. They do not wish to see it wasted. They would have wanted to stop the war, not let it continue forever. And they knew the Elder Gods would not stop."

"That's what the Elder Gods said about the Masters, too."

"The truth lies only with the original participants," Yenu said behind me, so close I jumped; I looked down into her sweat-soaked, luminous face, lit by the crawling glyphs of her wayfinding device. "But that should mean, Advisor, that quite soon you can ask one yourself."

He watched her go with something like horror.

"She's got very good hearing," I said.

"The other thing that concerns me—" he began, and glanced away as Ksajakra came around the far side of the stone and jerked his chin at us to get going again. But I knew what the Advisor had been about to say. It was always the same thing, when she was around.

AFTER ANOTHER FEW hours, and a pause to bandage up Sudworth and Itzlek after they were struck by rising rocks, the air began to warm perceptibly and the rain became a thick fog, smothering us as we struggled through the rocks towards what was undeniably becoming a solid and apparently inexplicable wall of heat. The vegetation grew hunched and faded as we approached, and the stone spires and spikes thinned out bit by bit until we were moving at last over ground nearly bare except for fallen leaves, swimming wearily as if through hot water.

"If it gets any hotter, this is where we stop," Ksajakra panted, draining his canteen and reaching into his pack for a full one, then pausing. Slowly and deliberately, he put the emptied canteen on the ground next to Yenu's boot. "We will turn back. Bring others to find and carry water. Perhaps if we repeatedly soak our clothing, we can go on a little further. But much worse and none of us will be able to go on. What does your spell tell you? Can we go around? Is there a way away from the heat?"

She didn't even look at the device, turned 'screen' side inwards against her opened coat, flat against her heaving chest. "There is something ahead," she murmured. "The heat... would turn back almost any living thing... I mean any living thing as weak as us..."

"Someone give her some water," I said, and took off my coat and pack. Boots too? No, might regret it. The tree we were leaning on leaned too, and I had climbed about ten paces up it before anyone realized what I was doing. The Advisor cried out, but the others must have restrained him from trying to fly or climb up to get me.

The first branches were just over my head; I reached, grabbed, hauled myself up, the air becoming cooler as I climbed. I had expected the hot air to rise, and the unexpected coolness was a relief. Sap oozed from broken branches as I snarled and crawled to the last thick branch, then parted the star-shaped leaves that still hid the view.

Nothing but heat shimmer at first, and the thinning ocean of trees, a surprisingly short expanse—we were nearly at the edge of the forest, beyond it a small curving plain of dark soil and rounded stones—and beyond that...

* * *

"So we *are* in the right place." Yenu stuffed her gadget back into her pack and strapped it shut.

"Did you miss the part where I said the prison was a solid brick in the middle of a moat full of giant burning fish?" I said.

"Amazing we were able to land the ship this close. We might have been walking for weeks if I had miscalculated," she added to Sudworth, who huffed and said nothing.

I put my coat and pack back on and drained my canteen, a sad few mouthfuls of hot water that tasted sweeter than honey. Every time I blinked I saw the flat oval of the moat again, burned onto my retinas in that first glimpse, until I had realized I could look at it better through a leaf, which cut its startling, malevolent light. It was like trying to look at a solar eclipse.

A mile-wide moat and at its centre, a tall terracotta-red building with no windows or doors, surrounded by the things, the fish, gold and white and red and amber, swimming slowly in an endless circle, packed fin-to-fin and each the size of a house, their fins poking up through a thin, syrupy layer of red-hot lava. We would never approach it; we couldn't even look at it. We would be killed by the heat if we moved any closer.

"Temporary retreat," Yenu said, standing shakily. "We need to cool down enough to figure out how we're going to get in there."

"We," I repeated before I could stop myself.

She rolled her eyes. "Sudworth, can I have some paper? Thanks." She scribbled as we pushed our way back the way we came, stumbling occasionally, until the canopy thinned and the temperature became manageable again; and then she sat on the ground, hunched over a lantern, while the rest of us gasped like landed fish and shed our outer layers. The Advisor spread his wings as best he could and slowly fanned them out, flapping them to shed the heat.

Sudworth's face was inscrutable in the dappled lanternlight. "No guards at the jail," she murmured. "You, 'Prophet.' I want to see it myself. You obviously don't know what to look for. Help me up."

"But—"

"Come on, you already did it once."

The others gave us no more than a cursory glance, but the Advisor padded after me as I got up and ushered Sudworth to the base of a likely-looking tree. She stopped and glared at him, but when this had no obvious effect, turned back to me and said "Well?"

I sighed. "I'll go first."

This tree was a slightly easier climb, though it took longer as I had to set my grip, turn, pull Sudworth up or let her haul on my arm or leg, and then climb again. At the top, I picked a leaf and handed it to her, then picked one for myself, so we could look at the moat. "Very romantic," I said.

"Atom bombs, right?" she whispered, a non sequitur so complete and perfect in its unexpectedness that for a moment I couldn't even think of a reply.

Before I could reply, she went on in a hurried whisper, "Look, Trinity. Right? None of my business, scientifically I mean, I was an archaeologist by training. I didn't know how they made the bomb and I didn't think to ask. It weren't till the Cold War started getting het up and everyone was like 'Ooh, let's dig a shelter in the back garden' that I got curious.

"How did they make such a thing? Now, the way you engineer any normal weapon, you come up with the idea, then a sketch, then maybe a model in clay or wood, and then a working version, and then if you want to make it bigger, you scale up, right? But Trinity, the first nuke, I couldn't see how they went from the idea to a small version then the big version, the one they set off in the desert. Wouldn't a small version have blown up the scientists and their lab? Could you even *make* a tiny little one?

"Let me tell you, sonny, the idea that they had gone straight from the sketch to the city-flattening version with nothing in between *did not even occur to me*. They couldn't test it before they used it. They just used it. Do you understand what I am talking about now?"

"Not even remotely."

She threw her hands to the sky with exasperation, and I quickly put a hand on her back to steady her. "There are spells you can't test before you cast them," she snapped. "There's no little version, there's no version with a safety catch or a limiter, there's no version that stays under control and doesn't start some kind of chain reaction. Or worse yet, people think there is, and later they find out there ain't.

"Like what Chambers did to the Earth, when she

told me about the spell, how she miscalculated. Neohexonomics is the development of all-new spells. *Not* tweaking an existing one, or combining two known ones, anything like that. It's practically unknown as a field because it *normally* results in the death of the person casting the untested spell. Plus sometimes their planet, solar system, galaxy, and/or universe. All right?

"But *Chambers can do it*. She's doing it right now as we speak, right at the foot of this tree, and from what she tells me, she's been doing it for years: big spells, small spells, whatever. My God, when she said that, I felt my blood run cold. And that makes her valuable to the Ancient Ones, and it also makes her perhaps the most dangerous valuable thing I can think of. She's like an atom bomb that can build more atom bombs. She is the world-destroyer, and she knows how to destroy worlds."

I lowered my leaf; my arm was cramping. I looked off in the other direction, over the stones and the trees and the indigo sky with its dark streak of dried blood along the horizon. "That's always been true," I said. "Why are you saying it now?"

"Because we're *here*. How in the hell did They *let* us get here? Why haven't They picked her back up? They want her with the heat of a thousand suns. Not just for Their use, but also to take her away from the Elder Gods, from humanity, from anyone else that might use her. They were the ones who made her a bomb that can make bombs, and now They have misplaced Their bomb, and you're telling me They aren't desperate to get it back? That They don't just *want* us to think They've misplaced it? Why would They let us get *so close* to breaking out a god?"

I swallowed; my throat clicked. Should I tell her Yenu's theory about the spy? Maybe Sudworth knew already. "They can't be everywhere at once," I said, just as I had before. "Maybe They really don't know she's alive, and... and pinballing around the universe trying to drum up an army."

"Bull-fucking-shit," she said. "And you remember I said that. When They come."

"You think she's... colluding with Them? That she'll let Them just pick her up, like you said?"

"I don't know what I think," she said grimly. "But none of us knows what she's up to. None. It'll be like those last minutes on Earth, kid. She'll fake us out and may God help us all."

"Dr. Sudworth," I said, turning back to her. Even out of the corner of my eye, the distant radiance of the prison burned my gaze. "Why did you come with us? Why didn't you go home?"

She breathed steadily for a moment, rolling the stem of the leaf between her fingers. "Look," she said. "I know what you want. You want revenge. You want to kill her, this impostor. And at the same time, you want to end this war. It's scribbled all over your face. I don't even have to listen to you arguing philosophy with your bodyguard or the other fellow down there. I can *see* it. Now listen to me closely: *you cannot do both*. You have to pick one."

My heart began to hammer again, though it had finally begun to slow after the climb. *That's not true*, I wanted to tell her. But she was right. I could feel the blood pound in my wrists against the branch we balanced on. "Answer the question."

"You can't do both," she said again. "You have to pick one. Do you understand? Tell me you understand."

"I understand."

"Good," she said. "Then you understand that whatever you pick, I am picking the other one."

Silence fell between us. Of course. I studied her hard, pale face, utterly resolute in the dim light, without a trace of the hatred I knew showed on mine. That was why she'd come with us. The moment Sudworth had seen Yenu and me together, she had known that she wanted these two things; known, too, that she couldn't have both, because to succeed at one precluded succeeding at the other.

But *together*, we might have a chance to do both. If we divided them up. I didn't know until she spoke which one I wanted more, but now I knew the answer was *both*.

"What should we do?" I said.

"Do what she says for now. Watch her. Wait for a chance." She threw her leaf, putting a full stop on the order. "Let's climb back down. And get some control over your face."

"Yes'm."

*   *   *

AT THE EDGE of the heat zone, Yenu played nervously with a piece of thick paper for a long time, before finally pressing it carefully onto the screen of her wayfinding device, tucking in the edges like a painting into a frame. Behind us, the sounds of the others cursing and chopping and squeezing through the underbrush back to the ship faded away.

I figured it out, she'd said when Sudworth and I climbed down. *It's a matter of movement, that's all. That's how we'll cross.*

Moving what?

Now she looked up at me, sweat beading on her forehead. Next to her, Sudworth and Ksajakra played uneasily with their weapons.

Just the heat, she'd said. *Nothing else. But it has to go* somewhere.

She hadn't added: *I can't manage more than that, and neither can the two of you.* But we had known. The others could not be protected under the spell, and had to get out of the blast zone, so she'd simply sent them back to the ship. I wished I was back there now, eating a piece of dried fish.

"So if your spell fails…" I said slowly.

"It'll be fine. I'm not trying to move the lava in the moat, Jesus Christ, that's millions of tons of stone, I'd need some kind of enormous boost, there are only a few artifacts in existence that could store that much raw magic. We're just… moving some of its energy somewhere else. I mean, *energy* you can move. It doesn't weigh anything, it wants to move anyway, you can feel for yourself how hot the air is. I just need to, you know. Keep it moving faster than the lava can generate it."

"It'll be fine," Ksajakra repeated, sounded a little strangled.

She lifted the device on its strap and put both her thumbs carefully on the sigil, then put her helmet close to it, whispering.

Neohexonomics. No one should have been able to come here and do this. Remember that. Only her.

The temperature began to drop at once, a rush of dry, lukewarm air blowing away the stifling heat. Around us, the plants began to crisp and curl, some even seeming to cry out, whistling as air escaped from hollow vines and broken branches. Yenu reeled, then steadied herself. "Now."

We crept leerily through the tunnel of cooler air. Around us the stones and sand began to tumble away, like the panicked flutter of pigeons. I found it oddly satisfying to watch, as some indication, if not an exact demarcation, of where our safe zone ended and the deathly heat resumed.

But the spell was working. Undeniably, and at who knew what cost, but it was working. At the edge of the moat we stopped, shading our eyes as best we could against the painful red light. This close, the fish were more frightening to look at: packed in tight as frogspawn, barely able to move but swimming anyway, their long serrated tails clacking against the armour of each neighbouring fish, like gnashing bread knives.

There was no lava at all, I realized; like the dragons

in the kingdom of the Burning King, they were not swimming in anything but each other, not floating on anything but each other, and all the heat emanated from inside of them so that they were red-hot and even white-hot at the tips of their spiny, glasslike fins, behind their large staring eyes that never moved and so seemed to see nothing but the fish ahead. Worst of all, there was a constant low noise—a clacking and rumbling, like stones falling down a mountain—of their scales rubbing against one another.

There was a drop of four or five feet from the ground to the backs of the fish, and about two hundred paces of fish lay before the doorless, windowless building. I looked questioningly at Yenu.

She murmured something, and around us rose a soft roar, building louder, the sound of wind carrying not merely danger but everything in the area, the sound of a tornado. And ahead of us, in a path just a few feet wide, the fish paused, writhed as if in agony, aligned themselves head-to-tail, damming the others who thrashed furiously against their sides, scissoring their mouths to chew a path through, to keep swimming.

The 'dam' faded to a stony gray as the path of fish froze in place, only their eyes rolling around to stare at us, quite normal fish eyes (I thought, aware that it sounded slightly crazed), an iridescent grayish-green with a round black pupil, in fact perfectly normal, like the daggermouth you could hook from Lake Daboloc next to the palace walls.

"Go," Yenu said faintly, "quick."

Sudworth shot her a look of worry that verged on pure terror; if Yenu passed out from the effort midway across, would the spell keep running? I did not think so. And I knew that Sudworth couldn't suddenly take it over. We could only hope that Yenu would realize she was fading in time, and grab at Sudworth to share the load, keep it going.

Still no one moved. In my head I seemed to see a timer ticking down, the second hand moving fast, Yenu's will and spell against all the laws of thermodynamics and the magic of the fish.

"I'll go first," I sighed. "I'm the heaviest. If they're going to move, they'll move under me."

Again, no one moved. I sat gingerly on the dirt lip and lowered myself down. It was hotter down here; not killing hot, but enough to make me gasp for air as I stepped tentatively onto the backs of the cold-immobilized fish. The heat shot through the soles of my boots as I walked along one flank, the next, this fish fin-up, edges as sharp as obsidian, the next on its side. That fish was too round to balance on, so I dropped to hands and knees and carefully shuffled along, distinctly hearing my coat catch and rip somewhere, audible even over the champing jaws of the fish a few feet away from my trembling hands. Their teeth were triangular, like a piranha's.

Were the others coming? I didn't dare look back. Pretty funny if I had volunteered to go first and they had just walked away. Gone back to the ship. I mean fair enough. Pretty elaborate ruse just to get rid of one person, but all right. Okay. A *little* insulted.

I couldn't laugh or I'd fall off the narrow path. Just walk and crawl, crawl and walk, don't look back. My clothes were drenched in sweat, heavy and sodden. *And just this, only this, to guard a god, supposedly. A sleeping, defeated god, long ago wounded and knocked out. All right. So she says. So she claims. And we none of us can refute her. Remember that, too. What if she's spent all this time trying to get us all to trust her, only so she could do something here that we'd never see coming? She always plays a long con. I know that. And Sudworth said so. She said it would be here. Here. The entire goal of the resistance, right here.*

Stop it. Keep moving.

I was light-headed and gagging by the time I reached the building, and instinctively put my palm flat on the hot reddish stone to steady myself, feeling near-invisible carving on it, words or sigils or both. There was no door here, no entrance of any kind, just as I had seen from the tree; I would have to stand on the increasingly agitated fish until we figured out how to get in or they threw us off. *Not* a very nice death. I giggled, unable to help it, and steadied myself again.

Yenu caught up several minutes later, clinging to Ksajakra's arm, and Sudworth last, swearing fervently and loudly, and bleeding from her hands and forearms where she must have slipped against a fin. Their faces were expressionless orbs inside the helmets, lit all in red and gold from the fish, light bouncing off the gleaming scales, polished from who knew how long—millions of years, maybe—of friction. The faces of the damned, I thought. From old movies. No face at all. Just a shape.

"There's no doors!" I said over the roar and the chew.

"There is a door," Yenu said. "It's just flush to the stone."

"But..." I stared up at the building again, then managed to catch myself just in time as the fish squirmed under me and nearly pitched me off. Heart pounding, I widened my stance and kept staring at the stone. No lines, no shadows. I remembered seeing a wall like this a long time ago, a lifetime ago, covered in mosaic tiles, and the design that had somehow jumped out at me and only me. This time there was nothing. The carvings were nearly invisible, the relief no higher than a dime. In the hot, uncertain light, they seemed to shift as if evading the eyes of a reader.

"Speak, friend, and enter," she said.

"Oh, fuck off."

She ignored me. "One of you boost me up. I need to reach the keyhole."

"Lift you *up*, you cannot be serious. We'll both fall," Ksajakra protested.

"Well, I can't fly. Figure something out," she said shortly.

No time to argue. I nodded to him, and carefully, by inches, we levered her up until she was standing very unevenly on our shoulders; I closed my hand around one booted ankle and put the other on the wall to steady myself again. The dam beneath our feet was trembling and rocking now. Some of the fish had been eaten entirely away behind us, and from the rumble I thought the flow was moving again. How would we get back? Was that the crux of her con? The return journey? No, don't think about it, not now. The stone scalded my palm but I was grateful for it, for the grit and heat that kept me attached to the moment.

"What's she doing?" Ksajakra said through gritted teeth.

"I'm not going to look," I said. "There's no way a prison built by the Ancient Ones would—"

And sound and heat vanished in a soft, petal-like bloom of cold, damp air.

CHAPTER THIRTEEN

THEY DON'T CARVE portraits of Themselves into mountains. Mortals do, sometimes. There are worlds where that's a commonplace practice: Earth, for example. But They don't. As discussed, there are very few portraits of Them. They like to put Their marks on the living who can suffer, not on the dead or anything that cannot.

All this to say: I was pretty sure we were looking at one now.

Anyone else would have called it a mountain. From most angles I suspected it would be. But from where we had come in, it gave me the impression of being a *thing*, something made. Maybe that was just the years spent at the palace, where nothing happened by accident. I knew, in my bones, that the shape of the mountain had not been caused by mere millennia of rain and wind, sand and gravity. It was a face, and not one you wanted to linger on.

Ksajakra had flung his arm across his helmet and was breathing heavily. "That," he managed. "I saw..."

"Bigger on the inside," Sudworth remarked laconically. "Huh. This don't seem so bad to be locked up in."

Yenu peeled the paper from the screen of her wayfinding device and activated it. "Jak, don't look," she said without looking up; her voice was thin and strained. "It's bad for you. The rest of us are a little more used to it, I think... It should be this way."

"How did...? Why would you...?" He slowly lowered his arm and looked around: a dark blue sky behind the gray mountain, squat hexagonal blocks of some shiny dark stone arranged around it, at their feet a forest of some graceful, silvery-leafed tree rustling softly and constantly despite a definite lack of wind. "Where are we?"

"In the jail."

"But..."

"It's in a different dimension," she clarified, moving her fingertip across the copper screen.

He stared at her expectantly. The word *dimension* translated straight across in Low Dath, which was handy, but I got the impression that there was supposed to have been a lecture about magical transportation before any of the rebels had even boarded the ship, and that had gotten skipped.

"Come on," she said, and we headed towards the mountain and its screen of gleaming columns. "Universes have a lot of dimensions. The vast, vast majority of them don't have anything inside them, not even stars. They all fit neatly together, though. I mean they touch, but they don't extrude into one another. What separates them is..." She hesitated, perhaps searching for more words in Dath she hadn't had to use yet. "Well, nothing."

"What? So they are all... one?" Ksajakra said.

"No, no. They're *extremely* separate. In fact, without magic you can't even cross between the dimensions, although that's a lot more feasible than crossing between universes, which as far as I know no mortal has ever done. No, it's like... soap bubbles pressed against each other."

"A very *thin* barrier?"

"No, it's like... there's no thickness to the soap at all. The bubble is touching the bubble but they're still separate and nothing can move from one to the other. Oh, forget it."

"What?"

"There's an absolutely impenetrable layer of nothing at all between them, and we just stepped through a door in it," I said.

"Yeah." Yenu hefted her pack and glanced around. "Wow, there is a *lot* of magic in the air here. Good Lord."

There was no horizon; the stones and hills surrounding us were, I sensed, the borders of the dimension. If you tried to go past them, you would find yourself where you came in. And where we had come in, of course, had closed behind us. It was a better jail than I had given Them credit for. But how had Yenu known anything about it, let alone how to get in? That hadn't been in a book, surely.

Remember that later, too, I told myself grimly.

INSIDE THE MOUNTAIN a cavity had been carved into an enormous and perfect dome, the walls gleaming and smooth as glass. Our hugely distorted reflections jumped and bobbed as we entered, our footsteps echoing too loudly on the slick stone. We were scaring ourselves, and there wasn't a single guard or creature or anything. Too easy, I thought again, before I could stop myself.

At thirteen points around the circumference of the dome, huge doors had been installed—identical, as near as I could tell—of some kind of greenish-silver metal. Each was intricately decorated with hundreds of spiral carvings and bits of gems or glass that glittered in the light of our lantern.

"The carvings," I said to Yenu. "That's some kind of code, right? Saying what's inside?"

She shook her head.

"Do we have to open all of them to find the god, then?"

"Definitely not." She held up a hand for silence, and we all listened; it was so quiet I could hear the blood inside my ears, amplified by the helmet. "There *are* guards," she said, "behind twelve of them. Supposedly. And the god only behind one."

"Guards," I said heavily. "You are using a job title, I cannot help but notice, instead of saying 'furiously angry monster that's been locked up in a prison cell for literally nobody knows how long.'"

"Wait a damn minute," said Sudworth. "You don't know which door, and that thing can't show you, can it? It's overloaded by the local magic here. Any spell wouldn't be able to pinpoint it. Not that close."

"I'm making an educated guess," Yenu said, leading us towards the nearest one. It took several minutes to get there.

"Educated, my entire arse," said Sudworth. "Where'd you even find out about this place? And don't tell me you knew how to open the dimensional door from a bunch of ripped-out pages in a book."

"Look, I can narrow it down, at least. When I developed the final phase of the spell I accounted for quite a bit of extra magic. Under the assumption that the proximity effects of a genuine Elder God would—"

"Or one of the Adversaries!"

"No, it's two *entirely* different signatures, it turns out."

Ksajakra looked with mild but increasing alarm between the two of them; even on his dark brown skin I thought circles were darkening under his eyes as I watched. "What is the problem now?" he said quietly to me in Low Dath.

"There are several problems," I said after a moment's thought. "Twelve, to be exact. What would you do if you didn't know which of the doors had a large angry monster behind it and which one had a god?"

He pursed his lips. "I would go bang on the doors until I found the one where the thing behind it did not attack the noise. Then I would open that one."

I stared at him. "Finally," I said, "someone on this mission with some damn common sense."

YENU DIDN'T LIKE the idea; Sudworth was all for it. We left them bickering over magical minutiae in the centre of the giant room while Ksajakra and I, swords drawn, cautiously went from door to door, hammering them with the handle of one of Yenu's daggers. Each door was a fifteen or twenty minute walk from its neighbours, and soon we could barely see the other two any more.

The metal of the doors was strange—it had so little resonance that it was not like striking metal at all, or even wood or stone, but some hyper-engineered material cooked up in a science lab intended to deaden all vibration and sound. Back on Earth when it existed, Chambers Labs might have developed this stuff for acoustic rooms. *The quietest room in the world! Listen to the blood cells move along the capillaries in your ears!*

"Somebody thought of this already," Ksajakra admitted, when we were at the third door. "They designed these doors to be resistant to sound."

"It's still better than nothing," I said, drawing my head back. I didn't like it, but the only way to hear anything behind a door was to press my helmet directly to it. Despite the thick, leaden silence of the domed room, whenever the glass touched the metal I could indeed hear something—but it was only a faraway song, bells and chanting that repeated again and again, a high, whiny chorus of voices. I drew an X on the door with a wax pencil. "Next."

When we returned to Sudworth and Yenu what seemed like forever later, my legs and stomach were cramping from dehydration. We sat uncomfortably on the slick stone floor, put the lantern between us, and quietly cobbled together a meal from our packs.

"We could definitely hear something behind six doors," I said to Yenu, chewing.

"And definitely nothing behind the other seven?"

"Definitely not definitely nothing," I said.

Sudworth squinted at us. "Are you two aware that you're the only people in the multiverse that can understand each other?"

"We're speaking English!" I protested.

"Barely."

"We marked them," I said, giving Sudworth back her wax pencil. "For what little good that'll do. Looks like we'll have to rely on your spell after all."

Yenu nodded, and played with the wayfinding device restlessly, turning it over and over in her lap. "It was a good idea. Nothing wrong with it. But we're not dealing with... I don't know. Guard dogs. You know. They won't necessarily bark at an intruder. It could be something silent. In fact, it's far more likely that They deliberately chose guards who would make no sound. For all we know there's a... a killer plant behind one of those doors. A cloud of poison gas. A neutron star."

We fell silent; Ksajakra looked at our faces, visibly opted to not ask what we had been talking about, and sipped from his canteen. I thought about opening a door and discovering a neutron star, and tried not to think about it any more, but of course it was impossible once my brain had seized on the initial thought. What was a neutron star, anyway? Would I die of radiation? Would I be sucked into it? Exploded by it? Cooked by it? Frozen? Crushed? Would I simply die of fright? They all seemed like reasonable options. Yenu probably knew; I didn't want to ask her.

I had spent enough time over the past several years thinking of the way I would have wanted to die, as well as wanting to die; I had hoped to simply go to sleep and never wake up. Painless, silent, dignified. A neutron star sounded like none of those things. For a moment I wondered if Yenu had spent the same amount of time thinking about death and dying, then shook my head sharply, as if it might dislodge the thought, throw it out onto the shiny stone floor.

Eventually we narrowed it down to two doors, so far apart I had to wonder how big the jail cells were behind them... or how big a god might be. The size of a mountain? The size of a virus? No size at all? Maybe it was nothing more than a burst of light, or three musical notes, or a hopeful thought.

And would it be happy to see us, even? What might happen once we freed it? What if it responded by lashing out at us?

"There's a ritual speech," Yenu said in response to my fretting, but she sounded like she wasn't really listening. She studied the door minutely, running her fingers

across the carved greenish metal and pressing her helmet
to it as I had. "It'll be fine. They protect life, they hold
life sacred. There's no oath they've sworn to fight the
Ancient Ones, but that's all they ever did."

"So it's said," I said.

"So it's said."

Said by who? I almost said, clamped my lips shut.
Now was not the time for doubt. Even so: "Will we
know it as soon as we see it? What if it looks like some
horrible dangerous thing?"

"I don't know." She ran her fingers along the spirals
again, then dug something out of her coat. "I suppose if
it tries to kill us immediately, it's a guard."

"And if it waits till you start talking to kill us, it's a god."

"Mmhm." She had brought a small glass flask of
something sluggish and inert, golden but gleaming like
mercury. It looked for all the world like the stuff that
had emptied out of her with that first spell to move the
ship. Maybe it was.

"What's that?"

"I'm still figuring it out," she said, and tipped the
flask against the door, sending a slow glittering stream
trickling onto the floor.

"You're... what?"

Sudworth took a large step backwards from the door.

Yenu said, "Look, I'm going to analyze it at some
point, I swear. It's not a *totally* unknown thing. It's... It
moves around, accompanying things, not a thing itself.
I think it's something that was once used in the past to
run certain spells. So I'm using it as if it were."

"None of that made sense. And you've done this before? You've read about this?"

"Not exactly." She stepped back too, and watched as the thin sparkling stream paused, found one of the carvings, moved slowly into it, began to climb back up, filling in the spirals and sending out tiny symmetrical tendrils, for all the world like a millipede, moving against gravity. "Educated guess," she said again, but more uncertainly.

It was *looking* for something, I thought: its movements had purpose. In the silence, the scratch and skitter of its movement across the pale metal made the hairs go up on the back of my neck. All at once it vanished into a nearly-invisible crack fifty yards up, nearly at the limit of the weak, wobbling circle of golden light from our lantern.

"Mm," Yenu said approvingly. "There's the lock."

"How did it know to look for a lock?"

"Beats me. You never know what things know."

Something creaked, then groaned, a metallic noise but uncannily like a voice. Yenu slowly replaced the empty flask. Behind me, out of the corner of my eye, I saw Ksajakra drawing his sword; I did too.

And the door slid upwards in little jerks, metal grinding against stone, screaming, inch by inch. The smile fell away from Yenu's face. I glanced at it only once.

"Run," I said.

This was something I had thought lost in the years I had spent pent up in the tower: me, the princess, never letting down my hair. But it was still in there somewhere, the ability to know danger for what it was, taught by the best.

Ksajakra barely hesitated; he swept Sudworth smoothly under one arm and took off, his form as perfect as any Olympian sprinter. I tailed him, arms pumping. The entrance was so far away, and whatever was behind us, *whatever* it was, would outpace us. But it was run or fight, and a single look at Yenu's face had told me we could not fight.

"Wait!" she screamed behind us in Low Dath, from another direction entirely, not behind us. "Not that way!"

I risked a look back: a darkness, of course, since we had the light, but also a new light, pinkish—in fact reddish, bloody—outlining a boiling mass of black tentacles, and a small shadow not running but scuttling across the floor. Yenu: heading for the other door.

I skidded to a stop, nearly cracking my head on the slick floor, and flailed for Ksajakra, too far ahead of me. "Did you hear her? This way!"

"What?" He kept running; I took off again to keep up with him, and finally snatched at his sleeve, tugging him backwards.

"This way!"

"Are you crazy?"

"Put me down, you fucking maniacs!" Sudworth screamed. "The way out is over *there!*"

We both got an arm on her instead and raced after Yenu, the tentacles rumbling behind us, snarling now, a voice behind them groaning, tendrils shooting out to stab at the other doors, a secret key. One by one they began to squeak and lift, up into the body of the mountain.

The room became a kaleidoscope and cacophony of pursuit. The usual nightmare: we were too slow, our pursuers too swift; we were small, they were large.

What saved us, I thought later, was only that Yenu had not started towards the entrance, even for a moment: had rushed, instantly, to the other of the two doors. It was the only one not opening.

She raised a hand and sent out a streak of green-blue light so bright that it burned into my retinas from top right to bottom left, like a knife slash, melting a round hole in the door. She slid through it like a snake.

It seemed to take forever to reach the door. Ksajakra pushed Sudworth through, then shoved me in the small of the back. "Go!"

"You first! I won't fit!" *She did that on purpose*, I thought clinically as he dropped flat and wriggled through. *Made a hole I wouldn't fit through*. I drew my sword and turned to face the darkness, feeling the stone floor shake as the things gathered, galloped, flew, soared towards us.

"Prophet! Get in here! I have to seal it up!"

I wavered, glanced back, saw nothing, not their faces, nothing. Just the darkness of the hole.

"*Nick!*"

All right. If she thought I'd fit... So much for death with dignity. I threw my sword through first, yelling "Heads up!" and then shucked off my coat, stuffed it through, dove in as best I could.

As I had calculated, my shoulders caught, then my stomach, but someone inside—impossible to tell who, maybe all of them—seized my wrists and dragged, and I kicked my way through into a cold, stale-smelling gray light, the same slick floor. Yenu shouted "Duck!" and loosed another blast of light.

The door rang to a thousand impacts from the outside: the sound of claws and fangs and feet and anger on the green metal. I backed away from it and climbed to my feet, gasping for air faster than the helmet could generate it. Sudworth handed me my sword, her hand shaking.

"And what was that, then?" she said critically as I stuffed it back into its sheath, which took several tries. "You were going to fight off the guards by yourself?"

"I was going to distract them for a few seconds while you two figured out how to seal up the door," I said.

"Well, she wouldn't let us till you were through," Sudworth said crossly. "Damn fool. Could've got us all killed."

"I mean, there's still time."

"That won't hold," Yenu croaked, padding past us; huge swathes of her coat had been burned away, leaving the charred lining holding it together in spots. I picked up my own coat and put it on, glancing back at the lumpy round patch-weld she'd put over our entrance hole. "Come on."

The god's cell, if that's what we were in, was the size of a cathedral, and the gray illumination that I had assumed was daylight was actually a small but brilliant light set high in the arched ceiling. The room was carved from dark blue stone, veined and slickly polished and warded from top to bottom, the wards inset in what looked like white glass or tile. The floor vibrated as the things outside scrabbled at the door.

I gave it another once-over. "It's..."

"Empty," Ksajakra said slowly, drawing it out. My stomach sank. Was this it? The end of the con? The betrayal Sudworth said we should watch for?

Yenu said, "No, it's in here. We just have to wake it up."

"We?"

She cleared her throat and began reciting something that I immediately recognized as the Old Tongue, whose real name you could not even say, lest it draw the attention of the Ancient Ones. Sudworth recognized it too, and froze in place, mouth open. *Stop!* I wanted to scream, but Yenu would not have used it lightly, and would not have used it at all if any other words of power would do, surely, *surely* this wasn't the double-cross... My blood ran cold just to hear it, and the wards began to whine, then shriek, till we had to cover our ears over their screams.

When they began to explode from the walls, there was nothing we could do but duck, the transparent shrapnel shattering into iridescent dust against the stone floor, pinging against our backs like thrown stones, clipping our exposed hands or sticking in our boots.

The sounds from outside grew muffled; Yenu's voice faded. A golden mist enveloped her, pure magic precipitating out of the air and snowing onto her clothes and skin, sticking to her helmet like powdered paint.

And then it was there. A narrow slit in reality reaching

from floor to ceiling, a slender darkness from one angle and invisible from the next, in which a few, faraway stars glittered.

Faintly, Yenu said, "We bid you greeting, and thank you for your kind regard in letting us live."

What language was she speaking? I was hearing it, impossibly, as every language I knew, layered on top of each other like the pages in a book. Was the god doing it?

The restraints are not completely broken, the god said, or somebody said; I seemed to *feel* it, in the bones of my jaw and up through my teeth and eyesockets, rather than hear it in my ears. Next to me, I saw but did not hear Sudworth swear.

"We released the guards," Yenu said. "Accidentally. I apologize. But our need was... is dire. And there's no time. Please hear us: the Ancient Ones are more powerful than ever, and They have started a new war of conquest. Millions of lives are at stake. They are killing even now, as we speak."

That is not a war. That is massacre. It is how they fight: one-sided.

"Yes," Yenu said meaningfully. "Unless someone could oppose Them."

If we are free, we will; we have sworn a secret oath to do so. But you should not have started with me, little mortal. I cannot even get us out of here.

The temperature seemed to drop; Yenu's mouth moved for a moment in sheer stunned surprise, and then she looked up at the god, gathering her thoughts. Below my growing panic, I allowed myself a dark moment of glee:

she hadn't been expecting this wrench in her plans. The others, maybe. *Maybe.* But not this. This was supposed to be the end of it, and she would dust her hands off and walk away the hero. This was the entire goal of the resistance... and now the god was trying to tag out.

I am weakened from this captivity. From the long enclosure. What time has passed, what power has left me, you will never be able to understand...

"Can we help?"

I will need a resting place to regain my strength and feed. Inside a mortal. My own is not enough.

"Then I volunteer."

Not you.

Ksajakra flinched; Sudworth blinked, tightened her lips. And again memory ambushed me: a dry, soft voice... a book speaking to me, or dozens of books, across dimensions and galaxies, through walls and angles real and imagined. *Not her. Never her.*

Not her. They didn't say why.

They didn't say why.

There are others here, the god said slowly, *who can access the etheric flow... one of them.*

Yenu nodded stiffly, disappointment as well as terror radiating off her every movement. Behind us, metal screeched; I glanced back to see the the patch bowing towards us, a grotesque sight, like a swelling boil. Already something sticky and probing was coming through the gaps.

Choose, I thought desperately, but said nothing. Yenu, for once wisely, also did not.

The books didn't say why. And I didn't ask them why, either. But why not her? A genius, a powerful practitioner of magic. Sudworth talking about—what's the word? Neosomething. That no one in history has been able to do, because they all died. Why not her? And my God, the venom in their voices, if I had heard it correctly. The books said: *Not her*. They said: *Never her*. They said *Never*.

Hurry, hurry, hurry...

You, the god said, and my back teeth clacked together.

I stared at the long streak of darkness as best I could, the tiny stars moving inside it, if stars they were. "I don't know," I said, and glanced behind myself again: the metal tearing now—grudgingly, like a thick sheaf of paper, but tearing anyway. What was coming in? A claw appeared, startling, stark white against the metal, and withdrew.

"Prophet," Ksajakra whispered urgently. "Just say yes."

I glanced at Sudworth, who shook her head almost imperceptibly, staring straight ahead at the wall, avoiding looking at the god.

And I thought very clearly, as if someone were saying it out loud: *Wait a minute. Weak. The god said it was* weak.

Maybe her plan does end here. She didn't know this was going to happen; she doesn't know what's going to happen next. Maybe I can still salvage this. Maybe there is something to salvage.

It doesn't *have* to be a war, even now. The presence of an enemy doesn't mean there has to be a fight. I could reason with the god, make it see sense, if it's inside me I might be the only one who can. Weak as it is. Maybe. You never know. Convince it; or fight it and control it, gain its power; or suppress it, refuse to let it act. I won't know until I...

"All right," I said. There would probably be a ceremony, and I hoped it would be quick, or the god would be trying to enter a dead body. "What do I—?"

And the darkness rushed in on me, all gladness and the distant sound of bells.

CHAPTER FOURTEEN

STARTLED, I FELL through void that should have held nothing to fall *through*, nothing for my skin to sense and resist, no air, no gravity, and yet I felt wind rush past my face and all the chemicals of fear and panic race through my blood and I screamed silently and the scream came out along frequencies of wave and particle that the void simply disregarded, and another emptiness behind this emptiness opened up like an eye, perceiving me until I was too close to perceive, and I fell through it, and another emptiness opened up again, perceiving me.

I was falling towards the god and the emptiness that had eaten everything inside of me, and when at last we met, it was nothing more than a small, golden mote, a sizzling little ordinary-looking spark, as if it had just been spat out of a fire.

If I could see the light and the colour, maybe I had

eyes. Did I have hands? I tried to hold them out in front of me and succeeded, though they looked odd: smooth, unscarred, unscorched. Their hair gleamed like gold filigree.

I reached for the spark, which jumped as if startled and jerked out of the way. "All right," I said. To stand, to speak, felt real enough: muffled, diluted, but real. "Where are we? We're in me, aren't we? In my mind. So now I'm going to be calling the shots. Can you understand me? Are you listening?"

I'm listening. The sound seemed to come straight into my head and march across whatever parts of my brain could hear and see, as if briefly imprinted across both my eyes and my ears like a projector.

"Okay, good," I said, nonplussed. Even embarrassed, I had to admit, but I tried to push it down. Lives, worlds were at stake. I found myself rushing, stumbling over my words. "I don't think Yenu—that woman out there, the one in the black coat?—really made it clear what was happening. Which is that she's trying to use you. Just like she's trying to use me. If she's not aligned with the Ancient Ones, I mean the Adversaries—"

I know who you mean.

"I... Yes, thank you. If she's not actually *allied* with Them, actively, right now, then she's as close as doesn't matter. Whatever she's choosing to do serves Them, and to me that means there's no difference. What she wants you to do is start rounding up the other gods, so you can create an army like the one in the last war, and fight Them again. But to me all that means is that a lot of innocent people are going to die. Not that the war will end. And *especially* not the way she wants it to."

The god hung silently, expectant, in what I slowly began to realize was not quite void—more like water, stagnant water full of some very fine particulate, like ash. The darkness around us was not a lack of light, only an inability for light to penetrate from outside.

Why does she feel that ending the war is her responsibility?

"That is a good question with a very, very long answer. But it doesn't matter. To stop her: that's something mortals can do. Gods don't even have to get involved. So that's what I'm doing. Don't do as she tells you, you understand? She'll give up on this, and that'll be that. Lives will be saved. Maybe including hers. And part of her *knows* that, part of her knows I'm right. She freed you. I get that you're grateful for that. But don't let it lead to another war. Are we clear?"

Silence again. Idly I wondered if I could fight it, the god. Overpower it maybe, if I had to. I was the one we were inside, after all; I should be able to control it if it didn't obey me. Not physically, but what did 'physically' mean anyway? We were in my mind. My place. My power. And the god was the one who was weak.

"All you have to do," I said, "is do nothing."

I am so weak now that nothing will be all I can do for some time.

"Good. Just keep it up then." And unbidden, I felt a flare of hope so sudden and bright that for a second I was surprised we both couldn't see it in here as something real, like fireworks. There was still hope for me, at least, no matter what Yenu said. And she was the one who had made it so. I could get the god to take me back to Aradec if she wouldn't, and maybe the King and the Queen would listen to me, understand that I had been taken hostage and forced to act under duress, and then I could turn over the god as a prized POW...

That is not who you are, the voice said gently.

"Excuse me?"

You think you would do anything to preserve your life... It's not true. I can see everything in you now. I see it before me in endless fields.

"In this darkness?"

I do not see it as dark. But I see that asking you whether you want to live or not is a more complicated question than I had originally anticipated when I came into this place...

I blinked.

What happened to you?

"What do you mean, what happened to me? Nothing did. You did."

I mean, the god said, *you're not alone in here.*

"I beg your fucking pardon?"

You are incomplete, the god said. *I have never seen anything like it. Whatever lives in you is as alive as you are, and it drinks you to stay alive. And it fights with the others...*

"There's *more than one thing*?"

Oh, yes. And me now, too. I do not know if you will have the strength to see this through to the end. I am sorry. With all this... you may die before what needs doing is done.

"Sounds like it."

You seem very calm about it.

"I might be in shock." I thought of a dim memory, years and lifetimes ago, dimensions ago, universes ago: a sandstorm, a girl falling, out of strength, emptied out like this, like me, emptied of everything to keep the spell going, the hungry spell. And a voice in my head saying something... I couldn't remember what. *Something* to keep me going. Something that urged me to move, to not stay still. And it wasn't her voice. And it wasn't my voice. What had that been? I had never thought about it. I had assumed it had come from outside me, not inside. "And I think I've died a few times before, anyway. Can you get rid of them?"

You can only get rid of an emptiness by filling it, the god said. *And this is beyond me to fill. I am sorry.*

"No, don't apologize. It's not your fault." I paused and looked at my hands again, the only thing I could see. A bit disconcerting actually, as if my body stopped just above my wrists. The hairs were standing on end like wires, like tiny antennae picking up the voice of the god, broadcast along wavelengths never before studied. "But it does suggest to me that you picked the wrong body to inhabit."

It suggests that to me too, the god said. *But you were still the best choice out of everyone here. And I am sorry for that, too.*

"Me too." I touched my face uncertainly, my beard,

my skin, my ears. "Where's my body, by the way?"

On a very strange vessel. And when I, as a god, say that it is very strange, I mean what I say... I feel stronger already now that I have eaten, but I need your body to survive a while longer.

I decided to disregard the eating comment, because eaten what, if there was nothing to eat but me? "I'm on the ship? Where are the others? How did we get here?"

I used you to get us out. We sail now on the Violet River... There are other names for it. I had never expected to see it again. To see anything again.

"You'll live to see many more things if you agree not to fight Them," I said.

The god went on, as if I had not spoken, *It is a way they used to use. During the war. But after it was over, it fell into disuse. As a way, I mean; a river flows whether it is being used or not, of course. I have never heard of mortals using it. Even knowing about it.*

"She had a theory," I said. "Yenu. About shapes in space. But then she also said this wasn't space, not really. It's just *like* space. I didn't understand all of it."

The gold light spiraled, moving in tight circles in front of me at waist level, then fell to my feet, below my feet (am I floating? don't think about it, this isn't real, it's not real), then back up. *It's so strange in here. I need information. Please, come with me. There are places I may venture and never return...*

"Inside my head? But you're a god. Nothing could hurt you in here."

Untrue. The light began to drift, and I followed it

uncertainly, muscle memory working my legs, both weightless and impossibly heavy, as if I were a cloud trying to move through a block of lead.

"I didn't think it would be so dark in here," I said after a minute. "You know, in movies and stuff it's usually... more busy. Inside someone's head."

We are not inside your head. We are inside your souls.

"Uh."

Mortals have two souls, the god said softly, drifting ahead of me. I realized with a start that I was barefoot under my long robe. My Prophet's robe, of all things. Was that how my soul saw me?

Soul is not the best word for it, the god said. *But in several tongues it is the one you will understand... and I see I am supplied with something like 'spark' and 'animus' from the words you know... There is one that makes you alive, rather than a lifeless collection of matter, and there is one that makes you who you are. They are entwined around each other, but they are separate. That is where we are now. That is where the divine can fit. Where magic draws from.*

"Which one?"

Both.

I looked around. "You'd think a soul would be made of light," I said.

Light doesn't tell you much. It's just a part of the spectrum that some mortals like. Darkness doesn't tell you much either. Optical sensors aren't even the best sensors that you have.

"What are the best ones?"

The ones you never listen to. It's very strange.

All the same, things were looming in the darkness both above and below us, just visible in the deep watery gloom outside the god's little circle of light: dark purple, dark green, every now and then a tiny flash of blue or white, like a single star being revealed for a moment before being covered again by clouds.

You're not alone in here, the god had said. All right. Don't think about it. I am legion, how long have I been legion? What does it mean? I had thought I was alone—if anything, I thought no one was more alone than me—and it turned out I was carrying a multitude inside of me the whole time...

Something sprouted out of the darkness in front of us, like a table with a tiny theatre set into the top. I paused, fascinated. Galaxies popped and sparkled like the flash of a camera, tiny motes flowed to and fro. Battle formations? Where they met, a constant thin detritus of something fell from them like sand. If they had been mortal, I would have thought of armour, weapons, letters, uniforms, bodies. Like the soldiers marching past my tower, on that morning that now felt so long ago.

At the end of the final battle, the god said, *we were going to join together. Myself and the other Elders. My friends, my family, my fellow fighters. Everyone together. To end the Ancient Ones and their reign of terror forever, and withdraw to let mortals live out their lives... But too many of us were already gone. Dead or captured.*

"I didn't know you could kill gods. Yenu said she thought it might be possible."

Now you know, the god said bitterly.

"WELL, THANK CHRIST," someone said loudly near my ear. "I'll go tell the others. Hang in there, brat."

Sudworth. Light returned, real light, hazy and golden. A lantern hung near my head, illuminating the wood beams of the hold. I was lying down—or so it seemed—and bound hand and foot—or so it seemed—and desperately thirsty. My tongue felt as big and shapeless as a pillow, and my whole body hurt, a strange pain, discrete bolts of it as if nails had been hammered into my bones. Two particularly big ones through my eyes. I stared up at the ceiling, listening to the ship: footsteps, voices, a faint sound of liquid. Were we still on the River? Or real water?

Unseen hands untied me, propped me up, and left; and I was alone again for a long time, listening to the slosh near my head like a bathtub. Footsteps again down the stairs: Yenu, so pale she seemed to carry her own light, with dark circles under her eyes, juggling a tray. She sat next to me and offered me a wooden cup with perhaps an inch of water in it.

"Sorry," she said. "It's been two-ish days. I don't really want you to chug a bunch of water and then puke."

I nodded, tried to rub my neck, failed at raising either hand, and sat there angrily while she fed me the few sips of water. My lips were so chapped that I saw flakes flap when I breathed. From the corner of my eye I spotted 1779, perched near my head and not moving except for his antennae, which spun in tight circles counterclockwise, giving him a slightly nervous air, like someone jiggling their leg under a desk.

"Um. How do you feel?" she said.

"Uh."

While I tried to come up with a coherent sentence, she refilled the cup and offered it again. I managed to get my left arm up this time, and only spilled a bit as I drank. It seemed to disappear onto the surface of my tongue rather than going down my throat. My bottom lip split as I drank, and the last mouthful was tinged with blood. I didn't care.

"I've been lying here for two days?"

"You kind of..." She shrugged. "You were thrashing around. Attacking people, the ship, the sails, everything. Everybody said to throw you overboard, that the god inside you was mad, or you were mad, or both, and we'd have to come up with something else. People said they didn't think the god was going to come onto the ship. But I convinced them to tie you up for a little while and wait. And then you blacked out."

"Everybody?" I said. "That's insulting." It felt as if lifting my arm had drained all the energy in my body; deep inside, a small but urgent voice cried out in alarm or despair, but there was no helping it. The god and I had spoken for a long time, arguing back and forth, unable to sway each other, apologizing, fighting again, trying to learn one another's histories. And he had, he said, been feeding the entire time. Off what? I still didn't know. It hadn't done him much good, anyway; he had burnt up the last metaphorical fumes in his gas tank getting us back to the ship. He wouldn't be good for much for a long time, and apparently neither would I.

"The books said not you," I murmured.

"What?"

"Never you... never..."

"Hey, no," she said, reaching out and hesitating. "Don't fall asleep again, you need to drink more water and eat something—"

But I was falling again, through the warm, dark waters of unconsciousness.

THE THING INSIDE me had teeth and I could not explain how it had teeth and there was no one I could tell. *What are you eating?* I screamed, but no one could hear me except the thing with teeth.

It is not your bones, the reply would occasionally drift back. *It is not your blood. It is not your brains.*

What then! What?

Sometimes I managed to get my eyes half-open, often when someone was trying to get water into me; it seemed they never attempted food. Wet cloths were pressed between my lips, squeezed over my tongue.

The thing inside me has teeth, I wanted to scream to them. *His voice is gentle, but there are teeth. Can you see it?* I pictured it sometimes as a piranha, so clean were the bites, only evident much later. But worse other times. Always an animal. A crocodile, taking messy bites with blunt teeth, spinning to rip and tear. A shark, eyes rolling back and lips peeling away from gums. A movie velociraptor, flitting through the undergrowth to bite from behind: the back of my neck, or lower on my spine. I screamed in silence. When my mouth opened, someone desperately dripped liquid into it. "Live," someone whispered somewhere: not inside me. Outside. Real air. "Live. Go on living. The Masters still speak through you."

Do They? Should They? Have They ever? No, I don't think that's true. Help me: I held out a hand, but no familiar paw was ever on the other end. Only the voice, and the faint, familiar, mineral smell of clock oil for his pocketwatch.

Someone's head. Got too used to it, living in that place. Bones all around. Whose skull was that? Had someone died for that watch to be made, or had they been dead a long time already? Did it matter?

Why had I never asked him?

Eventually the intrusion of a small strip of golden light, torn here and there with quivering lashes. And then motion, and then sound.

A voice near my ear: "Your Holiness. We are at a place that... that our captors say we must stop for a time. To repair the ship. Replenish supplies. And find a physician for you."

Don't let them touch me, I tried to say, and failed, as always. *I'm full of teeth*. But the light remained— morbidly, I thought perhaps my eyelids were too dry to stick shut—and I was lifted by many hands, transported from what I had not realized was dimness and warmth into cold, impossible light, and fresh air, wind smelling of salt and smoke.

THE PHYSICIAN—REASONABLY, I thought—refused to come aboard the ship; there was something otherworldly about it, and we had arrived at a place, I knew without being told, that did not get visitors from other worlds. Quite how we had gotten there I wasn't sure, but I was sure it had been through some back-door invisible to the residents of this world. The River had many mouths and tributaries; the shapes led to other shapes, and some of those shapes ended in a door.

I listened with my eyes closed, enjoying the bed beneath me, soft and stable. I had not realized how trying it had been to adjust, balance, stabilize itself, even while I had been asleep or unconscious, on the moving ship. Everything still hurt, but now there was localized pain: sewing up cuts, dabbing ointment on my burns, cleaning scrapes, and, to my surprise, inserting an IV. Yenu and the Advisor spoke Low Dath in the corner of the room, stiff and formal; she spoke another language to the physician, one I didn't know, and addressed nothing to me.

"Itzlek and Liandan went into the town for supplies," she murmured. "Everyone else is on the ship this time. I wish you'd stayed."

"People wish many things," the Advisor said.

Ah. A world of humans, must be. What a strange idea that was now. How strange to find it a strange idea, too. I wondered how people were coping with seeing the Advisor, how discreetly he and Yenu had managed to get me in here. Had we come at night? Could you pretend he was nothing more than a jet-black shadow? Let alone seeing the clearly inhuman patchwork quilt Yenu had become. It would have been like an alien landing on Earth. Like us, on Earth before the Anomaly...

Muffled conversation. The clink and jingle of metal against porcelain. Sound of meals, or dentistry. Forks against plates.

Where had I been when I was inside my head? Where was I now?

I vaguely remembered a time when I used to stay in the same place, and when I left it I would eventually come back to that place, maybe several hours or days later. A weird concept now.

I had a home, I told the god. *She took it away from me. Not once, but again and again. Because nowhere is truly home to her except her own head. And that head is full of demons and voices.*

Interesting noises now: whimpers, yelps, cursing in five or six languages. Yenu's voice. I pried my eyes open out of sheer curiosity and squinted across a long low room, hotly lit with white light from a wall of windows. Three people leaned over a table, each dressed in light, dove-gray robes splattered with what looked like ink. Her blood, I remembered belatedly, and not for the first time. Look at her: she bleeds words.

One pale hand flailed for a moment; the Advisor, unmoving in the corner next to the table, held out a paw for her to take. I laughed, an inaudible squawk.

From the crook of my left arm snaked a segmented translucent tube, pale green, more like the tendril of a plant than anything I expected to see in a doctor's office, which was attached to about one visible inch of a discomfortingly-large-bore bronze needle. The tube led to a round, valved tank the size of my head, suspended from a thin chain above the foot of my bed. Water or saline, probably. If it wasn't, I didn't want to know.

But I felt better, if nauseated and exhausted. How close had I been to dying of dehydration? What was the god thinking, letting me come so close to death, if I was the vessel he had chosen?

A fine passenger you are, I thought.

Silence in response. Had he eaten his fill of whatever he was eating? Had he overeaten, and fallen asleep at table? No way to tell. If I had indeed been depleted, I didn't know what he had taken.

A dark-haired, dark-skinned human woman put a glass carafe of water and a small tumbler on the table next to my bed and left almost before I realized she was there, her shadow quick and black across the tile floor. It was so bright here. How many suns did they have? Would I be allowed to stay here? No, probably not. Not now that I had the god in me. The next phase of the plan: a little golden spark somewhere inside me. Or not *inside* me, physically. Best not to think about it. At any rate, I was still useless to Yenu, probably, except as a vessel for her demands.

My thoughts felt strangely disconnected and distant. I sipped water and waited for Yenu's procedure, whatever it was, to end. I wondered how she would pay. I wondered what would happen if we could not pay.

Which begged the question: How had she paid for the building of the ship? Even the materials, all that wood, the sailcloth, the ropes. How had the resistance paid for their building? Maybe it was better to not know how she had been making money.

They left us alone after they were done, shutting and, I was fairly sure, locking the door behind them. An ordinary door, I noted: a rectangle with a plain brass knob. This place must have been colonized by humans long ago.

Let me stay here, I thought again, the notion insistent yet without weight or heft, as if knowing that I would not entertain it. I could not make a home here. There was nowhere I could make a home. Not to replace the one I had lost. I pushed the thought aside easily. It was a pathetic thing.

Yenu staggered over and sat in the chair next to my bed; her beige shirt bore a symmetrical bib of dark blood, though the doctors had cleaned up her face and neck. I could see the paler swipes of the cloth through the blue-black remnants under her ears and along her throat.

"Fixing your teeth?" I guessed.

She nodded.

"About time. Do they speak English here?"

She shook her head, raised her scarred eyebrows: *So what?*

"Yes, I know they're not here," I said. "They could be listening... look. The god. This god in me. He says his name is Ogruthon. It was something else when he was worshipped on Earth. Do you know who that is? Is that who you were looking for?"

She regarded me without expression, her swollen lips making her look petulant, but really she had simply ceased to move; a common tactic, and one she used to use far more effectively on anyone but me. It was a nod to our favourite movie and its finest scientific inaccuracy: don't move and the T-rex won't see you. I wondered if she was trying to avoid the attention of the god. At any rate, the answer to the question, whether she had said it or not, was 'I was about to say no, but I still need more information.'

"He says everyone fought," I said, and refilled my tumbler, still thirsty; every time I spoke it felt like my throat was drying up and swelling shut, and I had nearly finished the carafe. "They *all* fought in the last war. There were no noncombatants. *No one was a civilian*, he said, and he sounded so... I don't know. Proud. They call it that, you know, the last war. The 'most recent.' Not the final war. No one thought it would be final. Except that some gods can be killed, born, resurrected, rebuilt, broken, disabled, destroyed, put under—and some can't; and he thinks there might be prisons all over the universe with the gods that survived. The big and the small. But we can't break into them all. We don't have the numbers. And he thinks we don't have the time, either."

Yenu bowed her head, acknowledging it and already, visibly, beginning to scheme against it.

"You didn't get another weapon," I said. "You didn't get... an army, a hero, a bomb, a doomsday device, you didn't get something that will shift the balance of the war at all. Just accept it."

She shook her head.

"What did they do to your mouth, anyway?"

Carefully, wincing, she levered up her upper lip to reveal something gleaming in her mouth, still slick with her inky blood. I had gotten so used to the gaps in her teeth that I had stopped noticing; it seemed stranger to see something in the gap than not.

"They put in four new teeth," the Advisor said.

"Interesting," I said. "Anyway, I know this was where you thought everything stopped. Finding the god. And having him simply... roll downhill. A snowball picking up more snow. But it isn't. Or it is. The plan *does* stop here. Just not the way you wanted."

She shook her head, more vigorously this time. Blood oozed from the side of her mouth, unnoticed.

I sighed. Ogruthon had warned me that she wouldn't accept it. *How do you know?* I asked, and he said, quite mildly, in a way that had still somehow enraged me, *What are you talking about? It's all in here.*

"He says there was nothing wrong with your plan, though. You just need to modify it now. And I would like to go on the record as saying that I don't support this and I want to go home."

She nodded slowly, meeting my eyes with suspicion as

well as fear: the green, the blue, the red. At some point, I realized, all her eyelashes had been singed off.

"I know," I said, just to clarify, "I can't go home now. Not with the enemy literally inside me. So here's what he said."

The Advisor's hackles rose slowly, a menace all on their own, and did not settle back down. Yenu leaned away from him and put her elbows on the bed, lifting her bruised chin at me: *Go on. It's bad, you say? Don't hold back. I need data.*

"You wanted to start a chain reaction," I said. "You thought he would be enough: the one ping-pong ball that bounces, hits the mousetrap, and sends balls everywhere."

She snickered.

"Not quite," I said. "That was the mistake: only that he used to be heavy enough to set off the trap on his own, and now he's not. But he says he knows someone who can *for sure*. Another god. He says he even knows who, though he doesn't know where. He says between you, him, and the envoys, it can probably be found. Could I have some more water?"

The Advisor rose, took my carafe, crossed the long low room slowly and deliberately, so I could hear every footfall. I knew he could move silently when he wanted to; this was a message, meant for both of us.

I leaned my head close to Yenu's, reeling for a moment at the reek of her fresh blood, a strange and awful smell, not coppery like human blood. "He knows what you did," I said. "Ogruthon. He says he does, anyway. What do gods know, how do they know it? I still haven't figured it out. I thought this was going to make me powerful. Instead it's like I've eaten some fucked-up tapeworm. Listen. He knows what you did to Earth. He almost lost his mind."

She blinked, and something like fear crossed her eyes, moving from inhuman to human as if it were running behind the bone of her skull. Fear of hope. I knew I'd look the same. I coughed heavily, lowered my voice.

"He wanted to ask you about it. I think he had an idea, but he wouldn't tell me. Can you talk to him?"

She spread her hands eloquently: *You tell me.* Her palms shone with fresh sweat.

"No, he doesn't know how. He can barely talk to *me*, and every time he does I black out. He said you could figure something out."

At last she grinned: wolfish, bloody, and utterly familiar. The Advisor glanced once at her and slowly closed his eyes.

THE SPY IS on the ship or the spy is the ship, she'd said, *we have to talk somewhere else,* and I couldn't argue with that in terms of logic, but now, looking down at the thing she expected us to talk in, I wished I had. I could have said, "Hey, what if we just stayed near the doctor's office and got a bagel at a cafe or something." But that was the old days; she was far too paranoid for that now. And not for the first time, I wondered how much more extreme her precautions would become, and where they would stop. (More accurately: what would stop them. Because she would not be able to stop on her own.)

"I'll go first," she said, putting her hand at the top of the ladder.

"*I'll* go first. We've had this conversation."

"Yes, but you're not expendable any more."

"You said the quiet part out loud again," I said.

Ksajakra said, "I do not know what either of you are talking about, but *please* do not do this. Can we not land?"

"Nope," said Yenu. "Not if even half of what I've read about that ocean is correct."

"Then how did people reach this place in the past?"

"They didn't."

"But how was this *built?*"

"The gods," she said vaguely. "Look, just keep everybody fed and watered while we're gone, Jak."

"When will you return?"

"I'm not sure."

"What?" I said. They both ignored me. The Advisor's eyes bored into me with unpleasant intensity. He had gone into statue-mode again, sitting upright against the first mast like a sheet of black paper snipped out and pasted to the wood. Even his chest did not move as he breathed. I had not wanted to say to him *You could be the spy*, because to say it would have made it too true, even to myself. I had just mumbled something about at least one of us getting back to the palace to tell the truth, and very unconvincingly, too: we both knew we were never going home. But I had wanted him to think that at least one of us might live.

I took a deep breath—the air here was not only breathable but rich, something luxurious and silky about it even a hundred feet above the seething water—and swung my leg over the railing. The rope ladder creaked and stretched as I put my weight onto the first rung, far more than I had expected, and I froze, waiting to see if it would snap. Ksajakra had automatically reached out for my wrists at the noise; now he slowly withdrew his hands and put them on the railing next to the ladder.

"It's fine," I said in a strangled voice. "No problem."

"And at least it's a ladder, not a rope," Yenu said.

"You, shut up. I need to concentrate."

The climb down seemed to take forever; the ladder swayed in the wind, and each rung stretched so dramatically as I stepped onto it that I could not help but imagine the entire thing simply breaking at once, a knot or weak spot giving way that we had not noticed, and then... No, don't look down at the island, don't look up at the underside of the black ship, look at the *rope*. The rope is real, nothing else is real. Thick, pinkish soraza fiber. They took that from the trunks and cleaned it in vats; I had seen people doing it at the palace. Yes. Good. Something in it, the sap, sort of like a catalyst, polymerizing the shorter strands into long ones. You could get miles and miles of rope from a single tree.

Strong stuff. The best.

My foot slipped and I clutched the rung with both hands, heart hammering, till I could lift my free leg and carefully place it next to the other one. Itzlek had suggested, while we were making the ladder, that I do the climb with bare feet, and had even demonstrated, and it had made perfect sense, a very good suggestion, the others had all agreed, and I still hadn't done it. Die with your boots on. A good Albertan.

I laughed, slipped again, recovered, and kept descending.

At the bottom, I flopped into a heap and only got up slowly, dusting salt and dirt from my bandaged hands and looking up at the distant underside of the ship. Yenu hadn't started the climb down, and part of me thought that made pretty good sense, as there would be too much swaying with both of us, and part of me thought *This is it, this is where they laugh, pull the ladder back up, and sail off, finally rid of me.*

But she hadn't abandoned me yet; they did seem determined to keep what they had caught.

I walked around, hoping my legs would stop shaking. The island was a dot in the deep green water, an incongruous little blemish on the infinite smoothness; as we had sailed in, parting the veils at the mouth of its tributary onto the Violet River, I had wondered whether this was the only land on the whole planet. It was an irregular square about thirty paces across, slightly dipped in the centre, covered in short pale-blue grass, white around the edges from the spray of the waves.

Our destination was the centre of the dip, almost where I had collapsed: a baroque snarl of gilded metal, a bit tarnished, decorated with scrollwork and carved clouds and flowers, propping up, in the centre, a glass sphere of impossible transparency, marked deeply around its surface with incised lines and stars. Inside it shone a handful of smaller spheres, metal or stone, a thing that gleamed, all different colours.

It made me think (painfully, as always) of something my sister had had as a kid, something (more pain) Auntie Johnny had brought back for her from a trip to Japan, a crystal sphere with constellations on it that rotated on a little platform and projected stars onto her ceiling when she couldn't sleep. We had lost it in one of our hastier moves, and Carla had been so ashamed, blamed herself, begged me not to tell Johnny when I had suggested we ask her for a replacement... No, don't think about that. Don't think about it. Think about something else.

Yenu flopped onto the grass, and I waited patiently until she got up, spitting out bits of blue turf. "Son of a bitch," she croaked. "We should have landed."

"You said the ocean here would have dissolved the boat."

"Still better than that." She shook her head and pointed at the glass sphere. "Come on."

There was a door at the bottom, with a long, scrolled handle and no keyhole; it opened easily on silent hinges. The room below the sphere was cool and smelled faintly of seaweed, and nothing else. Not rust, not oil, not machinery really, although the room was filled with it top to bottom, gears and pulleys, ratchets and levers, and miles of thin brass chains.

In the middle of the room was a narrow staircase of intricately forged brass, each stair patterned with leaves and clouds, like outside; we squeezed up it and found ourselves inside the sphere, which from the sun and the glass should have been hotter than hell, but was just as cool as the room below. The coloured spheres inside it looked like glass too, all different sizes from as big as my fist to bigger than a car. They were attached to the ends of long brass rods that radiated out from the central mechanism. Six red velvet seats were attached to it too, like flower petals.

Yenu sat in one and gestured for me to sit across from her. It was so small I felt myself straining to balance on it like a tippy barstool. I stared up at the pale pink sky through the glass sphere, at the dotted and dashed and solid lines carved on it just visible, at the carven stars.

"What *is* this thing?" I whispered. "You said the gods made this? Did they make it just so people could talk to them?"

"No, not originally. It was just used for astronomical predictions, and to be perfectly technical, the gods didn't *make* it. They just moved it here and imbued it with the powers it has now. Like an artifact naturally able to store magic. They made it what it does, not what it is."

"But nobody can use it here. It can't *do* anything."

"Correct," she said.

"Doesn't that make you nervous? That they put it somewhere that it would never be used? It's like... those nuclear waste warning signs. You shouldn't need them if you've put it someplace that no one can get to, or that they don't know is there."

"There's no place *no one* can get to," she said, but drew her hand back from the lever she had been reaching for anyway and fiddled with the hem of her coat. "But I mean, if you're saying that the condition of only certain types of beings being able to access something means that the thing is inherently dangerous to every other thing that might show up there, you're not wrong. We definitely didn't come in through the door marked *Gods*. So yeah, it might take us apart into our constituent molecules."

"Pardon me?"

"It might not!" she said hastily. "Look, the important thing is that it isn't a spell, so if They're tracking us by watching for the flares of magic that I keep sending up with my name on them, They won't see one here. That alone makes this worth it."

I groaned. "I should have known," I said. "And by the way, it does not, and I would rather keep all my molecules where they are."

"Well, unfortunately you can't opt out and leave the god here," she said, sounding genuinely regretful. "So—"

Before I could reply, she reached for the lever and this time yanked it sharply.

For several seconds nothing happened at all; then I heard the subdued rumble and clatter of machinery below us, and felt the vibrations up through the seat. Above our heads, the glass globes began to rotate around the circumference of the sphere. It was a slow, beautiful dance, their greens and blues and grays and reds gleaming in the sunlight, sparking off the brass, swooping around us and spinning in place. Tiny moons I hadn't noticed before pirouetted around them, their whiteness soft and translucent as pearl.

I waited for the god inside me to speak as we watched the waltz of the planets, and Yenu, as if I had spoken out loud, whispered, "Not yet. We'll see when it happens."

"It?"

"Should be soon."

A moment later I saw what she had been referring to, and stared, open-mouthed: the brass rods, so clearly solid, were beginning to pass *through* one another, and so were the glass planets, beginning to leave swatches of one another's colours behind: an umber-brown planet passed me with a smear of blue on it, and following directly behind a blue sphere that had had a run-in with something bright purple.

By degrees the planets and the rods and the moons all danced each other into a single thing, and with a modest blink of white light, became a mirror. We both cried out, seeing ourselves reflected, hugely distorted inside the sphere, each of us the size of a house.

And there was a third reflection: faceless but not bodiless, a very curious thing, teardrop-shaped and studded all over with tiny spikes, brownish-gray, many-legged. And maybe, I thought in amazement as I studied the reflection, I had been wrong, and there was a face: two small dark specks gleamed out from under the rounded front edge of the teardrop.

"Ogruthon?" I said uncertainly.

The reply still came from somewhere below my sternum. *Yes, I am here. Well done to the both of you.*

"I had nothing to do with this," I pointed out.

Yenu said, "Look, we'd better be quick, I'm worried

about my molecules. What did you want to know?"

I need to see exactly *what happened in those final moments of your world*, the god said. *Neither of you alone has a full picture. I need to see both, and in here, that can be done.*

"I see," Yenu said uncertainly. "But why? It's..." She swallowed. In her mirrored throat the motion made me seasick, it was so big. I looked away. "It doesn't matter any more. I mean, it's over. Everything was destroyed."

Yes, I think it was, the god said offhandedly. We both winced. *But I would like to see how.*

"I... All right."

Ogruthon shifted slightly, the teardrop in the mirror becoming a sphere, then a bar, then a squashed oval, and then we all vanished and the mirror became a screen, showing the blue ocean, Earth's ocean, and the gray concrete island, and the little building on top of it, and the dull, bruised spot in the sky that slowly began to rip open like wet paper, and the things boiling out of the water next to it...

I shut my eyes, feeling only light move across them as everything replayed in silence. Ogruthon wanted the full picture; I did not. Watching it once had been bad enough. It had broken my mind in ways I had then been too broken to understand, and I sure as hell had not been able to fix it, only paper over it until I could cobble together the remnants into something that could bear the weight of everyday thoughts. I still could not bear the full weight of memory.

When the lights stopped, I opened my eyes again. Yenu

was crying silently, her face still. Ogruthon's reflection was a teardrop again, and the two little black glass beads under it had withdrawn till I could barely see them.

The spell you used would not have worked, he said, though his voice was kindly. *Even if you had not miscalculated. Because you did not know that the Manifestation was creating a gate in such close proximity. Your world was doomed one way or another.*

"All right," she said, and wiped her face, still weeping. "But in the end, it *was* me that destroyed it. Not him. Not Them."

Yes, Ogruthon said softly. *Looked at another way, you spared all the mortals on that planet the wrath of the Ancient Ones.*

"And looked at *another* way..." she began, but could not go on.

The god fell silent. Eventually he said, *What you said you would do... I mean, what you said to the others...? I did not understand everything I saw in your head, forgive me.*

"Strategic retreat," she said, not looking at me. "I said I was going to put Earth into its own pocket dimension. Create a shape around it that was cut off from magic forever, a dimension where there was no magic at all. So the magical prions would simply stop working."

As far as I can tell, that would have worked. The plan was sound.

I felt as if I had been stabbed, the pain so sudden and real that I jerked in the velvet chair and almost fell off. Would have worked! If she had just. If she could have resisted her own ego, just for *one more minute*. If she hadn't betrayed us. If...

The god seemed to not notice my flinch. *But instead, you tried to destroy Them? The opposite of what you claimed. An attack, not a retreat.*

She nodded, dabbing her nose with her sleeve. "I wanted to create a microsupermassive black hole and pull Them into it. Because nothing gets out, see. And the only way to do that was with a spell that could create it, target only Them, and then push it out of our dimension. And then They'd be gone for good. And I'd... "

The god—tactfully, I thought—said nothing about her covenant. Instead he said, *A very powerful spell.*

"Yes."

Perhaps the most powerful spell ever cast. I do not even think a god could have done it. We can only create a thing, not the absence of a thing.

"Yeah, that's why I had to use the reactor," she said, slightly nonplussed. "There wasn't enough local magic. And by local I mean like... our entire solar system, probably. Maybe further. Maybe our whole galaxy, I don't know, I didn't do the calculations. I knew right away it wouldn't be enough. But as soon as I figured out that magic has to be in motion to work, like electricity, I was able to hook the spell up to the reactor and overclock it to power the spell."

"So the spell can't be done now, to end the war?" I said, probing the hurt spots that were starting to form in the room. "Even by gods? Because that is... to be honest with you, that's where I thought that was going."

No. We could not. Not from what I saw. But...

Yenu opened her mouth, closed it again. For the first time, on the giant mirror of the sphere, I saw that they had replaced her missing teeth with stone. That was good. That was almost funny. The bluestone always used at Their altars, for sacrifices. You saw it on planet after planet. I had always wondered where Their quarries were. It was certainly traded everywhere They had touched. A mouthful of altar stones.

She shook her head. "Well, if a god can't do it, then that spell will never run again. The reactor was destroyed too," she said. "You saw. Everything was."

But if we could take you to it, he said. *Could you do it? Taking into account the gate?*

"What?"

I breathed in. Breathed out. She had only said *What* reflexively: we both knew what he was talking about.

If we could take you to it... The reactor was lost in space, but not entirely lost in time. Time travel, the way only a god could understand it. The reactor had been destroyed, and if Sudworth's logic held true, since that was the only universe that had ever contained the right Johnny Chambers, it also contained the only power source that could have possibly powered this spell.

But there *was* another universe that contained a working reactor: the one that had split off when Johnny had performed the spell, before it changed the shape of the universe.

I felt dizzy. "Wait a minute, wait a minute," I murmured, "won't eight years have passed in that universe too?"

"No," Yenu said; she sounded about how I felt. "I mean, yes and no. I mean, time is a place. That's the confounding factor. That's where you'd go back to—"

"When."

"*When* is a *where*," she said. "You'd just have to find it—which we can't do. And we can only move between dimensions, not universes. We would need the one universe with that exact confluence of... of split after split after split after split. To arrive at that one, at the same time as They were arriving, and the reactor still existed, and we were in the control room... "

Yes, said Ogruthon. *As you say. You could not go there. Only we could get you through.*

"We?"

Gods. Not only me. As many as we can find. Starting with the most important one, the one who strengthens me, and I strengthen her. We must find her next. If the two of us alone are not powerful enough to breach the barrier between our universe and that one, we will die trying.

His words seemed to hang in the air forever, like a bell tolling far away so that each individual note bled into the next. I realized suddenly that I was sweating, my shirt and britches soaked with it and cold.

Yenu said, "Recalculate the spell. Get the reactor online. Wait for the gate to begin to open. And then..."

Yes. Make your... your black hole. So interesting, he added with a chuckle. *As gods, we have seen them. But no one has ever made one. It is impossible.*

"Save the Earth," I said, just to make sure. "Ours."

Yes.

"In theory," Yenu said, automatically, the standard disclaimer she had always given moments before we did something that got us into trouble.

We all stared at each other for a while. "You know," I said, "I always thought you had some kind of brain problem, because you thought you were the most important person in the universe. And now I'm sitting here with a god telling me that you are. You're going to be impossible to live with from now on."

"I notice you're not taking back the brain problem statement," she said.

"Correct."

CHAPTER FIFTEEN

I WRAPPED BOTH hands around the railing and peered over it, down into what should have been an endless abyss of star-spattered darkness, but was instead, very clearly, a river. Dark violet, shot through with skeins of gold here and there, strangely coherent, like thread rather than liquid. Everybody else tended to avoid the railing, staying in their quarters below, or at the very least firmly in the centre of the deck, near the masts; but I, or the thing in me, could not stop myself from returning to stare at the stuff we sailed in, peering down into its murky ripples, the pulse and glitter of the gold inside it. I did not like that I didn't know which.

A tapeworm, I had said, but I didn't mean it. It was eating, all right; I could feel that much. I was constantly ravenous and thirsty, but also nauseated. As time went on, I could barely force myself to eat enough to keep my strength up. And I was constantly tired, bone-tired, in a way I had never felt in my entire life. Sleep didn't help. *It will lessen*, the god said, and I said *When?* and he did not reply.

Yenu had been insistent that we not tell the others about what we were doing. After all, she pointed out, at least the next step was the same as our original plan. But if we told them anything, who knew where that knowledge would spread? If the Ancient Ones—specifically the Manifestation, though we didn't say it—got so much as a whiff of what we were attempting, that would be the end of it. Gods or no, we'd never get back to that nexus of power. The *when* and the *where* that formed the fulcrum on which so many universes balanced.

I thought about it again and shuddered. The only time and place that had ever existed in which every element slotted into place to rid the entire universe of Them forever.

Of course, They'd still exist in the others, Yenu had said quietly. *So in order to keep Them from simply breaking through, if They ever figured it out and found us again, we'd have to fold the Earth into a pocket dimension too. Both spells. Not just one.*

You always remember where you are when your heart breaks, I had said. Because in a world entirely without magic, her covenant would not work; those things within her that we all considered superhuman, and she considered essential for who she was, would be gone. But we could not get around it. The only way to safeguard the Earth permanently was to cut it off from magic.

In the meantime, I would keep up my act of reluctant captive, longsuffering vehicle of the god only, and still seething or even scheming quietly to get home; the spy, if there was one, would never out themself to me, but that was something they could continue to pass on to the Ancient Ones.

If there was a spy.

The only people we were sure weren't the spy were myself and Yenu—and Ogruthon, who had, after all, arrived on the scene well after the paranoia-making coincidences. But no one else was exempt. Not the Advisor, not any of the resistance, not Sudworth.

Sudworth joined me at the railing, putting her hands firmly on the wood and squeezing tight. The vertigo increased the closer you were when you looked at the River, and we'd all figured that out long ago. "That god of yours say anything useful today?"

I shook my head. "He says he's still weak. Doesn't feel good."

She snorted. "You know, after all the trouble we took to find him and bust him out, I thought we'd all be... well, I don't know. Elevated in some way. Promoted. Demi-gods. It's in the historical records back home."

"Me too," I said.

"Not as payment, you understand," she stressed. "Not even as a sign of respect. As a mark of fucking gratitude."

"Those gods," I said. "On Earth. How real do you think they were?"

"You're askin' if I think they were all members of the Adversaries," she said. "Well, I don't. I think a solid ninety-nine percent of 'em were made-up. But the gods *we* came up with resembled us. Famous for it: Xenophanes. Motives too. Culture by culture, area by area. Now what I think we're seeing is what they didn't put in the stories. That the real gods are *absolutely irrational*. The good ones, the bad ones. Them and their games. No difference. In fact, makes me wonder where they came from. The Elder Gods, the Ancient Ones. The same place? Different? What's yours say, eh?"

I shook my head again. What was a Xenophanes? She'd be annoyed if I asked.

"What the hell kind of divinity doesn't know its own origins?" she said. "So much for all-seeing and all-knowing."

"Even if he did know I don't think he'd tell me," I said. "So far I think we are on a strictly need-to-know basis. Don't ask, don't tell. But also ask, don't tell."

"And how do you even know it's a he?"

"I don't," I said. "I asked him what I should say, if I was talking about him to others. And he said... I really can't describe it. I know a lot of languages now and I heard a word in all of them at the same time. I asked him to repeat it and the same thing happened. It was like having a truck horn blasting once right behind my head, *honnnnk!* It's like... *he, it, us, we, I, me.* All at the same time. So I just use he. I don't think the gods are very interested in gender. Or language, for that matter. Theirs, maybe. Not ours."

I looked down at her hands on the dark wood: the thin fingers, the veins thick and blue, protruding through the silken white skin, crisscrossed here and there with the neat cuneiform of fresh stitches. "You said absolutely irrational," I said. "Is that why they were always at war?"

"No," she said, after a moment's reflection. "No, I do think there would have been coexistence. Between them and us—mortals I mean. If no one had tried to impose their will on anyone else. But the Adversaries couldn't stop Themselves. It's not in Them to know what restraint is. You've seen that for yourself."

"Yes," I said. "But I haven't seen what the Elder Gods consider restraint either. What if they eliminate Them and turn out to be worse?"

She snorted. "Your bodyguard thinks that, you know. He won't come out and say *Might makes right*, but he thinks the Adversaries won the war because the war needed winning. He said to eliminate dissent eliminates conflict."

"He's not wrong," I said. "What part of that is wrong?"

She sighed, and seemed about to respond, then turned away from me and headed back to the others.

Yenu and Sudworth had kept mostly out of sight for a few days, or whatever felt like days as we sailed, working away in the hold. Unsatisfied with a mere device this time, Yenu had built a kind of wayfinding laboratory, all sorts of jury-rigged and string-fastened odds and ends of sigil-scribbled wood and slate.

Ogruthon had offered no assistance except for

informing Yenu of the other god's name, Caustur, and that one of the weapons we had stolen had been hers, and so bore a kind of magical fingerprint that could, with work, be extracted and engineered into a kind of homing signal. The spell was very complicated, and Sudworth had insisted that it could not be done. There simply wasn't enough information; we were like bloodhounds being offered a cloth with not even enough of a trace for their famous noses.

But we had no choice.

Hopefully, staying in the shadows, out of the searchlight of Their hatred, might buy us a little time. But what we needed more than time was power, and that we could not buy. We would have to dig it up, like a hidden seam of ore.

Footsteps behind me. Yenu came up out of the hold, tossed me a wary look, and moved to the bow, her shadow fuzzed and radiant from the weird multi-spectrum light of the stars here. "Everybody below," someone called, and I trudged back to the trapdoor with the others, heavy of heart.

And what if this god can't help us? I asked Ogruthon as I climbed down the steps. *Or what if she won't? What then?*

Silence. I sighed and sat against the wall, in the blanket-padded area we'd eventually accumulated next to the bunks. We waited together for the sound of the Violet River to change.

*   *   *

I STOOD BECALMED for a moment, trying to figure out what was so strange about what we were looking at. Yenu nudged me. "Blue sky," she said, as if she were reading my mind, her voice slightly warped through the helmet. "Blue water."

"Jesus."

That was it. I had been away from Earth so long I had basically talked myself into being weirded out by both. I stared up at the sky like I'd never seen the colour blue before, drinking it in. It tasted like home. If only we could...

"I know," Yenu said quietly. "But come on. This way."

"Are you sure?"

"God, no." She had the metal columns we'd stolen from the armoury in Bejurru in her pack, what Ogruthon had assured us was Caustur's particularly beloved weapon. In some way the wires and stones wrapped around it were supposed to alert us as we neared its imprisoned owner. Ogruthon had had to admit that inasmuch as his weakened and dulled divine senses could tell him, he would be no help here. Not until she had been freed.

Aside from the blue sky, it was a strange world. It resembled the sci-fi comics I had read as a kid: bizarre machinery littered the uncannily flat landscape. Oily-looking water had pooled in a few low areas, the pools perfectly rectilinear or circular. "Is this place in the future?"

"It's in the now," Yenu said. "Everything's in the now. I mean, you didn't really expect nowhere to have better technology than Earth, did you?"

"I don't know. Part of me must have."

"That's Terracentrism," she said, climbing over a small heap of glassy pebbles and broken circuitry. "I had to get over that too. The idea that Earth contains the most advanced non-magical technology in the universe."

"Con*tained*," I said, unable to help myself.

"Mm."

As I walked, I could not help feeling something strange, something I thought I had never felt before—that is, I *had*, but not for years, and that was what was strange about it. Not curiosity exactly, but hope. And hope for something like this specifically—that the Ancient Ones, so atavistic and possessive about Their conquered worlds, had spared or overlooked this one for long enough that a civilization that looked like something out of a particularly baroque 1980s comic book could exist. A world of the expected neoclassic architecture (look at those pillars and arches in the distance, fluted and ridged by the careful hands of someone used to working with marble) tangled with unbelievable inorganic complexity: like a railcar full of clock parts had crashed on Cybertron.

A sound approached us, familiar, almost friendly: water lapping softly against sand. Following it and Yenu's directions, we eventually came up a skinny stone bridge ending in a wide plateau.

In the middle of the plateau was a high gate, thirty storeys if it was an inch, built of smooth white stone that gleamed like glass, capped by a trapezoidal tangle of machinery and circuitry so complex I could barely look at it without giving myself a headache. Cables and wires dangled from the cap, blowing lightly in the breeze.

Yenu and I glanced at each other, and led the way around the gate; the Advisor and Ksajakra followed us. No way was I walking through that, though it might have been dead a billion years now. I wanted very badly to touch the stone, see how smooth it was, but even that I managed to resist. Maybe in some other universe some far more foolhardy Nick walked through it. Good luck to him.

On the far side of the gate was a flight of deep steps, which only the Advisor took easily; the rest of us had to awkwardly hop down or, in Yenu's case, turn and climb, lowering herself down step by step, grunting and snarling faintly in her helmet. At the bottom waited a beach encircling a still, slate-blue lake or inland sea. The water lapped modestly onto the white sand, perfectly clear.

Ksajakra picked up a handful of the sand; I could not resist doing the same. It wasn't really sand, but a mixture of rough-edged stones, gravel, and what looked like bits of glass—but far more than that, like the precisely milled assembly-line teeth of sharks. All were the same uniform white.

It has been a long time, the god inside me murmured. *I did not think this place really existed... See, this is Lake I'inausk, which they say has been here for ten billion years. The sand is the crumbled bones of sea serpents who fight each other without end. Beautiful.*

I stared out at the lake, and carefully let the handful of sand dribble from my fingers. "I could have done without knowing that," I said. No one responded. The water was so still; I wondered how deep the lake was, if these things were fighting somewhere in it.

Very deep, said Ogruthon. *I think deeper than you would like to be told about.*

Get out of my thoughts!

I am sorry. I am only trying to help. You have so many questions, and I have answers to some of them, and...

Yenu held up Caustur's weapon, began to say something, then cried out and dropped it; we jumped back as the wires around the metal columns melted into droplets, and the bound artifacts and gems simply disintegrated, the dust disappearing into the sand. The columns themselves glowed white, then returned to their normal colour.

She examined her palms minutely, her hands shaking. "Okay," she said slowly. "No problem."

"Except..." I prompted her.

"Except that you can't use magic to find the way in. There's warding somewhere... maybe inside the water. I'm guessing it's rigged to activate based on a certain type or magnitude of spell. Which makes sense."

"So," I said. "Problem."

"It's here," she said stubbornly. "We're close. I just have to figure out..."

I wandered off and found a rock to sit on, letting her voice fade as she lectured and gesticulated, picked up the now-cool weapon, waved it around. *Any tips?* I said to Ogruthon, without much hope.

I'm sorry. All I know about the place is the lake, the monsters. If I were the Ancient Ones, I would have placed the prison inside the lake, which you all know already. But the gate is probably on the shore, safe from the serpents. It could be anywhere.

Mm.

This place was formed when it was struck by something from the sky, the god went on, as if that helped. *It's perfectly round. You could go to a thousand worlds and never find a lake as round and as deep as this.*

Probably.

I shifted on my rock and glanced up and down the shores. Other stones were ranged along the shoreline for hundreds of paces, some vertical, some lying flat in the soft bone sand; they looked both natural and *placed* in some way, though I couldn't quite put my finger on it. Like landscaping rocks. As if...

And memory ambushed me, nearly tumbled me from my seat, something I had not asked for or dreamed or experienced, something delivered whole and solid into my mind by a consortium of books that had spoken to other books and taken over my consciousness while I had been in Sudworth's pocket dimension, before it had been blown apart by the worm—

"CAN YOU SLOW down and say it again?"

"Don't give me that look!" I wanted to take the helmet off, but settled for raising my voice instead. "I said, the stones are a message. The code is their location. I don't know how I know and I don't know who told me. It was just a flash of something, all right? I don't even know if the books meant for me to know."

"What does Ogruthon say?"

"He didn't disagree," I said, which was true; he had fallen silent. Her face worked. Ksajakra and the Advisor watched us closely, as if wondering whether they would have to work together to truss one of us up and take us back to the ship, frothing and mad. Strange that our entire complement of goods in the hold had no straitjacket in it. Or had she thought of that too?

"Hmm," she said. "A message encrypted in placement. But why shouldn't it be? Their distance from each other. Sitting or standing. Maybe some of them were standing and fell. That would complicate things. If I can figure out the code..."

She trailed off, glanced around. "Give me a minute."

THE SILENCE INSIDE the ship was thick, muffling, cold. From outside came the call and reply of unknowable creatures. I was glad there were no windows, less glad at the way voices bounced and resounded through the strange bluish metal. The floor was coated in a few inches of slimy water, but nothing dripped or flowed. In the light of the weak overhead bulbs, our faces and hands seemed drained of colour, chalky and dusty. Yenu moved ahead of us, catlike, putting her feet down carefully.

"I can't believe that worked," I murmured.

"I probably would have figured it out eventually

myself," she said. "But I mean, thanks for speeding things up. That was a good thing to remember right then. Do you remember what book told you that?"

She had never been good at gratitude; I ignored it. "No. Do you remember... that? Being at Sudworth's archive. Her home. And the books said they wanted to talk to me..."

"I remember." She paused and ran a hand along the perfectly flat, smooth metal wall, as if she expected a door to open up. "We sat outside. I could hear you crashing around in there, books falling onto the floor. And then nothing. You must have been writing then."

"What did you talk about?"

"We didn't talk." She frowned at the wall as if it had offended her, and kept moving. The shrieking cries outside had to get through the water, and then through the ship's hull, and then through our helmets to get to us, and I did not like that after all those barriers I could still hear them. They seemed too random and furious to be echolocation. Maybe it was just the screams of fights.

Fought without end, the god had said. Maybe the sea monsters screamed at each other first, and only then fought. Like displays of dominance. How long, how many generations, had they battled around this thing we were in? This thing like a spaceship, submerged at the bottom of the impossibly round lake, under who knew how much pressure, in the dark, perfect silence.

"I'm worried about her," I said, for something to say. "Sudworth. We shouldn't have left her with the others on the ship..."

"Frankly, I'd be more worried about them." We both slipped in the layer of muck and recovered our footing; behind me, Ksajakra swore. You'd think the place would have been sealed tight. In space it would have been airtight, tight against vacuum, the loss of any molecules needed for life; down here, as Yenu had pushed us through the thick, strange glassiness of the gate, it had seemed intact, perfectly so. But I supposed you only needed one tiny hole to let in water.

I thought about death by drowning down here and found myself not minding the idea too much. There would be pain, but not for long. And I had almost drowned before. Always missing that crucial final step, that was all.

"How did this get here?" Ksajakra said, looking around—particularly up, where the long flatworms of dull light lay along the metal ceiling.

"Hard to say," Yenu said. "My best guess? This god Caustur, and maybe others, were trying to use it to escape this place. Maybe they couldn't get away without it, or maybe the god simply didn't want to leave some mortals behind. Maybe they built it here, maybe it was from somewhere else. As for when? They must have known the war was over, or nearly over. And with this they intended to get away... and they just didn't."

"And the war ended," the Advisor said. "And the killing stopped. I urge you again, Yenu, to let this plan of yours go. It is not too late."

"Uh huh," she said, not looking back. "And do what, exactly? Go back to Aradec? Hand over two gods and what remains of the resistance back to the most evil creatures in the universe so they can be tortured, mutilated, killed, and eaten? Probably not in that order? And let the new war continue until every world they can reach is under their control? No thanks."

"You speak of them as if every world will face the same fate as yours," the Advisor said, pausing as she stopped again to feel the walls. "But from what the Prophet has told me... that fate was unique to your world."

She moved her hand more slowly on the metal, then kept walking.

"Consider Aradec," the Advisor said. "Ninety-nine of one hundred people living their lives in peace. Which you must have seen for yourself, if you were on our world for as long as you say you were. Perhaps the rules of the Masters were not to your taste. But supposing all the worlds They take were like that. Would that not be better than this?"

"This what?" she finally snapped, turning to glare at him. "Look, you're hardly here by invitation, and you *weren't* invited to share your opinion. You don't know what They're going to do this time, and you clearly aren't aware that I'm going to do whatever's needed to stop Their war. *Literally* whatever it takes."

"This war that you started," he said. "This war that began a blink of an eye ago, in Their time, because of you. Because you woke Them. Because you broke the long peace. Because you think the one in a hundred is worth imperiling the ninety-nine for."

Ksajakra stared at them both, mouth hanging open;

moments later I realized that the Advisor had been speaking in Low Dath since we had landed. "Is that true?" he finally said.

Yenu didn't even glance at him. "All the more reason to raise an army against Them," she said. "Not less. You thought I was going to say something else, didn't you? Look at your face. You thought I'd say *It doesn't matter who started it. It doesn't matter that it wasn't on purpose. It was in the past.* Well, I've had about eight years to think about whether it does or doesn't matter. I've looked at my own fucking fingers twitching in a pool of blood, thinking *Does this matter?* I'll give more than that to stop this. Alone, if I have to. Now are you going to help us or are you going to fight us?"

"I would like to hear you say it. I would like to hear that you acknowledge that you started this war. That it was you. As the Prophet said."

"I said. Help or no? You are not needed on the journey. So you should say now."

For a moment even the noises outside stopped, as if the serpents were briefly considering what dominance meant, or how to recalculate it given this new challenger.

And I thought, not for the first time: What I thought in those first moments of seeing her resurrected and mismatched eyes was true. We *could* stop her. Any of us. Not even together: any one of us, by ourselves, if we dared. She's not immortal; she's small, she bleeds, she can die. We could put the world right again. Stop dragging these half-dead divinities out of their rightful incarceration and put ourselves on a side. So why don't we?

Because you'd have to kill her to stop her. And none of us dares. Because we don't know what we'd be killing.

These people might kill my only chance to go home. Back to my *real* home.

I thought, too, more quietly, or at a lower level: If this was Their plan, if she is Their pawn, that was precisely what They would have her say. It would sound plausible. It does sound plausible. Coming from her. And it keeps us unswervingly on the path that They have chosen. It keeps us walking into Their traps, trusting that we will escape, regain confidence, and then be trapped forever in a final one. All this is planned. Every triumph, every disaster. Even us being trapped places that only she can get us out of. Even that. Planned. But by who?

In the silence of the Advisor's absent reply rose a new sound, much closer than the sound of the serpents: footsteps, racing towards us down the long flickering hallway, ringing on the metal floor. Ksajakra and I drew our swords a fraction of a second before the galloping forms collided, Yenu flattening herself against the wall and sprouting two daggers suddenly from either hand, snarling defiance as she dove to the floor and rose again, stabbing and retreating, snaking around the floor suddenly wet with both stagnant water and blood of several colours.

Guards? Maybe. Or just the crew of the ship, trapped and undying, inexplicably alive. Or semi-alive: they bled liquid as we fought, but also a pale gas that rose and filled the hallway, clouding our view. The Advisor howled, a sound I had never heard him make before, and tried to get out of the cloud, toppling instead into a dark heap on the floor. I cried out for him, found myself surrounded with uniformed bodies, clawing hands. They had no weapons, I realized, but were swarming us, trying to get close enough to punch, kick, claw.

Maybe *not* alive. Maybe semi-alive. No time to think about what or who we were fighting, only that they were fighting and wouldn't stop. My sword, blunt but heavy, was sort of a joke in this place, this futuristic flying palace. In a comic, this would have been Conan the Barbarian falling into a Buck Rogers issue.

A dozen deflated bodies lay on the ground when it was over, but all around us now the metal jingled and trembled, with new defenders coming for us, above or below us, or along the hundreds of hallways that branched from ours. I stooped and stupidly tried to raise the Advisor; he shook me off, but gently, and got up on his own. "What happened?" I gasped.

"I do not know—it went through the glass of this thing—the mist, the fog, it went *through* the—"

"Save your breath," Ksajakra said. "We're outnumbered, badly, much worse than this, I think. When they find us—"

"We go," Yenu said, "we have no choice but to go. Run."

"Where are we going? Do you even know?"

"It'll have been in the engine room," she said as we pounded after her down the hallway. "Powering the ship."

"You don't know how to find the engine room!" I said.

"Where the noises are loudest," she called back, glancing once over her shoulder. "What they're trying to guard. That way."

Again this sense of panic deep within me that I still could not say was a god or just my own common sense: the genius, the prodigy, relying on such a crude calculation. I swore foully in all the languages I could summon, and sped up, arms pumping.

BY THE TIME we reached what Yenu insisted was the engine room, we had fought off an uncounted number of the guards, or whatever they were. I still felt sure they were crew, and didn't want to think about how they were persisting down here, how they could still be alive, what being alive meant. They were more like puppets being powered by the whitish-green gas that puffed from them and choked the Advisor.

The engine room was a glittering monstrosity hung with long shreds of bioluminescent moss, or fungus, or something; Ksajakra and I barricaded the door we'd fought our way through, tugging down panels and forcing them into the narrow jamb, looking around for other points of entry, unable to see any in the dim and uncertain light.

"We cannot do magic here," he panted. "Can we? Any magic. Like she said. Or was she lying?"

"I don't know," I said. "I've stopped being able to tell. That blue thing over there, let's see if it will break off."

Outside, things hammered against the door; our barrier

vibrated, but held. A few minutes' respite? We brushed awkwardly through the dangling moss, shuddering as it touched our bare skin, to discover Yenu in the middle of a kind of spherical gantry or cage, like the kind (I thought at once, and laughed out loud, confusing the others) of iron cage you'd see motorcycle stunt riders in at rodeos and Klondike Days.

How had she gotten in there? I could barely fit an arm through the hexagonal openings, slick as they were with the glowing slime. She must have taken her helmet off, held her breath, eeled through, put it back on. Now she knelt in the centre, cradling something in her hand that I couldn't see, her body hunched over it. Protective, or had she simply buckled in despair? It triggered some memory deep in me, something painful but just at the edge of tolerance, as if I had held my hand near an open flame. I shook my head sharply. It was hard to concentrate through the banging outside.

"Yenu!" Ksajakra rapped his sword pommel on the cage. "Get out of there!"

"She's dead," Yenu murmured. "I didn't think it could... What does death mean to a god?"

Ogruthon! What now? I shouted inside myself, but there was no answer. I held down a stab of anger, knowing it was really terror. This wasn't his fault.

"All right," I said, when Yenu didn't get up. "All right, fine. We'll do something else, we'll... There are other gods. Forget it. We have to go. If we try to go the way we came, we'll have to fight those... things again. Is there another way out?"

Moving slowly, and showing no reaction to either of us whatsoever, Yenu opened her hand over the small box she had brought, shut it, fastened the catch, and put it back into her coat. Her hands were black to the wrists with her own blood. And then she simply knelt there, unmoving, as the noises behind us increased in volume and frenzy, accompanied by a strange, hollow howling that seemed to come from every direction at once.

"Yenu!" I hit the cage too, hoping to startle her. Nothing. "Come on! You got us in here, you're going to have to get us out."

Something has happened to her, Ogruthon said, so loudly that I reeled; I caught myself on the metal cage, vision gone, a whiteness hissing like television static.

"Her who? The god, or Yenu?"

Yes.

"...Can *you* get us out?" I said through the hiss, unsure if the others could hear me. The banging on the doors seemed very distant.

If all of you, not far, I suspect. This entire lake is a prison, a deep well of designed hungers, and it will eat the spell even as I cast it.

"We're not leaving anyone behind. Just get us to dry land," I said. "We can make our own way back."

It will cost you. It will cost us both.

"Thank you for the warning," I said, "but I think you understand as well as I do that we're going to have to pay whether we like it or not. Just do it."

A beat; my vision gradually returned, still fuzzed around the edges and crackling with invisible electricity, squirming in a disorderly mob so that I could only see in a tunnel directly ahead of myself. I took a deep breath, another, and rapped on the cage one last time. "Yenu, come on. We can't get in there to grab you. Ogruthon says he can get us out of here, but it'll be a near damn thing."

Inside me there was a tug, experimental, like the briefest muscle cramp, and then a long, steady pull, in a dozen places at once, at first only pressure, then building to pain. "Yenu! It's starting! What the fuck is wrong with you?" I added in English.

At last she stirred, gazing around as if she had just realized that we were all yelling. The floor began to vibrate up through the soles of my boots, so hard that my teeth clacked together. I locked my jaw and looked back at Ksajakra and the Advisor through my crackling tunnel: they were braced and ready, standing behind me a few paces away. Our makeshift barricade was giving way, the railings and panels beginning to slide across the slimy floor.

I lifted my sword again, wearily, my arms on fire, muscle, bone, something else, whatever the god was doing, whatever he was eating or ripping away from me to build the spell; my helmet filled with the rotting-fruit-and-solvent smell of magic. And above the cage, an orange spot began to glow on the ceiling, burning away the rags of mould and web that hung from it so that ash rained onto us, embers fluttering across the room and sputtering in the slime.

Yenu absently wiped the ash from her helmet, leaving

a long gray smear. "Get out of there!" Ksajakra shouted again.

We cannot leave her!

"I'm well fucking aware of that! Yenu! Get—" My voice left me in a wave of agony, rippling across me from inside to out, seeming to earth itself in my fingertips and head, so that I was only dimly aware that I was staggering, then falling. Someone caught me, and darkness covered my helmet. A wing, the black feathers smeared with filth.

From the ground I writhed and watched the orange circle grow, to redden in the centre like a sunset, and then suddenly open. A column of water slammed down, caving in the top of the metal cage like a fist, washing Yenu across it with a startled cry. My arm reached out for her without a single conscious thought, causing a fresh wave of pain that crisscrossed my body as if I had torn it off and set it on fire. I screamed, unheard in the din of the falling water.

The room was rapidly flooding, the thin trickle of water through the door its only release; everything we had not seized to barricade the door was beginning to float, and icy water lapped at my legs, rising with shocking speed.

Ksajakra was shouting something to the Advisor, who nodded, and they began to climb the half-crushed cage, the Advisor managing easily with three limbs, holding me with the fourth as I twisted and shrieked; Yenu, below me in moments, was no more than a scarlet mote in what vision I had left, paddling and kicking, trying to get to the walls of the cage.

What are you doing? I screamed internally. *We'll drown before you get that open! And she's still trapped!*

The god did not reply; the water torrented down as if forced through a firehose, under who knew what pressure, the ceiling bowing under it, metal beginning to tear like paper. The glowing strips in the ceiling went out. I waited for the cold to ease the pain, but it did not. The cost, he had said. The cost—

At last, the hole in the ceiling began to glow a blue-white, and I shut my eyes as we were yanked upwards through it, walloping briefly through a thin wall of water seemingly as hard as concrete, and dragged at skin-flaying speed through a glittering whiteness that left us washed up, gasping and shivering, somewhere else, but on solid ground, dry and flat.

I GOT UP sluggishly; my body felt loose, boneless almost, as if I had been a rubber band stretched too far. (Maybe I had? Best not to think about it.) My helmet was cracked—it looked all the way through this time, though the filters were still working, and I could breathe if I did it slowly. A spangled green arc interrupted my field of vision, which had returned more or less to normal, if a little pink where I must have busted some blood vessels.

"Where are we?" I croaked; the metal plain was featureless, no sign of the lake, and the few ruins far in the distance were plainly not the ship. "Ogruthon. Hey. Where did you put us?"

The ship is not far, the voice finally came back, faint

and tinny, as weak as when I had first heard him. I had to strain to hear him over the noise of the wind. *An hour's walk. Head towards the three-spired tower to our left and you will see it.*

"Stop saying *our*," I said. "That's *my* left and don't you forget it. If you don't have a body, you don't have a left."

Silence; then a faint chuckle.

I told the others, pointed at the tower, and went over to where Yenu was curled on the ground like a shrimp, poking her back with the toe of my boot. Her helmet was shattered like a car windshield held together with safety film. I had thought Ogruthon would break the cage open somehow, but he must have just given one tremendous yank to get her out. "What happened in there?"

"I don't know," she said, not getting up.

"Can you walk for an hour?"

"I don't know."

"And may I just say, it is very refreshing to hear you finally admit that you don't have all the answers," I said. "Come on. Your lieutenant will carry you if he has to."

"Okay."

She still didn't move, and I sighed and squatted next to her. "All right, so the god is dead," I said quietly. "It's a speedbump, not a dead end. You'll do what you always do. Pivot based on new information, pick a new direction, and go. It's not the end. What, did it fuck you up somehow?"

"I think so."

"Oh." That was interesting; but without even consulting the god inside of me, I knew it wasn't something we could fix. I leaned closer, closer, till our helmets touched, and pitched my voice just loud enough to go through them both. "Get up or get dragged."

She got up.

CHAPTER SIXTEEN

Around the ship, in the star-filled void, we began to see things like small tornadoes, tiny angry vortices of star-dust and pale flame. Yenu and Sudworth seemed to think they were ill omens; I leaned on the railing and watched them as the two discussed things from their personal treasure hoard of strange knowledge, their voices occasionally drifting back to me like dry leaves, a word here and there only. The dust devils were pretty, and they seemed harmless enough.

I did not know where Yenu was taking us now, only that we had to get away from the prison in the lake. We were forming patterns by what we were doing, and if there was any way to break up the pattern, we had to try.

And still I felt, without any evidence, that we were being pursued, and laughingly so; as if we were being tracked by something that saw our course like footprints on fresh snow, every part of the track visible.

The Advisor padded up next to me and sat back on his haunches. He smelled of the strong herbal soap we had brought onboard, and woodsmoke. "The others are eating at the fire," he said.

"Mm."

"I brought you food," he added. "I will eat with you, Prophet, if you will tolerate the company. It seems you wish to be alone."

"No. I thought I did. Maybe I just don't want to eat alone." I laughed bitterly, and unwrapped the packet of food: dried fruit, a rectangular slab of cheese crusted around the edges with crystals of salt and shards of pepper, a brick of compact, chewy black bread. At the bottom of the packet were several long shreds of jerky, dark red and fatty.

"Did... she tell you what happened in the ship of the god?" the Advisor said, unwrapping his own packet.

"No. But *something* did. You know, I truly think she doesn't know. That frightens her more than whatever happened. It wouldn't be correct to say that she knew everything, even back on... back when I first knew her. But it would be correct, I think, to say that she's rarely even had to *consider* that she doesn't know more than all the people around her."

"So she was wise? Or she surrounded herself with fools?"

"Both, I suppose." And again I had a flash of the past, unwanted, burning, brief: the bright little insects ambling along the hallways of her keep, that huge joke house like a fortress dug so deep into the ground I used to think it was warmed by the mantle, the insects looking for things to roll, unsure of what they were supposed to do with them afterwards.

"But not all who are wise can be trusted."

"No."

"Whatever happens…" the Advisor began, then paused.

"I know what you're going to say," I said. "So let me say it, because you'll dance around it and dance around it and dance around it and you'll say something next to it but it won't be what you meant to say. I'll say it for you. Listen, Advisor. She lied to me. She lied to save her image, then she lied to save her powers, and the world ended and I thought, *At least she cannot lie to me any more*. So now, no, I don't trust her. I trust nothing she says, nothing. And if the time comes that I think she is lying again and I must make a choice, it's you I'll save, not her."

"I—"

"She thinks she's a chosen one," I said, irritated. "And she's got the rest of them thinking that too… She isn't. She's a tool made by a malevolent blacksmith. If she says otherwise, that's a lie too. We have to save her *only* so he can't use her. She's not a chosen one. She's a made thing. Broken down and remade into something worse, not better. And chosen only because she survived the breaking. That's all. She doesn't deserve to live through this. Neither do I. You do."

He shook his head.

"Stop," I said. "You don't know her like I do. She'll betray us all, Advisor. It's what she was made to do. She fights it all the time. When she gets tired of fighting, it'll be the end of us."

"Then what should we do about it?"

"I don't know. Nothing, I suppose. Not without hard evidence. As we've been doing. The others will still defend her to the death. They really think she's some kind of saviour... They bought her whole act. I admit it's the one she's best at. She steps onto the stage and she plays it no matter what else she's supposed to be doing." I folded the empty paper carefully, put it in my pocket, and took out my canteen. Empty. They would probably have wine at the firepit, but I still felt unwelcome there.

"The problem is, we won't know she's about to betray us until the moment she does it," I said, leaning on the railing again, looking down into the eddies of the River. "Before that, what can we do? You can't arrest someone before they've committed a crime."

"You can if they say they will commit the crime."

"Only on Aradec," I said. "That won't fly here. And she hasn't said anything, anyway. And she won't."

He stretched his wings, resettled them flat against his back, a gesture he used as, more or less, punctuation. "Then we must wait."

"I don't see what else we can do." I put my canteen back, and added, "I suppose we could go get some wine. If we both go."

"Yes, we could do that." He smiled. "I'll go if you will."

*   *   *

WHEN WE SAT, Itzlek hefted the jug from its niche in the rim of the pit, poured, and handed me a wooden cup of wine, tea-hot, and supplemented both with herbs and, I thought, a healthy glug of something far more high-octane than wine. I sat, juggling my cup, and Liandan got up from next to me without comment and wandered off towards the heads.

Sudworth had gotten well into whatever the drink was; she was so pink her white eyebrows stood out like chalk. "Don't you start," she said, before I said anything.

"No'm."

Yenu was playing with something small, and staring moodily into the fire.

"What's that?" I said, and was surprised when she held it out to me; I took it automatically, somewhat out of surprise as well, and examined it closely: a wooden box, stained dark brown and with a simple brass clasp and corners. It looked like the kind of thing you'd put an engagement ring into, though less fancy. It felt empty. "That wasn't really an answer," I said.

"You can open it if you want," she said, still looking at the fire.

"Absolutely not," I said. "There was a whole movie warning people not to open strange boxes."

"I promise you the Cenobites will not show up."

"If they do, *you* talk to them," I warned her. "I am not even giving them the time of day."

"I will."

I flipped up the catch; everyone craned their heads to look. It wasn't empty, but its contents weren't what I had expected, either. Well, and how big was a god when it was alive, and how small did it become when it was dead, and what did size mean to gods anyway?

I held it up to my eye in case Ogruthon wanted to look, unsure as always whether he could look with or without me. Inside was only a droplet of something that looked like mercury, skittering around the lightly-incised sigils on the inner surface as I tilted it around. Unable to stop myself, I tipped the box over my hand and waited for the droplet to hit my palm, but it stayed stuck inside. I shut the box again and gave it back to Yenu.

"Did Ogruthon say anything?" she said.

"No."

She bowed her head over the box again, moved it between her remaining fingers slowly, easy with the lightness of it. As clearly as if she had spoken I thought: *She wants to toss it into the firepit.*

She wouldn't, I knew. Not in front of everyone. If she were going to do it, she would do it later, by herself. Rekindling the fire if she had to. Her life was still composed of this: succeed and only succeed in public; fail only in private. Certainly do not draw attention to the failure. There was still that about her. There was still that, and it still made her dangerous. And even with the small, hopeful flame of our plan burning inside me, this fear would not go away.

I had felt hope before, and she had killed it before.

"Yenu," Rhakun said softly, "please, where are we going now?"

"We are actively evading pursuit," she said. "We are putting distance between ourselves and the scene of this latest liberation. It is a tactical retreat."

"And then what will we do?"

"Then we will renew the fight."

"But how?"

"I'll figure that out," she said.

No you won't, I thought. Because we've finally been told that the task we have to accomplish is too big for you. For any single person. For any mortal. For all the mortals that still live. We need to do the impossible and there's no way you can get around it. When will they turn on you? Soon, I think. And what will *I* do when they do?

No one spoke for a long time. At last, Sudworth got up and stretched, unsteadily, and announced that she was going below; one by one, everyone got up and followed. Ksajakra was the last, and he and I both paused and looked at Yenu, alone by the fire, before we too walked down the steps.

I WOKE TO fire, to smothering smoke, falling through the clouds of a dream of a glassy black mountain with a single inhabitant, watching me, fire, fire, "Fire!" I tried to scream but no words came, nor breath.

Reality slammed back into place like a door: not fire but pain, a stabbing blade and a hand around my throat, and someone's hot, desperate, sour breath. I reached out blindly, felt the blade slash across my palm in the dark, snarled, used my other hand to pry away the hand squeezing my neck, and finally seized a handful of hair and ear and slammed a head against the wooden edge of the bunk.

In a moment I had slithered fully out of the bunk and, despite not being able to use my left arm properly, brought my full weight down on top of something that squirmed and flailed, and held it down on the floor, still silent. Blade. Where was it? Did they drop it? I groped for a throat, felt beard, stubble, scraping my hand, the sudden snap of teeth, saliva falling across my fingers.

The curtains were yanked aside, and lanterns appeared out of nowhere, dazzling me so that I couldn't see, and then it was a blur of golden light, red blood, voices, hands. Pain roared and shrieked where my neck and shoulder met, and something bobbed out of the corner of my eye, something bright, wet. There was a scuffle, the clang of metal against metal, and then, very near my ear, a man's voice saying in Low Dath, "Someone fetch a cloth, quickly!"

"Who was it," I said, or the god said, or somebody. "Who was it? *Who*."

No one answered; a white face passed close to mine, startling me so that I gasped and tried to recoil as if from a ghost. I felt drunk, despite only having a few sips of wine several hours ago. Had it been several hours? There was no time here on the river of darkness.

"Oh my *God*," said the face in English. Another flurry: my shirt being removed, then my undershirt, and then I was on the floor and someone was pressing on my shoulder with both hands. Underneath, it felt as if they had brought a live coal to hold against my skin. "Quit moving around! God. I need someone heavier—no, not you."

A darkness, a familiar face. The lanterns kept swaying. Were we being buffeted in the current? What current? I breathed, smelled blood. The Advisor reached out carefully with his right forepaw and pressed it down on the coal.

"Hear me out!" someone was shouting in Low Dath, a man. "Then let me finish what I began!"

"Who," I said again, aware that my voice was ragged and faint.

"Liandan," said someone next to me. Yenu, breathing fast. "He must have been trying to cut your throat. While you were. While..."

"Fucking incompetent," I croaked. "Did you put him up to this. Did you ask to have me killed. You son of a bitch. Did you think the god would go to you? Is that what you wanted all along? How long were you planning this, when did you tell him to do it?"

"Stop talking shit."

"You. *You.* You almost had me. You'd do anything, anything for power, not even money, *power*, we saw it for years, and then it was all taken from you, you were a vermin-infested skeleton in a dungeon, but you saw it swing by you again, close enough for you to touch—"

"Shut up," she said. "Stop it. You're not even making sense, and you'll say something you'll regret."

"Will I." It was becoming difficult to speak.

"Trust me or not, I don't care," she said, putting her face closer to mine. "The god had his chance. Anyway, if I wanted to kill you, I'd do it myself. And I don't want the spy to hear any of this. Shut *up*."

"Then why...?" The lights swirled, grew dark halos, brightened, became pink, became gold again. The Advisor's great face leaned over mine for a moment.

"I think he's blacking out," he said.

"No I'm—"

LIGHT RETURNED; I was still on the floor, and there was still shouting. Had I only been out for a minute or two? No, longer. A bandage had been wrapped across my chest, under my right arm and back over, as thick and stiff as plaster. I felt lightheaded and cold, and my whole body was covered in sweat.

Someone helped me sit up, and I swayed, accepted a scratchy blanket, smelling of wood chips. My left arm, the hand also bandaged, felt heavy but not paralyzed. That was something.

The others had formed a circle around Liandan, who had been bound at the wrists, and sat on the floor with his legs in front of him. Blood stained and stiffened his tawny hair. I hoped it was his, but the stuff on his shirt was probably mostly mine.

These people. Not that I had trusted them, no, but we had been through so much together, we had eaten, fought, even bathed together, there was nowhere else we could go, nowhere to hide, this ship was our floating refuge and the refuge was not safe—it too contained monsters. I couldn't believe it had taken this long, I thought bleakly. That was the only surprise really.

Maybe they had all wanted to do it. Maybe from day one. And had drawn straws, and Liandan had lost. Or won.

I glared at him. Ksajakra knelt in front of me, and unfolded a ripped piece of cloth to show the dagger: stunningly long, covered in blood from tip to hilt. I was shocked at how long it was. I don't know what I had been expecting. Yenu's daggers were barely longer than her hand. And the hilt brightly decorated with blue glass, that must have been what I saw sparkling and taunting me in the light, before they had pulled it out.

"Let me loose, you fucking fools!" Liandan snapped.

"What are we going to do with him?" Ksajakra said to me and, it seemed, Yenu, sitting cross-legged next to me, painted in crimson from her chin to her hips.

"Ask him why he did it," she whispered, taking the cloth-wrapped dagger. "Then we can decide."

"Why would that make a difference?" he said, then shrugged at her expression, and stood, returning to the prisoner. "You said to hear you out. Go on."

"The real question is why none of *you* have done anything!" Liandan shouted, spluttering blood in long, sticky strings onto his already-stained shirt. I hadn't realized I'd hit him so hard, and felt a split second of remorse before remembering that I had done so while he'd been trying to murder me. "That's the real question! For three nights now I've listened to the bastard talking in his sleep—yes, and you all would say you've heard nothing! I heard him! It's because he's *still on Their side*! He is! He talks, it's mixed with languages I've never heard before, old ones, evil ones, you can tell just by hearing—no, not the ones you people talk, I mean Their tongue, and who's he talking to, huh? There's—he stops, he talks, he stops again, he listens. I've heard it!"

His voice rose to a scream. "He wants to help Them find us, kill us all! And use that thing inside him to do it! It's no god, I tell you! It's no god! It's under his control and it's worse than any of Them! Now let me up so I can fucking finish the job!"

Ksajakra stared at him, mouth open, apparently genuinely shocked; and when he looked back at me, there was enough of a shadow of doubt in his eyes that fear pinned me to the spot for a moment, even the pain of the stab wound receding in a burst of adrenaline. Fight or flight, motherfucker, I thought. Or, of course, freeze.

No. What had Johnny told me all those years ago. They used to say fight or flight. Then fight, flight, or freeze. And one last one: appease. Not always an option, she admitted, but a good one when it was.

"I have no control over the god," I said. "And he *is* a god. Yenu spoke with him. Are you saying I'm lying? I understand that. But are you saying she's lying too?"

That stopped Liandan short, and he stared around at the others in mute appeal. Here it came, I thought clinically. Where we see what kind of control she has over them, where we see what kind of cult leader she really is... All of these people had known each other, and her, far longer than they had known me. It wasn't a matter of trust, only the snap judgement of soldiers at war wearing the same uniform. We were bonded by necessity, them and me, but they had been bonded by her, and this grand idea of resistance, of hope...

"We'll lock him up for the rest of the voyage," Yenu said, standing up. "We'll..."

"You better make sure those locks hold!" Liandan screamed. "Because he needs to die, and whatever thing is inside him! He'll kill us all! He'll sell us to his Masters for meat!"

"We're locking you up," Yenu said. "If you say we can't trust you not to try again, we'll stop somewhere and leave you there."

The others relaxed minutely but visibly; I saw it in their shoulders, in the dark circles beneath their eyes. We were all exhausted by death, surrounded by it. We did not need to add to it needlessly. Their brother-in-arms might be exiled, but he would not be dead, like all the others. And part of me wanted to say, "Hey, wait just a fucking minute, as the person he is trying to kill, do I not get a vote?" but my vote was the same as hers; Liandan wanted us to kill him, and that didn't sit right with me. He was capable of premeditated murder at close range. I did not think I was. Nor did I want to find out.

"Ceth," Liandan said as Ksajakra dragged him upright, kicking and trying to lash out with his bound hands. "Saloc! Sal. Come on! Look at him! He lies, you know he lies, look at his face! Look at his eyes! Just kill him and the thing inside him dies too! Do it! Or our plan comes to nothing, and he gets the war he wants!"

"We don't have anywhere to put him," Ksajakra said, struggling to hold him, skinny as he was. Itzlek came over and pulled the man's arms tightly behind his back. "I could tie him into a bunk for now."

"Well, we'll have to figure something..." Yenu trailed off, and the room fell into a hush, even Liandan's struggling ceasing. "No one's on watch."

I looked around, counting, rubbing my throat. She was right; we were all in the hold. Well, and so what? Aside from the infrequent golden things in the River that looked like fish, nothing was here with us. We sailed alone. The watch, which I had been exempt from anyway as an outsider, as had Sudworth and the Advisor, had been perfunctory, for things like broken lines, fires on the deck, that kind of thing.

Yenu looked at Ksajakra. "Tie him up," she said. "I heard something." In a blink she had eeled up the ladder again, snake-slick, leaving in her wake only the hushed, stuffy air below.

There were no screams, no cries for help. Only a sound I had not heard before: a bell ringing frenziedly, on and on, irregular as a heart stuttering to a stop, and then another silence, breaking off the bell's alarm mid-clang.

BEHIND US THE stars had vanished, or the things in the darkness that looked like stars, blotted out by a seething, roiling cloud, all pale blues and grays, and at its centre something writhing, enormous, an impossible serpentine creature, pale and faceless except for a gaping mouth lined with hooked silvery teeth. Inside lolled an obscene white tongue, glistening wet and visibly quivering, as if coated in pus.

I clung to the Advisor, wheezing, stunned. It would have been one thing if the creature were silent; but it made a low, thrumming roar, and something beat behind it. Again I thought of heartbeats. Or drums.

How far away was it? I wasn't sure, but it was catching up, twisting and coiling around itself like a snake climbing a tree, breaking up the River into so much fog, and carrying its own fog around itself like a cloak.

I was bleeding again; the stab wound, so recently and hastily bandaged, had not been stitched or packed with anything, and it did not like even the short trip to the deck, ten steps. I shouldn't be moved, the Advisor had said, and I said, Fine, then leave me down here with my murderer, and he said, Come on, then. I thought I was going to throw up from pain and vertigo. And then this thing. Coming after us in the void.

Fight, flight, freeze, appease. Well we couldn't freeze, could we? It had already seen us moving. And it was chasing us. And was it the reflex of a cat going after something darting across the floor, or had it been sent? It didn't matter now. It was catching up.

Good job dodging death for a whole twenty minutes, I told myself. Well, this would probably be better than dying of gangrene from the wound, anyway. And the god inside me would be silenced. Or further silenced.

Help us, I said.

No reply. Ogruthon had been weakened by getting us out of the ship inside the lake; had he been further weakened by the lake of blood I had left all over the bunk and the floor and the ceiling and the walls and the others? Had he been killed? Had Liandan, without meaning to, actually succeeded in his aim—killing the god that he thought made me so powerful? Was there a place inside me that the god physically resided, and had it been bisected by the dirty blade?

And I felt the rise of something else, something not-him, that felt powerful, a clean something that despite all my small, dirty, petty angers I had not felt for a long time: *rage*. I saw only the creature, a sickening impossibility approaching us like a spurt of pus, surrounded by infectious spores, I saw only the darkness that it contaminated, I heard silence inside myself, I saw the mouths of the others moving, screaming, swords being drawn, uselessly, and lanterns being lit, a little chain of light securing us to one another, and I did not hear myself screaming to the god, *You son of a bitch! You useless fucker! You said your only mission was to protect life, and now this? You call yourself a god? The word means nothing! You mean nothing!*

The blood-sodden bandages came away as easily as tissue paper, a clot flying across the deck and skidding several feet. Something enormous and velvety caught at my hand, and with my free one I calmly wound up and struck where I judged the face to be, hitting from my hip, the way I had been taught by the guards, striking solidly, and the blood came again, and still the god did not speak, still it did not save us.

"I know you're in there! Come out! You coward!" I screamed; warmth flooded down my bare chest, soaked into my beard, re-wetted my britches, cooling at once. The deck was going dark, the figures around me not paying the least attention.

My little drama did not matter. The great mouth approached. How it danced in its cloud, how it coiled and curled through space. We couldn't outrun it now that it had found us, and I had a sneaking suspicion that no one here could fight it. I waited for the voice of a deity to rise inside me and save us, or for all the old spells I had once known to sprout out of the concrete slab I had laid over my old life, but nothing happened, only blood, and the Advisor stunned a dozen paces away, obviously unwounded by my punch, staring at me who had never struck him in our entire acquaintance; I could see the sky-blue whites of his eyes, which you did not often see.

Life! *That* was what the thing inside me was eating. And now, dying, I jerked the plate away from his greedy hands: No more for you. I will not pay for nothing. You're the only one who can get us out of this. Yenu always thinks it's her. She's not even used the past few weeks to see how wrong she's been about that, again and again and again. It's you, it has to be you. It must be you, or I will end you.

Save these people. All of them. I demand this of you.

Not even a demurral, and the thing swung closer, and now it blocked out what I would have called the horizon if we had one; all I could see was teeth. Most sinister and disturbing about this was that I was sure it was still hundreds or even thousands of miles away, that when it eventually consumed us it would not be like a shark choking down a seal but like a whale somehow consuming a single speck of plankton. What we would have to be to evade it was anything but what we were: tiny, pitiful. Mortal.

And now a fresh horror, small, so small I actually laughed with what meagre strength remained. Liandan, trailing ropes behind him at a level that made me think for a split second they were loops of intestine, bloodied, frenzied, grinning in triumph. I was falling, landing elbows-first then ass, and he was still advancing. "Go on then!" I shouted over the noise of the drums, the roaring approach of the thing, the voices of the others. "Go on!"

Had he heard me? I didn't think so. I tried to rise, swayed, failed. My body felt very far away, controlled not even by strings but by spiderwebs, blown away and broken in the slightest breeze. There was light now: the monster had brought its own light. Fog began to seep through the railings. A herald.

Everyone else had gathered near the prow of the ship, screaming and fighting foes I couldn't see. Smaller things, thudding across the deck. The drumming filled my ears, something faint and high behind it, not screaming but a song. I was alone and I would die alone. Nothing but my rage was with me.

And then in the span of seconds, something else: Yenu,

running towards me, shouting something about a spell, not seeing Liandan until she was nearly on top of him, and then skidding, startled, caught between us, both of them still moving towards me. His hand came up, holding a blade, and hers came up empty, and in a split second I rose from the deck and arrowed towards them, the noise now so loud that I could not hear either of their screams, only see their mouths moving.

He was closer to her, but I was bigger, and in motion. Distantly, in the few seconds it took for us to collide, I imagined us from above like a physics problem in a textbook: three dots in straight lines, moving far too fast to change direction.

I hit her from behind with my deadened left side, twisted Liandan's wrist with my right hand, and came down on him with my full weight, landing so hard we slid across the deck for several feet.

Yenu rolled me off him, teeth bared. *Oh my God*, she said, unheard. We knelt at Liandan's side, the hilt of his knife protruding from his neck, blood flooding out, moving easily as water, meeting the seams of the boards and flowing between them. Fog blew across the deck, enveloping the lanterns, surrounding us in a golden glow till we could see nothing else, not the others, not even as far as the mast. Hiding this small tragedy in the larger one. His eyes were still open, flickering between the two of us, slowly beginning to dull, finally closing.

She put her mouth to my ear. "We have to—" she began, and screamed, leapt backwards, pawing at her coat. The wooden box with the dead god tumbled to the deck and exploded into light, spraying us with splinters.

Something clattered and unfolded, unseen at first in the fog, then visible: eight feet tall, nine, ten, vaguely humanoid, or at least two arms and two legs and a face like a helmet, all of it brassy and tarnished, a skeletal or insectile arrangement of strings and points like barbed wire, spikes protruding from its shoulders and back, two small spherical eyes, a glow within the brass like the coral and lilac of dawn. We stared up at it.

If it spoke in the din, we did not hear it. But I heard the god inside me awaken in response, roaring: *Yes!*

The ship shot forwards, the pursuing pale beast twisting futilely in the impossible distance, and then just as quickly up, flattening us to the boards, my face sticking to Liandan's blood. The darkness around us vanished, the River vanished, replaced with pale white light and silence, the drums receding, the chanting vanishing, leaving only silence, stunned and absolute.

THE NEW GOD declined to heal me; or at any rate she did not offer, and I felt that, there having been no offer, I would be out of place to ask. Sudworth heated a curved needle in a candle and, after the reopened stab wound had stopped seeping, stitched the edges together. I would have black carbon dots there for the rest of my life, she said.

She complimented me both on my survival after losing an amount of blood that would have killed a lesser man, and on staying still while she sewed. "Please trust me," I said, "the stitches hurt much less than the actual stabbing." It was true; I'd barely felt them.

"If it gets infected, you'll die," she said.

"I know. I suppose the god will have to move into his second choice of apartment then."

"Tacky," she said. "Secondhand god, too."

"Slightly used."

"Slightly." She pursed her lips, from which a fragment of the red thread hung, stuck with saliva to the corner. "I suppose there's no will."

"I'll write a will," I told her. "I'll leave you everything."

"Hmph." She stuck the needle into a folded scrap of leather, set it aside, and got out a glass screw-top jar of iridescent gray ointment. "I was supposed to tell you that this will sting."

"Again," I said patiently, "I suspect it will sting less than having eight inches of metal stuck into my torso."

"...Are you all right?"

"I think I may have gone a little more insane than usual," I said after a minute. "It'll wear off. It usually does."

She dabbed on the waxy stuff, and glanced back at where the others were talking. The new god, Caustur, unlike Ogruthon, was a talker; her voice came, slightly unsettlingly, from somewhere low on her torso rather than her head, but you got used to that quickly.

And unlike Ogruthon, Caustur had volume and mass— inexplicably, I thought, given that she had been a tiny droplet of nearly weightless metal inside the wooden box. The already-scratched deck was covered with thousands of tiny fresh scratches from her spiked feet.

Most importantly, she had snatched us away from the monster, though she cautioned us that she knew of this thing, that it would once again track us; our scent or signature or the marks we left by our very existence would be muddled thanks to her route, but eventually it would strike upon our trail again. We had paused to put ourselves back together, but we must keep moving.

She had taken us to a world where we could breathe, and I was thankful for that much. The air felt a little thin, but you didn't have to fight to breathe. Sudworth looked terrible: sunken and anemic. I suspected I looked worse. I certainly *felt* worse. I had apologized to the Advisor for striking him, and he had accepted it with his usual graciousness; and if he had asked me to explain why it had happened, I would not have been able to, and it seemed like a blessing that he had not.

Leaning on the Advisor, I returned to the firepit and sat carefully; Yenu and Rhakun moved to create a space for me. The Advisor settled behind me, and folded his forepaws carefully, claws in, like a sphinx. Around us was what looked like a desert, concrete-gray hardpan frosted here and there with fresh snow.

I studied the god that I could see, folded like a mantis with her knees practically at her ears, feet tucked in close to the strange pelvis that was like a child's drawing of a bicycle: a couple of awkwardly spiked wheels in a wonky frame, the openings filled with brass wires. When she spoke, it came out in every language at once in my head, like Ogruthon. I was still not used to it.

"Hello," she said when I sat, turning the smooth metal

face to me, the two small domes of the eyes—or I thought they were eyes, anyway. "Thank you for the weapons. And the sacrifice. The others have told me the story."

My stomach contracted. Even a moment's warning would have been useful before hearing *that*. "I didn't... I mean, you're welcome."

I didn't kill Liandan to give him to you, I meant; I killed him because he was trying to kill me. Or Yenu. Either way, not for you, not for your sake. Because do you know who *does* need human sacrifices? Who thrives on death, and the drinking of the soul? Or so I've been told? Not your side. The side of the enemy.

Someone will say something, I thought, but no one did. Next to me, Yenu's breath was slow and regular; she rubbed her hands together absently, extending them often towards the small, flickering fire.

"I don't know how much time has passed since the end of the war," the god said. "Time was very strange in that ship anyway. Do you know what that means, coming from one of our kind? I don't have the words in any language to explain it to you in a way that won't result in your brains coming out of your ears. I say 'strange' so you don't all go mad. I feel the same way about the things this one is telling me."

Yenu smiled, although it looked a bit as if someone had suddenly poked her in the back with a knife.

"That war—we only knew enough to call it a war when it was nearly over," the god continued; it was unnerving to hear a voice so animated coming out of something so still, like a statue playing a recording. "They were so disorganized, so chaotic. As they always have been. They fought us because they hated us and we them. They fought us because we defended mortals. They fought us because we did not lie down and surrender. They weren't even as coordinated as a swarm of eyks, and those don't actually have brains. But now... I don't understand it. What changed? They barely plan further than the ends of their noses. Now they *plan* a war? Them?"

As one, we looked at Yenu. I waited for her to shrug, in her old infuriating way: to say that what had happened was not important, and all that mattered was what was happening now, at this very moment. Not how it began, but what we planned to do about it. She rubbed her hands, she seemed ready to speak. Nothing came out.

I sighed. "She won't do it. Let me try. They *are* organized now. Systematic. It's a war of occupation and conquest and expansion, one world after another, each one providing troops to conquer the next. The great organizer, their general, used to be called the Corruption. Now the Manifestation. On Earth sometimes he was called Nyarlathotep. A made-up name he gave himself, like the others."

Caustur wheezed in seeming surprise. "Him! He was using that name in the first war. A messenger and cup-bearer, I think you would call it, of Azag-Thoth, and of *his* master in turn. He took orders between the generals. A little, shifty, servile nobody with a thousand faces. That was his only talent. I see his ambition was greater than we thought. How much he hid from us, and from his Masters. The *Manifestation*. Hark at him."

"So that's why we broke you out of jail," Yenu said when no one spoke again. "You and Ogruthon."

"To... what?"

"Fight the Ancient Ones. Like in the first war."

Caustur chuckled, or it sounded like it anyway: like spoons rattling in a drawer. "Two gods is not an army, little mortal. We are much stronger together, it's true. And with the addition of each new Quevereld, we will be stronger still. But there will never be enough of us to defeat them, or buy you more time than the few moments it will take for them to simply obliterate us. As for myself, I did not want to fight in the old days; and I do not want to fight now. And the others may not want to fight either. They may break their old oath; who knows."

"But now that you're out," I said, "you're a target. You're either with them or against them. Just like the rest of us. Your choices were to stay safe in prison, or be free and be the enemy. Those were the choices they gave you. They haven't changed."

"You cannot put me back in the prison, though."

"No."

"So you have removed the choice entirely. You have brought me here, and Ogruthon too, to save you; you have dragged us from our sleep and painted a mark on our backs for the enemies to spy across the stars in the hunt. Ha!"

"Will you help us?" Yenu said evenly, as if Caustur had not spoken at all. "You can still say no."

"I don't know. I must speak to Ogruthon." One spiky, insectile arm unfolded gracefully, reached across the firepit, and something like and unlike a hand at the end tapped me on the forehead, causing a little zap of electricity as if I had been shuffling across a carpet in socks. "Excuse me."

I braced myself for some kind of cacophony of divine voices inside me, but nothing happened. Caustur withdrew her hand and folded up on herself. After a few minutes of silence, Ksajakra said, "They are obviously having a... serious discussion. We should eat."

I had to admit that at this stage in the war, or the pre-war, or whatever it was we were doing (scouting? reconnaissance? something else?) almost all I thought about was food. Food, wine, and, more recently, the wound that began next to my neck and angled down, stopping just short of my heart. I felt it bubble and seethe inside me, like lava. Like the lava-fish, swimming around and around Ogruthon's monster-laden prison. The pain was constant and audible, a soft oceanic roar.

I wasn't surprised, much, to find myself not thinking about revenge or death or strategy or tactics. Just food and pain. It felt out of my control: the body thinking, not the mind. And the body thinking something very specific: I am going to die. Then garbling the signals on the way to my conscious mind so that it sounded like something else. But it was becoming increasingly evident. It felt as if the stab wound had closed my body off in some way, turned it from a city into a cage—no, an aquarium, sealed at every joint, inside which things were now shrieking and raging in a panic because they were trapped. Me, the infection that I suspected was already well under way, the god. Maybe other things. Like he said. That's what Liandan gave me: a lethal injection.

But since there was nothing anyone could do, I said nothing. I ate my food and drank several small cups of hot wine, and we waited for the god to speak again. I also waited for the god inside me to say something like *Be quiet, and let us talk*. Where were they talking? It was useless to think of their conversation as happening in a physical place, I supposed. Somewhere under my liver. Next to a rib. I would have to let go of all that at some point, and I was surprised that I hadn't yet. I mean thinking that things needed to physically exist, somewhere, anything.

CHAPTER SEVENTEEN

"I AM HORRIFIED by the plan," Caustur said, and Yenu nodded because, well. "But I agree with Ogruthon, my wise comrade. We owe it to our people to free them from the Ancient Ones' prisons, release them into a maelstrom though it may. It is monstrously cruel to keep them in these places. We will protect them if they do not fight. If they do not wish to be thrown under the Ancient Ones' war machine—how could we blame them?"

"Will you ask them to help with the final journey?" Yenu said. "I mean, the one to break through the barrier to the universe containing the necessary nexus, if we can find it."

"Yes, I will ask. We don't have a choice there. Ogruthon and I are not powerful enough to do so. Perhaps we will never regain our old strength. But the more of us there are, the stronger we are." Caustur laid her hands lingeringly on the ship's steering wheel, the spikes of her hands sinking into the hard wood as if it were cheese. She tugged them loose with a squeak. "Sorry. We must go, however. That thing that found us, that nameless thing, that was certainly *sent;* they are not natural trackers, nor are they intelligent creatures in the way we are. Now how did it find you in a place where supposedly things cannot be found? I don't know. But can it do it again? Yes, I think so. Someone aimed it very precisely."

"So either they found us," I said, "or they knew where we'd be at around that time."

"Certainly."

"Our plan is transparent," I said to Yenu. "From one step it's inevitable to guess what the next one is. They might have been tracking us from the moment you took the ship off Aradec. Or they might not have bothered; they might just have the MapQuest printout with our route marked on it in red pen."

She laughed, startled. "I hear you."

"We're not enough of a quantum."

"Wave," she said, moving her hand in the air. "Particle. I think about strategic relocation targets, don't you?"

"No," I said patiently. "I wasn't a politician with a football."

"Well, you know. It's not that we're assets; we're *targets*. Things don't want to abduct us, things want to blow us to smithereens."

I nodded dubiously. The second part of that was true. Was the first?

She said, "We need to move around more. I would say we even need to split up. Would that double our reach? Maybe. Would it make one group a decoy for the other? Maybe. Does it make it so a hit won't kill all of us at the same time? That's all we can say for sure."

Caustur touched the sigil in the centre of the wheel again, which glowed white for a moment, then faded. "What's in this? This is one of the most complicated spells for protection I've ever seen. Gods of course do not need sigils, but I can normally glance at these things and determine each individual component..."

"Please," I said, "do not shovel coal into the furnace of her ego, I beg you. It is bad enough that an entire coalition of eldritch creatures has for the first time in existence declared outright war on one person."

"She is proud of that?"

"Not that she'd admit."

"I am right here," Yenu said. "Anyway, listen. If we are being predicted somehow, we have to break out of a predictable pattern right away. If we're being surveilled, well, I suppose it won't help. What's being tracked? Me? You? The ship? Its magic? Something on it—a ward, a spell? Is there a magical tracking chip somewhere, like in a movie? Do such things exist? I don't have enough data to work with there. Where is everybody? Let's pull everyone together. Jak! Where are you?"

When they were gone, Caustur, inasmuch as she had an expressionless facade of bronze, gave me a look. "She's a devious little thing."

"Yes."

"And not as mortal as I had initially assumed."

"No," I said. "It's a long story. They can't kill her outright; it's part of her covenant. But you knew that already, didn't you?"

"Yes, Ogruthon told me what we know of her origins and that weapon and... well, several other things. I can see why they want her back. Why is she fighting them instead of rejoining them?"

"I couldn't tell you."

"She is like... there's a name for it. The end—"

"—of the world machine," I said. "Yeah. I know that one. Doomsday device."

"I cannot believe that a single mortal could be so dangerous, but she is, isn't she? Like some terrible isotope. A single fleck of it killing thirty mortals, forty. A handful of it killing millions. Imagine that. Passing her from hand to hand till everyone was dead. Instead of, perhaps, what I have seen—like an asteroid strike, smashing a planet into two. Like a great upheaval of the centres of worlds. No, just one little mortal."

I sighed. "Do you know the story of Prometheus?"

"No! Tell me. I love stories."

"Well, he stole..." I hesitated. Come to think of it, did *I* know the story of Prometheus? "He saw the gods using fire and humans suffering without it. So he stole it from the gods and gave it to humanity, and everybody's lives got better. Warmer, brighter, safer. Except his, because the gods were pissed off and punished him. I think an eagle had to peck out his liver every day but then it grew back every day too."

"Oh." She turned her blank, bronze face towards me. "But that was kind of him. Was he a god or a mortal?"

"I can't remember. I think he was a god. They punished one of their own."

"Then she too is Prometheus," Caustur said. "Your Yenu. It is not mortals that will catch and punish her in the end. What a good story."

"Can we talk about something else, please?"

Caustur made a brief clattering noise, like a laugh. "The universe isn't big enough for the both of you, is it? Let us find more of my people. At least we can outnumber her, if not overpower her."

YENU INSISTED THAT we not split up now, though she couldn't explain why without revealing her suspicion about the spy. But with no one permitted to stay aboard ship even to keep it from smashing against the rocks, we had to anchor far offshore and paddle in on an uncomfortably small boat. The water ran off the oars like paint, or something more viscous: rubbery and clinging, leaving a green cast on the wood. Whenever it splashed into the boat, it looked thick enough to pick up like a stone and toss back out.

"Very quiet," Yenu had said as we had packed. "No magic, no spells. Nothing. It's like sending up a flare. We sneak in, we break out the gods, we sneak out."

So we were sneaking, and so self-consciously it would have been funny if we hadn't been so terrified and sleep-deprived. Yenu had still not advanced her theory of a traitor on the ship; she hadn't given anyone a chance to confess, come clean. For once I thought she was right. No one would have. She had shown leniency to Liandan, maybe because the rest of the crew would have revolted. And because leaving him alive seemed as if it would not have repercussions for the war, for our lives... but now, the sentence would, probably, be death. And none of them would raise their hands against her. There were actual gods on this ship, but on this ship she was already a god.

Prometheus, I thought again, despite myself.

Landed and moored, we squelched through the damp sand, up through high, pale beach grass that switched at our clothes and left clinging white seeds. Around us, nothing moved; still we found ourselves unwilling to speak, as if our voices would draw down something waiting only for an unfamiliar sound to attack. The air was cold, damp, and rich; the sun was yellow. We could almost have been on Earth, next to an ordinary sea.

The beach grass petered out and became thick, pampered turf bordered with flowerbeds made of red brick, then topiaries in strange shapes that we gave a wide berth, as if they might come alive like statues. We wove through a sky-darkening hedge maze that soared above our heads. The smell of growing things and wet soil was reassuring: a smell of Earth, of home.

We pushed through the tight, glossy pale green leaves; it was a very simple maze, with only six or seven turnings, and no dead ends. A decoration rather than a true puzzle. We had to move in single file, but there seemed to be no danger in it. No minotaur in the middle, nothing waiting to savage us for intruding. I still felt so tightly wound up I was going to burst.

Leaving the maze, we brushed leaves from our hair and clothes, and looked down a long shallow slope of grass, studded at regular intervals with strange things. Or not strange. Strange only because of their placement.

Yenu moved instinctively towards the closest one, twenty or thirty paces away; Ksajakra reached for the back of her coat and missed. Shamefully, we stayed clustered near the hedge, as if keeping our backs to the wall.

At last curiosity overcame me and I followed her, my boots silent in the thick, closely-trimmed grass. (File that away for later: trimmed. Not overgrown. They have landscaping services at the jail. And no guards.) Nothing moved: not a bird, not a bug. Only the wind, bringing a clean scent of greenery and damp dirt.

The things were tables, incredibly unremarkable tables, or they would have been if I had seen them on Earth.

I stared at them, temporarily poleaxed, even after everything I had seen. Black plastic, rounded edges, the tops ridged in shallow, subtle marks, like restaurant tables designed to grip onto the tablecloth. I had worked for two summers at a bistro that had tables just like this.

Each was flanked by two chairs, also black plastic, sleek and modern-looking; they looked uncomfortable to sit on, but people who went to that kind of restaurant didn't care if they were comfortable or not, they just wanted to be seen. Most of the chairs were knocked over and lying in the grass.

Next to each table was a sculpted column that looked a bit like a chess piece, six feet high and made of what looked like frosted glass, decorated with flowers and leaves. Atop of each was a square metal platform, some covered with crumbs of what looked like dry dogfood. A double set of steel chains with shackles dangled from each. All the shackles were broken.

Yenu reached out slowly and touched one of the chains. Each bright link was as thick as her wrist.

I jumped as something touched my shoulder, and turned to see Caustur, leaning down far to get her head close to mine. "We must go," she said.

"I... What? But you're a *god*. And you said to free th—"

"We will never reach those gods," she said. "We must go. Now. In silence. This did not happen long ago. Go."

"This what?"

Yenu, who had been listening with her head cocked, looked around at the quiet landscape, the ranged tables. Still nothing moved. "But—"

"Now. Silently. As if we were ghosts. *Flee*."

We fled.

IN THE ADVISOR'S family, a long time ago on their homeworld, before They arrived, there had been a man they called the Negotiator, sometimes the Negotiator of Wars. He had been an unusual colour for their race, the Advisor told me. Pale blue in fur and feather, and lilac skin where pink had inexplicably mixed with the blue.

Thus he was very striking to look at when he stepped onto the battlefield, and all eyes were often on him. He would walk out into the thick of the fighting, and because he was moving slowly, people often stopped fighting around him; and then he would stand where it seemed useful, and hold up his strange pink forepaws, claws in, wings tucked, and he would speak; and he would ask both sides what they wished to accomplish, and then he would negotiate. No one ever attacked him and he was never wounded (except by accident). Those who could see him stopped fighting. It seemed like magic, though of course no Rhaokor could perform magic. There were many small border skirmishes and inter-tribal wars, so he was often busy. But it almost always worked. He saved many lives, when he could get there in time.

"It's a nice story," I said, leaning on the railing. I felt seasick for the first time, though I wasn't sure how much of that was the strange sea itself, which did not behave like normal water and was not treating the ship like a normal ship; and how much of it was the infection that was making itself increasingly undeniable, despite how often I had tried to tell myself that all I felt was the normal itch and fever of a healing wound; and how much was simply anxiety that we too were walking into a battle with no weapons and no plan. "A peacekeeper in the family... how did he die?"

The Advisor paused, his lips moving slightly. Had he ever lied to me? I did not think he was preparing to lie to me now. But he wanted to. He wished he could. "He was killed," he said.

"While he was doing this? Walking between armies?"

"Yes."

"Accidentally?"

The Advisor sighed, a rumble deep in his massive chest. "No. One of the generals had put a bounty on him. A soldier standing near to the front of the formation shot him."

I looked out at the horizon, trying to steady my stomach. "I suppose I shouldn't be surprised."

"That general subsequently won several other wars, and became king. He ruled for many years and united many lands."

"By united, you mean he killed anyone who didn't ally with him."

"Yes. He killed the leaders first if he could, and generally that was all that was required." He sat back on his haunches and put his paws up on the railing next to my hands; for just a second I got the sense that he wished he could have put a paw over my hand, the way his people reassured their children. "Prophet, we both know it is inevitable that one group will wish to dominate another. The strong wish to rule over the weak, and they also wish to rule over the strong: to have their strength to use as a tool, at will. There is no world, no race, no government, that does not have this wish. It is historical and universal. There are no examples, anywhere, of this desire being absent."

"There are plenty of examples where it isn't acted on."

"Yes, and all of those peoples became subjugated by others."

I turned at last and looked at him, his large, placid, dark eyes with their whites of sky-blue. "What are you trying to tell me, Advisor?"

"I am doing my duty," he said. "I am advising you of the way of the world. What the girl Yenu is doing—she cannot change the way things are. I know she greatly desires to. I respect that desire. But it will not work. It simply cannot. She may be able to change all the natural laws, she can change space, time, magic, I myself am in awe of what she does. But she cannot change the hunger for domination that lives in the heart of the Masters. Nor anyone else."

"I know that."

"Anywhere that power is removed, a thousand mortals, some perhaps even worse than the Masters in their desires and proclivities, will arise and say *Now I am the ruler*. It cannot be avoided."

"I know."

"Then why do you try to convince yourself otherwise?"

"I don't know." I couldn't think of anything else to say; and eventually he wandered off and lay down by of the masts, keeping an eye on me. I felt his gaze on my back like a cloak. 1779 squeezed out of my pocket, walked down my arm, and began to promenade up and down the railing, glinting in the light like a gem.

We were sailing, as Caustur had advised, non-magically and very quietly, under half-sail, till we were far enough from the prison and could rejoin the Violet River. She had refused to answer our questions about what she had expected to find there or what she clearly thought had happened—those tables, the chairs lying in the thick turf, everything so innocent and yet capable of terrifying a god.

The envoys had been sent out at last, but we did not know where to go next. "All is not lost," Caustur had said softly, and I had nodded, but why wasn't it? All surely *was* lost. We would never get back to the nexus, as we had begun calling it, without more gods; if not for their magic, then to slow down the Manifestation and his army while the others tried. Numbers, we needed numbers, and there was no way to get them.

Not for the first time, I went into myself and opened up all the books of my mind as best I could, seeing if I was ready to die, finding that I was, and that I had been for a long time. Yenu had, with Johnny-like cunning, tried to convince the enemy that we were blundering about, or at least acting on bad information, and therefore posed no real threat; the enemy, we agreed, was likely doing the same to us, having let us get this far to lull us into a false sense of competence or progress. What we did not say was that we *were* blundering about and acting on bad information. It was no act. We really did pose no threat. To me, this meant we should be spared; to Them, I knew, it meant only that we would be effortless to eliminate.

Maybe it was time to consider surrender. Whether we fought or not, we'd be killed; all we could do was hasten it or not.

I sighed. If someone was going to suggest it, it would not be me.

Something was zigzagging across the water towards us, and I squinted against the sun, then shaded my eyes with my good arm. A bird? An insect? No, a cloud— small, moving fast and jerky, as if it could not see (which was a ridiculous thought to begin with) but was instead scenting its way towards us. I tensed, tried to convince myself it was too small to harm us, remembered that size had become a useless concept several thousand lifetimes ago, and turned to yell to whoever was on deck—then turned back, shaking my head.

The envoy slid through the railings at my feet and lay there like a dirty puff of cotton candy, giving off an odour of artificial pines. "Hello," I said.

THE GODS WERE already beginning to arrive when we did, and for no reason I thought of something I had gotten into trouble with when I was a kid, attending Vital Grandin Catholic Elementary. *God is light*, they'd said, and I'd put up my hand (back when I still did such things) to say *So is Jesus light?* and gotten some hemming and hawing in response before I had pointed out that he did things like attend weddings and have nails hammered into him, and, *Well, but you said Jesus was God, so if God is light then—*

Had they called my parents? I felt pretty sure they had.

At any rate, many of the gods were indeed light, all different colours and shapes, some that I could not see at all but moved invisibly past the others and became for a moment visible, or like a cast shadow.

It had been a strange and even desperate several days—or several sleeps, at any rate. The envoy had returned with news not entirely good or entirely bad, but confounding. For just as we had hoped, some of them, working together, had been able to free a few smaller gods, who had had the situation explained (somewhat inaccurately, Ogruthon admitted, but it had worked) and rushed off to get others. So Yenu's chain reaction had started after all, though as the gods increased in magnitude, still they were not able to release many of what they called the *Great* Old Ones.

"English is so bad at this," I said to Yenu, who leaned next to me on the railing. "The Elder Gods. The Ancient Ones. The Great Old Ones. How are you supposed to keep anybody straight? Why not just call all the hockey teams Men Who Skate Good and Big Smelly Guys instead of giving them franchise names."

"A bunch of languages are super bad at it," she said, staring out at the moving shapes and lights. It was like going out at night during the Perseids, I thought: staring into the darkness, hoping for a shooting star. There was one. There was another one. After a while, your eyes became so exquisitely attuned to motion that you felt like you could see oxygen molecules moving around in your tears.

And darkness, pure darkness, was where we now hung, in a terrifyingly fragile bubble of air and gravity that I was trying very hard not to think about. *You think all is lost,* Yenu had said. *Not all,* I'd replied. *All is a lot.*

So we had come here, to space itself instead of a

world, to a place *between* worlds, and told the envoys to spread the word to meet us here. Gods and envoys alike were getting picked off as they tried to find our ship, which, after all, was in constant motion; so when Ogruthon and Caustur had suggested it, we'd all agreed to anchor the ship and let the army assemble around us, like growing a crystal. Strength in numbers. What was the use, they had argued, of an army spread out all over the universe? No one sent soldiers to war one at a time.

If you were the praying type now would be the time to pray, I thought. To summon the gods to you: nothing more. That would be the only purpose of the prayer. Not for worldly goods or wealth or even salvation, not for courage or fortitude or patience or forbearance. To say: *I pray that You might come here. I pray that You will fight.*

But prayer only worked on gods we had imagined. Not the real ones, who were perfectly capable of letting you down. Who did not want to fight a war with no rules of engagement, no propaganda, no encouraging speeches, no issues of troop morale being raised or lowered, no prisoners, no negotiation, no fair passage for medics, no rules about targeting civilians (the civilians being targeted was the whole point), and no truces, armistices, or surrenders. The whole sluggish machinery of both sides was revving up, waking up, sluicing in fuel and oil to charge at each other again, and it was inhuman, was simply not a human war. Humans would only be in the middle of it: where the two sides collided, and one side won.

I felt very small, and very mortal, and very tired.

Having all the gods here, I knew, was noticeable; the Ancient Ones would find us. It was only a matter of time. And if we could have avoided having Yenu here too, we would have; but she had tried to spin her presence as a good thing.

"You don't 'smoke out' the Ancient Ones," she murmured now, so low that I could barely hear her. "They don't give enough of a shit, or have enough fear, about anything. You can't... toss a burning branch through Their front door and expect Them to come running out. They hunger. You lure Them with hunger, not fear. If They know I'm alive and where I am, that's what They'll hunger for. Or the Manifestation will, anyway."

"I thought you were bait for a trap when you showed up at the palace," I said after a while. "And now you're bait on purpose. Incredible."

"Ain't it?"

I winced as I pulled my hair back and tucked it down my collar to get it away from my face. The stab wound woke and roared sleepily with pain, a dull red colour in my increasingly-disorganized mind, like blood, like embers. I said, "So it's like you said then. Instead of running around with the bomb and trying to hide it, we uncover the bomb. We make sure a satellite sees it. We start to drive..."

"They'll be thinking: *It's too obvious. It's an ambush. But at the same time, it would be a weak ambush, because they have no forces.*"

I considered that. "Well, we don't."

"Yeah."

"Do you still think there's a...?" I began, and she nodded before I could finish. She had made very sure that we all knew the name of the closest world—a string of syllables I could not pronounce or even remember—and had told only me, Ogruthon, and Caustur that it was incorrect. The false information would not draw out a spy if there was one, but it might mean that the Manifestation and his army would rush to the other place, buying us some time before they found us here.

We stood in silence for a while; I ran through the faces of those aboard the ship in my head. Everyone looked like a candidate. No one, I thought, had reason to be a spy, except for the reason that we all did, the reason that still lingered in my heart, though I felt it dying like a plant without light: there was going to be a winning side, and we were not going to be on it. Even the slightest amount of collusion might be rewarded—it was not a guarantee, They were too capricious and not interested in reciprocity—but there might be a *chance*. And we were so desperate that the slimmest chance seemed desirable now.

All of the resistance, in particular, had signed up to die; but how committed were they to the idea? How attached were they to life? People would do terrible things to live. Not even to do anything else: just to *live*.

It was still possible that we were simply being outguessed, outmanoeuvred, without any information at all. But you never knew, with strangers. Certainly they had all come this far; but that could be the desire to pass good intel to Them, not the desire to see Yenu's plan work. Or instead of 'anyone' perhaps I should have thought 'everyone': if one person was spying, the others might simply be looking away.

Consider even the Advisor: maybe he had been tasked with it long before the war came to Aradec. Maybe that had *always* been something he was prepared to do: serve the Masters, no matter what. Though I could ask him, I would never know if he were lying to me.

Or Sudworth, who had never repeated to me her assurance that we were dividing up our shared and secret goals, and who had never, not once, answered my questions about how she had known to get off Earth before its destruction, or how she had done so. An innocent historian in the wrong place at the wrong time? Something worse?

And Yenu had told me flat-out that she didn't think it was me. My loyalty was neither here nor there; she knew I had served Them for a long time, and that would have left a mark, a deep mark, in what I thought and did consciously and unconsciously, as doing anything merely to survive leaves a mark. It wasn't about loyalty. It was about ability: which she believed I lacked. *You, a spy*, she said. *Don't make me laugh.* If I were to betray her, it would be the work of a moment. Not a long, manipulative process.

I stared at the darkness, the moving lights of gods, trying to see them as soothing, looking out instead of in. Any of you. Any of you. Anyone here had the means and the motive. What would you say if you knew that I had been offered impossible things once to betray her? To drug her, bind her, and bring her to the creature that had made her. And I didn't. I refused. What would any of you say to that? Would you cheer? Would you curse my name, and point out that this is why we were here today? That your friends and family and comrades are dead because of what I failed to do, and so are mine? Maybe.

This is why she and I are still bound: complicity. Nothing like the rest of you. You loyal, devoted fools.

Something pale blue and triangular somersaulted past the railing and drifted off to join the others, something about its motion glad, even ecstatic. "There's one," Yenu said softly.

"Hope so."

"I asked you once to remember me as the real me," she said, out of nowhere.

"You did," I said. "And I said you were always the real you. And I was wrong, wasn't I? There was just a... a shell that looked like you. A cute smiling shell of a girl that fooled me like it fooled everybody because it was so hard and opaque. And underneath, something else. Something terrible. Something that would have fed us all into a woodchipper if it meant we would have looked up to you as a god."

She nodded. "What is beautiful is true, and what is... I don't know. Forget it. I don't think I'm more me now that I look like someone I'm not. I don't think I'm more true either. Or more good. Poets generally, I think, are full of shit. But listen. Don't remember the new me if we survive this. Don't remember the old me, either. Don't remember me as a little kid. Or a monster. Don't remember me with pity. Just... forget it all. That you knew me."

"I doubt I'll be able to."

"You never know," she said.

"Nobody ever loved you enough," I said. "And nobody ever said no to you. And this is what you became."

"But I'm trying to make it right."

"But you *can't*."

"Well, then I can make something *else* right," she said, and gazed off into the darkness, rubbing her hands together. "Maybe."

"I don't pity you," I said, after a minute. The liver, the eagle, the swooping shadow. "No one should pity you after what you've done in the name of your ego. Of your image. Of your *companies*. But maybe someone will show you mercy after all this. Not out of pity. Out of something else."

"What, then?"

"I don't know," I said, and meant it. "Hope, I suppose. That you could be someone better later. Even though your track record isn't great."

"No," she said. "I suppose it isn't. I suppose it doesn't look that way."

I couldn't think of anything else to say. After a while, I said, "We'd probably better go get some sleep."

"Yeah."

"You don't think, by the way, that you should maybe...?" I waved vaguely at the assembling gods, which felt a bit blasphemous. "I don't know. Give them a motivational speech or something? As their general?"

"Good Lord, no. Can you *imagine*."

DAYS PASSED, OR what seemed like days; we measured it only with the crude hourglass used for shifts on watch. Sudworth, when I questioned her, said something casually about how some deities carried time with themselves in a way that mortals didn't, and I resolved not to ask her about anything ever again, because even her theories gave me a migraine.

Godwatching had become my hobby now. And it was amazing, even after the last several years, how quickly something became normal: how quickly impending disaster and death became normal. I would wake up, eat two or three packets of food, clean my teeth, and go find a spot on the railing so I could watch the gods coming in. The crowd was gratifying somehow, even though I knew I couldn't see some huge percentage of them.

"This is good, right?" I whispered. "This is an army. A real army."

Numbers don't tell you much, Ogruthon said.

I barely felt a flicker of darkness across my eyes now when he spoke. Maybe staring out into the star-flecked dark sent the god sustenance. "What does tell you anything?"

Who survives.

I rolled my eyes. Someone came to lean beside me, at first an unrecognizable blob wrapped in scarves and wearing two hats, smelling of wine. Itzlek, yawning and sipping from his canteen. "Prophet."

I nodded at him. "A little early, no?"

"What *is* time? Anyway, I just got off watch. It's night for me." He gestured at the gathering army, what we could see of it between the stars. "I don't know how you stay out here and just look at it. It ruins all the tides in my gut."

"I've seen a lot of weird shit," I said. "This isn't so bad."

"And this world we're supposed to be so near... I can't remember the name of it. And I can't see it anyway. Don't like that either."

"Yenu said close was *relative*," I recited. "But we'd need a spyglass the size of a mountain to see it even as a pinprick from here."

"It's that small?"

"It's that far."

"And it's called what again?"

I told him, and he shrugged. "In a hundred years I'd never remember that. I don't think Dath even has most of those sounds," he said.

"Yeah," I sighed. "I nearly broke my tongue trying to do a spell that Yenu told me to do a while back. Dath isn't so bad. Mostly it sounds like what I already spoke."

He nodded. "Tells you a bit about who lives there," he suggested, though he sounded dubious; not for the first time I thought that if he had lived back on Earth, he would have been essentially both polite and doubtful about, say, overseas travel. Reasonably, I thought. Even if, back on Aradec, he had known that many other inhabited worlds existed, he had had no chance of seeing them himself, let alone visiting them physically, no matter what he did for a living, who he knew, or where he lived.

Saloc passed by us and nodded briefly, then handed Itzlek the red-shaded watch lantern. "Your shift, Lek."

"Thanks." Itzlek took one last look out at the stars, then shook his head and wandered off.

It wasn't till a few minutes later that I thought: *Wait. He just said...*

Honest mistake, I told myself. None of your business. Took a double shift to let someone else rest. After all, a lot of dead weight on this ship. Uh, he serves also who sits and...

But my stomach was churning, and although I had learned to mistrust my gut, I knew it would not settle till I looked.

He wasn't at the usual watch-station, a square platform set about halfway up the first mast, and he wasn't at the crow's nest either, which admittedly no one ever climbed. I moved around the empty deck, nodding to the others. The hold, then. Or the heads. Well, it didn't matter, it didn't mean anything, honest mistake.

Something something he serves also who *stands* and waits, wasn't it? Not sits. And prowls... Itzlek still had the red-glassed lantern, though he had closed it to nearly a slit. If my eyes had adjusted slightly more slowly, many things might have been avoided. Or, put another way, I would not have seen him at the far end of the hold, right in the stern, glancing around and then seeming to vanish.

Obviously not; he had just closed the lantern without me seeing. I moved quietly towards where I had last seen him, walking on the toes of my boots so the iron-clad heels didn't make so much noise. As always when no one was in it, the hold smelled of magic and rotting fruit, and the faint vinegary tang of spilled wine. One of the deck crystals contributed a minimal gleam of starlight, like a lightbulb about to fizzle out and die.

He *was* gone. I stood behind one of the support beams and stared for a long time. There weren't any rooms here, only the bunks, and all of those were uncurtained; the storage was small wooden lockers, big enough to fit a duffel bag. And why would he climb into one of those anyway? Let alone *how*…

Something must be covering the lantern. As I adjusted my position behind the wooden beam to look more closely, I saw something that made my heart sink. You could still be wrong, I said flatly, but even my internal monologue didn't sound convincing.

Half a dozen of the magical wards had been chipped out of the wood, the patterns destroyed with chisel marks. And one new sigil had been put in, so small I would not have seen at all if it had not been written in white chalk.

I breathed quietly. Moved towards the back of the ship, startled at something glittering faintly near my face, frowned. I had seen that before. In a forest ruled by the Burning King, I had tripped once over the edge of a perfectly real and solid stone altar because it had been placed inside an angle where I couldn't see it.

Now I knew to move very slowly, lest I hit some obstacle that would alert him to where I was, and I was still thinking *It's nothing, he came down here to eat a secret snack, or whack off, or just get some peace and quiet away from the rest of us, it's nothing—*

—when I stepped around, then through, the hidden angle.

I only saw him and his ritual for a second (candle, glass tile, paper and ink) before he spun with a gasp. I quickly put up my right fist, but he hadn't taken a swing at me, only held his hands up, palms out, his face very white in the light of the single flame. The folded compartment he had made was barely bigger than a bathroom stall, and our faces were nearly touching.

"Ah, Prophet," he began, and hesitated: far too long. Finally rallied: "Do you need anything?"

"I'd like to know what you're doing," I said. "And whether Ksajakra and Yenu know about it."

Itzlek licked his lips. His blue eyes were wide, but his overall expression was conciliatory, even conspiratorial, rather than horrified to be caught; his gaze darted back and forth as he lowered his hands. "Listen, Prophet, you know what? I am glad it was you that came to me and not one of the others. If it had to be anybody, you are the only one I would have picked. Or the Rhaokor, he's got the right idea. Like you. Like me."

I nodded, more to encourage him to go on, though he took it as agreement. (And who was to say even now that it wasn't? Ogruthon was silent inside me, listening too, or asleep, or feeding, or dying, stabbed. I felt and heard nothing.)

"No one can be guaranteed protection," he said quickly. "You have dealt with Them more closely than any of the others, so you know that better than they do. Am I right?"

"You're right."

"The innocent aren't immune naturally; they are not spared for any reason. The armies of the Masters are mindless, They don't know what They're doing, for most it is Their first fight of any kind, let alone Their first war. But some of Them have intelligence. Foresight. They are not merely walking weapons. They are gods, too. So why should we not pray to Them for mercy, eh? And why not make ourselves useful to Them?"

"Make ourselves useful," I repeated neutrally.

He swallowed, and tried a different tack. "Her out there, Yenu, I hear you talk to her now, but I've been talking to her for years. I'm from Aradec, lived there all my life. I left my butchershop to follow her. When I first met her I thought, She is a god, she is some kind of miracle! She cannot be explained even in a world where many things cannot be explained. The things she did, the things she showed us... When she told me months later that she was *not* blessed by the Masters and using those powers on Their behalf, I cannot tell you how shocked I was. And then worried, Prophet. *So* worried. For her, so young, her whole life ahead of her, for the innocent people she would pull into this vendetta of hers... It seems personal, doesn't it? She's hardly a hero. Hardly a peacemaker. You've heard her talk."

"All my life," I said. "She wants to be seen as a hero. But she's never out there just saving lives. What she's doing is being *seen* saving lives. She wants people to worship her, and they can't do that if they can't see her miracles. Then when she has worshippers, she has power."

He nodded eagerly, relief flooding his face. "So you see," he whispered, "it's better for everybody if... if I help the Masters. *He* has promised to spare me; he says he will put a mark upon me and no one will harm me, no matter what happens. He is trying to find us again, and despite all she's done to this ship, he *will* find us, and then our problems will be over. Life has gotten a little topsy-turvy, that's all. It can easily be turned right-side up. And it could be us, it could be *both of us*," he added in a hiss, staring up at me. "You don't have to say anything. You could help me, Prophet. Help Them. Very quietly. Without hurting anybody. Like this."

The candle flame seemed to flicker in his eyes—or behind them, the way it did sometimes in Yenu's. He was right in so many respects; he was saying exactly what the Advisor and I had so often thought. The room was so small I seemed to hear our heartbeats echo off the wooden walls. And yet... when had he joined the resistance, befriended the others? He had watched them die, he had *caused* their deaths by telling his Masters where we were, where we might be trapped.

"Yenu thought the ship itself was being tracked," I

said, as if I were thinking it over. "It would be easy to let her go on thinking it."

He nodded. "And she doesn't know about this place. I put up tripwires to let me know if anyone gets in when I'm not here. It could work. And *we* could be heroes on all those worlds."

All those worlds. Like Earth, writhing and erupting in those last few days, irrevocably changed, people panicking, in agony, watching one another transform into monsters, losing thought, memory, reason. Lives continuing, but not humanity. A brief, deranged twilight before utter dark.

My family, my home, everything and everyone I loved, over and over again, with no escape, in countless worlds.

The kids. The house. Our ordinary yellow sun. My heart.

Itzlek must have seen it on my face, for he instantly, visibly, gave up on me and went for one last transmission; I elbowed him in the mouth before he got out the first word of power, hard enough that his head rebounded from the wall and knocked the candle over, which luckily sputtered and went out instead of catching the paper.

The pain of his broken teeth would forestall any more magic for a minute. I scruffed him and dragged him whimpering back up to the deck, feeling nothing as his legs bumped up the stairs behind me. Anger made my steps light, made my pain fade.

*   *   *

GODS GATHERED CLOSE to watch, not out of vindictiveness (I thought) but curiosity. Though of course without faces—or faces I could interpret—I couldn't tell. I had told Yenu and the others what I had seen; Itzlek had not denied anything, nor had he confessed. Now he refused to answer Yenu's questions, kneeling indignant and bleeding at her feet next to the firepit. The others gathered, expressionless: numb rather than horrified, as in the aftermath of Liandan's death.

No, it is impossible, their faces said, but wearily so. I felt certain that Yenu had not been the only one to conclude that we were bleeding information on our 'secret' crusade.

No one defended him.

He said, mushily, "None of this will work. I don't even understand why you did this, knowing that it wouldn't work; it's an even worse insult to the Masters, it makes it seem you believe They are like these things... As if They could be killed by the little spirits that live in springs and crossroads. He won't like that, no."

"How long have you been spying for Them?" Yenu said flatly. "Since we left Aradec? Since we started building the ship? Before that?"

"It won't work," he said. "You're all going to die. It just... it just won't *work*. Look out there. This isn't an army. It's a children's choir."

Yenu fixed him with her gaze. The gods outside drew closer, a few pressing themselves against the dome of air surrounding the ship. Behind Yenu, Ksajakra stood with his arms crossed, his lips a thin, pink line, as if he were biting them on the inside. But he too said nothing.

And I thought, unable to help it, Itzlek had been right about one thing: he had been right about Yenu, about there being something wrong with her, deep inside whatever you would call either her mind or her heart, wherever you would say humanity lived. Something terribly wrong, something all the more unsettling for not knowing whether she would have been like this without her involvement with Them.

"You've caused thirty-six deaths," she said. "Resistance members, your comrades, friends. People who trusted you."

Itzlek raised an eyebrow. "Is it a competition?" he said. "Murders? You win."

She stared down at him. Not lost for words, I thought. Thinking of where to put him and how. You could not shame her with the number of lives she had taken, or else we would have by now.

"It's too late anyway," I said.

Yenu looked at me as if I had sworn at her.

"To make a difference," I said. "With all these gods gathered here... it can't possibly be a secret."

"Are you defending him?" she said evenly.

I blinked. "Did you miss the part where I was the one who caught him?" I couldn't remember if I was still supposed to be acting now that the spy had been found, or if she was, or what the hell was going on. The war felt very far away; Itzlek's hoarse, bubbling breath through his swollen nose and split lips was immediate and real. Not a field full of armies of millions of disembodied warriors. Just one man fuelled by cowardice as well as logic. Like me.

"Whatever you do to me," Itzlek said, and paused to spit blood onto the deck. "To me. You should do to him too. The Prophet. He is still Their servant as well. As loyal as me. As true."

Yenu ignored him. The others looked away: He is ours and not ours. She said, "Ksajakra, go below and get—"

She cut herself off as Itzlek rose, pulling something from his pocket; we hadn't tied him up, we should have tied him up, and of course he had been watching her for years with her deck of spells, and in the split second between her last syllable and his first, she raised her hand and a bolt of scarlet flame crossed the few feet between them, blasting a shallow crater in the deck and sending the rest of us backwards from the shockwave.

For several moments no one moved. The flame had been silent; all we had heard was the crunch and crackle as Itzlek's body was incinerated, the pitiful thud as the remains hit the deck. Bones, some teeth. A few metal things in his coat pockets. It was cold here, we wore our coats all the time, whatever you valued was always near you. I stared at the remnants: coins, keys. Keys to what? Nothing locked here. Must have been to his butchershop in Aradec. The traitor expected to go home safe and sound.

We looked at Yenu, staring at the body with her hands in her pockets now. The firepit cooled gradually from yellow-hot to orange and then merely red, the metal ticking and pinging like a clock. I imagined her saying

This is why I prefer to work alone, but I knew she didn't really. Solitude gave her no power over anyone else.

Like this, I couldn't help but think. The power simply to kill.

"I'll—I'll—I'll go get a blanket," said Rhakun, his voice trembling. His skin had gone slate-gray with shock.

"Prophet," said Yenu, still looking at the body.

"What."

"*Did* he send anything? When you came in."

"I don't know," I said, irritated. "I didn't see him for a few minutes. What does it matter? You gave us fake information anyway."

She nodded absently: a very unconcerned murderer, I thought. "Maybe it doesn't matter," she said.

The gods began to drift away from us, the show over. Rhakun still hadn't moved; I went over to him and said, "Come on. We have to gather it up."

He nodded, his large eyes glazed over, then abruptly focusing: not on, but behind me. "What is *that?*"

I didn't turn around. "Battle formations," I said.

CHAPTER EIGHTEEN

A REAL WAR—which I had never seen, admittedly—would have had uniforms. A real war would have had an easy way to tell friend from foe. Instead we lined up along the railing, Itzlek's corpse still untouched, and stared out at the starlit space around us, seeing nothing more than distant flares of light. As before, I could not tell how far away they were (millions of miles? more? less?) and as before, I knew it didn't matter.

"Stay together," Yenu said tonelessly under her breath. Who was she talking to? "Don't panic and split up. Stay together."

Stronger together, said Ogruthon inside me.

"They won't kill you," I said. She didn't look up. "They would take you alive. They must have orders to take you alive."

"They probably don't. Only Ny... the Manifestation

would. Him and his people. Why risk somebody else getting a hold of the nuke?"

"We should go," I said. "Get out of here, get you out of here."

"And go where? No, we need their protection for now; and we need enough power to get through to the nexus. Do we have that? Caustur says not yet."

Not yet, Ogruthon said.

"So that's it?" I said, and tried again, aiming my voice at a less strangled tone. "We just let the gods fight and die while we wait for the big guns to show up?"

She bobbed a shoulder. "That's always been the plan. You know. Like bullies at recess. Pick on somebody your own size. Not mortals."

The silence on the battlefield was unnerving, because I could clearly see the moving dots of light, and every now and then an unpleasant smear of unreality, surging back and forth and erasing the stars. It should have been accompanied by the noise of a fight. And the silence aboard ship was unnerving too. I thought about the gods sleeping, half-dead, more than half-dead, weakened, restrained, in all their various prisons and retreats. Where had they been, the large and the small? How many had escaped and hidden, like the Envoys, hoping to escape notice and malice? Mortals had written all the books and songs about that war... who had they learned it from?

"What do we do?" Ksajakra clutched the railing next to Yenu, breathing fast. "You! Prophet. Ask your god!"

"He's not *my* god. Anyway, all he said was *Not yet*."

"Not yet what?"

I narrowed my eyes at the middle distance, not quite hearing as Yenu and Ksajakra moved on to weaponry. In a movie, too, I realized, the thing flying towards us would have been making a whistling noise. Never mind the soundlessness of space. "Incoming!" I yelled instinctively in English; my stumble towards the centre of the deck completed the translation.

The thing never hit us. Several gods—or things on our side, anyway—flew to intercept it, also soundlessly, snatching the half-seen shape and tearing it to bits. Tentacles, eyes, and teeth flickered in and out of visibility as if they had attacked it with a strobe light. But it had gotten so close, so incredibly close. Even I could tell, despite the lack of landmarks and scale. No more than a couple of hundred yards from where we hung suspended in the void.

Caustur appeared out of nowhere, as she often did, although we should have heard her clicking across the wood. "Not yet, not yet," she said. "Well, we can defend ourselves here for a while. You look very worried, you mortals! You should save some worry for later. These are barely scouting parties."

"Scouting parties are dangerous too," I pointed out.

She made the noise that we had learned to interpret as laughter. "Yes, very! But I suspect these are new recruits. So to speak. And we are veterans. We have seen all this before."

"And lost."

"I don't know why mortals speak of winning and losing *war*, of all things. If a war happens, everybody's lost already."

The lights around us whirled, darkened, brightened, faded, returned. I felt as if we were in the eye of a tornado on a strangely sunny day, the spectral clarity of destruction that should instead have been filled with dirt and darkness. My heart was pounding and I reached stiffly for my sword, knowing it wouldn't help against spectral foes. May as well fight off a bear with a blade made out of fog. But if any of them were unlucky enough to suffer from mass and volume, well, I'd see what I could do.

Closer, closer. I could almost distinguish individuals now. Part of me wanted to scream *Just do it! Come here!* and part of me wanted to hide in the hold. Maybe reopen Itzlek's spy headquarters and shut the line of magic behind me: height and length only, no width for an enemy to slip into.

Christ. Itzlek. I closed my eyes against the maelstrom, opened them again. "I'm going to take the body below."

Yenu nodded; Ksajakra did too, and in a few minutes he and I had wrapped the still-hot puppet of bone and sinew into a blanket, tied it shut as best we could, and hauled it down the steps into the hold.

"We were supposed to have many more weapons," Ksajakra remarked when we were headed back up the stairs. I paused and looked down at him.

"Magical weapons, bombs," he said. "But we left before we meant to leave. We did not have everything we wanted on the ship. There was much still to load."

We're unarmed now because of you, he meant. *Because you escaped, and we had to chase you. And then you turned out to be useless for the purpose we stole you for.*

I didn't say that I would have sabotaged the ship early on if I had only thought of it. The involuntary sabotage was better than I could have hoped for at the time; if only they had seen sense and called all this off. "Things are moving in places we cannot see. Even now, right now. And while they move, They are moving us, too. Like puppets."

He took one more step, stopped, frowned.

"It doesn't matter that Itzlek was a spy," I said tiredly. "I always suspected, and still do, that every part of our plan, even where we corrected course, even where we failed and fled, has been arranged and scheduled in advance by the enemy. No matter what we did, we were meant to do it. Yenu must suspect it. She is lying to herself if she thinks she's been in charge this entire time. You'll see. No matter how much you hated the Masters, you were all wrong to follow her."

"I know."

We went back up, and tried not to think of the smell on our hands. Nothing more could be said. Johnny had always told me that nothing, *nothing* good comes for free. All we could decide was whether we wanted to pay the cost or not, and in what. If our lives were the cost for whatever she was doing, good or bad, I knew she'd pay it. And without asking us.

Wordless, I returned to Yenu, shuffling through her deck of cards. "Just let them *try* to board this ship," she muttered darkly.

"Yeah? What're you going to do, flamethrower them like Itzlek?"

"Could be. If it'd help." She shot me a look. "We have to live. All right? No, don't shake your head at me: this isn't ego. I'm saying, leave *wanting* to live out of it. I think for both of us that's up in the air anyway. Has been for some time. I'm saying, if what the gods say is true, we might be the *only* people, both backwards and forwards in time, that can rid this universe of the Ancient Ones. What if we are? What's our responsibility then? To lives that exist, and lives that will get a chance to exist...?"

She had stolen my words, my sentiment; I waited to feel angry that she was trying to turn them against me, and felt nothing. "What if we're not?" I said.

"I don't think we'll be alive to find out."

She moved three cards to the top of the deck, hesitated, then began distributing them amongst the pockets of her coat. The iron ring she still wore on a thin chain she carefully tucked down into her shirt. Metal, horn, bone, and glass glittered inside the coat. A walking armoury.

"You're really going to stab Them all to death, huh?"

"Maybe some of Them," she mused. "If They get within range. Depending on Their density."

"Did you say it was destiny?"

"I said density."

She shook her coat sleeves back, winced, rubbed her hands together and breathed on them. "I still wonder whether a universe is a computer. And whether it was designed and built, or allowed to be... random at first, and then steered, guided, later. And to do what? Maybe work out the answers to specific problems. Or not even *answers*. The universe is a certain shape because it has to be, but so are locks and keys, and a key isn't the answer to a lock. It just opens it. The presence or absence of certain people, acts, artifacts, ideas, I don't know: maybe those are all keys. Looking for their locks. The entire universe is full of them, but we don't know where the locks are until the key slides into place. That's *us* this time. For once. Maybe the only time it'll ever happen."

She patted her coat pockets, then, apparently satisfied, leaned on the railing again, balancing a dagger between her hands. "No surrender," she said, apparently to the dagger. "No negotiation. Are They... retreating?" She squinted.

"No," said Caustur. "Let me take out these old weapons... Ogruthon, do you think you can join the fight?"

If you and I fight, we will fight. I cannot fight alone.

"Yes, yes, very good!" She dug her spiked feet into the deck, clattering metallic laughter. "Like the old days. And let us see who else joins us. Here they come!"

She was right; she had seen it from a distance we could not. In the mingled starlight and the flare and spark of magic, the approach became clearer. The things flopped onto the dome around our ship and slowly, one by one, began to ooze through.

"Circle up!" shouted Ksajakra. "Circle, circle!"

I backed away from the railing and found myself pressed to the Advisor's flank; he had found or been given a sword from somewhere, and was holding it awkwardly, like a fork. His fur felt oven-hot even through my coat and shirt. On my other side was Ceth, armed with two thin swords like knitting needles.

"Oh, this is ridiculous," she murmured. "I feel as if I'm in a dream."

"Don't fight as if you were in a dream," said Saloc, and managed something like a laugh.

The dome was thick, and it seemed to be fighting Them itself, inasmuch as we could tell from the transparency. I thought about *Star Trek*: Shields up! We had no shields, we had only this, and things were coming through it, and I took a deep breath. Already you could smell Them: acid, sharp. "All right," I said, to everyone and no one, "let's put on a good show, yeah?"

And then they were on us.

Caustur had laughed about them being scouts but, I thought as I hacked easily through Them, wincing at the pain all along my left side, she had been right about them not knowing how to fight. The things were floppy, the usual disorganized tangle of teeth and eyeballs that you saw from the thralls and servants of the more cunning Ancient Ones, as if They had been put together out of leftovers.

I felt bad for Them, but not so bad that I couldn't kill Them. Yenu was hacking, slicing, and occasionally blasting Them with flames, just as she'd said she would; her clothes were covered with various shades and viscosities of ichor from the ones that had gotten within dagger range. And Caustur wasn't, as far as I could tell, using magic at all; she stalked like a praying mantis around the deck checking for any that had squeezed through, and simply picked Them up and tore Them apart. As she circled back around to me, I heard, almost like a passing train, a scrap of her conversation with Ogruthon:

can't let them

no, certainly not, the tales they'd tell

not even one may escape

one is too many

In a split second, with a decisive leap, Caustur shot up from the deck and scuttled around the outside of the dome, snatching at the smaller creatures that were apparently having trouble forcing Their way in. The other gods began to rally to us, capturing the now-fleeing creatures, crushing and burning and dissolving and compressing Them into nothingness.

I allowed myself a moment's hope past the fear, and even lowered my sword as the deck again fell silent.

Outside, against the darkness, the fight faded like the last moments of a fireworks show. I looked around: had we all made it? It seemed we had. It stank of burning chemicals, and the air felt dangerously depleted, making me lightheaded, but we few, the handful of resistance left, had resisted.

They will be back, Ogruthon said.

"Obviously," I said out loud. "We got lucky. We won't get lucky again. There might be more gods, but there'll for *damn* sure be more of Them."

"But if we leave, where can we go?" Caustur said, climbing back down the inside of the dome and reversing onto the deck. "I will not leave our people behind to fight while we flee, Ogruthon. Simply will not. You saw who's out there."

Yes. I saw, with love, with pride. Small gods. Spirits. Foot soldiers, scouts, couriers, light infantry, and talented little household sprites who guard the hearth. Brave and fey. And small. None like us. Did you?

"No. Not even sensed their approach."

Yenu, panting, said, "Do you know how to find the nexus now?"

We need more gods. We are stronger together: we can find it together, said Ogruthon.

Caustur made a brief, grating noise of distress. "Myself, I do not know. If we go towards it, the Manifestation will guess what we are doing and outflank and overpower us. If we stay we will only be attacked again. I do not see how we can move at all, little one."

The others watched us, baffled. "What bloody nexus?" said Sudworth.

I sighed. "You do the speech," I said to Yenu. "I'm going to go clean my sword."

Afterwards, the others joined me in the hold—a sad handful—to look after our weapons, nurse burns and wounds, get fresh clothes. I was shaking, but there was no shame in it; it was chemicals, adrenaline, that was all. And (I guessed) the perfect, screaming frustration that we had stepped into a glue trap, unable to move for fear of luring the enemy to our true goal, unable to stay lest we be encircled and cut down. What was one half-hour battle? It meant nothing. Even our survival meant nothing. Sudworth, helpfully, dug in our stores and returned to our lantern-and-crystal-lit circle with a ceramic flask of spirits, which we passed around.

Ksajakra and I could not help but look at Itzlek's corpse in its blanket wrapping, carefully and diligently bound in place so that it would not move around. We had accorded it so much more respect than Liandan's, even while skirmishes went on outside the ship. Why? Had we both liked Itzlek that much more? I didn't think so. And Itzlek had cost more lives, too. Liandan had only tried to kill me. But maybe that was it: the knife in the dark, the evidence of it in my stab wound, my fingers. What Itzlek had done still smacked of plausible deniability somehow: *They* did it all, not him. *Their* hands were bloodied. He had only ink on his.

The Advisor was ineptly sharpening (well, blunting) his borrowed swords; I took one, ran a wet rag along the sticky length, then tapped the whetstone in the cup of oil Ceth had brought, and began to sharpen it myself. No one spoke. It felt like last rites somehow, even though we had won.

"What's your name, anyway?" I finally said. "It's been eight years. I should know your name."

His face was inscrutable; he watched my hands on my sword, then began to imitate it at about quarter-speed. "Names are not important, Prophet," he said. "What we do is important."

"Well, you use names for everybody here."

"They have not told me their titles."

"We don't have them," Ksajakra said.

The Advisor frowned lightly. "You are not... Leader?"

"I might have said so once," he admitted. "But now..." He glanced at me, exhausted. "No. Whoever is leading... is not aboard this ship."

Silence fell again, punctuated only by the hiss of tearing cloth and the whine of stone along metal. "Well, never mind," I said. "I am the Prophet and you are the Advisor and that's how we'll stay."

BACK ABOVE DECK, I went to give Yenu some food and a fresh canteen; as I had expected, she was still fidgeting with her sticky daggers and leaning on the railing, watching the gods swirl in agitated circles, as if trying to mop up the last tiny speck of something from a countertop. Maybe they were.

She looked haggard, chalky: drained from the fireball spells, I figured.

Don't ever forget what it takes if there isn't enough around.

No, no, I said to Ogruthon hastily. I won't forget. I learned that early on. Everything has a price.

...Why are you feeding her when you are so full of hate for her?

"Because shut up, that's why," I said out loud. "How's anybody supposed to answer that?"

Yenu turned, confused. I thrust the paper packet at her. "Eat up," I said cheerily. "If you starve to death, you kill my last chance to go home."

"Oh. Well. Same."

"I already ate," I said. "And you're referring to the god, anyway, not me."

She bobbed a shoulder and began to unwrap the paper. "I... Is it very weird? Having him inside you. A person that isn't you at all."

"It's weird, but it's not bad," I said, putting the canteen into her least-stuffed coat pocket while she began to eat. The pocket's trim was sticky too, as if she had simply slipped and fallen into one of the less-cohered creatures. She smelled like a corroded battery. "It's like having an imaginary friend," I added thoughtfully.

"Yeah? You never had an imaginary friend though, did you?"

"Sure I did. You."

"I wasn't imaginary," she said.

"The friendship was."

This time she didn't even bother with the one-shouldered shrug, and simply continued to eat, using both hands to pinch the thin black bread around the salty cheese and fruit. I sighed hugely, although it seemed to deplete most of the oxygen left on the deck. "What are we going to do?" I said. "What? Someone has to make a decision. Not Ksajakra. Not the gods. You. Us. If we're the key."

"What if we're not? What if they're wrong about... about everything? This plan. The nexus. What if we can't find it, or we think we've got the right one and we don't, or they can't put us in the right place, and what if th—?"

"I guess we'll die. I don't know." I did not add that I didn't mind the idea of dying so long as, somehow, both of us did. The thought of her surviving me made bile rise in the back of my throat. At least if we were both dead, They could never get her. Disarmed nuke. So to speak. "Look, let me just say this once and then never, ever again, unless maybe I get cursed or something. For every time I've saved your life I only hate myself more now," I said.

"And it's been a few," she said, putting her chin on her wrist, nestling it between the thick metallic scales. "Anyway, I don't blame you."

"I don't care if you do or don't."

"I know." She tilted her head briefly at the Advisor, curled and wing-blanketed far down the deck, his face apparently sparkling with crystals of salt, though I knew it was just the effect of his skin. "You tell him any of those stories?"

"Just one. The pond."

She fell silent; tears cleansed a path down her face as I watched, gathering the starlight and godlight above us so it looked like she was weeping flames. "What did he say?"

"He said it was a noble thing to have done, but very unwise. Something only a child would do."

"That a man would have let me drown. Only a boy would have tried to save me. Because we both could have died. And you could have cut the fatality rate in half if you saved yourself."

"Yes."

"Mm." She wiped her face on the filthy shoulder of her coat. "Fair. Fair."

And that was back when I was still yours, I thought. *Your made thing. Before you told me the truth*. And what was I afterwards? A broken toy, something kept but not working the way it was supposed to, as I tried to unmake myself, get your fingerprints and maker's mark off me, not knowing how. Trying to be made by myself instead of you. Whether for good or bad, yours, your property. Your thing. And I had no way to learn how not to be that.

And even now I am not sure if I am mine. I am tired, so tired, of belonging *to* people, and yet never belonging. You don't know how it feels. You wanted to be what They made you. It gave you everything good in your life. I saved you then. And I wouldn't save you now. He was right: I'd let you die now. I'd save myself. I know I would.

Here is how the world is saved. One of us lives. One of us dies.

But you already know that, don't you?

"You know," I eventually said, "I always thought it was going to be one of your ridiculously fucked-up high-energy physics experiments that ended the world. Honestly."

"Actually, one time we—"

"My God, please do *not* tell me how close you came. Do not."

She smiled unexpectedly, exposing her altar-stone teeth. There was something strangely final about it: as if I'd never see her smile again, as if from then on it would always be a grimace of effort or a rictus of pain.

I shivered. Goose walked over my grave. In another universe.

"Remember what Dr. Jauffret used to call me? When I built that facility outside Rouen?"

"No."

"Her little strangelet." The smile fell away. "It was cute in her accent. I don't know. A strangelet is a hypothetical thing, it's like the... not the collective, but like the *unit* name for strange matter. A glob of it. Stuck together. Not particles on their own. Because, she said, I was so strange, and I collected strange things around me, and we all stuck together... It was a joke along a couple of axes. One, that you can only get strange matter under incredible pressure. In the core of certain types of stars, say. And two, that... that you can, maybe, cause a black hole to form around a strangelet. You need an accretion point. But then you also need the clumping, then the collapse, then the drawing in. And then..."

I looked out at the battlefield, where massive swathes of colour were beginning to fill up, like slow-moving water, on all sides. Loose spheres, lazy ovoids, lightning crackling inside them. Worlds of gods. Worlds of enemies. Lights in the darkness. I said, "That's you. I get it. You're the accretion point. The armies are clumping up here..."

"I don't *want* to be the accretion point!"

"Well, they need something to clump around, or they won't ever achieve anything. The collapse or whatever. It's us," I said, as she began to cry. "It's us. We're the emptiness that never fills. It's okay. Jesus. It's just a metaphor. Fuck *off*." I put my arm reluctantly around her shoulder, my far hand adhering to the disgusting fabric of her coat.

And Ogruthon? I added.

Yes?

You feed people you hate because they're *people*. That's why.

"It's happening," someone whispered behind me; I looked back briefly at Ksajakra, who'd come over to join us, then back out at the void in which we still floated. And there was sound now, impossibly, and I did not want to think of how that sound was reaching us. Not air. Something else.

Somewhere, far distant, a few notes on a trumpet. A call to war or a funeral salute. A sigh passed over the massed gods and I should not have heard that either but I still heard it, and under my arm Yenu stiffened.

I felt nothing from it, not worry or anticipation, not bloodlust. Who had lifted an instrument to his lips so far away? What was meant by it, and how had they done that? My blood felt cold and heavy, rising to roar in my ears so that I did not even hear the Advisor murmur his next words.

"What?"

"I said, we brought no music and no means to make it."

"No," I said. "Good. I don't know. War doesn't seem to be the place for it."

Sudworth nodded vaguely, cracked her knuckles the way the others were playing with the hilt of their swords or adjusting the last of our grenades. Her weapons were her hands. "Music's what makes us people," she said. "Instead of—what'd he say? A bag of chemical paste with a single spark buried inside the shit. It shouldn't be in a fight. Robs it of its magic."

But the trumpet had not been music, I thought. It had been a call, a signal. To strike a bell would have had the same effect. Half-automatically I looked down at Yenu, to ask her if she remembered the scene in *The Lord of the Rings* where the Horn of Gondor was blown, but found that I couldn't.

"We're doing the thing again," I murmured. "Just like you said. Not moving, because we think the do-nothing option is best. But it only benefits Them. Again. Let's get the fuck out of here." I looked up at Caustur, who had said nothing. "We don't decide for the gods. Like you said. Now that they're free, they can fight if they want. Or come with us while we run for the nexus. We'll just see who finds it first."

"Send the envoys," Caustur said, and laughed her clicking laugh. "I want to fight. Here, now. With all my people around me. But if you need me... I will go with you."

I sighed, watching the blurs leave our ship, and a thousand other points of darkness, and vanish into the general chaos. "I've been at a few last stands now," I said. "They never felt like this."

"What's a last stand?" said the Advisor.

I told him. He frowned. Sudworth laughed, a small, bitter sound barely audible under the trumpets and drums that approached us through soundless space.

Which were the Elder Gods, which the Ancient Ones? I didn't know. And was the Manifestation among them, the one we most wanted to draw out and defeat? I knew we'd never see him unless he showed himself on purpose. He always operated at a distance. The name: manifesting as anything.

"Let's go," I said again. "They can choose. I mean it. Don't stay for them."

Yenu nodded at last, and turned back towards the steering wheel in the bow that I still thought of as ornamental, even though I'd seen her use it a few times now. It just looked *fake*.

She blinked when she put her thumbs on the sigil in the centre. "I..."

"What?"

"It's not working."

"Get down!" someone screamed, and I looked up first, instinctively, but there was nothing, and a moment later I fell flat on my back, ass first then head, as we struck something unseen, or it struck us.

Whatever we had hit left the entire ship ringing like a bell, so that even my bones seemed to shiver when I got up, gingerly wiping scraped palms on my pants. The shuddering went on and on and on for far too long, as if somewhere below the insubstantial emptiness something was still hitting us, and then slowly faded. My teeth chattered on for a minute and then stopped.

The Advisor picked Yenu up by the back of her coat and set her on her feet; her nose was bleeding, sluggish and thick.

"The fuck," she croaked, and took a step towards the railing, then stopped. "I want to look but I don't want to look."

"Past experience tells me it would be a bad idea to look," I said, "but it's worse to not know."

"Are you coming then?"

"Nope." But I did, and we stood at the railing, hanging on tightly in case there was another collision. Only darkness, filled with stars. No shapes, no absence of shapes, no colour and no light.

"Who knows. But I don't like how it shook afterwards. I mean, it's wood, it's got no resonance. What's down there?"

"Something horrible," I said. "It's always something horrible."

She nodded, winding her hand nervously in a rope. It was quiet. Silent, I realized. The trumpets had ceased to blow. The messages being sent to us were no longer up for interpretation and argument, but had been delivered once, hard, to the hull of our boat.

It's just us. Just us mortals all alone here. Not for the first time I was struck by the vastness of the war we had embroiled ourselves in, and how horrifyingly small and fragile we were in comparison.

"We can't move at all, can we?" I said. Yenu didn't even look at me.

When the fins finally showed themselves, they were far distant; and at first, they looked like nothing more than star-flecked space itself. But they were approaching, for one thing, and growing for another, as something heaved itself briefly from the invisible spectrum to the visible, bladed like broken glass all along its back, jagged ridges of skin and scale like a mountain range, sliding sinuously towards us through absolute nothingness, paddling inexplicably through vacuum, fast, much too fast, closing the distance faster than something that big should have been able to move.

Someone screamed in a language I didn't know. I wrapped a rope grimly around my arm and closed my eyes.

This time the blow was deliberate, not a warning slap; I was wrenched backwards again, managing to stay upright by clinging to the rope. Something crunched, undeniably, I felt it up through the deck like my own bones had broken. Under my coat I felt my wound begin to bleed again, the blood clinging to my palm then dripping to the deck. Slow down there, I told it deliriously. This isn't over yet. I need that stuff.

And the thing wasn't even the main show. Had I hoped? It was only an emissary, testing with its void-hardened body the fragility of our wooden ship, the weakness of its protective wards. The stars seemed to boil all around us, coruscating as far as the eye could see, as if a million more giant sharks like this were gathering, shoving each other out of the way. I thought of the lava-fish in the moat around Ogruthon's prison, how it seemed a thousand years ago, how time was like distance, and we would never be further from home, and then the darkness parted in front of us laboriously, with a groan, like parturition, and birthed a mountainous thing entirely covered in writhing limbs, sickly white and glistening green, that reached out for us with spiders' limbs, tipped with claws and hairs.

It should have been louder, I thought dazedly; we should have all been screaming. Instead we were mostly frozen, staring up at it.

To think, I'd thought we would have to fight an *army*.

Yenu barked orders, telling everyone not to fight, to hang onto something, and then a flash of something white appeared in one hand—a card?—followed by a much larger flash, a roaring fireball of blue and black that careened up unevenly like a flare and splashed against the monster, to stick and burn with unpleasant, invisible flames.

The thing roared, again less loudly than I had expected, but the vibration came through the dome around the ship so hard that my teeth clattered together, subsonic. Its flesh boiled off in gobbets, hissing away from it in every direction, but it had a lot of limbs to spare, and though Yenu shot another, then another, then Sudworth launched a thing like a net of pale-pink laser beams that sliced off a hundred tentacles at once, it was relentless.

Its screaming now was ceaseless, as thick fluids poured out of it and vanished in an ever-increasing cloud around it, but it was still coming, still reaching. A spider with an insect trapped firmly in the net, I thought wildly: it can hear us buzz, see us kick, we are spitting out our little venoms, but we do no harm, we are prey. *We are prey*.

Without even meaning to, I brought my own hands up and sketched the simple shape in the air, shouted the words of power, sent a fireball of my own towards the thing; I had aimed high, and it reared back, startled, but only as much as a mountain could rear, as orange-and-pink flames burst in front of it. Its cry went up an octave; the ship too screamed, wood creaking and howling as it twisted apart against its own construction, against Yenu's spells protecting it from harm.

We should have been screaming, I thought again. Behind the creature came the other thing, the thing with the high glassy fins on its back, still unseen, still much worse than if we could see it. Just darkness, places where the stars weren't.

We couldn't move and we couldn't abandon ship and really, when you got right down to it, we couldn't fight. That made things easy, at least.

God, and I thought we were going to get to the nexus ahead of the actual war. I really thought it. I really let myself think it.

We hung onto ropes and masts and each other in grim silence, as the white-tentacled thing waited out our final, feeble, magical assault, and reached for the ship again.

And picked it up, easily, and drew us towards itself, the wounded, ragged, crawling surface of the creature fat with maggots and ticks, shelled things burrowing into the oozing skin to escape the cold and hunger of space, till someone finally did scream, their nerve gone. I could not see who. My entire vision was taken up with my fists, and the expensive, good ropes they held, how scarred my hands had become.

They are all ready to die for him, and I understand

that. What they think will be taken from them is worse than having life taken. With their own kind they will die, and they think that's a comfort, that it's better than a life bereft of whatever the Manifestation has promised them they will lose. Think of that. Think of us, think of them. Think of the lies on both sides. The lie that Yenu and I were telling people. The lie that we could win.

But the monster did not eat us. It turned, sending the whole sweeping battle past us like a painting, and floated through a round, flame-trimmed gate that formed even as we watched, something that blew towards us the scent of burning dust.

CHAPTER NINETEEN

LONG BEFORE WE arrived at our destination, while we seemed to be standing still, while motion seemed to be not happening, while only the dust came towards us, I knew who had summoned us: who had waited long enough, who had been laughing invisibly somewhere, and who had finally snapped shut his final trap. The laughter would go on, but not for much longer.

We had lost.

The ship, deposited ungently on hard ground, simply fell apart around us; we scrambled and leapt to get free as the masts came down, the railings bowed inwards, the deck crumbled, and the sails splayed. All our kegs of water, the remaining boxes of food, our clothes, timber, supplies, all spilled out and smashed, spreading across what looked like a pale, honey-veined marble floor.

There was light, thick and headachy, above us, a ruined

roof of stone circles and arches, in which perhaps glass had once been set. Through the vast stone openings shone only light from stars, seeming hot and close, not like the stars we had just left. And around us was a chuckling susurrus of sound, a shuffle and murmur as of bodies packed close together, the sound of a crowd. I looked at my rope-burned palms in the strange, slow light, and flexed my fingers, which cast no shadows on my palm.

No one said: *Kill the others; bring her to me.*

No one said: *You have your orders.*

No one said: *You know the plan.*

They simply came surging out from behind the tall marble pillars and the tumbled ruins, sliding across the great altar at the front of the temple, running down the slick steps, shouting in triumph. A mixture of things: flopping, scrambling, flapping, crawling. Some armed, many not. Humans, even, dressed in a wide range of clothing and armour. Probably the remnants of whatever armies had defied them to date.

The Manifestation, I thought bleakly, drawing my sword with a grunt, was efficient in war. Add to your coffers from the coffers of the enemy as soon as they were subdued enough to let you take it, and not a moment after. We had not thought they had reached so many worlds.

With the numbers they had, it was never going to be much of a battle. We formed up, shouting back at them, panting in the thin, salt air, killing the first wave mostly by the power of surprise and a few expertly-launched fireballs. Caustur sent out great swathes of greenish flame, cutting a path through the oncoming horde, but it was filled just as soon. Saloc fell in silence; Ceth screaming in rage, swinging an axe around her head and half-wading in the mingled blood of the things, stung by something that looked for all the world like a giant scorpion with claws dipped in copper.

Rhakun climbed the remains of the third mast to get to high ground and was cut down by a group of rat-like things working together, translucent green bodies apparently as soft as overripe fruit, but still overwhelming and suffocating him. I killed five, six, a dozen, but anything not in the immediate path of my sword paid me no heed. Indeed, nothing engaged me at all, which only added to the sinking feeling in my stomach entirely unrelated to the fight. Which began to feel less and less like a fight and more like a stage show. A play about war—a comedy actually, and us as the butt of the joke. A joke I knew had been a long time coming.

From the shadows behind the altar something colossal emerged and flowed towards us, or floated, more than walked: a roiling cloud at first, sparking lightning in its smoky depths, tightening, shifting, eventually becoming a very strange thing, a thing composed of thousands of smaller things, coarse-haired and glistening with some thick liquid, all of it moving at once so that you could barely stand to look at it, shifting again, liquefying, becoming a humanish form, humanoid, but built of broken mirrors, the shards reflecting everything back. In the glass I watched the thing's long casual gesture brush aside his army as if it were smoke, sending monsters toppling across the slick floor and crashing into the broken remains of our ship.

Him. At last. Not in his true form, because he did not have one, but the one he had chosen to show us. Part of the play. Part of the game.

And who had told me that the gods on both sides played games? Of unspeakable violence, over unfathomable aeons, with incomprehensible rules, for utterly depraved stakes. For amusement, to while away the years.

But there were more subtle games.

In front of him opened another stage prop: sluggish, something obscene about it, a circular pit that went down and down and down, and filled itself with voluptuous gulping noises. Real lava this time, not fish. The better to show off his mirrors, I thought. And for all I knew, an illusion, the heat too, no more able to harm us than a picture projected on a wall. Something seemed to grind inside it though, in silence, and unaffected by the molten stone: teeth, tongues. Purest white.

"Welcome, my Miscreation."

Yenu stared up at him: the long graceful gestures meant for her, his words meant for her. *Yours?* her face said. *Rude.*

His head inclined fractionally at me. "And to you too, the Conclusion. Welcome." He had no face, could not smile, but there was a warmth to his speech: a false, gloating warmth, a sickly heat as of fever. His voice was slow and slurred. "You; you, in particular, seem surprised. You should not be. Were you not told that your name was known to us? To all of us? Just as hers was? That was not a coincidence of proximity."

A jolt. I remembered a low, whitewashed building. Rugs everywhere, piled deep and soft, a smell of incense and the stench of magic not hidden by the air fresheners. Helen and Tariq: senior members in the Society, not believing us, or so they said, until they had tried to keep us there with a spell.

But also telling me: *Your name is known to Them.*

And something I had forgotten, too. Almost the moment I left. There had come a soft voice from the other room, from someone we had not seen. Telling them to let us go.

No, it could not have been him. One of his minions, certainly. No. But if it was, then his plan dated even to then, or before, he had already had us on the board, moving...

Inside, I screamed to the god: *Get us out of here!*

I cannot... not without Caustur... alone, we are...

What? Where the *fuck* did she go?

I looked up again; the god's voice was fading in and out. I said, "Someone was in the other room."

"I liked Earth," the Manifestation said. Too long on the final sound: *thhhh*, like he was sucking on it. "Liked to travel on it. Various guises. Human was very good. Or human enough; I didn't fool everyone. But what of it? No one who guessed correctly was of any consequence, and most of them immediately became the type of person no one would ever lend credence to again. I visited at odd times. Slept between. You know all this."

"Were you planning this even then?" I said, unable to stop myself. Even if he lied, I wanted him to say something. Some answer. Anything. "All this. This war."

"Oh, yes. Ever since her."

Yenu did not react; she was staring up at him. Or at her face reflected in one of his many facets. Strangely, I could not see it, even with the hundreds of mirrors and her standing near me. I could see myself, the temple around us, the sky, the hushed, waiting army. Far below a distant roar like rushing water, or an encroaching wildfire.

"Drozanoth's games and distractions were nothing to us," he said. "Not until *she* came about, and then I watched very closely indeed. Only around such a stone could I finally build a singular pearl. Nothing had ever worked out so beautifully before. Even come close."

"The reactor," Yenu said at last.

"Not the reactor," he told her. "You. You are the long-awaited weapon, the thing that brings about the end of worlds. *You* know that. But I watched; I waited. I thought: *Supposing now is the time to rise.* We are not a hierarchy, as you know. But there are elders and apprentices. There are servants and masters. And there is one, one atop us all... and I wanted to take the infinite universes from his hands."

Again a flash: the mountain of my dream spitting words like snow, and the low building, the standing stones, and someone sitting serenely in the storm, a piece of yellow silk blowing over a face that no one could look at. I seemed to hear the Advisor's words in my head once more. And where had *he* gone? He was not here either. They had all abandoned us. I was too weary to even feel betrayed. I was too close to death.

Fearing him without even knowing what they feared... the one who held the other end of the pantograph. The one who chose what crumbled and what flared into existence, and what the shape of a universe was: would it work, would it not. The one who could draw an original thing. And now this thing, the crawling chaos, the Manifestation, wanted that.

I could not imagine him being better or more just or kinder or more merciful or even more logical. I could only imagine him being worse.

"Why are you telling us any of this?" Yenu said. "It's so clichéd."

"There's no one around to talk to." He laughed, the sneer in it like a cut. "I am surrounded by animals. Like humans. All they want is to eat and shit and fuck. Boring. Boring. And now you, my Miscreation. Now this.

"You were created by chance, you became what you were by chance," he went on. "So you were worth monitoring simply out of curiosity... Chance runs so much more than you know. The brains of mortals *can't* know it. Not built that way. It is worth mentioning that in all the worlds, in all the dimensions, in all the universes I know of, you only existed in one. So Drozanoth watched you. And I watched you. I wanted to see what would happen. And then you stole my greatest prize from me... and I saw that you, my pearl, were not an ornament at all, but a tool."

"An accident."

"No matter. We believed you dead when your planet was destroyed. We did not know you had resurfaced till your latest arrest."

He let it hang. I wondered how he would kill us. The lava pit? There was something in there, too; would that be faster than lava? Slower? More painful? Or one of those mirrored shards. Throw a part of yourself into your enemy's soft mortal body like a spear...

"And *there he was*, waiting for you... Sometimes we have had to ensure that the threads of fate pulled you together. Sometimes we did not. Did you know that? Indeed, we never could have returned after you locked the gates if not for him."

Him who, I almost said, then froze: me. He was talking about me.

"What?" Yenu said faintly.

"Oh, yes. We had been shut out, we were insulted, we resorted to sniffing around keyholes and peeking through mirrors—not me, you understand, but so many others, hungry and prying and without dignity... and then he opened up a way. And we were able to pour in such spirits and servants as could fit through the opening, and we returned." He chuckled. "A circus through a keyhole."

At this, she stared at him with genuine confusion, visibly trying to work it out. But I knew what he was talking about, and my blood ran cold, as heavy as lead. Shame broke through my thick, glassy shell of numbness.

The watcher. The watcher I had snatched at, all

unthinking, to stop its lunge at my sister. Galaxies and lifetimes ago. You weren't supposed to touch them. You were never supposed to touch them. No one had ever said why. And of course it had hurt, and I had worried about it, but we had had other problems back then and...

Another flash: the forest we had run into by accident. That electric-green sea. We had been beneath Edinburgh Castle, and then suddenly we weren't, and the Burning King had looked at my upheld hand, and he had *stopped*... and I had never told her about that. I had passed off the wound as a bruise.

The whole time it had been a gate. Tiny, but big enough to let the Manifestation's magical prions, as she had called them, pour through. To start the invasion. To make a greater way.

I thought I had saved Carla's life. Instead I had doomed them all. It had been my fault. Or Johnny's. It depended on how far back you went, trading turns of guilt and causality, all the way to the beginning of time, whose fault it was. My heart stuttered, skipped beats. Felt like it might stop. I said nothing. At least if I died on the spot, the Manifestation could not kill me.

"So you did find a way in," she said. "And you came to the party at the castle as soon as you could... no. You sent your people. Your kidnappers."

"Very good. Now supposing I answered all your questions. As my new protégée, your first duty would be to tell when I was lying. And when I was telling the truth."

"Bernier let you into his apartment, and maybe that

time it really was you," she mused, as if he had not spoken. I could almost hear the whirl and click of gears in her head. That familiar, busy sound of childhood. "You took the face of someone he knew just long enough for him to open the door... but you didn't want us to have his data. You burned it."

Protégée, had he said? He still did want her. Alive. The greatest weapon of the war. He hadn't even said *join me*. You were supposed to say *join me* if you were really the villain. He had just taken it as a given. Talking as if the job offer had already been signed.

"It has all pointed here," the Manifestation said. He straightened, glittering, reflecting us, the temple, the silent army, sprouting a great razor-pointed crown that nearly touched the open arches far above us.

Yenu didn't back away. His fighters quailed and fled into the shadows, dropping weapons and shields. He didn't seem to notice.

"You already know your power is nearly limitless. Take away the *nearly*. Make it without limit. You could rule world after world—as many as you want, in my name. Do anything you wanted. Live forever. A new covenant could be written for you. See," he added slyly, "how I *offer* instead of *threaten*. Because you do not care if we torture and kill the Conclusion. Not any more. Once he could have been useful to us. Now you would not even notice."

She nodded dreamily, and I recoiled as if she had slapped me. Something about the look on her face. Untroubled by any care, not even an eyelash of worry between her brows. "Any world I wanted," she said. "Not just in this universe, but any universe."

"Of course."

"And to use the pantograph whenever I wanted. To make my own. And decide which ones would be destroyed after a spell. Or which ones could use magic at all."

"If you like."

"I mean, if you wrested control away from... *him*. Oh, and Drozanoth," she added. "I would want it killed. Tortured and killed. *Can* you torture it?"

"Nothing easier."

She was up to something. Had to be. *Was* she up to something? Would she... what? Agree to everything, get close to him, and then, I don't know, stab him? Zap him? Did she know how to kill him? My mind raced with a desperation I'd never felt. Seconds, I had seconds, she was giving me only seconds.

No, she could not do magic here. He was too careful for that. Had she truly spent her entire life, her death and resurrection and this second life, hungering and angling for power, as we had seen her do, as she had confirmed she was doing, only to betray him now? That would be his suspicion; but oh, he knew about hungers, They all did, and he knew about the hungers Their gift had created in her. No mere *world* could fill it. And so she had never been sated.

"A thousand worlds," he said, "would call us gods."

My entire body seemed to contract, shrinking away from him, from her, from the yawning red pit and its grinding teeth. Outside a strange wind picked up, a salty toneless whisper resembling song as it whirled through the broken roof, the crumbling walls.

Say it. She wanted to be a god. Not wanted, *wants*. She has always wanted to be a god. She destroyed our entire world in the hopes that she would not lose those qualities that caused us all to worship her. She had destroyed our entire world for *that*.

Look at her face. Look at the face you know. No one else could tell which decision she had made. Not even him. Only me.

"Yenu," I said.

She turned her back on me and stepped forward, her boot leaving the tawny stone. As she did so, a bridge began to form across the molten, spitting stone, I've seen this before, very theatrical, what trust you have to have to walk across it, to leave me, to walk to him, across the way he makes for you, cool and marble right to his very feet. "That's not my name," she said absently. "That's someone else... that's not who I am."

"Johnny, then. Get away from that. Come back. You can't *play* with him, you can't—"

"I'm done playing," she said; at last she paused though, and finally, slowly, turned to look at me, taking in my horror and astonishment. I seemed to see her mismatched eyes drink it in, gulping it. Always the hunger. "I'm a weapon. Weapons are meant to be used."

"To kill. And no you're not, you're not a weapon. You're a person. If you were... If you were an inanimate object, your existence would be immoral, yes. The process of developing you would be immoral. And your inability to prevent your own use would be immoral too. But *you* have a choice."

"Yes. I'm making it."

I thought: *We have been here before. It is as if we are always here. The villain makes a speech; we are both offered temptation; I resist.*

But I cannot resist this time. The cycle must be broken. This must be the last time. This cannot be allowed to happen again.

Something flickered at the corner of my eye: something bronze, gleaming. Did it mean...? No, it wasn't important, and I couldn't look away.

I took a deep breath. She turned from me again and took one more step across the marble. Her skin glowed rosily in the light from the pit. She almost looked healthy.

Say goodbye. Say goodbye to her for the last time. Say this is for your own good and for my own good and for the good of all the universes that will ever exist. Say that somehow, even in death, your ego that tells you that you are the most important person who has ever lived is not wrong. It's arrogant and evil but it's not wrong. Don't do it in silence.

"Goodbye," I said, and took two steps, closing the space between us. The Manifestation screamed, but it was too late, it was too late, and the wind rose and rocked around us, my way out already being prepared, my body already being lifted through it, so that I had to fight to get close enough, and she turned again, stared at me, her hands still empty at her side, face open, resigned rather than confused, *she knew,* I thought with greater grief than I had ever felt in my life, *she knew, she knows, she said sorry to me once and she was lying, she said she loved me and she was lying, this isn't personal but it is and it isn't and it is and it isn't* and I fought the wind till I could drive the sword around in a great sweep through her neck, entirely without resistance.

The blade emerged striped in blue and black, the head vanishing into the liquid abyss below us, and with my free hand I shoved her so that the body, *not her it's not her it's not her it's the body,* fell too, disappeared, something glittering briefly in the welter of blood, the thing wrapping itself around my hand.

And only the hysterical screams of the Manifestation convinced me that I had in fact done what I had done, it was real, it could not be taken back, and there was no way he could make it right, and for a moment my horror was replaced with relief and even something like wonder. For I had *wanted* to do it, hadn't I? For a long time. For years. Since that first moment in the desert, looking up at the ragged faceless abomination that had made her. A made thing. Don't ever forget that. Don't—

And then I was ripped backwards, pursued by his rage like a flock of furious birds. But sweet, no sweeter sound. Falling in my ears, all along my body, like the blows of a hammer. Receding in the distance to the pure high sounds of a trumpet. War, war. The last days. Sounding in my ears. Sounding all over me. Rolling across me in waves of space. Reminding me that the universe is cold and large, and the warm things in it will die and become cold. Sparks extinguished. Sparks extinguished forever. Unless I could put my body between the sparks and the extinguishing breath.

I closed my eyes and held on as tightly as I could and felt the spikes of Caustur's armour sink into my palms till they hit bone.

CHAPTER TWENTY

THE GHOSTS OF *Earth are not watching you*, the god said. *They offer you no benison for what you have done. But I do.*

I had no reply to that. I had never believed in ghosts. People did believe in them, of course, and some people said they'd seen them. But people are always saying things. Lying because they're grieving, or afraid, or guilty, or simply because they don't know they're lying.

But so many ghosts. She killed everyone on the planet, everyone except her and me and one furious old woman. Her own time was ticking down twice as fast as usual, and she had simply stolen the time of everyone left on Earth. Not on purpose, I knew. But that didn't make it any better. All those lives lost.

The darkness here is safe and warm and good, the god said faintly, as if it were receding from me. *The void is full of light and it is the light that kills. We will go between one and the other, Nick. Together.*

I nodded.

Remember the dead. Here is the only place they can live.

"I will."

I EMERGED SLOWLY from my own head, climbed out against all the grasping power of internal gravity, and for a brief, blissful moment there was only the sensation of warmth and safety. Then everything crashed back down on me, all edges and cold, like an iceberg. And worse yet, someone was attacking me, sobbing. I lifted a hand to bat them away, seeing only a silhouette bordered in orange and red. The sobs had a terrible, tearing quality to them.

The weight on me was lifted; I stood up cautiously. Two legs, two arms, brain, eyes. Where were we? There was air, there was gravity. It was strange that these were things I had to establish now.

And Johnny was dead. She was who she said she was, and she was dead.

So it seemed that everything I had ever done, while we were apart, while we were together, had been—though I did not know it—simply practice for that moment: for the moment when I had to put my full weight into the stroke, for the moment I had to be sure she was dead. For when I had had to take her away from the enemy.

You cannot have her; you will misuse her.

And she would misuse herself. She could not resist it. Not in the end.

It was Ksajakra who had attacked me, and someone was holding him back: yes, like a shadow, soft. The Advisor. So, two still alive at least. We stood in sand, deep and dark, like crushed sapphires; the sky was green, with three small, nearly-identical moons equidistant above, and stars glittering like crushed glass. Beautiful. Peaceful. Why peaceful? What was happening to the war whose armies we had placed just so onto the battlefield?

Someone had built a fire, and for a moment I wondered what we were burning from all this sand, then realized it was part of the ship. Caustur had been wise to seize the ship as she retreated: at least any mortal survivors would have a little shelter. Shadowy forms sat motionless around it. I walked past the struggling Ksajakra, and the Advisor, and I sat on the warm sand.

"How did we get away from that place?" I said after a while, when no one spoke to greet me.

Caustur said, her voice subdued and broken, "We gathered all we could. I started. I needed Ogruthon and he was not there. But we held each other and we shared and we amplified... Small gods and spirits. Envoys. Scouts. Whoever we could find... it wasn't enough. We saw that when he arrived. The armies of the Corruption—"

"He calls himself the Manifestation now."

"—fought us to keep us from him. And, it seems, from you... Oh, my friend. I thought: We must get you to the nexus. We must, we must. But while our single chance was gone many years ago, the new one is gone now. I saw at once what had happened. So all we could save was you."

"Thank you."

"Many small gods were sacrificed," she said. The fire—a large, burning chunk of gracefully-carved railing—crackled and popped, embers floating over our heads in the warm, still air. "They agreed to it, they did. They were very brave. It was still terrible. It hurt so badly. I felt it as if I were the one giving up my life... every one of them. But it was the fuel we needed to break his spell and get you out."

"Where are we now?"

"One of their worlds. An old one. They rarely come here; it is like Aradec, famous for it. A thrall world slavering to be a thrall. Obedient mortals. Sacrifices like clockwork. Magic, perhaps, to hide us a little while. Much magic in the air."

"Yes, I can smell it." I was shivering despite the warmth. Shuddering, actually. Once you start asking yourself *What have I done*, there is no way to stop. There is no end to the library of misdeeds. Murder felt like the least of it now.

The way her face had opened, like a blooming flower, as she spotted the blade. Could she still have dodged it? Had she *let* me do it? Hideous to not know. I felt it inside me as if I had swallowed a ball of barbed wire.

The jetting blood. I had had no idea it would leap so far. In the executions at the palace, the blade is left against the neck. All you see is the blood. Flooding out quiet and orderly.

What have I done. What have I done? More than just an atrocity to her. And more than just to myself. Oh God, what...?

"So we are back where we started," I said. "They are unopposed. The only thing They lack now is her. And They will go on without her."

Ksajakra croaked something I couldn't understand; his voice sounded closed-off, as if he had been crying so long he could no longer speak.

Just outside the ring of the fire, shapes swooped and flowed across the sand, camouflaged, blue feathers, blue scales, something like birds or bats. They did not approach us. Maybe they had never seen fire before but they knew vaguely what it could do.

"It was always headed towards this," I said dully. "It didn't have to end this way. But this is always where it was aimed. She knew that. Her existence was a threat to the entire universe. To every universe, if she had joined Them. I used to think that she was so... brave. For resisting the temptation. How she fought against it, year after year.

"But now I realize she was just waiting for the right moment. When They wanted her most. When They would offer the most. When she had nothing to lose. She had destroyed her empire on Earth. They would give her a new one. She betrayed us. I had to do what I did. I only wish I had done it earlier. Years ago. Then we wouldn't be here today. With nothing left to hope for."

Ksajakra's grief was palpable. Sudworth, huddled next to him, was an enigma; her face was perfectly still. The firelight lent her expressions that she was not making.

"What can we do now?" I said, after a long time, when no one else said anything; somebody had to say it. At least ask, even if the answer was *nothing*. "Caustur. Is there *anything* we can do?"

"I do not know. I would like to speak to Ogruthon. But he will not speak to me."

"He's doing something in there," I said. "I don't know what. But I can feel it. I don't like it."

The wind hissed across the dark, jewelled sand and made our fire flutter and kick. I got up, with difficulty, and walked away, trudging across the dunes. I was hungry, though the thirst was worse, and my stab wound ached and burned relentlessly, and I had lost my sword.

Absently I patted the pockets of my coat: no canteen, no food, the crystal dagger I had been holding so long ago when I had left Aradec. 1779, who crawled out, seeming dazed, from his pocket. "You *are* damage-resistant," I murmured, and put him on my shoulder so he could look at the stars with me. And something else, something sticky but hairy and a little alarming, as if I had put a dead animal in my pocket by accident, like the corpse of a mouse: but it was a piece of chain soaked in Johnny's black blood, sliced through a thumb's length from the catch, and still with her iron ring on it. It had wrapped itself around my wrist like a living thing in that last moment. I had thought it was no more than a splash of blood.

I knelt, feeling fever surge and slosh in me like vomit, and scraped away a few handfuls of sand, then buried both ring and chain. A curst relic. Let it lie on this planet till the end of time. At least They would not disturb it. They already owned this place.

Soft footsteps approached behind me. "Then you were loyal to her till the end," the Advisor said, his voice almost inaudible over the wind.

I tried to rise from my knees, found I could not, and simply remained there, both hands up to the wrist in the soft, warm sand. The Advisor padded over and lay down next to me, head high. "No," I said. "Maybe. That's the thing about loyalty. There's the kind where you're loyal because of self-interest—because if you stay close to someone till they trust you, your life will be better, maybe the lives of your family and friends, maybe the city, the country, the world, I don't know. And then there's the other kind. Where you get nothing. And it's because of love. And you die, in the end, with nothing but that. But love."

"There's a third kind," he said; he sounded as exhausted as I felt. "There's duty. Not someone saying, You must be loyal because I say you should be loyal, but because it's the right thing to do."

"Is that your kind?" I said. "I thought as much. Well, congratulations. It sounds stronger than the other two. Because it has a moral backbone. And the others have only self-serving greed. Or delusion."

"I am loyal to you," he said. "Not to those above you."

"Oh. I didn't know that."

"I assumed you did."

"No. No."

I dug my hands into the sand. It was strangely soothing. "Listen," I said into the dry darkness, speaking more to it, to the past, than to the Advisor. "She *was* beautiful. By anyone's standards. She was a cute kid that grew into a beautiful girl. And I loved her and I was *in* love with her. I felt all the different kinds of love that I thought existed in the world. I wanted to be her *and* I wanted to be with her *and* I wanted her to want to be with me. I thought she was beautiful like a cathedral is beautiful. And I thought she was beautiful like a hero is beautiful.

"But she was always a monster under all that. We just couldn't see it. None of us could. Because she was so busy telling us she was the hero. The bright light of the world. The one that was going to save everyone, make a better planet. So we'd all look up to her and say: There she goes, she's the best person in the world. So we'd never say: There she goes, the monster."

"So you hate her, then."

"What else is left?"

"Do you think you can remain loyal to someone you hate?" he said.

"Yes," I said. "Isn't that what we were doing? At the palace?"

"I suppose."

I thought about the Queen's questions so long ago: *Yes, no, never.* What had she asked? I'd never know. The wind moved across the sand, sending a thin skiff of it across the dunes crosswise from us, like a silk scarf. Already I could not see where I had buried the ring. "I never knew what it said," I said.

"What?"

"Nothing." I laughed mirthlessly then, remembering something she had said. "Nuclear winter. That was supposed to be the game-changer. Neither side would win. But They won. Help me up."

We returned to the fire, where I now saw the cloud of spirits, gods, and ghosts moving tentatively around the remains of the ship, hidden in the wreckage of the wood. I sat again.

Caustur said, "There may be something we can do with what remains. It may be that none of us will survive it. But the fact that there is only one point of pressure remaining to the universe is a fact. Thus the enemy knows it."

"So what," I said dully. "It's a war with one side still. No one will stop Them. Not us, not the planets They'll start invading. I mean, on the one hand, without Them sniffing after Johnny as bait, we're unobserved, and can go where we like. On the other hand, if we do somehow manage to get to the nexus unharmed and unhunted, which would be practically a miracle, and you manage to get me across, which we don't have enough gods to do, Johnny's *dead*. If I knew what the sigils were, if I knew the words, I could start them, maybe. But remember, she designed them. She's... would have been... the only one who could correct or adjust them on the fly. And she was the only one who knew how the reactor works. Anyway, They wouldn't bother coming after us. Because They know all that. And we would need Them to follow us from this universe to that one for this to work. So that in both universes, They would be destroyed. But They would only come if we were doing exactly what They think we were doing, which we can't. Now someone else talk, because I am going to throw up, I think."

My throat had tightened on the word *dead*, and I sat rubbing it painfully while Caustur tilted her head at me, a stilted and rehearsed but still-appreciated human gesture. The envoys crowded close, and I sneezed at their mingled smells, wiped my eyes. "Thank you for everything you did," I told them. They responded by drifting nearer and further from the fire in circles, over the toe of my outstretched boot, deep into the Advisor's folded wings.

Caustur said, "She is not dead."

I stared at her, for what little good it would do; the face was blank entirely, still, and I had long ago stopped thinking of the two brass knobs atop the smooth helmet as eyes. They looked like bolts, and probably were.

Inside me, a faint voice said: *No, she is not dead.*

I scrambled to my feet, involuntarily, as if I had been shocked. Sudworth gasped and covered her mouth.

"I killed her," I said, lips numb, mouth half-open. "I saw her die."

Yes. You killed her body; the animating soul perished. We saved the other. She is dead in a way that matters to you, and not dead in all the other ways that matter.

I felt my body buckle in half, all the poison and slop inside it curdling away from the god, from the small, implacable voice. The blood in my body seemed to turn to ice. "Tell me," I said out loud.

Caustur said, "She is in the little animal. Safe."

"If you're... joking..."

"No. It was there, it was receptive. It is very difficult to put a spark of life even temporarily in something that is not alive. The others could not take it. But we had this thing, we agreed at the very last moment." She paused. "Almost as the sword hit."

Fingers trembling, I brushed 1779 off my shoulder and held him in my open palm, as if I would look more closely and see... what? Her face? Her eyes? A laugh boiled up and I forced it back down. And for a moment I had an incredibly powerful urge to toss him into the fire, just flip my hand and watch the flames devour him. I resisted that too.

The beetle manoeuvred around to look at me, lifted his bright pink and violet wing cases, unfolded the wings beneath like green glass, neatly refolded them, and settled the cases back down. Everyone stared.

"Why the *fuck* didn't you tell me before?"

I could not speak. Caustur was too far. I am sorry.

"Did she... did she and you arrange this beforehand? Did she know this was going to happen? Was that why she let me do it? Why she didn't duck? My fucking *Christ*, you son of a *bitch*, you let me think I—"

"No," said Caustur. "We didn't."

I was breathing too fast. I tried to slow it down, and sat down again, dizzy and hot. How close was my own death, anyway? What was that infection doing in there? Did I have hours, days? "Jesus. I... I'm going to need a minute. My brain isn't working. I don't even believe you, I'm sorry, I'm going to be honest here. What does it mean? I don't understand. What do we do now? What can... Is it forever, the...?"

"Nick!" Sudworth caught me as I fell, and pushed me upright. Her arm against my back was a thin piece of steel. "Oh, Lord. Listen to the bubbling in your lungs. You—"

"I'll do whatever needs to be done," I said. "If you're not lying. If this isn't part of... some fucking game. Part of Their game. Part of his game. Or part of hers... You've all proven you can play for a long time. If this isn't it, then tell me what I need to do."

Ogruthon said, *You are waiting to be disappointed because you have been betrayed many times. But we mean what we say. We are grateful to you for our freedom, but there is so much more than that. Do you believe me?*

"I don't know."

Caustur and I have consulted. More gods are awakening still. They awaken others. That has not stopped. The envoys seek more. We have told them not to come here. We will go to them if we can. And if we can, we will join together to lure the Manifestation to an adjacency—

"A what?"

"A false place, near the nexus," said Caustur. "A decoy made to look like it."

"To look like..." I stared at her. I couldn't think. "The... Earth?"

"Yes. If he is fooled, you will have a little extra time. It will cost much—an entire world, even in illusion, is no small thing—and he will see through it, but then we will drop the illusion and... "

"Let the spell work on all of them at once," I said. My pulse felt sluggish, effortful; it wanted to race, but couldn't quite manage it. "Do you really think you can get us there?"

"Not all of us," Caustur began.

"Fine by me," Sudworth said. "I've had enough of this jaunting around bullshit."

I turned my head with some effort and stared at her. "But it's *Earth*. I mean it's *an* Earth. It's not different from the one we left. You could go home, you could..."

She shook her head. "There's nothing for me there, kid."

"There's the entire *planet*, ma'am."

"My archives are gone," she said. "I've been rebuilding them. It's the work of a hundred lifetimes and I don't have that many. I need to reassemble those books and I need to make sure they can still talk to each other. Don't you know they've been calling for help since the moment the brat activated that bullshit-machine? And my..."

I waited for her to say *my husband*, but she didn't. Again, I said, "Dr. Sudworth, please. I won't ever ask it again. Because we're almost out of time. How did you know to get off Earth before the end?"

"And I'm telling you again: I don't want to talk about it and I never will." Surprising me, she squeezed my arm tightly with both hands, and looked up at me; her face in the amber light was grim, but strangely serene. I tried to figure out what it meant and gave up. She was not sending me a signal I was meant to understand. "I will see you again," she said. "You'll see."

"Which one of the two things," I said carefully, "did you pick? Now that it doesn't matter."

"Not telling you that either. Nice try, though."

"I will stay and fight," Ksajakra said; he sounded shell-shocked. "With the others... I mean, I see that you are telling me I don't have a choice. But I wanted to say it anyway."

"So will I," the Advisor said. "I am not a fighting man, but I will too."

"I need a minute," I said, and staggered off again, shaking off their hands that grasped at me with concern. The Advisor followed me, as I had expected, and I was glad for it. Being with him was as close to being alone as I ever was, I realized. Perhaps he was a truer friend than I had ever given him credit for. And soon I would say goodbye and never see him again.

He walked after me for a long time, and when I finally stopped, he said, "Prophet. My people have a custom when one of us dies. It is meant to be done in a group. With all the family, the friends, the loved ones of the dead. The nobles do not do it, the royals. But everyone else does it. Country folk. Those in the cities."

"Mm."

"We find a place after the memorial," he went on, "like this. With sky. And we raise our voices. It sounds like noise at first: discordant sounds. Then it becomes one note. Loud, up into the clouds. That is where my people are said to go after death."

"Yes," I said slowly, unsure what I was agreeing to, then becoming more sure. "Good. Yes." I tilted my feverish, aching face to the sky. Blood still stuck my beard to my chest in patches and it hurt to do it. My neck hurt, my chest hurt. The sky was beautiful, each star so bright and clear it looked like a gem, so perfectly unsullied by clouds or dust that I could almost tell what each cut was. I thought about Johnny's ring again: no gem. I thought about leaving my body behind.

The noise seemed to come from high in my body at first, somewhere around my collarbone; then it lowered itself, spread out roots, and the faint wavering cry became a wail, then a howl. I drew in huge breaths of the warm air and sent them back out into the sky, and finally whatever last door inside me had been locked since the moment I first thought of killing her flew open, and I collapsed into sobs and incoherent screaming.

Some time later, the Advisor picked me up and laid me across his back. I felt emptied out, clean. I felt not even the small flickering presence of the god. My throat hurt.

"Were you weeping because she is dead?" he said softly. "Or because she is not dead?"

I wasn't sure. Exhausted, I let him carry me back to the fire and lay me down next to it, so I could still stare up at the stars.

THEY LET ME lie there while they talked, shivering occasionally, wrapped in a scrap of sailcloth scavenged from what remained of the third mast, mumbling to the beetle, trying to talk to Johnny if she was in there (I am so prepared for betrayal), trying to make him respond, occasionally snarling or roaring in frustration. The sand was a wonder at close range, even more than at a distance: not just dark blue but glittering with grains of gold, of green, of amber.

"And then the idea of dying," I said to 1779. "A good one. I cannot think of better. For either of us." The idea of it brought up no screams or cries of protest in my mind: I paused and waited for anything inside me to object, to cry out to live. Nothing. Inside me remained an echo of hatred and revenge, fading fast. But I thought the echo was good. It meant the emptiness had walls now, was bounded on the sides by something hard. I wondered what it was. If I believed in ghosts, I believe I would be surrounded by a cloud of ghosts, seven billion of them, telling me to join them. Telling me to bring her along. Better a ghost than a villain. Do you know what she's vulnerable to? they ask me. No, I tell them. What is it? If you know, please tell me. Because even if we return to a world where it was not all seven billion that she killed, the others will want to know.

The beetle did not reply.

"If people do not know what we did, they cannot forget it. But forgetting it is all I hope they would do if they did know. It is not right that the world should be cursed with this knowledge. Just the two of us is bad enough. And it's always been the two of us. I remember when you taught me about binary stars, which we did not learn in school. I remember realizing years later that that was what we were. You orbit me. I orbit you. And without love. And without will. When we are at the furthest points of our orbit we are lonely and safe and happy, and when we approach each other again it is because a malevolent force is exploiting the known curves of the ellipsis to do great evil. So we are glad to see each other, but only because of the recognition of the curse: that it requires both of us for the system to work. And because each of us is the only one who understands the other's curse. Not that there's sympathy: you for me, me for you. Not that there's pity or mercy. Just that we *know*, and no one else knows. And isn't that all we want from life? For one person to truly know us?"

I thought of the one with the yellow silk mask across his face, out there alone, touching everything, feeling the webs of his thread shiver. What was he feeling now? Were even the vibrations of my words reaching him? I hated to think of it. If we succeeded, the Manifestation would never move on his position, never usurp him. We would not be repaid for that in gratitude. But we might be repaid with solitude. The Earth a little blue-green, watery world, entirely innocent, entirely alone, and entirely without magic of any kind, forever.

Maybe that was too much to hope for. But I had to hope for something.

In the end there was only a moment for leave-taking; I shook Ksajakra's hand, embraced Sudworth, and gave the Advisor my crystal dagger, which after all was palace property. He watched me impassively, then reached up and touched my forehead with one paw, claws in. "Be who you are," he said. "That is the only way to defeat them."

"I will." I paused, then managed, "And thank you. For everything. If I thought I was going to live, I would wish to eventually turn into the man that you are."

"Thank you."

I glanced at Ksajakra one last time, not sure how to say what I meant to say. "You asked if I would have helped you if anyone else but her had been with you," I said.

"And?"

"Yeah," I said. "Sure. You. You, I would have followed, all on your own."

He waved as Caustur and I walked out into the desert, cooling now; I was stumbling regularly, unable to feel my legs, and she let me cling to her forearm, where the spikes looked fearsome but had enough room between them to fit my hand.

We stopped far out, with so many dunes between us and the fire that I could not even see the tip of the mast any more. The three moons had changed positions in the dance: still the same size, still the same colour, but two were much closer now. An isosceles triangle instead of equilateral.

Caustur grasped the back of my coat to keep me upright. "We will send you first," she said. "Ogruthon will lead the way. To smash the barrier between universes. Your body cannot go with you. Let it go, do not fight it. It is a shell only. What matters of you will travel, and it will travel to what you were calling the 'control room.'

Where you will both need bodies that can touch things. All right?"

"All right." I was holding 1779 lightly cupped in my left hand, feeling the legs skitter occasionally and slip between my fingers.

"Do you remember what you must immediately impress upon yourself upon arriving?"

"Yes. Or, I mean, there's going to be kind of a... a belief gap..."

"Don't be afraid," she said.

"I'm not," I said, surprised to discover that it was true. "And if this fails, if I die, that's all right. I forgive you in advance. And if you have to keep fighting Them forever because we failed, I ask you to forgive me in advance, too."

"Yes, I will do that," she said. "It's often said the gods do not forgive. But we do. That is why we do not answer prayers."

She put one cold, heavy hand on the top of my head, as gently as she could. Not for the first time I thought of how strange it must be for her to have mass and volume again, after so long as a tiny drop of metal in a submerged ship. "You will feel Ogruthon leave you," she added quietly. "And it may be that he too will die."

"Will I know?"

"I do not think so."

Goodbye, either way, I said inside me; there was no reply, only a spark of light, as if he had flicked on a lighter at a concert. I smiled.

"All right," I said. "I'm ready."

CHAPTER TWENTY-ONE

I WANTED TO take a deep breath and I couldn't, and for a moment there was only light, light perceptible even though I had no eyes, knowing I was only a mind, not even a brain, just a mind, wrapped around a spark of life, and I had thought the journey would take no time at all, but it was taking time, it was, and panic rose in me like something physical, an oncoming object in the wrong lane.

There was nothing to turn and no way to turn but I still did, to one side, following the curve of something ahead of me that I couldn't see, only sense, and then another turn, and then another, and then a voice inside me, not the god's, not mine, not hers: *Follow the magic, it's leading you through the spell. Don't get lost. You'll get there if you go together.*

Who are you? I tried to reply, but the light was

narrowing to a point, around it a hot ring of colours racing through the spectrum of what could be seen and what could not with human eyes, and then there was darkness, flickering, voices around us... and a forest.

I got up from hands and knees, stunned, weightless, despair already sinking my stomach. *Oh no, oh no.* This wasn't the control room of the reactor: it was grass, late spring flowers dotting the thick turf, bees roaming low over the clover blossoms, a smell of pollen, more overwhelmingly of trees, sap, clean air. A handful of aspens rose ahead of me, fresh young leaves. Green as saturated and wet as paint. And a boy: me. Staring.

Everything fell into place. "Oh Christ," I said. "We did make it. Is this it? You? I'm inside you, I mean me?"

He continued to stare: a tall boy less out of proportion than I had once believed myself to be, not grotesque at all, just big hands, big feet, skinny legs in baggy jeans, a black T-shirt, the beginnings of a gut that I knew he/I had already begun to feel self-conscious about, much smaller than he believed it to be, his black hair floppy, glossy. My heart ached, a keen pain like a blade.

"Who are you?" he managed.

"I'm you, there's no time to explain. You're in the control room, yes? With the reactor? Is that the last place you remember? And that fucking—no, look. I don't know how we're going to do this. You can't do it. You'll have to step aside."

"Step aside for you? What the hell?"

I glanced around desperately. "We're at the Creek, aren't we? I can't believe this. You could have the inside of your mind look like anything, you know, and you picked this! *Her* place! And you don't even love her!"

"I used to! And I'm allowed to love this property, even if I—" He shook his head and backed away from me. "Why are you wearing all that stuff? Are you one of Them? Sent to fuck up my mind?"

"I'm one of *us*. Sent to fuck up your mind," I conceded. "Look. There's *no time*. We have three or four minutes, maybe less, to save the world. You think that's what she's doing? She is not. She's about to betray you and everybody else on the planet. I can help. I'm from the place and time that that betrayal ended in. We're taking it back. We figured out how."

His eyes were round, dubious, and still with no sign of recognition whatsoever. But I had gotten through to him, I knew that. Before she had swapped the spells, part of him—of me—had known she wanted to. And had known that she never could resist doing what she wanted.

All he didn't know was that she had miscalculated her betrayal, gotten the spell wrong, that was all. "All right, man," he said. "I don't know how to let you drive. But do what you have to. Save what you can. Oh, and nice beard."

And somehow he retreated into the trees, and the scene around me shimmered, broke, and I opened my eyes—his eyes, our eyes—to a clean white room, and a thrum in the distance, and a panel full of switches and dials under my reeling fingertips. My whole body felt as light and empty as a plastic straw.

Next to me, Johnny—oh Jesus, blonde, ordinary, milk-white under her tan, as if she were about to be sick—was motionless, her eyes as vacant as mirrors.

Okay. Put yourself in place and time. Don't panic. Do not panic.

I spun to make sure I knew where I was. Yes, a few steps up onto the C-shaped control panel that took up most of this wall, bracketed by big rectangular windows, and then across the low spot on the floor, and then to the door where we had climbed up, where, incredibly, impossibly, maybe I hadn't believed it till now (no, I *know* I hadn't believed it till now) stood the dead: Sofia, and Rutger, and the Valusian in his gleaming cage. They were all staring at us.

Earth! *People from Earth!* People I *knew!*

"Nick?" Sofia's voice trembled. "What... just happened?"

"Nothing," I said. "Why?" My voice sounded weird, but I pushed that aside and tried to re-orient myself to the body. I felt the clock ticking down like one was implanted inside me, a real old-fashioned one with a loud second hand, my stomach churning with the urgency of it all, the actual desperation, but that wasn't what she was looking at. "Listen, you and—"

"You just... flickered," she said, and began to cross to me. "Like a lightbulb. What was that? And what's happening to Joanna?"

That was a good question, but the clock inside me continued to tick, and I took a couple of deep breaths. Strange air here: too wet, too rich, smelling of salt. Too much oxygen. "Get out," I said, trying to put as much authority as I could into my undeveloped voice.

"What?"

"Now. You and Rutger. Out, and quick. Get out of here. The pod is just up that ramp there. Call it in, then take it back to shore. Oh fuck, there's a code, you'll need to put it in or it'll lock. Hang on for just a second." I trotted over to Johnny and checked the window, worried: yes, last time (oh *Christ*, there was a last time, it's happening again, can we change this? Can we? Is this going to work?), our first clue had been something coming out of the sea, that horrible tentacle that had walloped the window. Because I had been looking down at the console instead of up at the sky: and now I looked up, and you could already see something small in the sky, a round white hole bordered with a ragged strip of red, like burning paper, the beginning of the gate that would fuck everything up.

My heart skipped a beat. And it was so strange to feel it, it felt like a stranger's heart, and it felt like a stranger's body: still with the taste of Gatorade in my mouth, but a strange mouth, and my beard gone, my face feeling cold and naked under its scruff, and the body too small, too light, utterly unfamiliar.

Quick. That hole still small. The light still dull.

Sofia turned, uncertain. "But you need our help for the spell. Don't you?"

"No! Get out! Something's about to happen. Okay, it sounds ridiculous, it doesn't seem like it now. But trust me, we only have a minute or two. Go!"

Rutger picked up the Valusian from the floor, watching my face closely. "Let's go. What is the code?"

"Right. Hang on."

Johnny was still frozen. Were they arguing in there? Had it turned into a fight? I wished I could be in there, slap some sense into her. The spark inside me had trusted me; but she would never trust herself. There was no one she trusted, and that included her.

I grasped her shoulder and shook her tentatively, then put my mouth close to her ear to ensure that the others couldn't hear. "Johnny. John! Hey! Are you in there? It's me." I swallowed. *Needs must.* "The M... whatever the fuck he calls himself. Nyarlathotep. He killed the you that just showed up. But she's the one that can fix this. We need a whole new spell stacked on top of another spell. Not this one. Do whatever you have to in there. You can sort it out later. I promise."

The light slowly returned to her eyes, the colour developing in her irises like a photograph. Who had won? I backed away and studied her face, heart still pounding, uneven and panicky with fear.

"Two four one," she said.

"What?"

"The code for the pod," she said. "Get them out, quick."

"But the Valusian—" Sofia protested again, turning to Rutger for support. "The spell won't work unless he's participating! You did all the calculations! You both did! What are you doing, what's happening?"

"It's fine, I promise," Johnny said, and turned back to the console.

The building trembled and rocked with the impact, the sound for a moment like a thunderclap, almost visible. Sofia cried out and fell to the floor.

"Two four one! Get out!" I shouted, and she and Rutger scrambled for the pod door, up the ramp into a hidden room; something hummed above us, the overhead lights flickering.

I turned back to Johnny, who was frantically punching at the console again. Above her, the big blue numbers ticked up, too slowly, it felt too slow: we were at 16. I counted breathlessly and had gotten to 24 before it reached 17. The room swam in front of my eyes. "We're not going to make it," I said.

She made a noncommittal noise; beads of sweat gleamed under her eyes.

"What was that?"

"It'll be close," she said. "It'll be close. It's all overclocked to fuck but I think the math is sound. I mean, as long as the components are sound." The building rocked again, the tentacle slapping the window, sliding down, leaving its snail-trail of colourless slime. I glanced at it once, then looked back at her. Not as far down as I was used to: I was back down to my height on that last day.

"That's what it is," she said softly, stepping back from the console and moving to the blank part of the wall I remembered: where with the Valusian she had not even written but simply spoken, and the sigil had appeared white-hot on the smooth cement.

"What what is?" I said, staring incredulously at the wall. How would she do it now?

"*That's* what it is," she said again. "I finally get it. The last pieces kind of... slotted themselves into their equations while I was, while... while I was dead. Because then I understood how Caustur felt while she was in the ship all that time. After she died. We both felt it settle into us like a... like a parasite."

"Felt what?"

"This thing. I was so close. Not only that magic is sentient, awake. But that it is *sapient*, and has will and a memory. It can be channelled into a spell and put to work with words of power... but it can also be persuaded to do things it wouldn't normally do. If you know how. That's it. That's the secret."

I stared at her, stared back at the wall, her small white hand on it. Something struck the building again, and behind me I heard the door slam open, something slobbering and snarling along the floor. I still couldn't look away. She would need a pen, I thought, a marker, or a piece of chalk or something, or she wouldn't be able to make the markings to—

"This will be the last spell ever performed on Earth," she said, and took her hand away. "Help me start it. Get it ready for the boost."

It won't work, I almost said, but how could I, now that everything was changed, that we were changed, that we were then and now and watching ourselves through today's eyes? I held out my hand; she took it, her fingers freezing.

And inside me, like a knot pulling free, a door opening, something rose, uncoiled, a silken ribbon cohering not out of weave or static but long knowledge, you could almost call it friendship, the particles of magic travelling smoothly together, the colour of blood: out through its home all around me, gaining velocity, and whirling entirely without resistance into Johnny's hand.

A design bloomed on the cement, small at first and too bright to look at, then expanding suddenly, bud to rose in three seconds flat, the white light sprinting across the cement and scribbling its way into an impossibly complex pattern, like and unlike any sigil I'd ever seen, full of thorns and ornaments that I instinctively felt should make the spell not work, it wasn't clean, wasn't neat enough.

She dropped my hand and ran back to the console, ignoring the window inches from her face, now crowded with grasping limbs and eyes, shockingly starred with cracks across the unbreakable nanoceramic, glanced up at the indicator—71—and started entering numbers until something popped up: a small switch, buried deep inside a metal housing. She reached inside and flicked it.

"Self-destruct," she said. "The reactor will be atoms. They'll never get Their hands on it."

"Good call," I said, and meant it. "Let's go, then. Now, before anything else gets in." The noise was rising outside, the roar of the waves merging with the multifold voices of the creatures racing in through the thin spot the Manifestation had created, as he worked to turn it into a gate.

She shook her head. "You go. The spell and the self-destruct aren't going to be far apart. Ten or fifteen seconds, by my best calculation. I mean it's a controlled explosion, but I have to make sure it goes off. I can't leave it to chance."

"The hell you are," I said reflexively.

"Well somebody has to, and you can't adjust either the spell or the reactor if it fucks up."

"No," I said. "Nobody has to. We're getting out of here." The ceiling began to creak and groan, bits of cement beginning to rain down around us. "They're through. They made it. This is it. This is when everything went to shit last time. *We have to go.*"

"You'd better get to the pod," she said, turning away from me.

"Joanna Meredith Chambers, don't you turn your back on me," I snarled, and she turned again, reluctantly; her face was wet with silent tears. "Is this the part where I argue that you don't have to die to pay back what happened? That your life can't bring back the lives of the people who died? Or that you're not, I don't know, Jesus or Aslan or whatever? That you don't have to die out of guilt or as capital punishment? That you're special and unique and the world would lose a precious gem if you did die? Or because people will miss you? Because I love you? Well, I hate you. That's not going to happen."

"Then why should I live?"

"Because enough people have died already. That's why. Because even one more is too many." I looked up at the number again: 97. As I did so, the roof ripped away in a ragged semicircle, exposing a startling sight: a sky dark as night, streaked with bluish clouds like flames, and behind it, the entire approaching army. Flames and claws, teeth and wings, segments, tentacles, tongues, and venom. And behind *Them*, the one thing we had been waiting for: the Manifestation himself, screaming and coming at us faster than even his screams from the great distance. The bait had worked. Somewhere nearby, the gods had swept away the decoy just in time.

"Just go!" she shouted, and shoved me towards the steps; I teetered on the edge for a second, feeling my feet beginning to lose contact with the ground from the strengthening wind. She was already a few inches up, her hands slack, lit through now by the glow of the spell so that I thought for an instant I could see her bones through her sodden, filthy clothing.

I took two clumsy steps towards the door. Paused. Inhaled. Exhaled. Turned back, and grabbed her wrist, and towed her towards the door.

We had almost reached it when the reactor blew.

I HIT THE water like it was concrete, head over heels, *sky sea sky sea sky sea* and my flailing legs ahead of me and clapping a hand at the last moment over my face because I knew I would try to breathe in the water and then I was up, floating, my clothes pulling me down but not harder than my flailing dragged me up. Things rained into the water around me, huge things, chunks of concrete that had mostly gone up and were now coming back down, go on and hit me then, see if I care, and

I wrenched my neck around to see if I was alone, if I would swim back alone, drown alone, die alone, but Johnny spluttered and surfaced next to me, a drowned rat, and gasped for air, and swam my way till we were close enough to clutch each other's sleeves while we treaded water.

The building was gone; half the island was gone. The sky was dark, but whether with smoke or fog or nanites or the end of the world I couldn't tell; it was just dark, like dusk, a blue-violet cast over everything.

"You said," I gasped, spitting icy water, "a controlled explosion!"

"That wasn't the self-destruct! That just melts the torus and two circuit boards!"

"So the reactor just *blew up?*"

"It's covered by insurance!"

I looked around, eyes burning from the salt and the impact. I had split my lip, and the salt was getting into that; all that I could keep above the surface of the water was my head, and the wind whipped the sea up like hands grasping us, trying to pull us under. I kept my hand locked on Johnny's wrist as the ocean yanked at us, trying to tear us apart. It was so cold and the water felt so heavy, it was like sheets of lead lapping at us, battering us with a force I didn't think water could possess. For a split second I thought of the desert, a long time ago; a desert, a shovel, a girl licking salt off her palm, a high clear voice, a voice I knew—

We couldn't tread much longer. It was so cold that my body alone, not even any part of me that had read about it, told me we had at most a minute or two before we went physically dead, our bodies curled up on themselves, and we sank. Scotland. February. Ocean.

Something huge and dark lunged out of the water next to me and I screamed and tried to protect my head before realizing what it was: not an animal or a monster, but two pieces of tubular carbon-fiber laced together with thin struts like black spiderweb. My teeth already chattering, I looked down its length, trying to gauge where it might have ended in the mist that near the shore.

Thoughts already getting cloudy. Misty. Like that. Think.

The pod. The track. Grab that, get out of the water. Climb it back to shore. Or at least nearer the shore. Near enough to swim. Black surface covered in tiny hexagons, each bearing the CI logo in fluorescent ink. Ha ha. No sign of the pod. My arms and legs screaming from the cold, feeling it pull me down. Johnny's head was gone.

Something washed over me: warmth, lassitude. Like being in a shower. We had won. We really won this time. If we died *now* it was all right. We had saved everyone else. Everyone. I could go under. Just as she had. And the track was bobbing away anyway, sinking away from us. Forming a more and more acute angle. It wouldn't hit the bottom here. Too deep. I could put my head back and sink forever...

No. Don't you dare.

A resident? An echo? No. A voice I had heard once, at the top of a crumbling temple, in a sandstorm. I kicked furiously till head and shoulders cleared the waves, gulped for air, and put my head below the water for a moment, so cold it was like being punched: but enough to let me see around myself, and Johnny still at the surface, her white face just inches below. Dead? Not sure.

I kicked over, forcing my wooden limbs to work, so cold I was sure they would simply snap, grabbed her around the throat and swam one-armed for the track again, using every ounce of power in my strange, thin, young body.

I thought: *I don't know you.* I thought: *Work with me. Save me. Save us. Save both of us, goddamn you. Kick, fight, swim. Kick, fight, swim. Breathe. Nice to not be stabbed, huh?*

The track cracked into my hand, hard enough that I thought it had broken fingers; it writhed out again, out of reach—come *on*, goddammit—and again. This time I sank my numb fingers into the plastic coating till my knuckles went white, bone-white under the water, and looked at the other end again, somehow out from under the darkness, in a strange foggy light. It might as well have been crossing the abyss of space.

(Which we did. This won't be so bad.)

Do it for Mom. Do it for Dad. Do it for the kids. Do it for the Earth, the future, a chance at something, a chance to *be* someone, a chance to be *anyone*. A chance to be free. Do it for myself. (Shove her under the waves and say she drowned. Tell everyone she died a hero's death.)

(Mm. Tempting.)

I clambered up onto the track, felt it give bonelessly under our weight, then bob up again. Once she was clear of the water I locked her arm around my neck and took her wrist, a cold bony adornment, then inch by inch, the same three points of contact for each inch, I dragged us down the track, or up the track, passing the pod itself which had bobbed to the surface—empty I hoped, I didn't look—up and up, clutching it as it swung to and fro in the waves, as it went up and down, as it tried to buck us off, all the way to the station at the end.

I felt like I had nothing left in me. Nothing at all. Not running on fumes but the memory of fumes. Johnny was silent, ice-cold on me. I couldn't feel her breath. But I was still breathing. I still had breath. Don't you remember this? I wanted to scream at her. I pulled you out. The pond. Remember? And your skates that seemed to weigh a hundred pounds. I got you. You lived. You can't die now. You simply don't dare.

He said be who you are, and I never knew who that was. He said be who you are. That is the only thing that will save you. He said you would both rather die than turn into each other, but that was never going to happen, and you feared it too much...

We crashed into a solid surface and for too long I couldn't even register it. My entire body shook as it tried to warm itself, scrambling the numbers each time I punched at the keypad. Nope. Not getting in. We hung suspended over the surf, the black stones below, in the icy fog. The temptation to let go and fall was still there,

I noted. Maybe it would never leave me. I put my thumb into Johnny's wrist, but both our hands were so cold I couldn't feel a pulse.

Beep

Beep?

I stared dully at the green light: the changed luck seemed actually farcical at this point. Then I dragged her into the shelter and draped us both across the track. The wind from the open door cut through my wet clothes like a knife, even though I knew academically it wasn't all that cold. I thought: Dry clothes. A warm bed. Hot soup. Not a hero's welcome, but a welcome. Back to a world that would have no idea what had just happened, again. A world that didn't know it had been a fulcrum for a moment, and that something had slammed down on the far side of the lever, catapulting it into obscurity. Maybe that was for the best.

"Come on," I said. "Almost there." Voices nearby: a girl, a man. Someone lifted me, and I let my head loll into the crook of his elbow. A familiar face. Rutger speaking, Sofia sobbing. Home.

"Aslan?" Johnny croaked somewhere near my shoulder. "*Seriously?*"

EPILOGUE

"THIS IS THE most awkward thing that's ever happened to me in my life. Lives."

"This might be the most awkward thing that's ever happened to anybody ever."

That was pretty rich, I thought, considering that it was her idea and therefore her fault. I morosely stirred what was left of my Slurpee—a dispiriting cup of blue syrup—and looked over at hers. "You gonna finish that?"

She shook her head and handed it over. I emptied my syrup over the bright-yellow slush and took a long sip. Funny how I wanted sugar all the time now. On Aradec there was usually nothing but honey (weird honey, from extremely ugly bees) and fruit.

We had chosen our perch in the hopes of hiding from the seagulls, who appeared out of the sky with no warning, like a thrown hatchet, if you made any gesture

543

resembling a hand being raised to your mouth. The rickety gazebo had been striped, when we found and claimed it, with bright orange tape marked *DO NOT USE*, but the steps seemed fine. The roof was busted but still provided shade, and let us watch the beach without having to deal with everybody else.

Everybody else being, thanks to Johnny: my dad and his fiancée Phyllis; my mom; Johnny's mom and *her* fiancé Sebastian; her dad; and my brothers and sister. And, because Rutger had insisted on it, five security personnel currently circling us in wide laps, supposedly in plainclothes, but in their aggressively bland matchy outfits, not very plainclothes at all. Huge discs of sweat darkened the backs of their pastel polo shirts and khakis as they walked.

Chris, Brent, and Carla had given up on their haphazard (not to mention uneven) game of beach volleyball, and were working together for once, slapping handfuls of dark sand onto a giant sandcastle looking a bit Disney princess on one side, and a bit Greyskull on the other. While they worked the adults watched them, surreptitiously eating fries and burgers hidden by sheets of newspapers held down with beach rocks. Mom had used a shell on one of hers; I watched resignedly as it got up and slowly began to walk towards the edge of their concrete picnic table.

"Nice to see everyone getting along," I said.

"Maybe it'll be less awkward in a couple of days," Johnny said. "I mean, it's the very first day."

"Eight to go."

"Eight to go." She yawned and stretched, salt flaking from her swimsuit and pattering audibly to the wood below us.

"You smell like a seaweed snack," I said.

"Why thank you."

"That's been left on a hot dashboard for about five weeks."

"Rude."

We had both changed into swim gear when we got up this morning, but she must have gone in when I'd been playing volleyball with the kids. Sitting as close as we were, her every breath blowing past me was redolent with iodine, as if she had inhaled the sea.

The sea, too, that had been her idea. I had wanted to go somewhere tropical, but she said the Maritimes were plenty hot in the summer—she'd been right about that, at least—and the kids would be just as happy here as with palm trees, and she'd been right about that too. Prairie kids. Awed by the ocean, wanting to be its friend or at least earn its respect, like some huge animal at the zoo that could kill them with a flick of its tail.

"I didn't even see you get in the water," I said.

"I had to get out. Something touched my leg."

"Johnny," I said patiently, "you've seen, chased, and killed creatures with more... tentacles, eyeballs, arms, legs, dongs, wings, fangs, antennae, and wiggly things than could possibly exist in our ocean, from the size of a ladybug to the size of Belgium."

"Yeah but none of them touched my leg, did they."

"Plus you used to have a *dorsal fin*."

"That was different. Mine was nice."

I gave up. "How was it?"

She took a deep breath, blew it out slowly. "Beautiful. Clean. I mean it *felt* clean somehow. The salt. The light inside of it."

"Maybe I'll go swim later." I glanced down the beach to our left, where the single lifeguard in her tower seemed more alert than any of us. The lines of the tower lay on the sand as crisp as black ink. After what had happened in February, people were slowly beginning to travel again, but the beach was virtually deserted this afternoon. A couple wandered past, paused to chat with the kids about the sandcastle, it seemed, and then wandered on, hand in hand. Gulls dipped, glanced at the gray sheets of newsprint, swooped away. It seemed peaceful, safe.

And it *was* safe. The world. Of course, there was a kind of burnt spot, or a blob of mould, in people's memories—a trauma toxic yet indistinctly delineated. No one had any way of knowing that we were in a world without magic, that the invisible film around us that had nothing to do with space or time or velocity had changed its shape. So no one had any reason to believe we were really safe this time. And there remained a heavy cloud of fear and uncertainty, of people mistrusting their memories, their relationships, their governments, militaries, and selves. Too many people had seen too many other people become their worst selves, and in many cases, twice. Trust was over. It seemed like a new Cold War had begun, but this time no one knew which sides were playing, or what the stakes were.

Any remaining physical artifacts suggesting magic, monsters, plague, invasion, and transformation could not be verified; they seemed without meaning. Video seemed like proof, but wasn't; books and newspaper articles did too, and also weren't. Not if nobody remembered it properly, not if the witnesses weren't sure. The dead were still dead, the missing still missing. Time had been lost, the one thing we could not create, with all our technology. Time and life.

It had felt important to take the kids somewhere nice. Somewhere we could decompress and make some memories, take back souvenirs and stories, before school started again in a few weeks. For all of us, actually. Carla was starting grade nine; the twins grade seven; and I was headed into my first undergrad year at the University of Alberta, hoping to come out in four years with a psychology degree. I hadn't told Johnny that. There was a lot we hadn't told each other since we came back. A lot (I suspected) that we both knew the other person knew and didn't want to say.

The main one for me was, *Were you really going to go over to the Manifestation?* Because either a yes or a no would, I thought, ruin our lives forever if it were to be said out loud. Even rehearsing the conversation in my head made me feel sick and shaky. A *yes* meant she was the monster I had always suspected she was; a *no* meant I had cold-bloodedly taken her life for no reason. It was very easy to say, *Well, we all make our choices based on what we love most; who are we to judge what others love?* when what you loved most was peace. In me, all that had looked like was cowardice. It was very different if the answer was power or fame or money or immortality. Just a qualitative difference that hurt me in every part of my body. And I didn't want to know.

There were safer things to ask. Whole areas that might not *kill* me to speak of. I was determined to stay on those.

As if she could hear me thinking it, she said quietly, "You know, I don't think the Ssarati disbanded?"

"Yeah?"

"I think they just, you know…" She dipped her hand vaguely in the air next to me, already scratched by the broken edges of seashells. "Went underground. Really far underground. And when they come back up, it'll be like they meant to be. Or, I mean, some of them meant to be."

"Librarians. Archivists."

"Yeah. Like that. Guardians. Not dragons, sitting on their hoards."

I flinched, and we both laughed weakly. Not that *dragons* was a dirty word, exactly, but some things were more easily said than others. I didn't want to say *Sofia*, who had politely but very firmly told me she hoped our paths would never cross again, and whom therefore I had not spoken to since March. I didn't want to say *Dr. Sudworth*, because it hurt me too badly.

Even Johnny and I had barely spoken in months, until she had proposed this holiday. And even then we'd mostly been talking about where to stay and how to keep the kids entertained. Not, for example, about the

Valusian, who was living apparently happily enough in one of her sub-basements, still in his armature.

"What are you going to do now?" I said.

"I dunno. Maybe see what the lunch special is, then go to the—"

"Not today. I mean... everything."

When she didn't respond, I glanced over to where she had curled up on her step, bare toes hanging over the edge. The garish board shorts she wore over her swimsuit were too big, and that seemed deliberate now, as if she were trying to retreat into them. "Well, all the work on the reactors is still under a construction moratorium... "

"Understandably, I think you'd have to admit? No?"

"The investigation is ongoing," she said stubbornly. "And anyway, I think it'll be finished soon. This report from the IAGRE or whatever that's supposed to come out in December. After all, the reactor was *clearly* running well outside specified parameters at the time of the incident, so—"

I laughed entirely without meaning to, an incoherent squawk. We both froze as something heavy landed on the gazebo roof and splapped around for a minute, as if daring its rival to call out again. At last it flew away.

"And I explained to Rutger that... I..." She shook her head.

You can't even make yourself say it, I almost said, then stopped. We'd hurt each other enough.

That her ill-gotten gift was gone, she meant. Her entire life had been built around the molten core of that secret, and like the Earth's core, it had driven everything she did and planned to do. The weather cycles of her hungers and angers, the fields that protected her secrets, that shielded her vulnerabilities, her burgeoning empire, the things that only she could do. Now she was just like the rest of us: on her own, exposed.

"What did he say?"

She smiled bitterly. "He said it was fine. That it didn't matter. That I would still and always be the head of the company. That I could move into more of a... an administrative, figurehead role."

"Well, that doesn't sound so ba—"

"I'll show *him*," she muttered. "I mean, who's the one with the house full of books and equipment? I'm going to become a real scientist. I don't care how long it takes. I've got all the stuff. I just need to study it."

"This is going to end in disaster," I said.

"Mm. Say something nice at my funeral."

"You still really want to save the world, huh?" I said. I set the Slurpee cup next to me, stomach churning.

"No. Just help. If I can."

"That doesn't sound like you," I said.

"It doesn't, no."

"On the other hand," I mused, "we did save the world already, technically."

"We did."

"From you."

"Shut up."

I closed my eyes and let the cool, damp breeze hit my face and arms. This; we had saved this. Every day we knew more than we knew before, and the hole left by the absence of magic would matter less and less. Soon the Chambers Reactors would start going up again. We could decarbonize. Clean the air till it squeaked. Quit coal and oil and gas, and plant trees where the companies had ripped up the land. With Johnny's new molecular construction facilities, it might be a millennium before we had to start extracting resources from the ground again. Everything humanity had thrown out could be broken down and repurposed. After the Anomaly, she'd tried to help the people affected by it: bionic eyes with nano-adjusting lenses; brain implants for a whole new crop of neurological disorders; new water purification tech and food supplements for hard-hit areas, electrified shelters, evacuation vehicles like tanks that made their own tracks. Ultra-rapid treatment of sewage (and human remains).

We'd get better. We'd get better than better; we could build a utopia out of green concrete and no-waste particleboard. Paradise at zero cost.

Or zero cost unless you knew what we'd done.

"What's really fucked up," I said after a minute, "is how no one else knows the truth. Only us. It's like being on a country of two. A planet of two."

"And you're not sure you want to stay on the planet. Not if it's me you have to stay with."

I shrugged. It wasn't her fault she was no longer who I had known—my childhood friend had turned out to be a fraud, and even that fraud was gone forever, just another impurity vanished in the crucible of the war.

And I wasn't who she had known either. I'd strayed too

far to return to that. And who I had been was something
she'd created anyway. It was so tempting to agree. To
just say, *Yes, after this, let's just end everything. Let's
be who we are instead of the monsters we made out of
each other.*

I waited, breathed: Johnny's skin, the salt-crusted
wood, the metallic, rusty odour of the ocean. Like
blood. She was staring fixedly out at the water, the sides
of her mouth trembling. I knew what it had cost her to
say that out loud. I wouldn't have been able to.

I looked at her fingers, whole again, tanned. What she
had done for the sake of knowledge, out of my sight.
What I had done for power out of hers. Who was I, who
was she? Who had we become? Could we ever say to
each other, *Do you miss it?*

"Nick!" Carla was waving to me, pointing at her sand
bucket while the twins stood expectantly behind her.
Needed someone tall. Willing to wait. I smiled shakily
and stood up.

"There in a minute!" I yelled back, and looked down
at Johnny on her step, small and uncertain as a moth
caught out in daylight. "Can I ask you a question?"

"I guess," she said listlessly, clearly expecting the
worst.

"What does it say inside your ring?"

She blinked. Slowly removed it, turned it over and over
in her fingertips. "It says *1668. You and I are earth.*"

Had I heard a capital E on the word? Maybe I was
losing the ability to catch those now. I felt strange, as
if some tank inside me that I had never known existed

had just had a small amount of fuel poured into it. I felt
its energy, its potential. And its strangeness: why had I
never known it was there?

"We could start over," I said.

"How do you mean?" Her voice was lightly suspicious.

"I don't know. We can't pretend that... all this didn't
happen. That we can just go back to being family like we
used to be. But we *could* pretend we had a clean slate.
See if we're worth trusting. Maybe not by everybody.
Just each other. Starting from right now." I took a deep
breath. "If you want."

She smiled, and it lit up her face like a candle. "Yeah.
Yeah, okay. Here." She held out her hand. "Pleased to
meet you. My name is Johnny."

"Nick." I shook the small hot hand.

"And what do you do, Nick?"

I laughed. "I'm still figuring that out."

The kids were waving at us, impatient. Quartz glinted
off the sun on their palms. "Come on," I said. "We got
construction work to do."

We dusted ourselves off, put our sandals on, and side
by side walked towards our people, laughing as we
stepped from the darkness into the light.

ACKNOWLEDGEMENTS

As ALWAYS I would like to thank my loyal and enthusiastic agent Michael Curry, and my indefatigable editor David T. Moore, who did an astonishing job on the sodden brick of words I threw at his head in September 2021. I would also like to thank our copyeditor Paul Simpson, publicist Jess Gofton, and my treasured readers and fans. This third book in the duology would not exist without you.

ABOUT THE AUTHOR

Premee Mohamed is an Indo-Caribbean scientist and speculative fiction author based in Edmonton, Alberta. She is the author of novels *Beneath the Rising* (finalist for Crawford Award, Aurora Award, British Fantasy Award, and Locus Award), *A Broken Darkness*, and *The Void Ascendant*, and novellas *These Lifeless Things*, *And What Can We Offer You Tonight*, and *The Annual Migration of Clouds*. Her short fiction has appeared in many venues.

www.premeemohamed.com
@premeesaurus

FIND US ONLINE!

www.rebellionpublishing.com

/rebellionpub   /rebellionpublishing /rebellionpublishing

SIGN UP TO OUR NEWSLETTER!

rebellionpublishing.com/newsletter

YOUR REVIEWS MATTER!

Enjoy this book? Got something to say?

Leave a review on Amazon, GoodReads or with your
favourite bookseller and let the world know!